THE NEW WINDMILL SERIES
General Editors: Anne and Ian Serraillier

14

THE FLIGHT OF THE HERON

This stirring historical novel, the first
of a trilogy on the fortunes of Bonnie
Prince Charlie and his companions, is
concerned with the '45 rebellion itself
and the escape of Prince Charlie (1745–
6). For older readers who enjoy dramatic
and romantic stories with a convincing
Scottish historical background. It gives
a clear picture of the conditions under
which the Jacobites remained loyal to
a hopeless cause. The story is continued in THE GLEAM IN THE NORTH
(no. 19 in this series) and completed in
THE DARK MILE (no. 20).

THE FLIGHT OF
THE HERON

BY

D. K. BROSTER

'But the heron's flight is that of a
celestial messenger bearing important, if
not happy, tidings to an expectant people.'
—'V.' *As You See It.*

HEINEMANN EDUCATIONAL BOOKS
LONDON

Heinemann Educational Books Ltd
LONDON EDINBURGH MELBOURNE AUCKLAND TORONTO
HONG KONG SINGAPORE KUALA LUMPUR
IBADAN NAIROBI JOHANNESBURG
LUSAKA NEW DELHI

ISBN 0 435 12014 X

First published by William Heinemann Ltd 1925
First published in the New Windmill Series 1952
Reprinted 1953, 1955, 1956, 1958, 1960, 1961,
1962 (Reset), 1963, 1964, 1966, 1968, 1970,
1975

Published by
Heinemann Educational Books Ltd
48 Charles Street, London W1X 8AH
Printed and bound in Great Britain by
Morrison and Gibb Ltd, London and Edinburgh

Contents

Those desirous of following the subsequent fortunes
of the chief characters in this book can do so in its
sequels, *The Gleam in the North* and *The Dark Mile*,
both published in this series.

AUTHOR'S NOTE

For the purposes of this story a certain amount of licence has been taken with the character of the Earl of Loudoun in Part IV, Chapter V.

A Promise of Fair Weather

I

THE sun had been up for a couple of hours, and now, by six o'clock, there was scarcely a cloud in the sky; even the peaked summit of Ben Tee, away to the north-east, had no more than the faintest veil floating over it. On all the western slopes the transfiguring light, as it crept lower and lower, was busy picking out the patches of July bell-heather and painting them an even deeper carmine; and the mountains round were smiling (where sometimes they frowned) on Loch na h-Iolaire, today a shining jewel which tomorrow might be a mere blot of grey steel. It was going to be a very fine day, and in the West of Scotland such are none too plentiful.

Loch na h-Iolaire, the Loch of the Eagle, was not large – little more than a mile long, and at its greatest breadth perhaps a quarter of a mile wide. It lay among the encircling hills like a fairy pool come upon in dreams; yet it had not the desolate quality of the high mountain tarns, whose black waters lie shoreless at the foot of precipices. Loch na h-Iolaire was set in a level space as wide as itself. At one end was a multitude of silver-stemmed birches, of whom some loved the loch (or their own reflection) so dearly that they leaned over it until the veil of their hair almost brushed its surface; and with these court ladies stood a guard of very old pines, severe and beautiful, and here and there was the feathered bravery of a rowan tree. Everywhere underfoot lay a carpet of bogmyrtle and cranberry, pressing up to the feet of the pungent-berried junipers and the bushes of the flaming broom, now but dying fires. And where this shore was widest it unexpectedly sent out into the lake a jutting crag of red granite, grown upon in every cranny with heather, and crowned with two immense Scots pines.

The loch's beauty, on this early summer morning of 1745, seemed at first to be a lonely and unappreciated loveliness, yet it was neither. On its northern shore, where the sandy bank, a little hollowed by the water, rose some three feet above it, a dark, wiry young Highlander, in a belted plaid of the Cameron tartan, was standing behind a couple of large juniper bushes with a fowling-piece in his hands. He, however, was plainly not lost in admiration of the scene, for his keen eyes were fixed intently on the tree-grown islet which swam at anchor in the middle of the loch, and he had all the appearance of a hunter waiting for his quarry.

Suddenly he gave an exclamation of dismay. Round the point of the island had just appeared the head, shoulder and flashing arm of a man swimming, and this man was driving fast through the barely rippled water, and was evidently making for the shore in his direction. The Highlander dropped out of sight behind the junipers, but the swimmer had already seen him.

'Who is there?' he called out, and his voice came ringing imperiously over the water. 'Stand up and show yourself!'

The discovered watcher obeyed, leaving the fowling-piece on the ground, and the swimmer, at some six yards' distance, promptly trod water, the better to see.

'Lachlan!' he exclaimed. 'What are you doing there?'

And as the Highlander did not answer, but suddenly stooped and pushed the fowling-piece deeper into the heather at his feet, the occupant of the loch, with a few vigorous strokes, brought himself in until he was able to stand breast-high in the water.

'Come nearer,' he commanded in Gaelic, 'and tell me what you are doing, skulking there!'

The other advanced to the edge of the bank. 'I was watching yourself, Mac 'ic Ailein,' he replied in the same tongue, and in the sulky tone of one who knows that he will be blamed.

'And why, in the name of the Good Being? Have you never seen me swim before?'

'I had it in my mind that someone might steal your clothes,' answered Lachlan MacMartin, looking aside.

'*Amadain!*' exclaimed the swimmer. 'There is no one between the Garry and the water of Arkaig who would do such a thing, and you know it as well as I! Moreover, my clothes are on the other side, and you cannot even see them! No, the truth, or I will come and and throw you into the loch!' And, balancing his arms, he advanced until he was only waist-deep, young and broad-shouldered and glistening against the bright water and the trees of the island behind him. 'Confess now, and tell me the reason in your heart!'

'If you will not be angry I will be telling you,' replied Lachlan to his chieftain Ewen Cameron, who was also his foster-brother.

'I shall make no promises. Out with it!'

'I cannot shout it to you, Mac 'ic Ailein; it would not be lucky.'

'Do you think that I am coming out to hear it before I have finished my swim?'

'I will walk in to you if you wish,' said Lachlan submissively, and began to unfasten his plaid.

'Do not be a fool!' said the young man in the loch, half laughing, half annoyed: and, wading to the bank, he pulled himself up by the exposed root of a birch tree, and threw himself unconcernedly down among the heather and bog-myrtle. Now it could be seen that he was some inches over six feet and splendidly made; a swift runner, too, it was likely, for all his height and breadth of shoulder. His thick auburn hair, darkened by the water to brown, was plaited for the nonce into a short pigtail like a soldier's; his deepset blue eyes looked out of a tanned face, but where the sunburn ended his skin was as fair as a girl's. He had a smiling and determined mouth.

'Now tell me truly why you are lurking here like a grouse on Beinn Tigh,' he repeated.

The half-detected culprit glanced from the naked young man at his feet to the only partially concealed fowling-piece. 'You will not be pleased, I am thinking.'

'All the more reason for knowing, then,' responded his chieftain promptly, hugging his bent knees. 'I shall stay here until you tell me . . . dhé, how these vegetables prick! No, I do not want your plaid; I want the truth.'

'I am here,' began Lachlan MacMartin with great unwillingness, 'because there is something in the loch which may bring you ill-fortune, and—'

'In the loch! What, an each uisge, a water-horse?' He was smiling.

'No, not a water-horse. But my father says—'

'Ah, it is a matter of the two sights? Angus has been 'seeing' again! What was the vision?'

But at that moment the speaker himself saw something, though not by the supernatural gift to which he was referring. He stretched out a wet, accusing arm and pointed towards the juniper bush. 'What is that gun doing here?' And at the very plain discomposure on its owner's face a look of amusement came into his own. 'You cannot shoot a water-horse, Lachlan – not with a charge of small shot!'

'It is not a water-horse,' repeated his foster-brother. He suddenly crouched down in the heather close to the swimmer. 'Listen, Mac 'ic Ailein,' he said in a low, tense voice. 'My father is much troubled, for he had a "seeing" last night across the fire, and it concerned you, but whether for good or ill he could not tell; neither would he tell me what it was, save that it had to do with a heron.'

'It is a pity Angus cannot be more particular in his predictions,' observed the young man flippantly, breaking off a sprig of bogmyrtle and smelling it. 'Well?'

'You know that I would put the hair of my head under your feet,' went on Lachlan MacMartin passionately. 'Now on the island yonder there lives a heron – not a pair, but one only—'

The young chieftain laid a damp but forcible hand on his arm. 'I will not have it, Lachlan, do you hear?' he said in English. 'I'll not allow that bird to be shot!'

But Lachlan continued to pour out Gaelic. '*Eoghain*, marrow of my heart, ask me for the blood out of my veins, but do not ask me to let the heron live now that my father has seen this thing! It is a bird of ill omen – one to be living there alone, and to be spying when you are swimming; and if it is not a *bòchdan*, as I have sometimes thought, it may be a witch. Indeed, if I had one, I would do better to put a silver bullet—'

'Stop!' said the marrow of his heart peremptorily. 'If my father Angus has any warning to give me, he can tell it into my own ear, but I will not have that heron shot, whatever he saw! What do you suppose the poor bird can do to me? Bring your piece here and unload it.'

Out of the juniper bush and the heather Lachlan, rising,

pulled the fowling-piece, and, very slowly and reluctantly, removed the priming and the charge.

'Yet it is an evil bird,' he muttered between his teeth. 'You must know that it is unlucky to meet a heron when one sets out on a journey.'

'Yes,' broke in Ewen Cameron impatiently, 'in the same way that it is unlucky to meet a sheep or a pig – or a snake or a rat or a mouse, unless you kill them – or a hare, or a fox, or a woman, or a flat-footed man . . . and I know not what besides! Give me the gun.' He examined it and laid it down. 'Now, Lachlan, as you have not yet promised to respect my wishes in this matter, and a gun is easily reloaded, you shall swear on the iron to obey me – and that quickly, for I am getting cold.'

Startled, the Highlander looked at his young chieftain to see whether he were serious when he suggested the taking of so great and inviolable an oath. But, unable from his expression to be sure, and being blindly, fanatically devoted to him, he obediently drew his dirk from its sheath, and was about to raise it to his lips to kiss it when his foster-brother caught his arm.

'No, I was jesting, Lachlan. And . . . you do not keep your *biodag* very clean!'

'Not clean?' exclaimed its owner, lowering the formidable, hiltless blade. Then he bit his lip. '*Dhia gleidh sinn!* you are right – how came that rust there?'

'Rust? It is blood!' Ewen took it from him by its black handle of interlaced design and ran a finger down it. 'No, I am wrong; it was only the early sun on the steel.'

For the weapon lay across his palm, spotless and shining, the whole foot and a half of it.

The dark Lachlan had turned very pale. 'Give it to me, Mac 'ic Ailein, and let me throw it into the loch. It is not well to keep it if we both saw . . . what we saw.'

'No,' said his master with more composure, 'it is a good dirk, and too old a friend for that – and what I imagined can only have been some memory of the times when it has gralloched a deer for us two.' He gave it back. 'We are neither of us *taibhsear* like your father. I forbid you to throw it away. Nor are you to shoot that heron – do you hear?'

If his young chief was not, Lachlan MacMartin was plainly shaken by what had happened. He thrust the dirk deep into the heather as though to cleanse it before he returned it to the sheath. 'I hear,' he muttered.

'Then see that you remember!' Shivering slightly, the young man sprang to his feet. 'Now, as you have forced me to land on this side of the loch, Lachlan, I shall dive off the *creag ruadh*. A score of times have I meant to do it, but I have never been sure if there were enough water below. So, if a water-horse gets me, you will know whose was the fault of it!' And laughing, disregarding entirely his foster-brother's protests, which went so far as the laying of a detaining hand on his bare shoulder, he slid down the bank, ran along the narrow strip of sand below it, and disappeared round a bend of the shore. A moment or two later his white figure was seen clambering up the heather-clad side of the red crag which gave the whole property its name. A pause, then he shot down towards the lake in the perfect dive of the athlete; and the water received him with scarcely a splash.

'The cross of Christ be upon us!' murmured Lachlan, shutting his eyes; and, though he was no Papist, he signed himself. When he opened them the beloved head had reappeared safely, and he watched it till the island once more hid it from his view.

Still tingling with his dive, Ewen Cameron of Ardroy, when he had reached the other side of the little island, suddenly ceased swimming and, turning on his back, gave himself to floating and meditation. He was just six-and-twenty and very happy, for the sun was shining, and he felt full of vigour, and the water was like cold silk about him, and when he went in to breakfast there would be Alison, fresh as the morning, to greet him – a foretaste of the mornings to come when they would greet each other earlier than that. For their marriage contract was even now in his desk at Ardroy awaiting signature, and the Chief of Clan Cameron, Lochiel 'himself, Mac Dhomhnuill Duibh, Ewen's near kinsman by marriage as well as his overlord, was coming tomorrow from his house of Achnacarry on Loch Arkaig to witness it.

Lochiel indeed, now a man of fifty, had always been to his young cousin elder brother and father in one, for Ewen's own father had been obliged to flee the country after the abortive little Jacobite attempt of 1719, leaving behind him his wife and the son of whom she had been but three days delivered. Ewen's mother – a Stewart of Appin – did not survive his birth a fortnight, and he was nursed, with her own black-haired Lachlan, by Seonaid MacMartin, the wife of his father's piper – no unusual event in a land of fosterage. But after a while arrived Miss Cameron, the laird's sister, to take charge of the deserted house of Ardroy and to look after the motherless boy, who before the year had ended was father-less too, for John Cameron died of fever in Amsterdam, and the child of six months old became 'Mac 'ic Ailein', the head of the cadet branch of Cameron of Ardroy. Hence Ewen, with Miss Cameron's assistance – and Lochiel's supervision – had ruled his little domain for as long as he could remember, save only for the two years when he was abroad for his education.

It was there, in the Jacobite society of Paris, that he had met Alison Grant, the daughter of a poor, learned and almost permanently exiled Highland gentleman, a Grant of Glenmoriston, a plotter rather than a fighter. But because Alison, though quite as much in love with her young chieftain as he with her, had refused to leave her father alone in exile – for the brother of sixteen just entering a French regiment could not take her place – Ewen had had to wait for four long years without much prospect of their marriage. But this very spring Mr Grant had received intima-tion that his return would be winked at by the Government, and accordingly returned; and so there was nothing to stand in the way of his daughter's marriage to the young laird of Ardroy in the autumn. And Alison's presence here now, on a visit with her father, was no doubt the reason that, though her lover was of the same political creed as they, never ques-tioning its fitness, since it was as natural to him as running or breathing, he was not paying very particular attention to the rumours of Prince Charles Edward's plans which were going about among the initiated.

With deliberate and unnecessary splashings, like a boy, Ewen now turned over again, swam for a while under water, and finally landed, stretched himself in the sun, and got without undue haste into a rather summary costume. There was plenty of time before breakfast to make a more ordered toilet, and his hair would be dry and tied back with a ribbon by then. Perukes and short hair were convenient, but, fashionable or no, he found the former hot. When he was Lochiel's age, perhaps, he would wear one.

Before long he was striding off towards the house, whistling a French air as he went.

2

Between the red crag and the spot where he had rated his foster-brother that morning Ardroy stood alone now with his betrothed. The loch was almost more beautiful in the sunset light than when its waters had closed over his head all those hours ago, and even with Alison on his arm Ewen was conscious of this, for he adored Loch na h-Iolaire with little less than passion. So they stood, close together, looking at it, while here and there a fish rose and made his little circle, widening until it died out in the glassy infinity, and near shore a shelduck with her tiny bobbing brood swam hastily from one patch of reeds to another.

Presently Ewen took off his plaid and spread it for Alison to sit upon, and threw himself down too on the carpet of cranberries; and now he looked, not at the loch, but at her, his own (or nearly his own) at last. Alison's hand, waited for so patiently . . . no, not always so patiently . . . strayed among the tiny leaves, and Ewen caught the little fingers, with his ring upon the last but one and kissed them.

'And to think,' he said softly, 'that by this time tomorrow we shall be contracted in writing, and you not able to get away from me!'

Alison looked down at him. In her dark eyes swam all kinds of sweetness, but mischief woke and danced now at the corners of her small, fine, close-shut mouth, which could be so tender too.

'Oh, Ewen, does the contract make you more sure of me? You'd not hold me to a bit of paper if I were to change my mind one fine morning and say, "Ardroy, I'm sweir to tell it, but wed you I cannot"?'

'Would I not hold you to it! Try, and see!'

One of Alison's dimples appeared. 'Indeed, I'm minded to try it, just for that, to see what you would do. What would you do, *Eoghain mhóir*?'

'Carry you off,' replied Ewen promptly.

'And marry me by force?'

'And marry you by force.'

'There speaks the blood of Hieland reivers! I'd think shame to say such a thing!'

'And are you not Hieland yourself, Miss Grant?' inquired her lover. 'And was there never cattle lifting done in Glenmoriston?'

'Cattle!' exclaimed Alison, the other dimple in evidence. 'That I should be likened, by him that's contracted to be married to me, to a steer or a cow!'

'I likened you to no such thing! You are like a hind, a hind that one sees just a glimps of before it is gone, drinking at the lake on a misty morning. Oh, my heart's darling,' he went on, dropping into Gaelic, 'do not make jests upon our marriage! If I thought that you were in earnest – Alison, say that you are not in earnest!'

Alison Grant looked into the clear blue eyes, which had really grown troubled, and was instantly remorseful. 'Oh, my dear, what a wretch am I to torment you thus! No, no, I was teasing; Loch na h-Iolaire shall run dry before I break my troth to you. I'll never force you to carry me off; 'tis like I'll be at the kirk before you.' She let him draw her head without words upon his shoulder, and they sat there silent, looking at happiness: both the happiness which they knew now, and the greater, the long happiness which was coming to them – as stable and secure in their eyes as the changeless mountains round them.

Yet Alison knew her lover's mind, or at least a part of it, so well that she presently said: 'And yet I am not jesting, Ewen, when I say that I think you would be hard put to it to choose between me and Loch na h-Iolaire – Loch na h-Iolaire and the house of Ardroy.'

His arm tightened round her. 'Alison, how can you—'

'But you'll never have to choose, *m'eudail*. I love this place most dearly already. I have never had a home like it to love, living as we have for so long, now in France. now in Holland.

But your heart is as strongly rooted here as . . . the red crag yonder.'

Ewen gave a little sigh. 'You see a long way into my heart, you that are the core of it. Indeed, when I am dying I think this is the last place I shall have sight of in my mind. I hope I may be seeing it with my eyes also.'

Alison did not shudder or change the subject, or implore him not to speak of such things, for she was Highland too, with her race's half-mystical preoccupation with the dead. But she thought: 'I hope I'll die the same day, the same hour. . . .'

The shadows on the loch crept a little farther. Behind them Ben Tee changed colour for the hundredth time; his pointed peak seemed to soar. It grew cooler too, and Ewen wrapped the ends of the plaid about his lady.

'On Wednesday we will spend the day at Loch Arkaig,' he announced. 'We will take ponies, and you and Mr Grant shall ride.'

'And Miss Cameron?'

'Aunt Marget detests such jaunts. Meals for the parlour, and the parlour for meals, that is her creed. – Alison, are you not cold?'

'In this?' She fingered the plaid where it hung over her shoulders, and added after a moment: 'How strange it will be, to wear another tartan than one's own!'

'You shall always wear the Grant if it pleases you better.'

'No, it does not please me better,' answered Alison softly. 'I feel . . . very warm in the Cameron.'

He kissed her for that, smiling, and, raising his head from his kiss, became aware of a dark object beating towards them out of the sunset sky. It was the solitary heron of the island, winging his strong way home with a deceptive slowness. The sight reminded Ewen of his morning's encounter with Lachlan, and he was about to tell Alison of it when Fate's messenger, who for the last five minutes had been hurrying round the loch, came past the red crag of Ardroy, and Ewen's quick ear caught the snap of a breaking stick under the deerskin brogues. He looked quickly round. A bearded Highlander was trotting towards them under the birches and pines.

'It is Neil – what can he want? Forgive me!' He rose to

his feet, and Neil MacMartin, who was Lachlan's elder brother and Ewen's piper, broke into a run.

'Mac Dhomhnuill Duibh has just sent this by a man on horseback,' he said somewhat breathlessly, pulling a letter from his sporran.

Ewen broke the seal. 'Perhaps it is to say that Lochiel cannot come tomorrow,' he observed to his betrothed. But as he read his face showed stupefaction. 'Great God!'

Alison sprang to her feet. 'Ewen! Not bad news?'

'Bad? No, no!' He waved Neil out of hearing and turned to her with sparkling eyes. 'The Prince has landed in Scotland!'

She was at first as amazed as he. 'The Prince! Landed! When . . . where?'

Ewen consulted his letter again. 'He landed at Borradale in Arisaig on the twenty-fifth. Lochiel desires me to go to Achnacarry at once.'

'He has come – at last!' said Alison to herself, almost with awe. 'And you will go with Lochiel to kiss his hand, to – Oh, Ewen, how I envy you!'

The light which had come into her lover's eyes died out a little. 'I do not know that Lochiel is going to Arisaig, darling.' He glanced at the letter again. 'He is troubled, I can see; there are no troops with the Prince, none of the hoped-for French help.'

'But what of that?' cried the girl. 'It is not to be thought of that Lochiel's sword, of all others, should stay in the scabbard!'

'Lochiel will do what is right and honourable; it is impossible for him ever to act otherwise,' answered Ewen, who was devoted to his Chief. 'And he wants speech with me; I must set out at once. Yes, Clan Cameron will rise, not a doubt of it!'

And, youth and the natural ardour of a fighting race reasserting themselves, he snatched up his bonnet and tossed it into the air. 'Ah, now I know why Lachlan and I thought we saw blood on his dirk this morning!' Then he caught Alison to him. '*My dearest on earth, give me your kiss!*'

It was the title of one of the ancient pibrochs that he was quoting, and the Highland girl put her arms round his neck and gave him what he asked.

Loch na h-Iolaire, bereft of the echoing voices, sank into a silence that was not broken until the heron rose again from the island and began to fly slowly towards the sunset. Then the stillness was rent by a sharp report; the great bird turned over twice, its wings beating wildly, and fell all huddled into the lake. A little boat shot out from the side of the *creag ruadh*, and in a moment or two Lachlan MacMartin, leaving his oars, was bending over the side with the end of a cord in his hand. There was a splash as he threw overboard the large stone to which the cord was fastened; and having thus removed the evidence of his blind effort to outwit destiny, he pulled quickly back to the shelter of the crag of Ardroy.

Soon the same unbroken calm, the same soft lap and ripple, the same gently fading brightness were once more round Loch na h-Iolaire; yet for all those who today had looked on its waters the current of life was changed for ever.

I

Through English Eyes

'One of them asked . . . how he liked the Highlands. The question seemed to irritate him, for he answered. "How, sir can you ask me what obliges me to speak unfavourably of a country where I have been hospitably entertained? Who *can* like the Highlands – I like the inhabitants very well." '
    —BOSWELL. *Journal of a Tour to the Hebrides.*

Chapter One

I N all Lochaber – perhaps in all the Western Highlands – there was no more bored or disgusted man this sixteenth of August than Captain Keith Windham of the Royal Scots, as he rode down the Great Glen with a newly-raised company of recruits from Perth; and no more nervous or unhappy men than the recruits themselves. For the first time in their lives the latter found themselves far north of 'the Highland line', beyond which, to Lowland as well as to English minds, there stretched a horrid region peopled by wild hill tribes, where the King's writ did not run, and where until General Wade's recent road-making activities, horsed vehicles could not run either. Yesterday only had they reached Fort Augustus, two companies of them, and this afternoon, tired and apprehensive, were about half-way through their thirty-mile march to Fort William. As for the English officer, he was cursing with all his soul the young Adventurer whose absurd landing on the coast of Moidart last month had caused all this pother.

Had it not been for that event, Captain Windham might have been allowed to return to Flanders, now that his wound of Fontenoy was healed, to engage in real warfare against civilized troops, instead of marching through barbarous scenery to be shut up in a fort. He could not expect any regular fighting, since the savage hordes of these parts would probably never face a volley. Nevertheless, had he been in command of a column, he would have judged it more prudent to have a picket out ahead; but he had already had a slight difference of opinion with Captain Scott, of the other company, who was senior to him, and, being himself of a temper very intolerant of a snub, he did not choose to risk one. Captain Windham had no great love for Scotsmen, though, ironically enough, he bore a Scottish Christian name and served in a Scottish regiment. As it happened, he was no more responsible for the one fact than for the other.

It was hot in the Great Glen, though a languid wind walked occasionally up Loch Lochy, by whose waters they were now marching. From time to time Captain Windham glanced across to its other side, and thought that he had never seen anything more forbidding. The mountain slopes, steep, green and wrinkled with headlong torrents, followed each other like a procession of elephants, and so much did they also resemble a wall rising from the lake that there did not appear to be space for even a track between them and the water. And, though it was difficult to be sure, he suspected the slopes beneath which they were marching to be very nearly as objectionable. As a route in a potentially hostile country, a defile, astonishingly straight, with a ten-mile lake in the middle of it, did not appeal to him.

However, the mountains on the left did seem to be opening out at last, and General Wade's new military road, upon which they were marching, was in consequence about to leave the lake and proceed over more open moorland country, which pleased Captain Windham better, even though the wide panorama into which they presently emerged was also disfigured by high mountains, in particular by that in front of them, which he had been told was the loftiest in Great Britain. And about twelve miles off, under those bastions, lay Fort William, their destination.

But where was the river which, as he knew, they had first to cross? In this wide, rough landscape Captain Windham could not see a sign of it. Then, farther down the slope and about a mile ahead of them, he discerned a long, thick, winding belt of trees, and remembered to have heard an officer of Guise's regiment at Fort Augustus say last night that the Spean, a very rapid stream, had carved so deep a channel for itself as almost to flow in a ravine, and that Wade must have had some ado to find a spot where he could carry his road over it. He had done so, it appeared, on a narrow stone structure whose elevation above the river-bed had earned it the name of High Bridge. Indeed the Englishman now saw that the road which they were following was making for this deeply sunken river at an angle which suggested that General Wade had had little choice in the position of his bridge.

Ahead of Captain Windham on his mettlesome horse the scarlet ranks tramped down the gently sloping road through the heather; ahead of them again, at the rear of the foremost company, Captain Scott sat his white charger. The English officer looked with an unwilling curiosity at the great mountain mass over Fort William; it actually had traces of snow upon it . . . in August! What a country! Now in Flanders— What the devil was that?

It was, unmistakably, the skirl of a bagpipe, and came from the direction of the still invisible bridge. But if the bridge was not to be seen, something else was – tartan-clad forms moving rapidly in and out of those sheltering trees. Evidently a considerable body of Highlanders was massing by the river.

The senior officer halted his men and came riding back. 'Captain Windham, I believe there is an ambush set for us down yonder.'

'It does not *sound* like an ambush, egad!' replied his colleague rather tartly, as the heathenish skirling grew louder. 'But I certainly think there are Highlanders posted at the bridge to dispute our crossing.'

'I'll just send forward a couple of men to get some notion of their numbers,' said Scott, and rode back again. Keith shrugged his shoulders. 'Somewhat of a tardy precaution!' he thought to himself.

A sergeant and a private were thereupon dispatched by Captain Scott to reconnoitre. Their fate was swift and not encouraging, for they had not gone far ere, before the eyes of their comrades, they were suddenly pounced upon by two Highlanders who, with a yell, darted out from the trees and hurried them out of sight.

The intimidated recruits began to shuffle and murmur. Cap-

tain Windham spoke vigorously to his subaltern, and then rode
forward to consult with his senior.

Captain Scott wheeled his horse to meet him. 'This is unco
awkward,' he said, dropping his voice. 'The Deil knows how
many of those fellows there are down yonder, but do you
observe them, Captain Windham, skipping about like coneys
among the trees? The bridge, I've heard, is uncommon narrow
and high, with naught but rocks and torrent below. I doubt we
can get the men over.'

'We *must*!' retorted Keith. 'There's no other means of reaching Fort William. The Royals to hesitate before a few beggarly
cattle-thieves!'

Alas, the Royals did more than hesitate. Even as he spoke
there were signs that the half-seen 'cattle-thieves' on the bridge
were preparing for a rush, for loud orders could be heard, and
the piping swelled hideously. And at that the scarlet-clad ranks
on the slope wavered, broke, turned, and began to flee up the
rise as fast as their legs would carry them.

It was in vain that their two captains endeavoured to rally
them. A man on a horse cannot do much to stem a flood of
fugitives save perhaps on a narrow road, and here the road had
unlimited space on either side of it. Helter-skelter the recruits
ran, and, despite their fatigue and their accoutrements, never
ceased running for two miles, till they stopped, exhausted, by
Loch Lochy side once more.

By that time Captain Windham was without suitable words
in which to address them; his vocabulary was exhausted. Captain Scott was in like case. There was another hasty consulta-
tion beneath the unmoved stare of those steep green mountains.
Scott was for sending back to Fort Augustus for a detachment of Guise's regiment to help them force the bridge, and
Captain Windham, not seeing what else was to be done, con-
curred in this opinion. Meanwhile the recruits should be
marched at an easy pace in the direction of Fort Augustus to
their junction with these reinforcements, which were, of
course, to come up with all speed. There had been no sign of
pursuit by the successful holders of the bridge, and it might
be hoped that in a little the morale of the fugitives would be
somewhat restored.

Captain Scott thereupon suggested that Captain Windham
should lend one of the lieutenants his horse, which was much

faster than his own white charger – no other officers but they being mounted – but Keith objected with truth that a strange rider would never manage his steed, and offered to make over his company to his lieutenant and himself ride back to Fort Augustus if Captain Scott thought good. And Captain Scott hastily agreed to what both officers felt was a somewhat unusual course justified by circumstances.

To a man who, three months ago, had borne his part in the wonderful retreat at Fontenoy, that epic of steadiness under fire, and who had even been complimented by the Duke of Cumberland on his conduct, the last half-hour had been a nightmare of shame, and Keith Windham, glad to be able to extricate himself from it with the confidence that he was not abandoning his men on the eve of a fight, set spurs to his horse with great relief.

He had gone about five miles along the loch – always with those abominable mountains on either side of him – when a report echoed soundingly among them, and a bullet struck the road a little ahead of him. His pulling, nervous horse reared and plunged; and Keith swore. He was not unobserved, then, and might very well be picked off by some unseen marksman up there. Bullets, however, did not discompose him like cowardice, and, cramming his hat farther down upon his head, he merely urged the animal to greater speed

In the next few miles, as occasional bullets winged their way at varying distances past his person, Keith Windham began to think that the hapless Royals behind him were perhaps being outflanked by some enemy marching parallel to them on the hillside – and marching much faster. The prospect of their being attacked seemed by no means so remote. Still, in any case, it was now his business to go on. But when he came in sight of the village beyond the end of Loch Lochy through which they had passed that morning, he could see armed Highlanders there in such numbers that it was unlikely he would be allowed to ride through it. Gad! he thought, the rout at the bridge had served, then, as a spark to all this tinder! For a moment – since under a mask of indifference and cynicism he was a very hot-tempered young man – the sting of that knowledge prompted him to attempt cutting his way through regardless of consequences. Then common sense triumphed. Better to avoid the enemy altogether by crossing to the farther side of the smaller lake just ahead of him (he did not know its name) on the wide flat isthmus which separated it from Loch Lochy. If there were no ambushes on that side he would yet reach Fort Augustus, since, as the Highlanders did not appear to have horses, he was safe from mounted pursuit.

It became, however, a question whether he would get to the isthmus in time to evade the enemy ahead, of whom half a dozen or so, suspecting his intention, were running down the road towards him, targe on arm and broadsword in hand, to cut him off. Keith spurred his horse hard, fired at the foremost figure (which he missed) and next moment dropped his own pistol with an exclamation, his arm tingling to the shoulder. A bullet had struck the barrel, ricocheting off Heaven knew where; in any case it was one of the nearest escapes which he had ever experienced. For the moment his right arm was useless; but here, at last, was the end of the waters of this interminable Lock Lochy. He turned his almost frantic horse and galloped like mad across the green, spongy isthmus, pursued now only by ineffectual yells which he soon ceased to hear.

The neck of land, though narrow, was longer than he remembered; there were perhaps two miles of it before the next lake came to separate him from his enemies. But, whether or no the fact of his having a fast horse deterred them from pursuit, not one Highlander attempted to cross after him. Possibly they were reserving their forces undiminished for the attack on the main body of the Royals, a thought which caused the Englishman to maintain his headlong pace. Fortunately this side of the lake seemed deserted; no man was going to stop him now!

And no man did. But he had not gone a mile by the lake side when a large grey-and-white object flapped up suddenly from the water's edge almost under the nose of his excited horse; the beast shied, swerved, crossed its legs and came heavily down, flinging its rider against a fallen tree with a force which knocked him senseless.

Captain Windham was not stunned for very long, though to him it was an unknown space of time that he lay sprawling in the dust by the side of the pine-trunk. When he dizzily raised himself and looked about him no human being was in sight, but there on the road, within a few feet of him, with snorting nostrils and terrified eyes, lay his unfortunate horse, trying desperately and repeatedly to get to its feet again, despite a broken foreleg. Keith stared at the poor sweating, plunging brute, then, passing a hand over his bruised and bleeding forehead, he got to his own feet. There was only one thing to be done; though the sound of a shot would very likely draw undesirable attention upon himself, he could not leave the animal there in agony. His remaining pistol was in his holster, and during the process of extracting it he realized that he had twisted an ankle in his fall. A moment or two later the sound of a shot went ringing over the waters of Loch Oich, and the troubles of Captain Windham's charger were over.

But his were not; indeed he fancied that they had but just begun. Dismounted, his brilliant scarlet-and-blue uniform rendering him in the highest degree conspicuous, his head aching, and in one place excoriated by contact with the tree-trunk, he saw that he could never summon reinforcements in time now; it was doubtful whether he would reach Fort Augustus at all. His ankle, as he soon discovered, was swollen and painful; moreover he had somehow to get back to Wade's road when he reached the end of this lake. With his hand to his head he glanced in disgust at the prostrate trunk with which it had just made such painful acquaintance. Detestable country, where even the wildfowl and the vegetation were in league with the inhabitants!

Hearing a sound of water, he looked about till he found a tiny ice-cold spring between the track and the lake, and, dipping his handkerchief into this, bathed his forehead. Had he known of the seven gory severed heads which had been washed in that innocent-looking little source less than a hundred years before, perhaps he would not have done so. Hardly had he reloaded his pistol, his next care, when a distant noise, like many running feet, sent him hurriedly to the shelter of the steep, tree-clad hillside on his left. Here, among the scanty undergrowth, he crouched as best he could while, some minutes later, a score of armed Highlanders poured past on the track below him. So this side of the lake was gathering, too!

Captain Windham waited in his concealment until the way was clear and silent again, and then descended, since it was impossible for him to keep in cover if he meant to reach Fort Augustus – and where else should he make for? Leaning on the branch of oak which he had broken off to assist his steps, he began to trudge grimly forward.

There soon came in sight, on its rock by the lake side, the keep of Invergarry Castle. Captain Windham did not know that it belonged to the chief of Glengarry, but he was sure that it was the hold of some robber or other, and that he himself might not improbably see the inside of it. It looked ruinous, but that was no safeguard – on the contrary. And here were some dwellings, little, roughly thatched buildings, but obviously inhabited. Yet all he saw of their occupants were a few white-haired children who ran screaming away, and one old woman at her door, who crossed herself devoutly at sight of him. So, to add to all their other vices, the people of these parts were Papists!

The next obstacle was a river, which he had to cross as best he could on insecure and slippery stones, and the difficulties of doing this with an injured ankle took his mind off remoter possibilities, so that when he was safely over he was surprised to find the ominous tower well behind him, and he went on somewhat cheered. The sun was now getting lower, and though the other side of the glen was in full warm light, this side felt almost cold. Another peculiarity of this repulsively mountainous district. Gently swelling hills one could admire, but masses of rock, scored with useless and inconvenient torrents, had nothing to recommend them. He did not wonder at the melancholy complaints he had heard last night from the officers quartered at Fort·Augustus.

And what would the garrison there say when they heard of this afternoon's disgrace? Captain Windham's thoughts went angrily back to it. What, too, had happened to those chicken-hearted recruits by this time? He pulled out his watch; to his surprise it was after six o'clock. And he still had the watch in his hand when his ear was caught by the sound of horse's hoofs behind him. He stopped to listen. The pace, a smart trot, did not seem hurried; the rider might be some unconcerned traveller. But he might on the other hand be an enemy. Keith Windham looked for cover, but here there was none convenient as a while ago, and the best he could do was to hobble on ahead to where a solitary oak tree reared itself by the side of the road, for he was minded to have something to set his back against if necessary.

When he was nearly there he looked round, and saw the rider, a big Highlander on a grey horse. He was not alone, for at his heels came another, keeping up with the horse with long loping strides like a wolf's. To Keith one tartan was as yet like another, so, for all he knew, these two might be of a friendly clan. He awaited them by the oak tree.

As the horseman came on Keith saw that he was young, vigorous-looking and well armed. He wore trews, not a kilt like the other. But as he came he rose in his stirrups and shouted something in which Keith clearly caught the word 'surrender'. So he was not friendly. Very well then! Captain Windham raised the pistol which he had ready, and fired – rather at the horse than the rider. The young Highlander, with a dexterity which he could not but admire, pulled aside the animal in the nick of time, and the shot missed. Keith's sword leapt out as, with a yell, the man on foot flung himself past the horse towards him, dirk in hand. But the rider called out something in Gaelic, which had an immediate effect, for the gillie, or whatever he was, came to an abrupt stop, his eyes glowering and his lips drawn back, as like a wolf about to spring as possible.

Meanwhile, to Keith's surprise, the horseman sprang to earth, flung the reins to his henchman, and came forward empty-handed – a magnificent specimen of young manhood, as the soldier could not help admitting.

'I advise you to surrender, sir,' he said courteously, lifting his bonnet, in which were fastened two eagles' feathers. 'I am sorry to take advantage of an injured man, but I have my Chief's orders. You are completely cut off, and moreover your men are all prisoners – indeed Captain Scott is at this moment in Lochiel's custody. If you will give up your sword I shall be honoured to take you into mine.'

'The deuce you will!' exclaimed Keith, secretly astonished at the polish of his manner – a man who wore a plaid! 'And who are you, pray?'

'Cameron of Ardroy,' answered the young man. 'Lochiel's second cousin,' he added.

'I don't care whose second cousin you are, Mr Cameron of Ardroy,' returned Captain Windham to this, 'but if you think that you are going to have my sword for the asking, you and your cut-throat there, you are vastly mistaken!'

For provided – but it was a big proviso – that the two did not rush upon him at once he thought that he could deal with each separately. Splendidly built as this young Highlander was, lean too, and doubtless, muscular, he probably knew no more of swordplay than was required to wield that heavy basket-hilted weapon of his, and Captain Windham himself was a good swordsman. Yes, provided Lochiel's second cousin did not use the pistol that he wore (which so far he had made no motion to do) and provided that the wolf-like person remained holding the horse . . .

'Come on and take me,' he said provocatively, flourishing his sword. 'You are not afraid, surely, of a lame man!' And he pointed with it to the rough staff at his feet.

Under his tan the large young Highlander seemed to flush slightly. 'I know that you are lame; and your forehead is cut. You had a fall: I came upon your dead horse. That is why I do not wish to fight you. Give up your sword, sir; it is no disgrace. We are two to one, and you are disabled. Do not, I pray you constrain me to disable you further!'

Hang the fellow, why did he behave so out of his cateran's rôle? 'You are considerate indeed!' retorted Captain Windham mockingly. 'Suppose you try first whether you *can* disable me further! – Now, Mr Cameron, as I don't intend to be stopped on my road by mere words, I must request you to stand out of my way!' And – rashly, no doubt, since in so doing he no longer had one eye on that murderous-looking gillie – he advanced sword in hand upon his reluctant opponent. Frowning, and muttering something under his breath, the young man with the eagles' feathers at last drew his own weapon, and the blades rang together.

Thirty seconds of it, and Keith Windham knew that he had attacked a swordsman quite as good if not better than himself. Breathing hard, he was being forced back to the trunk of the oak again, and neither his aching head nor his damaged ankle was wholly to blame for this. Who said that broadsword play was not capable of finesse? This surprisingly scrupulous young barbarian could have cut him down just then, but he drew back when he had made the opening. The certitude of being spared irritated the soldier; he lost his judgment and began to fight wildly, and so the end came, for his sword was suddenly torn from his hand, sailed up into the oak tree above him, balanced a moment on a branch, and then fell a couple of yards away. And his adversary had his foot on it in a second.

As for Keith Windham, he leant back against the oak tree, his head all at once going round like a mill-wheel, with the noise of a sluice, too, in his ears. For a flash everything was blank; then he felt that someone was supporting him by an arm, and a voice said in his ear: 'Drink this, sir, and accept my apologies. But indeed you forced me to it.'

Keith drank, and, though it was only water, sight was restored to him. It was his late opponent who had his arm under his, and who was looking at him with a pair of very blue eyes.

'Yes, I forced you to it,' confessed Captain Windham, drawing a long breath. 'I surrender – I can do nothing else, Mr . . . Cameron.'

'Then I will take you home with me, and your hurts can be dressed,' said the Highlander, showing no trace of elation. 'We shall have to go back as far as the pass, but fortunately I have a horse. *Lachuin, thoir dhomh an t'each!*'

The gillie, scowling, brought forward the grey. His captor loosed Keith's arm and held the stirrup. 'Can you mount, sir?'

'But I am not going to ride your horse!' said Keith, astonished. 'It will not carry two of us – and what will you do yourself?'

'I? Oh, I will walk,' answered the victor carelessly. 'I assure you that I am more accustomed to it. But you would never reach Ardroy on foot, lame as you are.' And as Keith hesitated, looking at this disturbing exponent of Highland chivalry, the exponent added, hesitating a little himself: 'There is only one difficulty. If you are mounted, I fear I must ask you for your parole of honour?'

'I give it you – and that willingly,' answered Keith, with a sudden spurt of good feeling. 'Here's my hand on it, if you like, Mr Cameron!'

Chapter Two

I F to ride along a road in these mountain solitudes was distasteful, to be following a mere track (and that a very steep one) in amongst their very folds was worse. When first he had seen the path which they were to ascend, and the V-shaped depression, sharp against the sunset sky, up to which it led, Captain Windham had with difficulty repressed an exclamation of alarm. However, he could not really believe that Mr Cameron of Ardroy was taking him up this terrifying route in order to slay him, since he could already have done this with so much less trouble on level ground. Therefore, though he had raised his eyebrows, he had said nothing. After all, it was the horse, and not he, who had to do the climbing. And now they were half-way up.

The wolf-like attendant, carrying the surrendered sword, kept in the rear, but Captain Windham was almost physically conscious of his frown behind him. This unattractive person was, he felt, no willing party to his capture; he would much have preferred that the redcoat should have been left cold beneath the oak tree. Meanwhile his master, the young chieftain, or whatever he was, walked with a mountaineer's elastic step at the horse's head, occasionally taking hold of the bridle; rather silent, but uncommonly well-made and good-looking, thought his captive again, glancing down at him.

Captain Windham's own dark, rather harsh features were not unpleasing, save when he frowned, which he was somewhat given to doing, nor were they devoid of a certain distinction, and he had really fine hazel eyes. But his mouth had already taken a cynical twist unusual in a young man of thirty. If he had a passion left in life, it was military ambition. Earlier he had known others, and they had brought him nothing but unhappiness. As a boy he had had an extraordinary devotion to his lovely mother – whom he had not been alone in thinking fair. But she, too, was ambitious, and her second marriage, to the Earl of Stowe, with its attendant advantages, was more to her than the claims of her own son. Then the beautiful boy she bore to Lord Stowe usurped the place which Keith had never had in her heart. So, in respect of affection, sometimes even of ordinary attention, he had passed through a neglected childhood and a starved boyhood, and they had left an indelible mark on him – more indelible, though he did not guess it, than the scars of another woman's betrayal of him four years ago.

The consequence was that at thirty, with a nature at bottom passionate and impulsive, he had become as disillusioned, as little prone to enthusiasms, as a man of twice his age. His creed was that it was a mistake to desire anything very much – a fatal mistake to desire a place in any person's affections, or to admit anyone, man or woman, to a place in your own. By the end of life, no doubt, every human being had discovered this truth; he had done so early, and could count himself the more fortunate.

At the same time it needed a rather different kind of detachment to take his present situation philosophically; and yet, to his own surprise, Keith Windham knew that he was doing so, even though he had by now gleaned from his captor the later history of the day's disaster, and had learnt its mortifying completeness. Matters had fallen out for the unfortunate recruits almost exactly as Captain Windham had afterwards feared; for another body of Highlanders *was* following them unseen on the hillside, and near the head of Loch Lochy further progress had been barred by those who had attempted to stay Keith himself. Though Captain Scott too had tried to cross the isthmus, it was impossible, since more Highlanders were hastening to the spot from that direction also. Too tired and panic-stricken to use their muskets to good effect, the redcoats had, on the contrary, received a fire which had killed five of them and wounded a dozen, including Captain Scott himself. Some leader called 'Keppoch', Captain Windham heard, had then called on the Royals to surrender, or they would be cut to pieces, and to save his men Captain Scott had done so. Immediately on this had come up Ewen Cameron's chief, Lochiel (who had been asked for assistance), with a number of his clan, including the present narrator, had taken charge of the prisoners, and marched them off to his house of Achnacarry. But as the Highlanders from the far side of Loch Oich reported having seen a dead charger on the road, and one company of the redcoats was plainly captainless, Lochiel had sent his young kinsman, since he happened to be mounted, in pursuit of the missing officer. (And at this point the officer in question had remarked rather stiffly that he trusted Mr Cameron knew that his absence from the scene of conflict was due only to his having gone for reinforcements, and Mr Cameron had replied politely that no other explanation had even occurred to him.)

They were at the top of the pass at last, and had a fine view before them; but the captive did not find it so, the mountains being too high for his taste and the downward path too steep. Stones rolled away from beneath the grey's hoofs; now and then he slipped a trifle, for which his owner, leading him carefully by the bridle, apologized. He would not have come this way, he said, but that it was the shortest from the spot where he and Captain Windham had 'chanced to meet', as he put it. And then all at once the descent was less steep and they were looking down on a glen among the mountains, with a little like some signs of cultivation, grazing sheep and cattle, and, in the midst of trees, the roof and chimneys of a house, whence a welcome smoke ascended.

'There is Loch na h-Iolaire,' said the young Highlander at Captain Windham's bridle, pointing to the sheet of water: and he paused after he had said it, because, though Captain Windham could not guess it, he never came upon the loch from any point of the compass without a little fountain of joy bubbling up and singing to itself in his heart. 'And there is the house of Ardroy, our destination. I am sure that you will be glad of a meal and a bed, sir.'

Keith admitted it, and the descent continued, in the face of the sunset afterglow. His captor did not live in a cave, then – but the Englishman had abandoned that idea some time ago. Indeed Mr Cameron was apparently a landed proprietor with tenants, for besides sheep, goats and cows, there were a good many roughly constructed cottages scattered about. By and by, skirting the end of the little lake and its birch trees, they struck into another track, and Keith saw the house in front of him, a simple but not undignified two-storeyed building of which one end was slightly lower than the other, as if it had been added to. Over the porch was a coat-of-arms, which successive layers of whitewash had made difficult to decipher.

'I expect that my aunt, who keeps house for me, and my guests are already supping,' observed the young owner of this domain, assisting his prisoner to dismount. 'We will join them with as little delay as possible. Excuse me if I precede you.' He walked in and opened a door on his right. 'Aunt Margaret, I have brought a visitor with me.'

From behind him the 'visitor' could see the large raftered room, with a long table spread for a meal, and a generous hearth, by which were standing an elderly man and a girl. But in the foreground was a middle-aged lady, well-dressed and comely, exclaiming: 'My dear Ewen, what possesses you to be so late? And what's this we hear about a brush with the Elector's troops near Loch Lochy? . . . Mercy on us, who's this?'

'A guest whom I have brought home with me from the Glen,' replied the latecomer. 'Yes, there has been a skirmish. – Captain Windham, let me present you to my aunt, Miss Cameron, to Miss Grant, and to Mr Grant, sometimes of Inverwick.'

Keith bowed, and the two ladies curtseyed.

'You are just going to sit down to supper?' queried the master of the house. 'We shall be glad of it; and afterwards, Aunt Margaret, pray find some bandages and medicaments for Captain Windham, who has met with a bad fall.'

'I had perhaps better tell you, madam,' interpolated Keith at this point, holding himself rather erect, 'that, though Mr Cameron is kind enough to call me a guest, I am in reality his prisoner. – But not one who will put you to any inconvenience of wardship,' he added quickly, seeing the look which passed over the lady's expressive countenance. 'I have given Mr Cameron my parole of honour, and I assure you that even "the Elector's" officers observe that!' (For he believed so then.)

Miss Cameron surveyed him with humour at the corners of her mouth. 'Every country has its own customs, Captain Windham; now I warrant you never speak but of "the Pretender" in London. You are English, sir?'

'I have that disability, madam.'

'Well, well,' said Miss Cameron, breaking into a smile, 'even at that, no doubt you can eat a Highland supper without choking. But take the Captain, Ewen, and give him some water, for I'm sure he'll be wanting to wash off the traces of battle.'

'I should be grateful indeed,' began Keith uncomfortably, wondering how much blood and dirt still decorated his face; but his captor broke in: 'You must not think that I am responsible for Captain Windham's condition, Aunt Margaret. His horse came down as he was riding to fetch reinforcements from Kilcumein, and he was disabled before ever I overtook him.'

'An accident, sir – or was the poor beast shot?' queried Miss Cameron.

'An accident, madam,' responded Keith. 'A heron, I presume it was, rose suddenly from the lake and startled him; I was riding very fast, and he came down, breaking his leg. I twisted my ankle, besides being stunned for a while, so that I must apologize if my appearance—' And this time he put up his hand to his forehead.

'A heron, did you say?' exclaimed Ewen Cameron's voice beside him, surprised and almost incredulous. 'A *heron* brought your horse down?'

'Yes,' replied Keith, surprised in his turn. 'Why not, Mr Cameron? An unusual mischance, I dare say, and none of my seeking, I assure you; but it is true.'

'I don't doubt your word, sir,' replied the young man; yet there was something puzzled in the gaze which he turned on his prisoner. 'It is . . . yes, unusual, as you say. Herons, as a rule—' He broke off. 'If you will come with me, Captain Windham, you shall refresh yourself before we eat.'

Captain Windham sat down to a better supper than he had met since he left London, and even in London he would not have tasted such trout and venison, and might well have drunk worse claret. Out of regard for him, perhaps, or out of discretion, the conversation never touched on political matters, though he thought that he could feel a certain excitement simmering below the surface of the talk. (And well it might, he reflected; had not the master of the house this day committed himself to overt hostilities against His Majesty's Government?) The elderly gentleman in the grey wig, who appeared to have been living recently in Paris, discoursed most innocuously of French châteaux and their gardens, with frequent references to Versailles and Marly, and appeals to his daughter —'You remember the day of our little expedition to the château of Anet, my dear?' Keith would have thought the deserted shrine of St Germain a more likely goal of pilgrimage, for he took Mr Grant, from his mere presence here, to be a Jacobite.

But surely his daughter would have preferred to this mild talk of parterres and façades a recital by Mr Ewen Cameron of his afternoon's prowess! As far as their personal conflict went, Captain Windham was perfectly willing that this encounter should be related by a victor who was evidently disposed to allow the fullest weight to the physical disabilities of the vanquished; yet he was grateful for the tact with which

Mr Cameron (in his presence at least) had glossed over the flight of the Royal Scots from the bridge. Only questions, indeed, drew from him the partial information which he furnished. He would tell them more afterwards, no doubt. . . . Who was this pretty Miss Grant with the blue fillet in her dark hair – a kinswoman? If she was the future mistress of the house, young Cameron had good taste. So, to be just, had the lady.

But, despite the courtesy shown him, the unwilling guest was not sorry when, very soon after supper, it was suggested that he should retire, for his ankle was painful and one shoulder ached, though he protested that he could look after his own hurts. His conqueror showed him to his bedchamber exactly as a host might have done. The room was of a fair size, and had good old-fashioned furniture; and, presumably because it had been for some time unused, there was even a fire burning. An elderly woman brought up a crock of hot water, a salve and linen for bandages, and the Englishman was then left to her ministrations. And it was not long before his discreet questions had drawn from this dame, who was not very communicative, and spoke English as though it were a foreign tongue to her, the information that Miss Grant was to marry the laird in the autumn. Keith privately hoped that the prospective bridegroom might not find himself in prison before that time, as a consequence of having laid hands on himself – if of nothing worse – though, after that venison, he resolved that he would not lift a finger to send him there.

When his ankle had been bathed and bound up, and the elderly servant had withdrawn, the soldier removed his sash, coat and wig, and extended himself in a comfortable chair in front of the fire, with his bandaged foot on another. There were books to his hand, as he discovered by reaching up to a shelf on the wall; but, having pulled some down, he did not, at first, find that the effort had repaid him. He had captured a Terence, a Horace, *Télémaque*, and Montesquieu's *Lettres Persanes*. They all had Ewen Cameron's name written in them.

Keith whistled. He was turning over the leaves of the *Lettres* when there was a knock and his host – or gaoler – re-entered.

'I hope that Marsali has made you comfortable, sir? – Those books are not very entertaining, I am afraid. If you intend reading into the night – which I fear must mean that your foot is paining you – I will see whether I cannot find you something else. I believe that my aunt has Mr Fielding's novel of *Joseph Andrews* somewhere.'

'Pray do not trouble, sir,' replied Keith. 'I intend to go to bed and sleep; it was only idleness which directed my hand to that shelf there. I see that you read French and Latin, Mr Cameron?' And even as he uttered the words he thought how ill-bred was the remark, and the surprise which he had not been able entirely to keep out of his tone.

But the young Highlander answered quite simply, in his gentle, rather slow voice: 'I was partly educated in France – for that, you know, is easier for us Jacobites. As to Latin, yes, I can read it still, though I am afraid that my hexameters would only procure me the ferule nowadays.'

Captain Windham's ideas about the Northern barbarians were undergoing startling changes. He had already noticed that none of the inmates of this house used the vernacular which he was accustomed to hear in the Lowlands; they spoke as good English as himself, if with an unfamiliar and not displeasing lilt. A little to cover his annoyance at his own lack of breeding he remarked: 'France, yes; I suppose that your connection is close. And now that the . . . that a certain young gentleman has come thence—'

'Yes?' asked the other in a slightly guarded manner.

'No, perhaps we had best not engage upon that topic,' said Keith, with a slight smile. 'I will imitate your own courteous discretion at supper, Mr Cameron, in saying so little about the episode at the bridge, of which indeed, as a soldier, I am not proud. – By the way, having myself introduced that subject, I will ask you if you can make clear a point in connection with it which has puzzled me ever since. How was it that no attempt at pursuit – or at least no immediate attempt – was made by the body posted there?'

'That is easily explained,' replied Ewen Cameron promptly. 'The Keppoch MacDonalds there dared not let you see how few they were, lest your men should have rallied and crossed the bridge after all.'

'How few?' repeated Captain Windham, thinking he had not heard aright. 'But, Mr Cameron, there were a quantity of Highlanders there, though, owing to the trees it was impossible to form an accurate estimate of their numbers.'

'No, that would be so,' said his captor, looking at him rather oddly. 'You may well have thought the bridge strongly held.'

'You mean that it was not?' And, as his informant merely shook his head, Keith said impatiently, but with a sudden very unpleasant misgiving: 'Do you know how many men were there, Mr Cameron?'

Mr Cameron had taken up a fresh log, and now placed it carefully in position on the fire before answering. 'I believe,' he said, with what certainly sounded like reluctance, 'that there were not above a dozen there – to be precise, eleven men, and a piper.'

Keith's fingers closed on the arms of his chair. 'Are you jesting, sir?'

'Not in the least,' replied the young man, without any trace either of amusement or of elation. 'I know it to be a fact, because I spoke afterwards with their leader, MacDonald of Tiendrish. They used an old trick, I understand, to pass themselves off as more than they really were.'

He continued to look at the fire. Captain Windham, with a suppressed exclamation, had lowered his injured foot to the ground, and then remained silent, most horribly mortified. Two companies of His Majesty's Foot turning tail before a dozen beggarly Highlanders with whom they had not even stayed to exchange shots! The solace, such as it had been, of reflecting that the recruits had in the end been surrounded and outnumbered, was swept clean away, for he knew now that they would never have come to this pass but for their initial poltroonery. Keith had lost all desire for further converse, and every instinct of patronage was dead within him. Why the devil had he ever asked that question?

'I think, sir,' observed his captor, turning round at last, 'that it would be better, would it not, if you went to bed? I hope that you have been given everything that is necessary?'

'Everything, thank you,' replied Keith shortly. 'And also, just now, something that I could well have done without.' He tried to speak lightly, yet nothing but vexation, he knew, sounded in his tone.

'I am sorry,' said the Highlander gravely. 'I would not have told you the number had you not pressed me for it. Forget it, sir.' He went to the door. 'I hope that your injured ankle will not keep you awake.'

That ill office was much more likely to be performed by the piece of news which he had presented to the sufferer. 'Eleven men and a piper!' repeated Captain Keith Windham of the Royal Scots when the door was shut; and with his sound leg he drove his heel viciously into the logs of Highland pine.

Chapter Three

CAPTAIN KEITH WINDHAM, unwillingly revisiting the neighbourhood of High Bridge, which was populated with leaping Highlanders about nine feet high, and permeated, even in his dream, with the dronings and wailings of the bagpipe, woke, hot and angry, to find that the unpleasant strains at least were real, and were coming through the window of the room in which he lay. He remained a moment blinking, wondering if they portended some attack by a hostile clan; and finally got out of bed and hobbled to the window.

In front of the house a bearded piper was marching solemnly up and down, the ribbons on the drones of his instrument fluttering in the morning breeze. There was no sign of any armed gathering. 'Good Gad, it must be the usual reveillé for the household!' thought the Englishman. 'Enough to put a sensitive person out of temper for the rest of the day.' And he returned to bed and pulled the blankets over his ears.

At breakfast, an excellent meal, and a pleasant one also, where very civil enquiries were made concerning the night he had spent and the state of his injuries, Miss Cameron expressed a hope that he had not been unduly disturbed by Neil MacMartin's *piobaireachd*, adding that he was not as fine a piper as his father Angus had been. Keith was then thankful that he had not heard Angus.

When the meal was over he strayed to the window and looked out, wondering how he should occupy himself all day, but determined upon one thing, that he would not let these Camerons guess how bitterly he was mortified over the matter of the bridge. Outside the porch his host (save the mark!) was already talking earnestly to a couple of Highlanders, in one of whom Captain Windham had no difficulty in recognizing the 'cut-throat' of the previous day; the other, he fancied, was the musician of the early morning. 'I wish I could persuade myself that Mr Cameron were putting a ban upon that performance,' he thought; but he hardly hoped it.

Presently the young laird came in. He was wearing the kilt today, and for the first time Keith Windham thought that there was something to be said for that article of attire – at least on a man of his proportions.

'Is not that your attendant of yesterday out there?' remarked the soldier idly.

'Lachlan MacMartin? Yes. The other, the piper who, I am afraid, woke you this morning, is his brother Neil. – Captain Windham,' went on the piper's master in a different tone, 'what I am going to tell you may be news to you, or it may not, but in either case the world will soon know it. Today is Saturday, and on Monday the Prince will set up his standard at Glenfinnan.'

There was a second's silence. 'And you, I suppose, Mr Cameron, intend to be present . . . and to cross the Rubicon in his company?'

'All Clan Cameron will be there,' was the reply, given with a probably unconscious lift of the head. 'And as in consequence of this I shall be pretty much occupied today, and little at home, I would advise you, if I may, not to go out of sight of the house and policies. You might—' Ewen Cameron hesitated for a moment.

'I might find myself tempted to abscond, you were going to say?' struck in his captive . . . and saw at once, from the bleak look which came into those blue eyes, that his pleasantry did not find favour.

'I should not dream of so insulting you,' replied Ardroy coldly. 'I was merely going to say that it might not be over-safe for you, in that uniform, if you did.' And as he was evidently quite offended at the idea that he could be supposed to harbour such a suspicion of his prisoner, there was nothing for the latter to do but to beg his pardon, and to declare that he had spoken – as indeed he had – in the merest jest.

'But perhaps this young mountaineer cannot take a jest,' he thought to himself when they had parted. 'I'll make no more – at least outwardly.' But he was not to keep this resolution.

And indeed he had little but occasional glimpses of young

Ardroy or any of the family that morning. The whole place was in a bustle of preparations and excitement. Tenants were (Keith surmised from various indications) being collected and armed; though only single Highlanders, wild and unintelligible persons, appeared from time to time in the neighbourhood of the house. Miss Cameron and Miss Grant seemed to be equally caught up in the swirl, and Mr Grant was invisible. The only idle person in this turmoil, the captive Englishman sat calmly on the grass plot at a little distance from the house, with *The History of the Adventures of Mr Joseph Andrews* in his hand, half amused to see the inhabitants of this ant-heap – thus he thought of them – so busy over what would certainly come to nothing, like all the other Jacobite attempts.

And yet he reflected that, for all the futility of such preparations, those who made them were like to pay very dearly for them. Ewen Cameron would get himself outlawed at the least, and somehow he, whom Ewen Cameron had defeated yesterday, would be sorry. The young Highlander had certainly displayed towards his captive foe the most perfect chivalry and courtesy, and to this latter quality Keith Windham, who could himself at will display the most perfect rudeness, was never blind. And yet – a sardonically comforting reflection – a rebel must find the presence of an English soldier not a little embarrassing at this juncture.

It was partly a desire to show that he too possessed tact, and partly pure boredom, which caused Captain Windham, in the latter half of the afternoon, to disregard the warning given him earlier, and to leave the neighbourhood of the house. He helped himself to a stout stick on which to lean in case of necessity, though his ankle was remarkably better and hardly pained him at all, and started to stroll along the bank of the loch. Nobody had witnessed his departure. And in the mild, sometimes obscured sunshine, he followed the path round to the far side, thinking that could the little lake only be transported from these repellent mountains and this ugly purple heather into more civilized and less elevated surroundings, it would not be an ill piece of water.

Arrived on the farther side, he began idly to follow a track which led away from the lake and presently started to wind upwards among the heather. He continued to follow it without much thinking of what he was doing, until suddenly it brought him round a fold of the mountain side to a space of almost level ground where, beside a group of pine trees, stood three low thatched cottages. And there Captain Windham remained staring, not exactly at the cottages, nor at the score or so of Highlanders – men, women, and children – in front of these dwellings, with their backs turned to him, but at the rather puzzling operations which were going forward on top of the largest croft.

At first Captain Windham thought that the man astride the roof and the other on the short ladder must be repairing the thatch, until he saw that, on the contrary, portions of this were being relentlessly torn off. Then the man on the roof plunged in his arm to the shoulder and drew forth something round and flat, which he handed to the man on the ladder, who passed it down. Next came something long that glittered, then another round object, then an unmistakable musket; and with that Keith realized what he was witnessing – the bringing forth of arms which should have been given up at the Disarming Act of 1725, but which had been concealed and saved for just such an emergency as the present.

Now there came bundling out several broadswords tied together and another musket. But a man in a bright scarlet coat with blue facings and long white spatter-dashes is altogether too conspicuous a figure in a mountain landscape, and Keith had not in fact been there more than a minute before a boy who had turned to pick up a targe saw, gave a yell, and pointing, screamed out something in Gaelic. Every face was instantly turned in the intruder's direction, and moved by the same impulse each man snatched up a weapon and came running towards him, even he on the roof sliding down with haste.

Captain Windham was too proud to turn and flee, nor would it much have advantaged him; but there he was, unarmed save for a staff, not even knowing for certain whether hornets upon whose nest he had stumbled were Mr Cameron's tenants or no, but pretty sure that they would not understand English, and that he could not therefore convince them of his perfect innocence. Deeply did he curse his folly in that moment.

He had at any rate the courage not to attempt to defend himself; on the contrary, he deliberately threw his stick upon the ground, and held out his hands to show that they were empty. The foremost Highlander, who was brandishing one of those unpleasant basket-hilted swords, hesitated, as Keith had hoped, and shouted something; on which the rest rushed forward, and as many hands as possible laid hold of Captain Windham's person. He staggered under the impact, but made no resistance, for, to his great relief, he had already recognized in the foremost assailant with the broadsword the scowling visage of Lachlan MacMartin, and beside him the milder one of his brother Neil, Mr Cameron's piper. Even if they did not understand English, these two would at least know who he was.

'I am your master's prisoner,' he called out, wishing the others would not press so upon him as they clutched his arms. 'You had better do me no harm!'

In Lachlan's face there was a sort of sullen and unwilling recognition. He spoke rapidly to his brother, who nodded and gave what was presumably an order. Reluctantly the clutching hands released their grip of Keith, their owners merely glowering at him; but they did not go away, though the circle now opened out a little. A couple of women had joined the group, and a small child or two; all talked excitedly. Keith had never thought to feel gratitude towards the wolf-like Lachlan, but at this moment he could almost have embraced him, since but for him and Neil his own might well have been the first blood on those resuscitated claymores.

His preserver now advanced, his hand on his dirk, and addressed the soldier, rather to his surprise, in English.

'You may be the laird's prisoner,' he said between his teeth, 'but why did you come up here? – You came to spy, to spy!' He almost spat the words in the intruder's face. 'And with spiess, who haf seen what they should not haf seen, there iss a ferry short way . . . either thiss,' he unsheathed an inch or two of his dirk, 'or the lochan down yonder with a stone round your neck!'

'I am not a spy,' retorted Captain Windham haughtily. 'I knew nothing of there being cottages here; I was taking a walk, and came upon you entirely by accident.'

'A walk, when yesterday your foot was so hurt that you must ride the laird's horse!' hissed Lachlan, bringing out all the sibilants in this not ineffective retort. 'All thiss way for pleasure with a foot that iss hurt! And then you will pe going back to the *saighdearan dearg* – to the red soldiers – at

Kilcumein and pe telling them. . . . Ach, it will certainly pe petter . . .' And his fingers closed round the black hilt at his groin; Keith had never seen fingers which more clearly itched to draw and use a weapon.

But at this point Neil the piper intervened, laying his hand on his brother's arm, shaking his head, and speaking earnestly in their native tongue, and Keith, concluding that a professional musician (if that term could possibly be extended to one who produced sounds like this morning's) would be a man of peace, felt more secure, not knowing that in a fray the piper habitually gave his pipes to his boy and fought with the best. But he heartily wished himself back at the house again; it would have been far better had he taken his host's warning to heart instead of making a foolish jest about it.

During the colloquy, however, there approached the group a handsome, venerable old man whom Keith had not previously noticed. He came towards them tapping the ground with a long staff, as if of uncertain sight, and said something first to Lachlan and then to Neil. The piper appeared to listen with attention, and on that turned to the captive.

'My father iss asking you,' he said, in a manner which suggested that he was seeking for his words in an unfamiliar tongue, 'to permit him to touch you, and to pe speaking with you. He iss almost blind. He hass not the English, but I will pe speaking for him.'

'Certainly, if he wishes it,' replied Captain Windham with resignation, thinking that 'permission' to touch him might well have been asked earlier, and not taken so violently for granted.

Neil took his father's hand, and led him up to the interview. The old man, who was obviously not completely blind, peered into the Englishman's face, while his hands strayed for a moment or two over his shoulders and breast. He then addressed a question to his elder son, who translated it.

'He asks if you wass meeting a *curra* yesterday?'

'If I had any notion what a *curra* was,' returned Keith, 'I might be able to satisfy your father's curiosity. As it is—'

'A *curra*,' explained Neil, struggling, 'iss . . . a large bird, having a long . . . a long . . .'

'It iss called "heron" in the English,' interposed Lachlan. And he added violently: '*Mallachd ort!* wass you meeting a heron yessterday?'

The Erse sounded like an objurgation (which it was) and the speaker's eyes as they glared at Keith had turned to dark coals. It was evidently a crime in these part to encounter that bird, though to the heron's victim himself it wore rather the aspect of a calamity. Ignoring this almost frenzied query he replied shortly to the official interpreter: 'Yes, unfortunately I did meet a heron yesterday, which by frightening my horse led to – my being here today.'

Lachlan MacMartin smote his hands together with an exclamation which seemed to contain as much dismay as anger, but Neil contented himself with passing on this information to his parent, and after a short colloquy turned once more to the Englishman.

'My father iss *taibhsear*,' he explained. 'That iss, he hass the two sights. He knew that the heron would pe making Mac – the laird to meet with you.'

'Gad, I could wish it had not!' thought Keith; but judged it more politic not to give this aspiration utterance.

'And he asks you whether you wass first meeting Mac 'ic Ailein near watter?'

'If that name denotes Mr Ewen Cameron,' replied Keith. 'I did. Near a good deal of "watter".'

This was passed on to the seer, involving the repetition of a word which sounded to Captain Windham like 'whisky', and roused in his mind a conjecture that the old man was demanding, or about to demand, that beverage. None, however, was produced, and after thanking the Englishman, in a very courtly way, through the medium of his son, the soothsayer departed again, shaking his head and muttering to himself; and Keith saw him, when he reached the cottages, sit down upon a bench outside the largest and appear to fall into a reverie.

Directly he was safely there, Lachlan MacMartin reverted with startling suddenness to his former character and subject of conversation.

'You haf seen what you should not haf seen, red-coat!' he repeated fiercely. 'Pefore you go away from thiss place you shall be swearing to keep silence!'

'That I certainly shall not swear to do,' replied Captain Windham promptly. 'I am not accustomed to take an oath at any man's bidding, least of all at a rebel's.'

Again the dark flame shone in the Highlander's eyes.

'And you think that we will be letting you go, Sassenach?'

'I think that you will be extremely sorry for the consequences if you do not,' returned the soldier. 'You know quite well that if you lay a finger upon me you will have to answer for it to your master or chief, or whatever he is!'

'We are the foster-brothers of Mac 'ic Ailein,' responded Lachlan slowly. ('What, all of you?' interjected Keith. 'I wish him joy of you!') 'He knows that all we do iss done for him. If we should pe making a misstake, not knowing hiss will . . . or if you should fall by chance into the loch, we should pe sorry, but we could not help it that your foot should pe slipping, for it was hurt yessterday . . . and you would nefer go back to Kilcumein to tell the *saighdearan dearg* what you haf peen seeing.'

He did not now seem to be threatening, but rather, with a kind of gloomy satisfaction, thinking out a plausible course of action with regard to the intruder, and it was a good deal more disquieting to the latter than his first attitude. So was the expression on the faces of the other men when Lachlan harangued them volubly in his own language. His brother Neil alone appeared to be making some remonstrance, but in the end was evidently convinced, and almost before the unlucky officer realized what was toward, the whole group had launched themselves upon him.

Keith Windham fought desperately, but he had no chance at all, having been surrounded and almost held from the outset, and in a moment he was borne down by sheer weight of numbers. Buttons came off his uniform, his wig was torn bodily from his head by some assailant who probably imagined that he had hold of the Sassenach's own hair, he was buffeted and nearly strangled, and lay at last with his face pressed into the heather, one man kneeling upon his shoulders, while another tied his hands behind his back, and a third, situated upon his legs, secured his ankles. Outraged and breathless, the soldier had time for only two sensations; surprise that no dirk had yet been planted in him, and wonder whether they really meant to take him down and throw him into the lake.

The struggle had been conducted almost in silence; but conversation broke out again now that he was overpowered. Only for a moment, however; then, as suddenly, it ceased, and the

heavy, bony knees on Captain Windham's shoulder-blades unexpectedly removed themselves. A sort of awe-struck silence
succeeded. With faint thoughts of Druids and their sacrifices
in his mind Keith wondered whether the patriarchal soothsayer were now approaching to drive a knife with due
solemnity into his back . . . or, just possibly, to denounce
his descendants' violence. But he could not twist himself to
look, for the man on his legs, though apparently smitten
motionless, was still squatting there.

And then a voice that Keith knew, vibrating with passion,
suddenly shouted words in Erse whose purport he could guess.
The man on his legs arose precipitately. And next moment
Ewen Cameron was kneeling beside him in the heather, bending over him, a hand on his shoulder. 'Captain Windham, are
you hurt? God forgive me, what have they been doing? *Tied!*'
And in a moment he had snatched a little knife out of his
stocking and was cutting Keith's bonds. 'Oh, why did I let
you out of my sight! For God's sake tell me that you are not
injured!'

He sounded in the extreme of anxiety – and well he might
be, thought the indignant Englishman, who made no haste to
reply that, if exhausted, he was as yet unwounded. He made
in fact no reply at all, while the young chieftain, white with
agitation and anger, helped him to his feet. When at last he
stood upright, hot and dishevelled, and very conscious of the
fact, Captain Windham said, in no friendly tone:

'You were just in time, I think, Mr Cameron – that is, if,
now that you are here, your savages will obey you.'

From pale the young man turned red. 'I warned you, if you
remember,' he said rather low, and then, leaving Captain
Windham to pick up his hat and wig and to restore some
order to his attire, strode towards the silent and huddled
group of his retainers, who had retreated in a body nearer to
the crofts. Angry and humiliated as Keith felt, it was some
consolation to him, as he brushed the pieces of heather off
his uniform, and pulled his wig once more over his own short
dark hair, to observe that, whatever their master was saying
to them in the Erse, it seemed to have a most salutary and
withering effect. Even the redoubtable Lachlan, who hoarsely
uttered some remark, presumably an excuse was reduced to
complete silence, either by the very terse and vigorous reply

which he drew upon himself, or by the threatening attitude of the speaker.

All this time the prophetic elder had sat at his cottage door listening, with his head tilted back in the manner of the blind, but taking no part in the reckoning which was falling upon the offenders, just as (presumably) he had sat throughout the assault. And having made short work of the culprits, the rescuer now seemed in haste to remove the rescued, and came towards him, his eyes still very blue and fierce.

'If you will allow me, Captain Windham, I will take you back to the house, away from these savages, as you rightly call them.'

'Thanks, I can return safely enough, no doubt,' replied Keith indifferently, pulling down his waistcoat. 'There are no more encampments of them, I believe, on the way back.'

'I should prefer to escort you,' returned Ardroy, most acutely vexed, as was evident. And, since his vexation did not at all displease the Englishman, he picked up his staff and preceded him in silence off the plateau.

They had gone some way down the montain path before Ewen Cameron spoke again.

'I had no right to accept your sword,' he said, in a voice still bitter with mortification, 'if I could not protect you against my own followers. I would not have had this happen for a thousand pounds. I can offer you no apologies that are deep enough for such an outrage.'

'Except for the loss of some buttons, I am not much the worse,' replied Keith dryly without turning his head.

'But I am,' he heard the Highlander say behind him in a low voice.

Nothing more passed between them until they had arrived at the level of the loch, but by that time a rather remarkable change had come upon Keith. Much better and more dignified to make light of the outrage which he had just suffered than to exaggerate it by sulking over it. Besides, he was beginning to be sorry for the palpable distress of that punctilious young man, Mr Cameron of Ardroy, who could not in very justice be blamed for what had happened.

So he stopped and turned round. 'Mr Cameron,' he said frankly, 'I have no one but myself to thank for the rough handling I received up yonder. You warned me not to go far afield; and moreover I acted like a fool in staying there to watch. Will you forgive my ill-temper, and let me assure you that I shall think no more of the episode except to obey your warnings more exactly in future.'

Ardroy's face cleared wonderfully. 'You really mean that, sir?'

'Assuredly. I ran my head into the lion's mouth myself. I shall be obliged if you will not mention my folly to the ladies; a soldier's self-esteem, you know, is easily hurt.' His smile went up a little at the corner.

A sparkle came into Ewen Cameron's eyes. 'You are generous, Captain Windham, and I am not deceived by your plea for silence. I am so ashamed, however, that I welcome it for the sake of my own self-esteem.'

'But I mean what I say,' returned Keith. (He was quick enough in the uptake, this young chief of the barbarians!) 'It was the act of an utter fool for me, in this uniform, to stand gaping at . . . at what was going on up there. You know what it was, I presume?' he added, with a lift of the eyebrows.

'Naturally,' said Ewen without embarrassment. 'It was that which brought me up there – most fortunately. But now,' he went on with a frown, 'now I am not sure that I shall allow those arms to be carried by men in my tail who have so disgraced themselves and me. – Let us go on, if you will, for when I have escorted you to the house I shall return to deal with that question.'

'You seemed,' observed Keith, as they went on once more, 'to be dealing with it pretty satisfactorily just now!' (so he proposed, as a punishment, to debar the offenders from the pleasures of armed rebellion!)

'At least, before I consent to their following me on Monday,' said the dispenser of justice, striding on, 'they shall all beg your pardon!'

'Oh, pray excuse them that!' exclaimed Keith, not at all welcoming the prospect. 'I should be horribly embarrassed, I assure you. Moreover, I can almost sympathize with their zeal – now that there is no prospect of my being thrown into the lake here with a stone round my neck.'

His captor stopped. 'Was that what they were going to do?' he asked in a horrified tone.

'They spoke of it, since I would not promise to keep silence on what I had seen. They were quite logical, you know, Mr Cameron, for what I saw was certainly not meant for the eyes of an English officer!'

'You were my prisoner – my guest – they had no excuse whatever!' declared the young man, wrath beginning to seize on him again. 'Neil and Lachlan knew that, if the others did not. And Angus – what was Angus about not to stop them?'

'Is that the blind veteran who takes such an interest in the natural history of these parts?'

'What do you mean?' asked his companion.

'Why,' answered Keith, who was after all enjoying a kind of secret revenge by quizzing him, 'that he was particular to inquire, through his estimable son, your piper, whether I had encountered a heron before I made your acquaintance yesterday.'

The mention of that fowl appeared for the second time to startle his host, though until that moment Keith had forgotten its effect upon him last night). 'Ah, my foster-father asked you that?' he murmured, and looked upon the Englishman with a rather troubled and speculative gaze. But Keith had found a new subject of interest. 'Is the old gentleman really your foster-father?' he inquired. 'But of course he must be, if his sons are your foster-brothers.'

'I think,' said the foster-son somewhat hastily, 'that you can return safely from here, so, if you will excuse me, Captain Windham, I will now go back to Slochd nan Eun.'

'To execute judgment,' finished Keith with a smile. 'Indeed, I am not so devoid of rancour as to wish to hinder you. But if you do condemn your foster-relations to stay at home,' he added rather meaningly, 'you will be doing them a good turn rather than an ill one.'

It seemed doubtful, however, if Ewen Cameron had heard this remark, for he was already striding lightly and quickly back in the direction of the mountain path, his kilt swinging about his knees as he went.

It was an odd coincidence that at supper that evening, after Angus MacMartin's name had come up in some talk between Miss Cameron and Mr Grant, the former should turn to Captain Windham and ask if he had seen their *taibhsear* or seer? Seeing instantly from Ardroy's face that he was regretting the introduction of his foster-father's name into the conversation, Keith made malicious haste to reply that he had contrived to get as far as the soothsayer's dwelling, and that his reception there had been a memorable experience. Immediately the ladies asked if Angus had 'seen' anything while the visitor was there, to which Keith, with a glance at his host, replied with great suavity that such might well have been the case, since he appeared, towards the end of the visit, to be entirely withdrawn from outward events.

'He left the honours to his interesting sons,' he explained with a smile, 'who entertained me so . . . so whole-heartedly that if Mr Cameron had not appeared upon the scene I might be there still.' But at this point Ewen, with a heightened colour, forcibly changed the conversation.

Chapter Four

I N spite of a certain amount of turmoil earlier in the day, almost the usual Sunday calm lay on the house of Ardroy between five and six that evening, and in it Alison Grant sat at one of the windows of the long living-room, her arms on the sill, her cheek on her joined hands. Her father had gone to Achnacarry, Ewen was she knew not where, her aunt, she believed, in her bedchamber. It would be better, Alison thought, if she were in hers, upon her knees.

But she could pray here, too, looking out on this blue and purple loveliness of distance, and here she might get a passing glimpse of Ewen, busy though he was, and would not thus be missing any of these precious last moments of him. The sands were slipping so fast now . . .

Alison pulled herself up. The sands were indeed running out, but towards how glorious an hour! Prayed for and wrought for with so much faith and selfless devotion (as well as with so much crooked counter-plot and intrigue), it was to strike tomorrow, when his banner would proclaim to all the winds that the fairy prince of the hopes of a generation was here at last on Scottish soil. And tomorrow Ewen would lay his sword at those long-expected feet. Happy Ewen – happy to be among the faithful, when many were forsworn; happy in that he was a man and could play a man's part. For what could a woman do but hope, and what has she to give but prayers!

Again Alison checked her thoughts, or rather, a new thought came to her. Why, *she* gave what no one else in wide Scotland had to give. Ewen himself!

For a moment she saw herself, as it were, irradiated by the splendour of that priceless gift; then, with a sudden terror, she knew that her will was not to a gift, but to a loan. She was only lending Ewen to the Prince. A gift is gone from one's hands for ever; a loan comes back. She made this loan willingly – more than willingly; but as a free gift, never to be resumed – no, no!

The door in the far corner of the room opened, and Alison swiftly withdrew the hands that she was pressing over her eyes. Miss Cameron came in, looking exactly as usual in her Sunday paduasoy, not a hair out of place beneath her cap, and no sign of agitation or excitement on her firm-featured, pleasant visage. By only one thing was this Sunday of last preparations marked off from any other, that she wore at her waist the capacious silk pocket in which she kept the household keys.

'Ah, there you are, child! Your father is not returned, I suppose? Where is Ewen?'

'I do not know, Aunt Margaret.' Alison's voice seemed to herself a little unsteady, so, with some idea of covering this deviation from the usual she added: 'Nor do I know where Captain Windham is got to either.'

'Captain Windham is down by the loch, my dear; I saw him set out in that direction. And I have my reasons for thinking he'll not have gone farther.' There was an odd tone in Miss Cameron's voice, and a twinkle in her eye, as she sat down on the window-seat by the girl, plunging her hand into that capacious pocket of hers. ' 'Twas our redcoat that I came to speak to you about. Alison, do you know what these are?'

She laid on the window-sill between them two buttons covered with gold thread.

'They look,' said Alison, studying them, 'like the buttons on the lapels of Captain Windham's uniform. I noticed this morning that some were missing. How did you come by them, Aunt Margaret?'

'Neil MacMartin brought them to me about half an hour ago. Before that they were reposing in the heather up at

Slochd nan Eun, where their owner also reposed, very uncomfortably, I fear, yesterday afternoon. I can't keep from laughing when I think of it!' declared Miss Cameron. 'And Alison, are not men the sly creatures! To think that Ewen knew of this yesterday evening, and said never a word!'

'Knew of what, Aunt Margaret?'

'I will tell you,' said Aunt Margaret, with visible enjoyment of the prospect. 'It seems that yesterday afternoon my fine Captain very incautiously walked up to Slochd nan Eun by the lane, and arrived there just as the arms were being taken out of Angus's thatch. Not unnaturally the MacMartins and the others thought that he was a Government spy, so they fell upon him, tied him up, and might have proceeded to I know not what extremities if Ardroy had not appeared in the very nick of time.'

'Oh, what a dreadful thing!' said Alison, aghast.

'Exactly Ewen's view, as you may imagine. He has not yet forgiven the two MacMartins, whom he holds most to blame. Neil, in the greatest despair, has just been to beg me to intercede for him and Lachlan, and seemed to think that the restoration of these buttons, torn off, so I gathered, in the struggle, would go to prove their penitence.'

'Was Captain Windham at all hurt, do you think?'

'No, I do not think so, though I can quite believe that it was not his mother's bosom he was in – you know the Erse saying. Neil admits that they had him on his face in the heather when they trussed him up, and that two of them sat upon him. Well, they are paying for it now. As you know, Ardroy is not in general easily angered, but when he is, he is not easily pacified neither. Neil looks like a whipped dog; 'tis really comical, and I dare say Lachlan is ready to cut his own throat. I think you had best do the interceding, my dear; and you can give Ewen the buttons to return, for we women cannot restore them to Captain Windham without his knowing that his misadventure is no longer the secret that he and Ewen hoped it was.'

'Never fash yourself about Captain Windham, my lass; I warrant he can fend for himself. Ewen should not have brought him here at a moment so inopportune – just what a man would do, without thought of consequences! At the least he might have locked him up somewhere out of harm's way, and not made all this parade of his being a guest and the like.'

'*I* think it fine of Ewen to have behaved so,' retorted Alison rather mutinously.

'Bless you, child,' said Miss Cameron, smiling, 'so it is. I'd not have him a churl. But they must have made a compact, the two deceitful bodies, not to let us know. And to think that I asked the Captain at supper last night had he seen our *taibh-sear* – do you mind of it? And he smiling and saying he was well entertained up at Slochd nan Eun!'

'But Ewen did not smile,' amended Alison. 'He was displeased; I saw it, and wondered why.'

'Now that you mention it, I remember I saw him glower a wee. He's not so deep as yon Englishman, I'm thinking. All the same, he can keep a secret. . . . Alison, my bonny lass, do you think he'll have secrets from you when you are wed?'

'No,' said Alison, shaking her dark curls with a half-secret smile. 'Or if he has, I'll know 'tis something I had best be ignorant of.'

'Then you'll make a dutiful wife, my dear,' pronounced Miss Cameron, smiling too.

'If ever I am a wife at all!' suddenly came from Alison with a catch of the breath, and she turned her head away.

Margaret Cameron, who was never known to show much emotion, who even now, at this last hour before what might prove so tremendous a dawn, seemed mainly occupied with amusement at Captain Windham's misfortune, gazed at that little dark head, so beautifully and proudly set on its long neck, and a profound change came over her cheerful and practical face. Thirty years ago, in the Fifteen, she too had stood where Alison stood now, and had seen her lover go from her down the dark defile. She had never seen him return. . . . Alison did not know this, and even Ewen, though he had heard the story, thought that Aunt Margaret had long ago forgotten her tragedy.

'Oh, my dear, do not say that!'

Struck by the unfamiliar note in the elder woman's voice, Alison turned her head quickly, and met the look in those eyes, nearly as blue as Ewen's. It was a surprise to her, and yet – how could she have imagined that Aunt Margaret did not realize what she, Alison, risked . . . what they both risked!

'I did not mean that,' she exclaimed rather tremulously. 'To be sure Ewen will come back, and we shall be wed some day;

but I cannot help knowing, as he does, how even Lochiel himself has been torn in two by the Prince's coming without the aid that was promised. But when Ewen goes tomorrow he shall never guess how cowardly my heart is.'

Miss Cameron bent forward and kissed her.

'That's my brave lass! We shall both be as gay as the laverock, I dare say, till he's fairly away, and then we can be as hare-hearted as we please, with no one to see. Hark, there's the boy's step! I'll leave you, my dear; don't forget to put in a word for poor Neil!'

'Till he is fairly away.' It echoed in the girl's ears as Miss Cameron slipped from the room. Why, one could not even imagine what the house of Ardroy would be like without Ewen!

'Heart's darling, are you there?' He had come in by the door from the hall, and now threw himself down beside her on the window-seat. 'Hardly a word have I had with you this live-long day! And now I must ride over to Achnacarry for Mac Dhomhnuill Duíbh's final orders, and shall not be back till late, I fear me. But all's ready here, I think.'

'I wish I were more ready,' thought Alison, devouring him with her eyes. His bright hair grew down in such an enchanting square on his wide forehead, and a desire came upon her to pass her hand over some of its thick waves. 'Ah, to see the Prince at last, at last, Ewen, with one's own eyes!'

'You'll see him yourself before long, Alison, I hope, in Edinburgh, or maybe Perth – or even, before that, at Achnacarry, if he honours it. Who knows? Meanwhile you can be practising your curtsy, m'eudail!'

'You do not know what His Royal Highness will do after the standard is set up?'

'I've not a notion. But I shall contrive to send you word of our movements, never fear. I suppose that somewhere or other we shall be obliged to try conclusions with Sir John Cope and the Government troops.'

The words reminded Alison of the commission just laid upon her. She took up the buttons from the window-sill and held them out towards him.

'Ewen, these have just been brought down from Slochd nan Eun.'

Her lover looked at them with a surprise not quite free from embarrassment. 'They must have come off Captain Windham's uniform,' he observed non-committally. 'I will give them back to him.' And he took them from her.

'I must tell you that I have just heard how it was that he lost them,' confessed the girl.

Ewen's mouth tightened. He laid the buttons on the sill again. 'How came that? I had hoped—'

'Yes, dearest, I know; but the matter came out by reason of Neil's bringing the buttons to Aunt Margaret this afternoon as a kind of peace-offering, it would seem. But, Ewen, what a shocking thing to have happened! I do not wonder that you were angry.'

By the laird of Ardroy's looks, he was angry still. Alison trusted that he would never look at her, on her own account, in that stern way; and perhaps indeed Ewen realized that he was frowning on the innocent, for his brow relaxed and he took her hand into his as if in apology.

'Indeed, Alison, my heart was in my mouth when I came upon the MacMartins and the rest up there yesterday; for all I knew they had dirked Captain Windham. It seems they had thought of throwing him into the loch. He should not have gone so far from the house; I warned him against it. But he behaved very well over the affair, and we agreed not to tell you or Aunt Margaret, so you must neither of you say a word to him about the matter this evening.'

'But he must have been greatly offended and incensed. It is true that he was very agreeable at supper, even though Aunt Margaret asked him had he seen Angus.' She paused, wrinkling her brows. 'Ewen, do you think that he was only feigning?'

'No, I do not think so, although he was very angry at first – and naturally. Afterwards he made to treat the affair almost as a joke. But I do not think that in his heart he can have considered it as a joke. And considering that his person should have been held sacred, it was a very black disgrace for me, and I did well to be angry. I am still angry,' he added somewhat unnecessarily, 'and I have not yet resolved whether I shall allow the two MacMartins to accompany me tomorrow.'

'Not take Neil and Lachlan to Glenfinnan – not take your piper and your right-hand man!' exclaimed Alison, almost incredulous. 'But, Ewen, dearest, you will break their hearts for ever if you leave them behind! That punishment is too great! It was surely in ignorance that they sinned; you yourself said that Captain Windham should not have gone there, and in that uniform they must naturally have thought—'

'Neil and Lachlan did *not* sin in ignorance,' interrupted Ewen sternly. 'I had particularly told them that morning what was Captain Windham's position here. The others, if you like, had more excuse, though why Angus did not prevent their setting upon him, as he could have done, I cannot think. The reason he gave was so—' He broke off, and pushed about the buttons on the sill for a moment or two, then, raising his head, said: 'I have not yet told you, Alison, how Angus "saw" last month that this fellow Windham and I would meet.'

'Angus "saw" that you would meet!' repeated Alison, wide-eyed. 'Oh, Ewen, why did you not tell me?'

'Because I forgot all about it till last Friday night. Yes, and what is more, it appears that we are to keep on meeting, confound him!'

'Do you then dislike Captain Windham so much?' asked Alison quickly.

'I do not dislike him at all,' Ewen assured her, 'though I confess that I cannot quite make him out. But I have no desire for the continual rencontres with him which Angus promises me. And I am sure that Captain Windham cannot possibly view me with anything but dislike for capturing him—and now comes yesterday's affair. Don't look so troubled, my heart!'

'Tell me what Angus said.'

Ewen looked at her a moment as if considering. 'But you must not believe it too implicitly, darling; I do not. Though I admit,' he added, as though wishing to be quite just, 'that the old man's predictions have sometimes fulfilled themselves in an extraordinary way. . . . This one began by something about a heron.'

'That, then, was why you were so much surprised on Friday evening,' interpolated Alison in a flash. 'I mean, when Captain Windham said that a heron had brought down his horse. I saw it, Ewen. But how—'

'I will tell you from the beginning,' said her betrothed. He got up and put a knee on the window-seat. 'It was that day at the end of last month when Lochiel's message came about the Prince's landing – you remember? Early that morning Lachlan

had been very troublesome, wanting to shoot the heron that
lives on the island in the loch, because his father had been
having a vision about one. I forbade him to do it. – That re-
minds me, I have not seen the bird of late, but I do not think
that Lachlan dare have disobeyed me. – After I had taken leave
of you that evening, darling, and was just about to set off to
Achnacarry, I met Angus by the Allt Buidhe burn. He had
come down from Slochd nan Eun on purpose to see me, and
he told me very solemnly that I should soon meet with a man
whose destiny would in some unknown way be bound up
with mine, and that I should meet him through the agency of
a heron. Angus went on to say: "And as the threads are twisted
at your first meeting, foster-son, so will they always shape
themselves at all the rest – a thread of one colour, a thread of
another." I said on that: "At all the rest, Angus? How many
more then?" and he thought a while and answered: "I saw you
meeting five times. The first time and the last were by water
. . . but always the place changed. Oh, my son, if only I could
know what it means!" I asked then whether I ought to avoid
this man, and Angus said: "You will not be able to avoid him;
the heron by the waterside will bring you to him." "Ah,"
said I, "that then is why Lachlan wanted to shoot the *curra*
this morning!" But Angus shook his head and muttered: "A
man cannot change the future in that way. What is to be
will be."

'I thought at the time, Alison,' went on Ewen explanatorily,
looking down at her intent face, 'that I should come on this
man some day, if ever I did, when I was out with a fowling-
piece, or something of the sort, and then, to tell truth, I forgot
all about the matter in the stir of the news from Moidart; and
thus it never crossed my mind when I encountered Captain
Windham that he could be the man . . . till he mentioned
the heron which startled his horse, and so indirectly – or
directly, if you will – led to my overtaking him by Loch Oich,
and our fight.'

'And is that all that Angus said?' asked Alison breathlessly.

'There was one thing more, I remember, for when, after he
had assured me that I should not be able to avoid this man, I
said: "He is an enemy, then?" Angus replied: "That I cannot
see. He will do you a great service, yet he will cause you bitter
grief. It is dark." You know how vexatious it is when one with

the two sights cannot see any more. It is like beginning to read a book of which the last pages are lost.'

'I do not think that I should wish to read any more,' said the girl, shivering a little, and she too got up from the window-seat. 'I have never before met anyone who had the gift so strongly as Angus, and indeed it is not canny. You are used to it, Ewen, since you have known him all your life, and I think you do not believe in it very much, either.'

'No, I do not,' admitted her lover. 'But it would not be kind to tell my foster-father so.'

Alison looked out of the window for a moment, biting her lip hard. 'Ewen, when a *taibhsear* "sees" any person it is nearly always a warning of that person's imminent death!'

Ewen put his arm round her. 'No, you are wrong, my dear. A *taibhsear* has been known to see a man's future wife – sometimes, his own. I wonder Angus never "saw" you, sitting by the hearth here in the days when you were in Paris . . . long days those were for me, *mo chridhe*! Moreover, in this matter of the heron he "saw" two people, and neither Captain Windham nor I can be going to die very soon, can we, if we must meet each other four times more?'

She looked up and met his expression, tender but half quizzical. 'No, that is true.'

'Angus said nothing about death,' went on Ewen reassuringly. 'And he seemed completely puzzled by his vision – or visions. If it were not for that heron by Loch Oich, I vow I should think that he had dreamed the whole business.'

'Have you told Captain Windham any of this?' asked Alison.

'Not I. He would only laugh at it, and I am sure, too, that he has no desire to meet me again, so that I should not be telling him anything to pleasure him.'

'Do you think,' suggested Alison slowly, 'that Angus did not hinder his sons and the others from attacking Captain Windham because he thought that he would be better out of the way – on your account?'

Her lover looked at her with a rather startled expression. 'I never thought of that. . . . But no, I do not believe that was the reason – it would not have been, unless he was lying over the reason he gave me.'

'And what was that?'

'It was outrageous enough. He said that there was no cause

for interference, because he knew that the *saighdear dearg* and I had yet several times to meet, so he would take no harm! What do you think of that? Had he not been an old man, and nearly blind, and my foster-father to boot, I declare that I could have shaken him when I went back to Slochd nan Eun and upbraided him and was given that for justification. It might very well have been Captain Windham's wraith that I was to tryst with!' He glanced at the clock. 'I must go, darling.'

'What will become of Captain Windham tomorrow?' asked Alison with a tiny frown.

'I do not know; it is a question I have to ask Lochiel.'

'One thing more, Ewen; did not Angus, after he had seen Captain Windham in the flesh yesterday, as I suppose he did – did he not tell you any more about him . . . and the future?'

'Not a word. No, as I say, the last pages of the book are torn out . . . but then it is so with every book in which our lives are written.'

He had both his arms round her now, and Alison hid her eyes against his breast, for he was so tall that even the top of her head was scarcely level with his chin. 'Why do you say that, Ewen? Oh, Ewen, why do you say that?'

'What ails you, heart's darling?' he asked, looking down at the dark head tenderly. 'It is true. You're not thinking, surely, that at the end of the book I can care for you any less, little white love? That's impossible . . . and I think it's impossible that I should care for you more, either,' he added, and put a kiss on the soft hair.

Alison clung to him, saying nothing, mindful of her proud promise to Aunt Margaret, but shaken with the knowledge of the red close of many a life across whose pages the name of Stuart had been written. Devotion to that name and cause was the religion in which she had been reared; but the claims of religion can sometimes make the heart quail . . . and Ewen was so splendid, so real and so dear! She forced a smile and raised her head; her eyes were quite dry. 'I must not keep you from Lochiel; but when you return, Ewen, will you not tell your foster-brothers that you have remitted their punishment?'

'For your sake, Alison?'

'No, for his who is waiting for them! Is he not needing every sword that we can bring him?'

Ewen smiled down at her appreciatively. 'You find clever

argument, miss! I never said that they should not join me later.'

'As ghosts? You may find yourselves trysting with wraiths, as you spoke of doing a while ago! Are they not capable of drowning themselves in the loch, particularly Lachlan, if you put that shame upon them, Ewen?'

'Yes,' said Ewen after a moment's silence, 'I'll not deny that Lachlan, at least, might throw himself into Loch na h-Iolaire. I suppose that I must allow them to come with me, and if you see them before my return, you can tell them so, rose of my heart.'

The room was empty once more, almost as empty as it would be tomorrow. And, since there was no one to see, Alison put her head down upon her arms on the window-sill.

When she raised it again after some moments a small object rolled off the sill and fell tinkling to the floor – one of Captain Windham's unfortunate buttons, which Ewen had forgotten after all to take with him. As Alison stooped to recover it the thought of its owner came sharply and forbiddingly into her mind, accompanied by all that she had just heard about him. Ewen's destiny bound up with his . . . and he, yesterday, disgracefully handled by Ewen's followers! Surely, however he had passed it off, he must retain a grudge about that, and it might be that in the future he would seize an opportunity of repaying the outrage. Alison wished for a moment that she were not Highland, and that belief in second sight did not run so in her blood. She could not shake from her mind the conviction that for old Angus to have seen the doubles of Ewen and the English officer meant the death of one or both of them within the year. It was true that the prediction had not seemed to trouble Ewen much, but he was a man, and had his head full of Glenfinnan at present. Yet there was Captain Windham, with nothing to do but to brood over the injury. Already, as Ewen had felt, he might well have a dislike to his captor. And did it not seem as though he had a horrid gift for dissimulation if, so soon afterwards, he could pretend to find amusement in the mortifying thing which had happened to him? What sort of a man was he really, this stranger who was to cause her Ewen bitter grief?

Alison jumped to her feet and stood with clasped hands. 'I'll go along the loch side, as though I were taking a walk, and if he is still there I'll engage him in talk, and perhaps I can find out a little about him.' For in the house she could not so easily get speech with him alone, and tomorrow he would surely be gone altogether. Yes, she would do that; Captain Windham would never guess that she had come on purpose. She slipped the buttons into her pocket and left the room.

Chapter Five

I T was not difficult to find Captain Windham by the loch, for the delicate veils of birch foliage made no effective screen for his strong scarlet. Alison saw him, therefore, before he was aware of her presence. He was sitting a yard or two from the edge of Loch na h-Iolaire, on the stump of a felled pine, with his arms folded on his breast, staring at the water. Was he thinking of yesterday – meditating some revenge? She would never know, because she dared not refer, even indirectly, to that unlucky contretemps. The buttons were in her pocket only for safe keeping.

Alison came very slowly along the ribbon of track through the heather, her eyes fixed on the soldier's unconscious figure. Ewen's destiny in *his* hands! No, Angus had not said that exactly. Nor had Angus said that he was an enemy; on the contrary, he was to render Ewen a great service . . . . Technical enemy of course he was. She had his profile now, clear against a reddish pine trunk; he looked rather sad. He was an enigma, neither friend nor enemy, and she would find out nothing, do no good . . . and wished she had not come.

Then the best was to turn and go back again. No, it was too late for that now. At that very moment Captain Windham must have heard her step, for he turned his head, sprang up, and uncovering, came towards her between the pines.

'Pray do not let me drive Miss Grant away,' he said civilly.

'I . . . I fear I disturb you, sir,' said Miss Grant, really discomposed.

'Disturb me! But I was not asleep, I assure you, and in breaking into my meditations you may have been doing me a service.'

He smiled a little as he said it, but Alison looked at him warily, wondering what he meant by that remark. Here they were, alone together, and neither could see what was upper-most in the other's mind. *He* did not know that strange thing prophesied of him, linking him to an enemy, nor could she in the least read what were his feelings with regard to Ewen, although it was a matter which concerned her so vitally. But, notwithstanding that she had a moment ago turned away like a coward from this interview, now she resolved to pursue it. Surely her wits could point out some roads by which she might arrive at Captain Windham's real sentiments?

Quite close to her was another convenient pine stump, so she sank down upon it murmuring about resting for a moment. Captain Windham stood beside her, his hands behind his back and his head bent, and before she had settled upon her own line of attack startled her by saying slowly, and even a trifle hesitatingly, that he had for the last hour been greatly wish-ing for the privilege for a few minutes' conversation with her.

Considerably surprised at this reversal of parts, Alison glanced up at him. Was this remark a prelude to compliments or gallantry of some kind? No; Captain Windham's manner quite disposed of that idea. Yet he said again, gravely: 'I desire to ask a favour of you, Miss Grant.'

'Pray ask it, sir,' replied Alison, just a trifle stiffly.

There was a moment's pause. 'I believe that Mr Cameron – Ardroy, I suppose I should say – has ridden off to see his Chief, has he not?' said the soldier.

'Yes,' said Alison, still less encouragingly.

'And by this time tomorrow—' Captain Windham left the sentence unfinished, and, to her surprise, walked away from her with bent head and stood at a little distance carefully pushing two or three fallen pine cones together with his foot. Finally he stooped, picked up one, and came back, twirling it in his fingers.

'Miss Grant,' he said, studying it with apparent absorption, 'I wish that I could make Ardroy some return for his generous treatment of me. This is not a mere figure of speech; I am in complete earnest. But the only return that I can make he would never take at my hands.' He raised his eyes and looked at her musingly. 'What I wonder is, whether he would take it at yours.'

'What do you mean, sir?' asked Alison, lifting her head a

trifle haughtily. Surely he was not going to offer Ewen money!
She must prevent that at all costs, or Heaven knew what might
happen!

Captain Windham threw away the fir cone. 'Will you
believe, Miss Grant, that in what I am going to say I speak as
a friend might (though I dare not presume to call myself one)
and that I have but one aim in speaking – Mr Cameron's good
and yours?'

Alison met his eyes, and they convinced her of his sincerity.
She had scarcely time to be amazed. 'Yes, I do believe it,'
she said in a softened tone. 'Please say what you wish, Captain
Windham.'

'Then let me ask you,' said the Englishman earnestly,
'whether you and Ardroy realize on what a hopeless adventure
he is embarking? Is it possible that, on the strength of having
captured two wretched companies of raw recruits – for indeed
they were no more than that – the clans of these parts think
that they will be able to defy the whole military force of the
Crown? Yes, Miss Grant, it is advice that I should like to give
Mr Cameron, if he would only take it. Cannot you use your
interest, with him? Forgive me if I trespass on delicate ground,
but . . . this is to be your home together, is it not? Think
again before you let him stake it on so hazardous a throw!
You know what happens to the property of a declared rebel.
And he stakes more than his property, Miss Grant!'

His voice was very grave. Alison, who had heard him
through, answered firmly: 'Yes, I know that.' But the lovely
colour was gone from her cheeks, and her hands were holding
each other tightly.

'It is not too late, even now,' urged her companion. 'If I
choose to suppress the fact that I was brought here as Mr
Cameron's prisoner, who is to gainsay my assertion that I
came as a guest? Only keep him back from this crazy
rendezvous tomorrow, which can but herald disaster, and he
may be able—'

'Keep him back!' exclaimed Alison. She had got up from
her tree-stump. 'Do you suppose that I could? Do you suppose
that if I could, I would?' Her voice trembled a little.

'But, Miss Grant, consider! If this young man, this Prince
of yours, had come with an army—'

'Then it would have been safe to declare for him!' broke in

Alison, and her dark eyes flashed. 'Oh, if that is the English way of thinking, it is not the Highland! Because he comes alone, and trusts himself to us, is not that the best of reasons why we should follow him who has the right, Captain Windham, and who may yet prove to have the might also?'

There was a short silence between them. On the other side of the loch a curlew uttered its plaintive, liquid cry. Captain Windham drew himself up a little.

'If you feel thus about the matter, Miss Grant,' he said rather dryly, 'there is no more to be said. I see that you will not take my offering. The best I can wish you, then, is that the affair may burn itself out as quickly as possible, for the longer it lasts the more victims there are likely to be . . . afterwards. And I would give much, believe me, to know that Mr Cameron of Ardroy will not be among them.'

Alison held out her hand impulsively. And she had been thinking that he was brooding on revenge! 'I thank you for those words, sir,' she said with great sweetness, 'because I believe that you mean them. But, though I shall not easily forget your kindness, it is – forgive me – useless to discuss the matter further.'

Captain Windham kissed her hand in silence, and offered her his arm back to the house, if she were returning thither. Alison took it readily enough, and as they left the loch, conversing on indifferent topics, she had time to taste the surprise and relief which had come to her there. If Fate's chosen instrument – supposing he were really that – were so well disposed towards Ewen, how could he in the future be used against him?

And yet, later in the evening, waiting for Ewen's return, she found that, unreasonably perhaps, she disliked Captain Windham's presumption that she could, if she tried, influence her lover to betray his convictions even more than the supposition that she could be induced to try. She felt that the soldier understood neither Highlanders nor Jacobites. But for his kindly and even generous intentions she had nothing but gratitude.

As for Keith Windham, whose meditations by Loch na h-Iolaire had moved him to an effort which surprised him, he told himself that he had never expected any other result.

They were all blinded and besotted, these Jacobites. He wondered whether Miss Grant would tell her betrothed of his attempt. With Ardroy himself he naturally should not think of expostulating; to do so would be mere waste of breath.

There was no Ardroy at supper, though it appeared that he was expected back at any moment, and Keith shortly afterwards excused himself and withdrew to his own bedchamber, having no wish to be an intruder on the lovers' last hours together, rebels though they were. But it was too early to go to bed, so once more he pulled a couple of books at random from the shelf on the wall, and settled down by the window to read. One of them he opened before he realized what it was, and found himself staring at 'Most heartily do we beseech Thee with Thy favour to behold our most gracious Sovereign Lord King—' but 'James' had been neatly pasted over the 'George'.

Captain Windham smiled. He held in his hand the Book of Common Prayer as used and amended by the nonjuring Episcopalian Jacobites, and saw with his own eyes the treason to which his ears might have listened earlier in the day. For though, on rising, he had forgotten that it was Sunday, this was a fact of which he had not long been suffered to remain ignorant, since after breakfast Miss Cameron had said to him in matter-of-fact tones – they were alone for the moment: 'I doubt you will wish to attend Morning Prayer with us, Captain Windham, even if you be an Episcopalian, like most of the English, for I must not disguise from you that we pray, not for King George, but for King James.'

' "Morning Prayer," ' Keith had stammered. 'Is – do you – I had thought that you were all Presbyterians hereabouts . . . or Papists,' he added, suddenly remembering the old woman on Friday.

'Ah, not at all,' replied Miss Cameron composedly. 'The MacDonalds of the mainland and the most of the Frasers indeed are Papists, but we Camerons are Episcopalians, and so are our neighbours, the Stewarts of Appin. But we can get to kirk but rarely, and today in especial, being, as you will understand, somewhat throng, we shall be obliged to worship at home.'

'And who—'

'Why, my nephew the laird, naturally,' replied Miss

Cameron. 'Though as Mr Grant is with us, 'tis possible he may read the service today.'

'Leaving your nephew free to preach, no doubt?' suggested Keith, trying to control a twitch of the lip.

'Now you are laughing at us, sir,' observed Miss Cameron shrewdly, but with perfect good humour. 'No, Ardroy does not preach. But I have the habit of reading a sermon to myself of a Sunday afternoon, and if you scoff any more 'tis likely the same exercise would benefit you, and I'll be happy to lend you a volume of some English divine – Bishop Jeremy Taylor, for instance.'

Keith bowed, and gravely assured her that if she saw fit to do this he would duly read a homily. But he had gone out into the garden smiling to himself. That model young man – he could not be more than five- or six-and-twenty – reading the Church service every Sunday to his household! He thought of the young men of his acquaintance in the army or in the fashionable world of London, the careless, loose-living subalterns, the young beaux of White's. Ye gods, what ribald laughter would have gone up at the tale! . . . Yes, but not one of those potential mockers could have beaten Ardroy in stature or looks or at swordplay. Keith would not forget Loch Oich side in a hurry.

But he had not attended Morning Prayer.

Now he was rather wishing that he had done so, for he supposed that he would never again have the chance of seeing a young man who could fight in that style acting as chaplain. But perhaps Mr Grant had superseded him; Keith had not inquired. At any rate Ewen Cameron was not engaged on particularly prayerful business at this moment, over at his Chief's house, nor would he be on his knees tomorrow. Afterwards . . . well, it was likely that his relatives would have need to pray for *him*!

He turned over the Prayer Book idly, and it opened next at the feast of the Conversion of St Paul, and the words of the Gospel leapt at him: 'Every one that hath forsaken houses, or brethren, or sisters, or father, or mother, or wife, or children, or lands, for my Name's sake . . .'

Though not much of a churchgoer himself, Captain Windham was shocked at the analogy which occurred to him, and closing the Prayer Book hastily, fell to wondering what was going to be done with him tomorrow; also, whose hand had retrieved and laid upon his dressing-table the two missing buttons from his uniform which he had found there a short while ago.

It was nearly ten o'clock when he heard the beat of hoofs. They stopped in front of the porch, but he did not look out. Someone dismounted, then Keith heard Miss Grant's voice, with her heart in it: 'Ewen, you are come at last; it has been a long evening!'

'And will be a short night, Alison,' came the half-exultant reply. 'We march at daybreak for Glenfinnan.' And from the sudden silence Keith guessed that the girl was in her lover's arms. He moved away from the window and began to pace up and down. So there was to be no holding back. Ah, what a pity, what a pity!

Half an hour later he was back in his old place reading, but with a lighted candle at his elbow now, when there was a knock, and Ardroy himself came in, a big branched candle-stick in his hand.

'You are not abed, Captain Windham! I must apologize, none the less, for so late a visit.'

There was a kind of suppressed elation about him, and his eyes were as blue as the sea.

'Your Highland nights are so light,' returned Keith, as he rose to his feet, 'that it is hard to believe it late.' Why should he, who cared for no human being, feel regret that this young man was going to destruction?

'My excuse,' went on Ewen, setting down the light he carried, 'is that I leave this house again in a few hours, and must speak with you first on a matter that concerns you.'

'You will be setting out for – the rendezvous of which you told me?'

'Yes. And before I go—'

'Mr Cameron,' broke in the Englishman, 'you gave me a warning yesterday to which I should have done well to listen. I suppose it is too much to hope that, at this eleventh hour, you will listen to one from me?'

As he said it he knew that he was a fool for his pains; that his words, uttered on that astonishing impulse, so contrary to his intention, were as useless as the little puff of air which at that moment entered by the open window and set the candles a-quiver. And over the bending flames the Highlander, looking very tall, gazed at him straight and unyieldingly.

'You are too kind, Captain Windham. But if the matter of your warning be what I suppose, you must forgive me for saying that you would only be wasting your time.' His tone was courteous but very cold.

Keith shrugged his shoulders. After all, if a man *would* rush on his doom it was his own affair. 'My time is far from valuable at present,' he replied flippantly, 'but yours no doubt is precious, Mr Cameron. On what matter did you wish to speak to me?'

'I have come to tell you from my Chief, Lochiel, that you are free from tomorrow – on one condition.'

'And that is?'

'That you engage not to bear arms against the Prince for the remainder of the campaign. Lochiel will accept an assurance given to me.'

'"For the remainder of the campaign"!' exclaimed Keith rather indignantly. 'An impossible condition, on my soul!' He gave a short laugh. 'It is true that your "campaign" is not like to be of long duration!'

Ewen ignored the sneer. 'You cannot tell, sir,' he replied gravely. 'But those are the terms which I am to offer you. Captain Scott has accepted them, and has today gone to Fort William to have his wound cared for.'

'Precisely,' retorted Keith. 'Captain Scott is wounded; I am not.' There was still indignation in his voice; nevertheless he was thinking that if he accepted the offer he would be able to leave the Highlands and return to Flanders and real warfare. It was a temptation. But some deep-rooted soldierly instinct revolted.

He shook his head. 'My sword is the King's, and I cannot enter into an indefinite engagement not to use it against his enemies. Indeed it is fully time that I should ask you, Mr Cameron, to restore me the parole of honour which I gave you. I should prefer henceforward to be your prisoner upon ordinary terms.'

But at this his jailer seemed taken aback. 'I fear that is impossible at present, sir,' he replied with some hesitation. 'If I left you behind here there would be no one to guard you. As you will not accept your freedom on the condition which is offered you, I have no choice but to take you with me to-morrow – still on parole, if you please,' he added, looking his captive straight in the face.

'I have requested you to give me back my parole, Mr Cameron!'

'And I have already said that I cannot do so, Captain Windham!'

Once more they were facing each other across the candle-flames. Keith began to feel annoyance.

'Am I then to go ranging the mountains with you for ever? You will find me a great nuisance, Mr Cameron.' (Mr Cameron looked at that moment as if he shared this opinion.) 'But perhaps this is your way of forcing Lochiel's offer on me, for, by Gad, that is what it comes to!'

'No, no,' said Ewen hastily, and with a frown. 'I had no such intention. I will consult Lochiel again about the matter to-morrow, and—'

'Can't you do anything on your own responsibility, Mr Cameron of Ardroy? Must you always consult your Chief?'

He had goaded him at last. Ardroy's head went up. 'Had you not a commanding officer in your regiment, Captain Windham?' he inquired haughtily.

'Touché!' said Keith, with good humour. (It was a mutual hit, though.) He liked to see his civilized young barbarian on the high horse. 'But suppose, Mr Cameron, that I do not choose to wait so long, and tell you frankly that, if you will not re-store my parole to me, I shall myself withdraw it from mid-night tonight?'

'In that case,' said the barbarian with great promptitude, 'I shall put two of my gillies in here with you, lock the door and sleep across it myself. . . . Do you tell me that you with-draw it?'

There was a second or two's silence while Keith envisaged himself thus spending the remainder of the night. It was on the tip of his tongue to inquire whether the amiable Lachlan would be one of his guards, but he suppressed the query. 'No,' he said with a little grimace, 'you may keep my parole and I will keep my privacy. Let us hope that your "commanding officer's" wisdom will be able to cut the knot tomorrow. I am to be ready, then, to accompany you at daybreak?'

'If you please,' said Ardroy stiffly. 'I am sorry that I can do nothing else. Good night.' He took up the candlestick and stalked out.

Captain Keith Windham remained staring for a moment at the closed door and then began to smile rather ruefully. 'A droll captivity, 'pon my honour! Had I known that I was to be trailed about in this fashion my attempt at warning might have been less disinterested than it was. But I shall not make another.'

Chapter Six

F O U R days later Captain Windham was sitting at evening in a dark little hut on the shores of Loch Eil, studying a pocket-book by the light of a small lantern hung on the wattled wall behind him. A pile of heather was all his seat; outside it was pouring with rain, but he, unlike almost everyone else, was at least under cover and secure, as he had not been lately, from the attentions of the rapacious Highland midges.

It was Thursday, 22 August, and since Monday he had gone with Clan Cameron wherever it went. First of all Ardroy and his contingent had rendezvoused with the main body of the clan at the very place where Keith Windham now found himself again, Kinlochiel, at the upper end of Loch Eil. Here, on that eventful Monday, Keith had had his first meeting with the courteous and polished gentleman whom Clan Cameron followed, Donald Cameron of Lochiel, nineteenth of the name. And Lochiel had appeared so much distressed at the idea of the English officer's continued conveyance with them under guard, even possibly in bonds, for they had no place in which they could conveniently leave him behind, that Keith had been prevailed upon to extend the parole which he had tried to take back from Ardroy, and to regard it as given for the space of one week, dating from the day and hour of his capture in the Great Glen. When that week was up, his jailers seemed to think that they would be able to make other arrangements about his custody.

After the rendezvous the clan had proceeded westwards, in the direction of the coast, along a difficult road between close-pressed craggy mountains, where the grey rock pushed in a myriad places through its sparse covering, and came at last in the afternoon to the trysting place at Glenfinnan. Though he was treated with every civility, and rode in comfort on a horse of Ardroy's, it had been a mortifying journey for Captain Windham. Between the ranks of Camerons marched sulkily the captured recruits of the Royals, without their arms – like himself – and even Captain Scott's white charger formed part of the procession, to be offered to the 'Prince'. As well, thought the Englishman, be the prisoner of wandering Arabs.

So, scornful but half interested too, Keith Windham had been present at a scene which, a week ago, he could little have imagined himself witnessing; when, on the stretch of level ground at the head of Loch Shiel, among that wild and lonely scenery, a thousand Highland throats acclaimed the fair-haired young man standing below the folds of his banner, and the very air seemed to flash with the glitter of their drawn blades. It was very romantical and absurd, of course, besides being rank rebellion; but there was no denying that these deluded and shaggy mountaineers were in earnest, and Lochiel too, who was neither shaggy nor – so it seemed to the observer – deluded in quite the same sense . . . and certainly not absurd.

None observing or hindering him during the following days, Captain Windham had taken the opportunity of keeping a fragmentary journal in his pocket-book, and it was these notes which, for want of anything better to do, he was now reading over in the wet twilight.

'What an Army! 'tis purely laughable!' he had written on 20 August. 'The Men are fine, tall Fellows enough, particularly the Camerons – but their Weapons! I have seen Muskets with broken Locks, Muskets with broken Stocks, Muskets without Ramrods, and Men without Muskets at all. There can't be more than a Score of Saddlehorses all told, and the Draught Horses are quite insufficient for Transport over such a Road. Moreover, the so-call'd "Army" is as yet compos'd of two Clans only, the Camerons and some Part of the Mac-Donalds, its Number being, I suppose, about thirteen hundred Men.

'The Pretender's Son I must admit to be a very personable young Man indeed, with the *Bel Air*; they all appear craz'd about him. My own young Achilles, still very well-bred and agreeable, like his Chief. I never looked to see so much native polish as Lochiel exhibits. Achilles, if I mistake not, pretty well adores him. There is also a younger brother of the Chief's, whom they call Doctor Archibald; with him also my Warrior seems on very friendly Terms.'

Captain Windham turned over to the next two days' records, which were briefer, and brought him up to the present date.

'August the 21st. Set out at last from that curst Spot, Glenfinnan. But, after an Advance of one Mile, the Road was found to be so bad, and the Horses so few, that the Rebels were oblig'd to leave twelve out of their Score of Swivel Guns behind, and spent some Hours burying 'em in a Bog. As their total March today to a Place call'd Kinlocheil, was no more than four miles, it looks as though 'twould be some Weeks before the Breechless reach Civilization.

'August the 22nd. At Kinlocheil all day. Prodigious Rain. Much-needed Attempts seem to be going forward to organize the Transport, Wagons and Carts of all Sorts being collected. Have scarce seen E.C. all day.'

But he had hardly come to these last words, when a tall, wet figure appeared without warning in the low doorway, and the diarist restored his notebook somewhat hastily to his pocket. Ardroy stooped his head to enter, taking off his bonnet and swinging it to remove the raindrops. The dampness of the rest of his attire appeared to give him no concern.

'Good evening, Mr Cameron! Have you been burying any more cannon?' inquired the soldier pleasantly.

Ardroy, reddening slightly, made no reply beyond returning the 'Good evening', but hung up his bonnet on a nail and began to unfasten the shoulder-brooch of his plaid. There was not a very great deal of satisfaction for Captain Windham to be got out of baiting this 'young Achilles' of his, because Achilles kept so tight a hold upon his temper and his tongue. Or was it that he was naturally impassive? Hardly, for Keith was sure that he felt the points of the darts which he contrived from time to time to plant in him. Perhaps Ardroy thought that the best way to meet his captive's malice was to appear unaware of it; and indeed the archer himself had to confess that this course rather baffled him. He followed up his first shaft by another.

'You must admit that you should not have brought me here if you did not wish me to learn your military dispositions – if such I am to call that measure!'

And if the Highlander went on pretending that the unpin-
ning of his plaid was engaging his whole attention Keith
would feel that he had drawn blood. He knew that his own
conduct verged on the puerile, but the pleasure of pursuing
it was too strong.

The big brooch, however, was undone at last, and Ewen
said rather dryly: 'I am glad that your spirits are not suffering
from the weather, Captain Windham.'

'On the contrary,' said his prisoner cheerfully, leaning back
against the wall of the hut, his hands behind his head, 'I am
entertaining myself by trying to recall any other great commander who began his campaign by burying most of his artillery in a swamp; but I have failed. Yet, by Gad, the plan might
work a revolution in warfare – in fact 'twould end it altogether
if it were carried out to its logical conclusion. Armies would
take the field only to bury their muskets – and perhaps,' he
added, maliciously, 'that *will* be your next step. I protest
that some of them would not take much harm by the in-
terment!'

Ewen swung off his plaid. 'Your mirth at our lack of equip-
ment is very natural,' he replied with complete equanimity.
'But perhaps our ill provision may not be widely known to
our enemies. And is it not a fact within your own military
experience, Captain Windham,' he went on, looking him in
the face, 'that it is what one supposes an enemy's forces to be
rather than what they actually are which sometimes turns
the scale?'

It was the Englishman who coloured this time. In its absence
of specific reference to the mishap at High Bridge the retort
was just sufficiently veiled to enable him, had he chosen, to
affect unconsciousness of its sting. But he was too proud to
do this.

'I deserved that,' he admitted, scrambling to his feet with
the words. 'I am not such a dolt as to be unaware to what you
allude. That you feel obliged to remind me of last Friday's
disgrace proves that my own remarks were not in the best of
taste – and I apologize for them.'

But his tormentor's apology appeared to embarrass Ewen
Cameron much more than his thrusts. 'I am sorry I said that,
Captain Windham!' he exclaimed, with a vivacity which
rather astonished the other. 'I ought not to have taunted you

with a calamity for which you were not to blame. That was in worse taste still.'

'Egad, Mr Cameron, you are punctilious,' said Keith carelessly. 'But if you are of that mind – I don't say that I am – we may fairly cry quits.'

'For after all,' pursued Ewen, throwing down his plaid, 'since you are not witnessing our preparations of your own free will, I suppose you are at liberty to make what observations you please upon them.'

'You seem bent upon making allowances for me!' returned Keith with a smile. 'However, I do not complain of that; and if Fate should ever reverse our positions, and give you, for instance, into my hands, I hope I may be able to show the same generosity.'

Ardroy, who was now unbuckling his broadsword, stopped and gazed at him rather intently in the feeble lantern-light, feeble because it still had to contend with a measure of wet daylight. 'Why, do you then *anticipate* our meeting again, Captain Windham?' he asked after a moment.

'I anticipate nothing, Mr Cameron. I am no wizard to foretell the future. Yet, but for the fact that we could not meet save as enemies, I vow 'twould give me pleasure to think that we might one day encounter each other again.' But, feeling somehow that the young man standing there looking at him took this for a mere *façon de parler*, he added, with a return to his bantering tone: 'You can have no notion how much this tour – albeit a trifle too reminiscent of a Roman triumph – has been alleviated by having so agreeable a cicerone. Though indeed in the last twenty-four hours my glimpses of you have been few – too few.'

So expressed, his sentiments had of course small chance of being taken for sincere. The Highlander, indeed, for all reply gave a little shrug that was almost like a Frenchman's, spread his plaid upon the bare earth floor and laid his broadsword beside it.

'Surely you are not going to sleep in that plaid!' exclaimed Keith, stirred out of his levity. 'Why, 'tis drenched! Take my cloak, I have no mind to sleep yet, and shall not need it.'

But Ewen, without stiffness, declined, saying that a wet plaid was of no consequence, and indeed but kept one the warmer. Some he added, and the Englishman gasped at the information, wrung them out at night in water for that reason. All he would accept was some handfuls of heather for a pillow, and then, lying down, his sword convenient to his hand, he wrapped himself in the folds of damp tartan and in five minutes was fast asleep.

But Keith, as he said, was not sleepy; and after a while, feeling restless, he strolled to the doorway – door the hut had none. When he got there he was aware of a rigid figure, muffled in a plaid, standing in the rain, just out of the direct line of vision – the inevitable Lachlan watching over his master's slumbers. He turned his head, and Keith could see a contraction pass over his dark features. But the English officer was not to be intimidated by a scowl from studying, if he wished, the sodden, cloud-enfolded landscape, and the sheets of rain driving in the twilight over the waters of Loch Eil, though it was not a cheerful prospect.

What was going to happen to him when his parole expired tomorrow? At the far end of Loch Eil, Loch Linnhe joined it at right angles, and on Loch Linnhe was Fort William, with its loyal garrison. Tomorrow the Highland force would proceed along Loch Eil, and every step would bring him nearer to his friends. . . .

He left the doorway after a few moments, and looked down at the sleeper on the floor, his head sunk in the bundle of heather and his arm lying across his broadsword. 'The embraces of the goddess of ague seem to be agreeable,' he thought. 'I shall be sorry to say farewell tomorrow, my friend – deuce take me if I quite know why – but I hardly think you will!'

Then at last he went and lay down on his heap of heather, and listened to the sound of the rain, always since he was a boy, connected with the worst memories of his life. There was the dismal day of his father's funeral; he had been but five then, yet he remembered it perfectly; rain, rain on the nodding plumes of the great black carriage which had taken his father away; the day some years later on which his childish mind first realized that his adored mother cared nothing for him – rain, a soft mist of it. And the night in London, four years past now, the night that he had discovered what Lydia Shelmerdine really was. Against the closely-curtained windows of her boudoir it could be heard to dash in fury (for there was a great wind that evening) every time that there came a pause in her high, frightened, lying speech, which ran on the more that he stood there saying so little. The rose had slipped loose from her close-gathered powdered hair, her gauze and ivory fan lay snapped at her feet . . . and the rain sluiced pitilessly against the windows.

Into that tempest Keith Windham had presently gone out, and, once away from the scented room, had known nothing of its fury, though it drenched him to the skin; and he had forced his way all dripping into the presence of the man who had seduced her . . . no, the man whom she had seduced . . . and had told him to his face that he was welcome to his conquest, that he did not propose to dispute it with him, nor even to demand satisfaction. The lady was not worth fighting about; 'not worth the risking of a man's life – *even of yours*!' There had been witnesses, vastly surprised witnesses, of conduct so unusual. But he thought his way of dealing with the situation more effective than the ordinary; and perhaps it was. He never saw either of the two who had betrayed him again.

Riding behind his young Achilles next afternoon Keith Windham kept looking at Loch Eil, now shining and placid, the seaweed of its level shore orange in the sun, and the great mountain miles away over Fort William mirrored, upside down, as clear as the original. If only he could reach Fort William! But Ardroy, to whom his word of honour still bound him, would certainly see to it that at the expiry of his parole this evening he was secured in some other way. 'I dare say he will make it as little irksome for me as he can,' thought Keith, looking at the tall, easy figure sitting the horse just ahead of him, on whose gay tartan and ribbon-tied autumn hair the westering sun was shining full. 'He's an uncommon good fellow . . . and we shall never see each other again, I suppose.' And again he thought: 'Not that he will care – and why the devil should I?'

Then the stream of men and conveyances began to leave the loch side, making towards Mr John Cameron's house of Fassefern, standing where Glen Suilag made a breach into the mountains; though Lochiel's burgess brother, who would not join the Prince, had carried his prudence to the length of absenting himself from his property lest he should be open to the charge of having entertained that compromising guest. It was not until they came to the gate in their turn that Ardroy slewed round in his saddle to speak to the captive, and said that he would do what he could for him in the way of accommodation, if he did not object to waiting a little. So Keith gave up his horse to one of Ewen's gillies, and, working his way through the press, waited under a tree and revolved plans. But in truth he could make none until he knew how he was to be secured.

Sooner than he had expected his warden reappeared and, taking him in at a side entry, conducted him to the very top of the humming house.

'I thought this little room might serve for us,' he said, opening the door of a small, half-furnished garret, and Keith saw that their mails were already there. 'I do not know how many others may be thrust in here, but there is at least one bed.' And so there was, a sort of pallet. 'You had best establish your claim to it at once, Captain Windham, or, better still, I will do it for you.' And, mindful as ever of his prisoner's comfort, he unfastened his plaid and tossed it on to the mattress. 'I will come and fetch you to supper; I suppose there will be some.'

Keith could not help looking after his departing figure with a smile which held both amusement and liking. He could not, however, afford to let sensibility interfere with what was in his mind now. Whatever were the reason, Ardroy seemed to have completely forgotten that in – Keith consulted his watch – in another twenty minutes his captive's parole would expire, and he would be free to take himself off . . . if he could. Or was it that he had not mentioned the coming change of conditions from some feeling of delicacy, because it would involve setting a guard?

The Englishman sat down upon the pallet and considered his chances. They depended almost entirely upon whether in twenty minutes' time there was a Highlander posted at the door of this room. But Ardroy had spoken of fetching him to supper. Heaven send then that supper was delayed! Perhaps he could creep out of the garret and conceal himself elsewhere until he found an opportunity of getting clear away later in the evening. Yet there was no special advantage in waiting for nightfall (even if Ardroy's forgetfulness extended so far) because the nights were apt to be so disconcertingly light. No, the great difficulty at any hour was his uniform. . . .

And here he found himself looking at the roll from Ewen Cameron's saddle, lying on the solitary half-broken chair.

But Keith Windham was much too proud a man not to have a strict regard for his pledged word. He could hardly prevent the entrance of a plan of escape into a brain which was, as yet, on parole, but he would not take the smallest step to put it into execution before the appointed hour should strike. To pass the time he would scribble a note to explain his conduct; and, wondering the while whether he should not have to destroy it even before he had finished it, he tore out a leaf from his pocket-book and began:

'DEAR MR CAMERON,—

'To justify my unadvertis'd Departure I am fain to put you in Mind that I gave my Parole of Honour for the Space of a Se'nnight from the Day and Hour of my Capture by you in the Evening of last Friday. In ten Minutes more that Period will have expir'd, and I trust you will not think it any infraction of Military Honour that, without having previously recall'd that Fact to your Memory, I intend at half after six to attempt my Freedom.

'I shall always retain the most cordial Remembrance of your Hospitality, and though the Pilgrimage of the last few Days has been somewhat prolonged, it has enabled me to be present upon a more interesting Occasion.

'Adieu, and forgive me for supposing that when you are more accustom'd to a military Life, you will not repeat the Oversight by which I am hoping to profit.

'Your most obedient, humble Servant,
'KEITH WINDHAM, *Captain*.'

When he had finished this effusion, of which the last paragraph, it cannot be denied, afforded him a special pleasure, he still waited, watch in hand. At half-past six exactly he rose from the pallet and, feeling remarkably like a footpad, opened Ardroy's modest baggage with hasty fingers. It proved to contain a clean shirt, a pair of stockings, a few odds and ends and – a kilt. The plunderer held this up in some dismay, for he would very greatly have preferred trews, such as Ardroy was wearing at present, but it was this nether garment or his

own, and in a remarkably short space of time he was surveying his bare knees with equal disgust and misgiving. No knees
that he had seen this week under tartan were as white as that!
Happily the garret was dusty, and therefore his legs, if not
respectably tanned, could at least look dirty. He thought at
first of retaining his uniform coat, which he fancied could be
fairly well hidden by Ardroy's plaid – how he blessed him
for leaving it behind – but the skirts were a little too long,
and the blue cuffs with their galons too conspicuous, and so
he decided to go coatless. Thereupon he began experiments
with the plaid – what a devil of a lot of it there was! He wished
he had a bonnet to pull forward on his brows . . . but one
could not expect everything to be provided. The want, however, reminded him of his incongruous wig, and he took this
off and placed it, with his discarded uniform, under the
mattress. And so there he was, clad in a costume he would
as soon have assumed as the trappings of a Red Indian – and
clad very insecurely too, he feared, for Ardroy's kilt was too
big for him, and he could not fasten it any tighter.

Still no sign of any person coming. Keith looked doubtfully
at his host's rifled baggage. It was his duty to regain his liberty
by any lawful means, but he had certainly acted the part of a
pickpocket. The only compensation in his power was to pay
for the clothes he had taken, since those he had left behind
were no adequate exchange. He pulled out his purse, having
small idea of the worth of the purloined garments, and still
less of how Ardroy would view the payment; he suspected
that the Highlander might not relish it, but for his own peace
of mind he felt constrained to make it. And so he wrapped
three guineas in his farewell letter and laid the letter on the
chair. Then he softly opened the garret door, went to the head
of the stairs, and listened.

The immediate neighbourhood of the little room was
deserted, and the sounds from below suggested that the bustle
which existed in Fassefern House that evening was more likely
to help than to hinder a pretended Cameron who desired to
slip out unnoticed. Captain Windham settled the plaid more
to his satisfaction and began with an unconcerned air to
descend the stairs. But he was clutching nervously at the top
of the philabeg, and his legs felt abominably cold.

·   ·   ·   ·   ·

Some three-quarters of an hour later Donald Cameron of Lochiel and Alexander MacDonald of Keppoch, he whose clansman had held High Bridge, were talking together outside the front of Fassefern House. About an hour previously it had been arranged that the heavy baggage was to go forward that night along Loch Eil side with a strong convoy of Camerons; a large escort was required because at Corpach they would have to run the gauntlet of the neighbourhood of Fort William on the other side of the water – a danger which the Prince and the rest of the little force would avoid next day by taking a route through Glen Suilag impossible to the baggage train.

'And I am sending my young cousin Ardroy in command of it,' concluded Lochiel, 'though the news was something of the suddenest to him. But he will be ready; he is a very punctual person, is Ewen.'

And they went on to speak of other matters: of Macleod of Macleod's refusal to observe his solemn engagement to join the prince (even if he came alone), which was still more resented than the withdrawal of Sir Alexander MacDonald of the Isles; and of what Sir John Cope would do, and where he would elect to give them battle. For that the English general would take his alarmed way up to Inverness without daring to face them had not occurred to the most sanguine.

Lochiel, indeed, was looking very grave. Keith Windham's flash of insight had been correct; he was not deluded. His was the case of a man who was risking everything – life, fortune, lands, the future of his young family – against his better judgment because, more scrupulous of his plighted word than the Chief of Macleod or MacDonald of Sleat, he felt himself too deeply engaged to draw back without loss of honour. Yet, unlike Macleod's, his engagement only pledged his support in the case that the Prince came with French assistance – and he had come without it. The fate of his whole clan lay on Lochiel's shoulders – more, the fate of every man in the rising, for if he had held back the spark would have been quenched at the outset for lack of fuel. That knowledge was a heavy burden to be laid on a man who, far from being a freebooting chief, had striven all his life for the betterment of his people.

'Yes,' he was saying for the second time, 'if we can reach

and hold the pass over the Corryarrick before Cope—'

At that moment there was a rapid step behind the two men, Lochiel heard his name uttered in sharp accents, and, turning quickly, beheld the young commander of the baggage convoy in a state of high discomposure.

'My dear Ewen, what is wrong?'

'He's gone!' And so agitated was Ardroy's tone, so black his brow, that Lochiel's own colour changed. 'Who – not the Prince!'

'The English officer – my prisoner . . . he's escaped! His parole expired at half-past six this evening, and I, fool that I was, had forgot it over this business of the escort. He'll go straight to Fort William with information of our numbers and our arms. . . . Oh, I deserve you should dismiss me, Lochiel! He's been away near an hour, I suppose. Shall I ride after him! . . . No, I cannot, unless you give the convoy to someone else – and truly I think I am not fit—'

Lochiel broke in, laying a hand on his arm. ' 'Tis not worth while pursuing him, my dear Ewen, nor any very great loss to be rid of him. I doubt not, too, that they have already at Fort William all the information that Captain Windham can give. But how, with that uniform, did he get away?'

The enraged young man ground his teeth. 'He was not wearing his uniform. He stole some clothes from me – a philabeg and my plaid. And he left me a damned impertinent letter . . . and these.' He unclosed a hand and held out three gold coins. 'Isn't that the final insult, that he must leave so much more than the things were worth, as though to—' He appeared unable to finish the sentence. 'If ever I meet him again—' Back went his arm, and Captain Windham's guineas hurtled violently into the shrubbery of Fassefern House.

Flood Tide

'To wanton me, to wanton me,
Ken ye what maist would wanton me?
To see King James at Edinburgh Cross,
Wi' fifty thousand foot and horse,
And the usurper forced to flee,
Oh this is what maist would wanton me.'

—Jacobite Song

Chapter One

T H E dusk of early October had fallen on the city of Edinburgh,
that stately city, which for some three weeks now had been
experiencing a situation as old as any in its varied and turbulent history. For Prince Charles and his Highlanders held the
town, but not the Castle, secure on its lofty and impregnable
rock; this they could neither storm, owing to its position, nor,
from lack of artillery, batter down, while King George's
military representatives in the Castle were, for their part, unable to regain control of the city below them. The stalemate
thus established was perfectly in harmony with the spirit of
unconscious comedy which had reigned throughout these
weeks, beginning with the ludicrous indecisions and terrors of
the city fathers on the news of the Highland advance, and the
casual method by which the city had suffered itself to be
captured, or rather walked into, by Lochiel and his men. For
the opening of the Netherbow Port very early on the morning
of 17 September, just as the Highlanders outside were preparing to withdraw disappointed, was due to nothing more
momentous than the exit of a hackney carriage on its way to
its stable in the Canongate – though it is true that it was the
carriage which had just brought back the discomfited envoys
sent to interview the Prince at Gray's Mill.

Yesterday only had come to an end the latest (and not
entirely humorous) episode, of some days' duration, when,

the Prince having 'blockaded' the Castle, in other words, having cut off daily supplies, the garrison had retaliated by firing on the town, killing some innocent inhabitants, striking terror into them all, and making it very undesirable to be seen in the neighbourhood of the Castle in the company of a Highlander. Violent representations on the part of the city to the Prince, embodying 'the most hideous complaints against the garrison', had brought this uncomfortable state of affairs to an end by the raising of the 'blockade' – itself originated, so the story went, by the discovery of smuggled information in a pat of butter destined for the valetudinarian General Guest, for whom milk and eggs were permitted to pass daily into the Castle. Yet the old gentleman's treacherous butter was only one of the many whimsical touches of the goddess Thalia, who had devised, during these weeks of occupation, such ingenious surprises as the descent of a soldier from the Castle by means of a rope into Livingstone's Yard, where he set a house on fire, and returned in triumph, by the same method, with a couple of captured Jacobite muskets; the discomfiture, by a sudden illumination from above, of three Camerons sent experimentally to scale the Castle rock under cover of darkness, and – perhaps the most genuinely comic of all – the solemn paying out to the cashier and directors of the Royal Bank of Scotland, within the very walls of the Castle, and in exchange for Prince Charles's notes, of the ready money which had been taken there for safety, but the lack of which inconvenienced the Edinburgh shopkeepers as much as anybody. This transaction had taken place, under the white flag, during the blockade itself.

But tonight, the guns being silent, and General Joshua Guest once more in possession of his invalid diet, the lately terrified citizens in the high, crammed houses with their unsavoury approaches were preparing to sleep without fear of bombardment next day by their own defenders. Those outposts of the invading foe, which always kept a wary eye upon the Castle and its approaches – and which had not passed through a very enviable time the last few days – the Highland guard at the Weigh-house, the West Bow, and elsewhere, had received their night relief, and Mr Patrick Crichton, saddler and ironmonger, was writing in his diary further caustic and originally spelt remarks anent these 'scownderalls', 'scurlewheelers' and 'hillskipers'. Inside the walls all was quiet.

But at the other end of the town Holyrood House was lit up, for there was dancing tonight in the long gallery under the eyes of that unprepossessing series of early Scottish kings due to the brush of an ill-inspired Dutchman . . . and under a pair of much more sparkling ones. For the Prince was gay tonight, as he was not always; and though, following his usual custom, he himself did not dance, it was plain that the growing accessions to his cause during the last few days had raised his spirits. For, besides all those who had joined him soon after Glenfinnan – Stewarts of Appin, MacDonalds of Glengarry, Grants of Glenmoriston – two days ago had come in fierce old Gordon of Glenbucket with four hundred men, and the day before that young Lord Ogilvy, the Earl of Airlie's son, with six hundred, and Farquharson of Balmoral with two hundred, and his kinsman of Monaltrie with more. And others were coming. Whatever the future might hold, he was here as by a miracle in the palace of his ancestors, having defeated in a quarter of an hour the general who had slipped out of his path in August and returned by sea to the drubbing which awaited him among the morasses and the corn stubble of Prestonpans.

So there, at the end of the gallery nearest to his own apartments, in a costume half satin, half tartan, stood the living embodiment of Scotland's ancient dynasty, and drew to himself from time to time the gaze of every lady in the room. But it was to those of his own sex that he chiefly talked.

At the other end of the gallery, which looked out on to the garden and the chapel, Alison Grant, very fine in her hoop and powder, her flowered brocade of blue and silver, with a scarf of silken tartan and a white autumn rose on her breast, was talking with animation to three young men, one of whom, in a French uniform, bore a strong resemblance to her, and was in fact her young brother Hector, just come over from France. The others were distant kinsmen, Grants of Glenmoriston and Shewglie respectively. Right in the corner, on a gilded chair, sat Mr Grant in a not very new coat (for it was more fitting that Alison should go braw than he). His hands rested on his cane, and his lined face, half shrewd and half childlike, wrinkled into a smile as he saw the likelihood that neither young Glenmoriston nor young Shewglie, who seemed to be disputing in a friendly way for the honour of the next dance,

would obtain it, since someone else was making his way between the knots of talkers to this corner. To judge by the
glances cast at him as he passed, it appeared that Alison was
not the only lady there to think that a certain tall cadet of
Clan Cameron, a captain in Lochiel's regiment and one of the
Prince's aides-de-camp, who wore powder for the nonce and
amber satin instead of tartan, was the match of any other
gentleman in the room – except, of course, of him with the
star on his breast.

Yet Alison, for some reason, gave the newcomer the briefest
glance now, though it was a sweet one enough; then her eyes
wandered away again. The two Grants, evidently thinking
their cause hopeless, took themselves off.

'Alison, here is your cavalier come to claim you,' said her
father from his corner.

'Alison has not a look or a thought to give to me nowadays,'
observed Ewen, looking at his love from behind, at the back
of her white neck, where the sacque fell in imposing folds
from the square of the bodice, and where two little unruly
tendrils of hair, having shaken off their powder, were beginning to show their true colour. 'Like the rest of the ladies, she
has eyes only for the Prince. 'Tis pity I am not a Whig, for
then she might pay me some attention, if only in order to
convert me.'

At that Alison turned round, laughing.

'Well, sir,' she said, looking him up and down, 'your
costume, I vow, is almost Whiggish. In those clothes, and
without a scrap of tartan upon you, you might be an Englishman?'

'Or a Frenchman,' suggested her father from his corner.

But this accusation Alison repudiated somewhat indignantly.
'No; Frenchmen are all little men!' Yet, having lived so much
in France, she must have known better.

'No one could call Ardroy little, I admit,' agreed Mr Grant.
'And he has not the French physiognomy. But in that dress
he has quite the French air.'

'Thank you, sir,' said Ewen, bowing, 'since I suppose I am
to take that as a compliment.'

'There are some tall fellows in my regiment,' declared
Hector Grant, drawing up his slim and active figure. 'For my
part, I've no ambition to attain the height of a pine tree. Alison,

is it customary in Scotland, think you, for a brother to lead
out his sister?'

'Not unless they are so unlike that the company cannot
guess the kinship,' responded Ewen for his betrothed. 'Not,
therefore in this case, Eachain!'

'Proprietary airs already, I see,' retorted the young soldier,
a smile in the dark eyes which were Alison's too. '*Eh bien*, if
I may not have Alison, I vow I'll dance with the oldest dame
present, I like not your young misses.' And away he went,
while Ewen, offering his hand, carried off his lady for the
minuet which was just about to begin.

And, intoxicated by the violins, the lights, the shimmer of
satin and silk – with just enough tartan to show the gathering's heart – thinking of Cope soundly beaten, Edinburgh in
their hands, Ewen distinguished by the Prince for Lochiel's
sake, Alison felt that she was stepping on rosy clouds instead
of on a mortal floor. Her feet ached to dance a reel rather than
this stately measure. And Ewen – the darling, how handsome,
though how different, he looked in powder! – did he too know
this pulsing exhilaration? He always kept his feelings under
control. Yet when his eyes met hers she could see in them,
far down, an exultation profounder, perhaps, than her
own.

The music ceased; her betrothed bowed low, and Alison
sank smiling in a deep curtsy that spread her azure petticoat
about her like a great blue blossom. Then she took his hand
and they went aside.

'Now you must fan yourself, must you not, whether you be
hot or no? What are these little figures on your fan – Cupids
or humans?' asked Ewen.

'Mercy on us!' exclaimed Miss Grant suddenly, looking towards the end of the apartment, 'the Prince is no longer
here!'

'Is he not?' responded Ewen calmly. 'I had not observed.'

'And you one of his aides-de-camp! Fie on you!' cried
Alison, and took her fan out of his hand.

'I was looking at you, *mo chridhe*,' said her lover in his deep,
gentle voice, and offered no other excuse.

'But where can His Royal Highness have got to?'

'My dear, His Royal Highness is under no vow that I know
of to watch us dance any longer than he pleases. However,

there's another of his aides-de-camp, Dr Cameron; perhaps he can assuage your anxiety, Archie!'

Dr Archibald Cameron, Lochiel's brother, turned round at his kinsman's summons. He was a man only a dozen years or so older than Ewen himself, with much of Lochiel's own wisdom and serenity, and Ewen had for him a respect and affection second only to that which he bore his Chief.

'Archie, come and protect me from Miss Grant! She declares that I am a Whig because I am wearing neither trews nor philabeg, and unworthy of the position I occupy towards the Prince because I had not observed his withdrawal, nor can tell her the reason for it.'

But already the fiddles had struck up for another dance, and one of the young Grants had returned and was proffering his request anew. So Ewen relinquished his lady and watched her carried off, sailing away like a fair ship.

'Taken to task so soon!' said Dr Cameron with a twinkle. He was a married man himself, with several children. 'No doubt if my Jean were here I should be in like case, for though I knew the Prince had withdrawn I have not fashed myself about it.'

Neither did Ewen now. 'Is it true,' he asked, 'that Donald will not be here tonight at all?'

'Yes; I left him by his own fireside in the Canongate.'

'He's not ill, Archie?'

'No, no; he's older and wiser than we, that's all.' And giving his young cousin a nod and a little smile Dr Cameron went off.

Ewen abode where he was, for it was too late to secure a partner. Suddenly, hearing his name uttered in a low tone behind him, he turned to see Mr Francis Strickland, one of the 'seven men of Moidart', the gentlemen who had landed with the Prince in the west.

'Captain Cameron,' said he, coming closer and speaking still lower, though at the moment there was no one within a couple of yards or so, 'Captain Cameron, the Prince desires that in a quarter of an hour you will station yourself at the door of the ante-room leading to his bedchamber, and see to it that no one approaches his room. His Royal Highness finds himself indisposed, and obliged to withdraw from the ball; but he particularly wishes that no attention shall be called to his absence. Do you understand?'

Ewen stared at him, a good deal astonished at this com-misson. There was something furtive too, about Mr Strick-land's manner which he did not relish, and, in common with many of the Highland chiefs, he was coming to dislike and mistrust the Irish followers of the Prince – though Strickland, to be accurate, was an Englishman.

'This indisposition is very sudden, Mr Strickland,' he observed. 'A short while ago the Prince was in the best of health and spirits.'

'I suppose, sir,' retorted Strickland tartly, 'that you scarcely consider yourself to be a better judge of the Prince's state of health than he is himself?'

'No,' returned Ewen, his Highland pride all at once up in arms, 'but I do conceive that, as his personal aide-de-camp, I take my orders from His Royal Highness himself, and not from any . . . intermediary.'

Mr Strickland's eye kindled. 'You are not very polite, Cap-tain Cameron,' he observed with truth. Indeed he seemed to be repressing a warmer retort. 'I am to tell the Prince, then, that you refuse the honour of his commands, and that he must find another aide-de-camp to execute them?'

'No, since I have not refused,' said Ewen with brevity, and he turned upon his heel. But Strickland clutched at his arm. 'Not yet – you are not to go yet! In a quarter of an hour's time.'

And Ewen stopped. 'The Prince intends to be indisposed in a quarter of an hour's time!' he exclaimed. 'Then indeed 'tis a very strange seizure; I doubt Dr Cameron would be better for the post.'

'For God's sake, Captain Cameron!' said Strickland in an agitated whisper, pulling Ewen by the sleeve. 'For God's sake show some discretion – moderate your voice!' And he mur-mured something about a delicate task and a wrong choice which only inflamed Ewen's suspicions the more. What intrigue was afoot that the Prince's door should be guarded, under plea of illness, in a quarter of an hour's time? He was expecting a visit, perhaps – from whom? Ewen liked the sound of it very little, the less so that Strickland was plainly now in a fever of nervousness.

'Pray let go my arm, sir,' he said, and the Englishman not at once complying, added meaningly, 'if you do not wish me to be still more indiscreet!' On which Mr Strickland hastily removed his grasp, and Ewen turned and began to make his way down the room, careless whether Strickland were following or no, since if that gentleman's desire for secrecy were sincere he dared not make an open protest among the dancers.

As he went Ewen very much regretted Lochiel's absence to-night, and also the indisposition of Mr Murray of Broughton, the Prince's secretary, who had delicate health. Mr Strickland must be aware of both those facts. . . . And if Strickland were in this business, whatever it might be, it was fairly certain that Colonel O'Sullivan, the Irish Quartermaster-General, was in it also. For a second or so the young man hesitated, and glanced about for Dr Cameron, but he was nowhere to be seen now. Then he himself would try to get to the bottom of what was going on; and as when his mind was made up an earthquake would scarcely have turned him from his path, Mr Cameron of Ardroy made straight for the Prince's bedchamber with that intention.

The drawing-room leading directly from the picture gallery had about a dozen couples in it; the ante-room which gave at right angles from this was fortunately empty, although the door between was open. The investigator went quietly through, closing this, marched across the ante-room and knocked at the Prince's door.

'Avanti!' cried a voice, and Ewen went into the bedchamber which had once been the ill-fated Darnley's. The Prince was sitting on the other side of the gilded and embroidery-hung bed, with his back to the door, engaged, it seemed, in the absence of Morrison, his valet, in pulling on his own boots. A black cloak and plain three-cornered hat lay upon the gold and silver coverlet.

'Is that you, O'Sullivan?' he asked without turning his head. 'I shall be ready in a moment.'

Ewen thought: 'I was right; O'Sullivan is in it! . . . Your Royal Highness. . . .' he said aloud.

At that the Prince looked quickly behind him, then, still seated on the bed, turned half round, leaning on one hand. 'My orders, Captain Cameron, were for you to post yourself at the outer door. There has evidently been some mistake, either on your part or on Mr Strickland's.'

'On mine then, may it please Your Highness,' admitted Ewen coolly. 'As the order puzzled me somewhat, I have ventured to ask that I may receive it from Your Royal Highness's own mouth.'

The mouth in question betrayed annoyance, and the Prince arose from his position on the bed and faced his aide-de-camp across it. '*Mon Dieu*, I thought it was plain enough! You will have the goodness to station yourself outside the farther door and to let no one attempt to see me. I am indisposed.'

'And the quarter of an hour's interval of which Mr Strickland spoke, sir?'

'That is of no moment now. You can take up your place at once, Captain Cameron.' And with a gesture of dismissal the Prince turned his back and walked across the room towards the curtained window. It was thus plainly to be seen that he had his boots on.

He was not then expecting a visit; he was going to pay one! Hence the sentinel before the outer door, that his absence might not be known. Ewen looked at the cloak on the bed, thought of the dark Edinburgh streets, the hundred and one narrow little entries, the chance of a scuffle, of an encounter with some unexpected patrol from the Castle, and took the plunge.

'Your Royal Highness is going out – at this hour!'

The Prince spun round. 'Who told you that I was going out? And if I were, what possible affair is it of yours, sir?'

'Only that, as your aide-de-camp, it is my great privilege to watch over your Royal Highness's person,' answered Ewen respectfully but firmly. 'And if you are going out into the streets of Edinburgh at night without a guard—'

Charles Edward came nearer. His brown eyes, striking in so fair-complexioned a young man, sparkled with anger. 'Captain Cameron, when I appointed you my aide-de-camp, I did not think that I was hampering myself with a—' He bit off the short, pregnant word, the aide-de-camp's suddenly paling face evidently recalling to him whither he was going. But he instantly started off again on the same road. '*Dieu me damne!*' he said irritably, 'am I to have your clan always at my elbow? Lochiel may have walked first into Edinburgh, but he was not the first to declare for me. He sent his brother to beg me to go back again! I think you Camerons would do well to remem—' Again he broke off, for there had come a knock at the door.

But Ewen, white to the very lips, had put his hand behind him and turned the key. 'Will your Royal Highness kindly give your orders to some other man?' he asked, in a voice which he did not succeed in keeping steady. 'I'll not endure to hear either my Chief or myself insulted, no, not though it be by my future King!'

The Prince was brought up short. His aide-de-camp might have taken upon himself a good deal more than his position warranted, but to offend a chieftain of Clan Cameron at this juncture was madness. Charles was not yet a slave to the petulant temper which from his boyhood had given anxiety to those about him, and which in later unhappy years was to work so much disaster, and his great personal charm was still undimmed.

'Wait a little!' he called through the door, and then looked with appeal in his beautiful eyes at the tall figure in front of it, rigid with the stillness of a consuming anger. 'Ardroy, forgive me for a moment of irritation! I scarce knew what I was saying. You cannot think that there is any thought in my breast for my good Lochiel but gratitude – all the greater gratitude that he knew and weighed the risk he ran and yet drew that true sword of his! And as for you, how did I insult you?'

'I think,' said Ewen, still very pale and haughty, and using to the full the physical advantage which he had – not very many had it – of being able to look down on his Prince, 'I think that your Royal Highness was near calling me . . . something that no gentleman can possibly call another.'

'Why, then, I could not have been near it – since I hope I am a gentleman!' The Prince smiled his vanquishing smile. 'And to prove that you are imagining vain things, my dear Ardroy, I will tell you on what errand I am bound tonight, and you shall accompany me, if you still insist upon your right to watch over my royal person.'

Ewen was not vanquished. 'Your Royal Highness is too good,' he answered, bowing, 'but I should not dream of claiming that right any longer, and I will withdraw.'

'I always heard that you Highlanders were unforgiving,' lamented the Prince, between jest and earnest. (Devoted though they were, they were certainly not easy to manage.)

'Come, Ardroy, you are much of an age with myself, I imagine – do *you* never say in heat what you designed not – and regret the moment after?'

Their eyes met, the warm Southern brown and the blue.

'Yes, my Prince,' said Ewen suddenly. 'Give me what orders you will, and they shall be obeyed.'

'I am forgiven then?' asked the Prince quickly, and he held out his hand as though to clasp his aide-de-camp's. But Ewen bent his knee and put his lips to it.

During this touching scene of reconciliation it was evident from various discreet but not too patient taps upon the door that the excluded person on the other side still desired admittance.

'Open the door, *mon ami*,' said Charles Edward, and Ewen, unlocking it, did so; and in walked Colonel John William O'Sullivan, not too pleased, as was obvious, at his exclusion. He carried a cloak over his arm.

'I thought your Royal Highness was admitting no one except—' He stopped and looked in dumb annoyance at the intruder. Ewen showed a stony front. There was no love lost between the Quartermaster-General and the Camerons whom he had posted so badly at Tranent before the recent battle.

'Strickland has not come yet,' observed the Prince, and added, with a spice of malice: 'I think it well to take an aide-de-camp with me, O'Sullivan. We shall therefore be a *partie carrée*.'

'As your Highness pleases, of course,' said O'Sullivan stiffly.

'And in that case,' went on his Royal Highness, 'he had best know whither we are bound. We are going, my dear Ardroy, to pay a visit to a lady.'

Ewen was astonished, for he had seen enough since their coming to Edinburgh to make him conclude that the Prince was – perhaps fortunately – very cold where women were concerned, no matter how much incense they burnt before him. Then disgust succeeded to astonishment: was this the time for intrigues of that nature? But the latter emotion, at least, was very transitory, for the Prince went on almost at once: ' 'Tis the Jacobite widow of a Whig Lord of Session – an old lady, but no doubt charming, and certainly loyal – who dwells at the corner of the West Bow and the Grassmarket.'

'So near the Castle!' broke from Ewen in spite of himself.

'*Donc*, the last place in which I shall be looked for! More-over,' said the young Prince gaily, 'I am borrowing Murray's name, since Lady Easterhall is his kinswoman, and is expecting a visit from him – though not, I'm bound to say, tonight. You look blank, Captain Cameron' (and Ewen had no doubt he did). 'See then, read the old lady's letter to Murray.'

Ewen took the paper which the Prince drew from his pocket, and read the following, written in a slightly tremulous hand:

'MY DEAR JOHN,—

'It will no doubt be your Labours in His Royal Highness's Service that have hitherto hindered you frae waiting upon an old Woman who has not set Eyes upon you since you were a Lad. I see I'll e'en have to bid you to my House, and maybe set a Bait to bring you there. Well then – do you mind of William Craig of Craigmains, him that's sib to your Uncle Dickson on the Mother's Side, with a pretty Fortune, and Kin that went out, severals of them, in the Fifteen? He comes to Edinburgh today on Affairs, and will likely stay two-three Days with me; and I'm thinking that could he be gained for the Good Cause others of the Fife Lairds might follow his Example. Forbye there's his Siller. Try then could you not dine with me the morn at three of the Clock, and have a bit Crack with Craig-mains, and tell him how well Things go for our bonny Prince, and you'll maybe do as good an Afternoon's Work as writing Proclamations.
                    'Your loving Great-aunt,
                              'ANNA EASTERHALL.'

This letter was superscribed 'To Mr John Murray of Broughton at Holyroodhouse', and was of the same day's date. Ewen gave it back to his royal hand in silence.

'Mr Murray is indisposed and keeps his room, and I am going to pay his great-aunt a visit in his stead,' said the Prince, going to the bed and taking up his cloak. 'And "our bonny Prince" himself will have the necessary bit crack with this Fife laird of the moneybags. You can see from the letter that Lady Easterhall thinks a little persuasion might induce him to open them, and I flatter myself that he'll yield to me sooner than to Murray.

'But your Royal Highness could cause this kinsman of Mr

Murray's to come here, instead of venturing yourself in the Grassmarket,' objected Ewen, to whom this Haroun-al-Raschid scheme – unknown, he felt sure, to the secretary himself – did not at all appeal.

'Not before he had made up his mind, man! He would not; your Lowland Scot is too canny.'

'But would not a visit to this lady tomorrow—'

'Would you have me approach the Castle in daylight, my friend?'

'But consider the other dwellers in the house,' urged Ewen. 'Your Royal Highness knows that nearly all Edinburgh lives pell-mell, one above the other. Lady Easterhall's neighbour on the next land may well be a Whig gentleman or—'

'My dear Ulysses,' said the Prince, laying a hand familiarly on his aide-de-camp's arm, 'you may have an old head on young shoulders, but so have I too! Lady Easterhall is very singular; she has a whole house to herself. I found this out from Murray. And if report says true, the house itself is singular also.'

At that moment there was another discreet tap at the door, and O'Sullivan, who had been listening to this conversation in a sardonic silence, opened it to admit Mr Francis Strickland in a cloak. In response to the displeased query on the last-comer's face the Quartermaster-General observed that Captain Cameron was going with them, 'though one gathers that he disapproves.'

'He has my leave to disapprove,' said the Prince lightly, 'provided he comes too.' He was evidently in great spirits at the prospect of this escapade, as pleased as a boy at stealing a march on his bedridden secretary – relieved too, perhaps, at having laid the storm which he had himself raised; and when Ewen asked him whether he should not procure him a chair, scouted the idea. He would go on his own feet as less likely to attract attention. 'And when I have my cloak so' – he threw it round his face up to the very eyes – 'who will know me? I learnt the trick in Rome,' he added.

But his gaze then fell upon his aide-de-camp's attire. 'Faith, Ardroy, you must have a cloak, too, to cover up that finery – nay, you cannot go to fetch one now. I know where Morrison keeps another of mine.'

'And the sentinel at your Royal Highness's ante-chamber

door?' inquired Strickland in an injured voice.

'The door must go wanting one after all – unless you your-self covet the post, Strickland? In that case you can lend *your* cloak to Captain Cameron.' And at the look on Strickland's face he laughed. 'I was just jesting. Like the man in the Gospel, I have two cloaks – here, Ardroy, if 'twill serve for that exces-sive height of yours. . . . Now for my great-great-great-grandsire's private stair!'

Chapter Two

THE three men followed him in silence down the narrow, twisting stair, Ewen bringing up the rear, and wondering why disapproval made one feel so old. And, after O'Sullivan had given the word of the day and passed them out of Holyrood House, they were soon walking briskly, not up the Canon-gate itself, but up the slope parallel to it, the 'back of the Canongate', the Prince in front with the Irishman, Ewen be-hind with Strickland, both the latter very silent. Flurries of the October wind plucked at their cloaks as they went in the semi-darkness, sometimes swooping at them from the open grassy spaces of the King's Park on their left, at others appear-ing to originate mysteriously in the tall line of houses of the Canongate with their intervening gardens on the right. They met nobody until they came to the Cowgate Port, and, O'Sullivan again giving the word to the guard, were admitted within the town walls and the nightly stenches of Edinburgh proper.

In the Cowgate there were still a few folk abroad, and a couple of drunkards, emerging unexpectedly from a close, all but knocked into the Prince. As he moved quickly aside to avoid collision, a man passing in the opposite direction was obliged to step into the gutter. It was quite natural that this man should turn his head to see the reason for being thus in-commoded, but unfortunate that the Prince's cloak should at that instant slip from its position. Ewen could only hope that the passer-by had not recognized him; there was at least nothing to indicate that he had. He went on his way without a pause, and the four adventurers resumed theirs.

As they emerged into the Grassmarket the great mass of the

Castle Rock, half distinguishable against the sky, and crowned with a few lights, lifted itself as if in menace; but a few steps farther and it was blocked from view by the houses on the other side of that wide open space. Lights still burned in some of these but everything was quiet.

'That is the house,' said the Prince in a low voice, but it was not easy to know at which he was pointing across the Grassmarket, since they all adjoined each other. 'The entrance, however, is neither here nor in the West Bow, but up a close leading out of the Grassmarket, so Murray says.'

Holding their fluttering cloaks about them they crossed the Grassmarket. Away to their right, when they were over, wound the curve of the West Bow. At the mouth of the close which the Prince indicated Ewen, seeing that O'Sullivan seemed to be going to allow his master to walk first up the dark passage, strode forward, and without apology placed himself in front, and so preceded them all up the alley, his hand on his sword. He liked this place not at all.

In a moment he felt a twitch on his cloak from behind. 'This will be the door of the house,' said the Prince's voice. 'See if you can summon someone. They keep uncommonly early hours hereabouts; I trust the household is not already abed.'

But Ewen, tirling the risp on the door in the gloom, welcomed this suggestion with delight, since, if it were so, the Prince would be obliged to go home again. And for some little time it did appear as if his hope were to be fulfilled, for no one came in answer to his summons. He peered up the close; it seemed to him possible that its upper end debouched on the Castle Hill itself. It was madness to have come here.

The Prince himself then seized the ring and rasped it impatiently up and down, and very soon Ewen's heart sank again as he heard bolts being withdrawn inside. An old servingman opened the door a little way and put his head out.

'Will Lady Easterhall receive her kinsman, Mr Murray of Broughton, and his friends?' asked Mr Murray's impersonator.

The ancient servitor opened the door a little wider. 'Ou, ay, Mr Murray o' Broughton,' he said, stifling a yawn. 'Mr Murray o' Broughton,' he repeated, in an owl-like manner which hinted at recent refreshment. 'An' Mr Murray's frien's,' he added, with another yawn but made no motion to admit the

visitors. 'Hoo mony o' ye wull there be then – is yon anither?'
For footsteps had been coming up the close, and at the words
a man passed the group, walking quickly. He did not glance at
them, and it was too dark in the alley to see faces; but Ewen
felt an uncomfortable suspicion that it was the same man who
had passed them in the Cowgate and had looked at the Prince.
But no, surely this man was shorter; moreover he had betrayed
no interest in them.

'Come, man, conduct us to Lady Easterhall,' said O'Sullivan
sharply. 'Or is she abed?'

'Nay, her leddyship's taking a hand at the cartes or playing
at the dambrod wi' Miss Isobel. Come ben then, sirs. Which
o' ye wull be Mr Murray?'

But nobody answered him. They followed him towards the
staircase, up which he began laboriously to toil. 'Forbye her
leddyship's no' expectin' Mr Murray till the morn,' they heard
him mutter to himself, but soon he did little save cough as he
panted and stumbled upwards, pausing once to announce that
whiles he had a sair hoast.

'Take heart, my Nestor,' said the Prince in Ewen's ear, as
they arrived at the first floor. 'It may be difficult to get into
this house, but I have heard that it is easy to get out of it.'

Before he could explain himself the old man had opened
the door of a large room, economically and most insufficiently
lit by the flickering firelight and a couple of candles on a small
table near the hearth, at which sat an old lady and a young
playing draughts. There was no one else in the room.

'My leddy, here's yer leddyship's kinsman, Mr Murray o'
Broughton, and a wheen frin's tae veesit ye. Wull I bring some
refreshment?'

From the island of light the old lady looked up surprised.
'Ye veesit ower late, nephew,' she said in a little, cracked, but
authoritative voice, in the Scots common even to persons of
breeding. 'Nane the less ye are welcome. But did ye no get my
letter the day? Saunders, light the sconces and bring wine.'
And, as one or two candles on the walls sprang to life and the
Prince took a few steps forward, she leant from her easy chair.
'Eh, John, ye've made a finer figure of a man than aince I
thocht ye like to do! But hae ye the toothache that ye are sae
happed up? Come and present your friends, and I'll make ye
acquainted with Miss Isobel Cochran, your aunt Margaret's

niece. Bestir yersel' now wi' the candles, Saunders – dinna don'er, man!'

The Prince removed his cloak from the lower part of his face. 'Madam,' he said, bowing, 'I must crave your pardon for having used your great-nephew's name as a passport. I am not Mr Murray, and – though I hope indeed that you will not be so cruel – I await only your word to have your good Saunders show us the door again.'

The old lady peered still farther into the only half-dispelled dimness. 'Presairve us – wha's gotten intil the hoose?' she exclaimed. 'What is't . . . I canna see . . .'

But the girl was on her feet, the colour rushing into her face. 'Great-aunt, great-aunt, 'tis the Prince himself!'

Even Ewen's disapproval was hardly proof against the scene that followed. Old Lady Easterhall rose tremulously on her ebony stick, her face working almost painfully, and attempted to kneel, which the Prince of course would not allow; while Miss Cochran, from pale that she was become, had the colour restored to her cheeks by the salute which he set on her hand as she rose from the deepest curtsy of her life. In a short time Saunders, babbling joyfully, had lit every sconce in the room, till the candle-light swam and glittered on the well-polished furniture and the half-seen satins of the visitors' coats, seeming to concentrate itself upon the winking star of St Andrew which – most ill-advisedly, thought the aide-de-camp – still adorned the Royal breast. And when chairs had been set, and wine brought, then at last, in a warm atmosphere of loyalty and emotion, the Prince tactfully explained his errand.

Lady Easterhall shook her becapped head. 'Ah, I jaloused 'twas not to see an auld woman that your Royal Highness came here! But Craigmains is no' come yet; he wasna to reach the toun till noon the morn. I thocht I had writ that in my letter to my nephew. Sae your Royal Highness has come here for naething.'

The Prince's face had indeed fallen, but he recovered himself quickly. 'Do not say that, madam. Have I not gained the pleasure of your acquaintance, and of Miss Cochran's, not to speak of drinking the best claret I have tasted since I came to Edinburgh? So let us pledge the missing guest, gentlemen, and the real Murray shall deal with him tomorrow.'

On which, lifting his glass, he drank again, and Colonel O'Sullivan and Mr Strickland followed his example. But Ewen did not; he had risen, and now remained standing behind the Prince's chair, as one awaiting the signal to depart. Now that he had learnt the uselessness of his escapade His Highness would no doubt speedily withdraw. But that young gentleman showed no sign of such an intention. On the contrary, he began in an animated manner to question Lady Easterhall on her recollections of the Fifteen, while Miss Cochran's hand played nervously with the neglected draughtsmen on the little table, though her eyes, wide and glamour-stricken, never left the unbidden guest. She at least, even if she knew it not, was uneasy.

And after a few minutes the Prince became aware of his aide-de-camp's attitude. He turned his head.

'What a plague ails you, Captain Cameron, standing there like a grenadier! Sit down, man, and do not so insult our hostess's excellent vintage.'

'I had rather, with Your Highness's and Lady Easterhall's leave,' replied Captain Cameron, 'post myself in some part of the house whence I can get a view of the approach to it. Does not the close run up towards the Castle Hill madam?'

'You are very nervous, sir,' commented O'Sullivan, half-sneeringly. 'Why should the nearness of the Castle trouble Lady Easterhall, since his Royal Highness's presence cannot possibly be known there? And of what use is the guard at the Weigh-house – your own clansmen, too – if they cannot prevent the garrison from coming out?'

But Lady Easterhall herself seemed of Ewen's opinion. 'The young gentleman is verra richt,' she declared. 'He shall keep watch if he's minded tae, though, as ye say, sir, the Castle's little likely to trouble my hoose. Isobel, gang ye with Captain Cameron and show him the best windy for the purpose. Though even if they should send a picket here,' she added, smiling, 'His Royal Highness and all could be oot of the hoose before they could win entrance. There's a secret stair, gentlemen, leads frae this verra room doun under the hoose to a bit door in the West Bow, and the entry to't lies ahint yon screwtore at the side of the chimley, sae ye may be easy.'

All eyes turned towards the spot indicated, where, not far from the hearth, an ebony writing-table with inlay of metal

and tortoise-shell – evidently a French importation – stood
against the panelling. 'A secret stair!' exclaimed the Prince,
and, in a lower tone, '*ma foi*, rumour was right! – You hear,
Ardroy? So now you need not deprive us of your society . . .
nor of Miss Cochran's.'

'Miss Cochran's I need not in any case take from your Royal
Highness,' responded Ewen, preparing to leave the room, 'for
I doubt not I can find a suitable look-out without troubling her.
But, even with the secret stair, I think it would be better to
post a sentry.' A laugh from O'Sullivan followed him as he
closed the door, and stirred his simmering wrath against the
Quartermaster-General and Strickland to a still higher tem-
perature. That they should without remonstrance allow the
Prince to remain here, under the very shadow of the Castle,
for no more valid object than to drink Lady Easterhall's claret
– and, of course, to give her pleasure by the honour done to
her – was monstrous! It was true that it needed a certain
amount of skill and courage to make a dash from the Castle,
on account of the Highland guards in its neighbourhood, but
it was dark, and he was still uneasy about the man who had
passed them in the close.

The landing and stairway were ill lit, and he hesitated; he
had better summon Saunders, perhaps. Then the door behind
him opened and shut, a rather timid voice said: 'Captain
Cameron!' and turning, he beheld Miss Isobel Cochran with
a lighted candle in her hand.

'I came, sir, because I thought you would need this.' She held
it out none too steadily. 'Oh, sir, you are the only one right of
all of us! The Prince should not bide longer; it is too dangerous.'

'So I think,' said Ewen, looking down at her gravely. 'I
thank you, Miss Cochran.' He took the light from her. 'Could
you not persuade Lady Easterhall to hasten his departure?'

'Hardly,' answered the girl regretfully. 'You can see what
it means to her to have the Prince under her roof . . . . If
you will go along that passage, sir, you will find a window
out of which you can see some way up the close. . . . Stay,
I will show you, since I am here.'

She slipped along the passage in front of him, and he
followed with the candlestick.

'There,' said Miss Cochran, 'this window.' She unlatched it,

Ewen setting down the light at some distance. He saw the girl put her head out . . . and then draw back, her hand over her mouth as though to stifle a scream. 'Too late, too late already! Look, look!'

Ewen leaned out. Down the dark alley, already echoing to the quick tramp of feet, a file of soldiers were advancing two by two, an officer leading. He drew in his head.

'Go back at once and warn the Prince, madam. I will stay a moment to watch. Blow out the light, if you please; I do not want them to see me.'

Obeying him, the girl fled, while Ewen, crouching by the open window, held his breath as the heavy, hasty footsteps drew nearer and nearer, and he was looking down at last on three-cornered hats and tilted bayonets. There were fully a score of soldiers, and they *were* stopping at Lady Easterhall's entrance; he saw the officer raise a lantern to make sure of the door. Waiting no longer, he ran back along the passage and pelted down the stairs. 'Saunders, Saunders!'

Fortunately the old man heard him at once and emerged from some lair of his own on the ground floor. 'What's to do, sir?'

'There are soldiers from the Castle at the door. Don't admit them, on your life! They are after . . . "Mr Murray". Is the door stout?'

'No' by-ordinar' stout. Dod, they'll be for coming in; nae doot o' that!' For a sword-hilt, it might have been, was clamouring on the door. 'If I'm no' tae open, they'll ding the door doun!'

'Let them,' commanded Ewen. ' 'Twill take some time to do it. And remember, you know nothing at all about her lady-ship's visitors!'

He ran up again, thanking Heaven with all his heart for the secret passage and its exit in a spot where the redcoats would never dare to show their faces – since there was a Highland post in the West Bow also.

Three minutes, perhaps, had elapsed since the first discovery and Miss Cochran's return to the drawing-room; Ewen hoped, therefore, as he burst into that apartment, to find no one but the ladies remaining. To his dismay, however, they were all there, in a group against the wall on the right of the hearth. The writing-table had been pushed aside, Strickland was holding a candle close to a panel, and O'Sullivan seemed to be struggling with something in the carving of this. Lady Easterhall, looking incredibly old, was clinging to her great-niece, and the eyes of both were fixed agonizedly on the Irishman and his efforts. The Prince, though he too was watching O'Sullivan narrowly, appeared the most unconcerned of the five.

'Ah, Ardroy, it seems you were justified of your nervousness, then,' he observed coolly. 'And the spring of the panel is unfortunately stiff. It is long, evidently,' he added in a lower tone, 'since a lover left this house by that road!'

'The soldiers are at the door,' said Ewen in a stifled voice His heart felt like hot lead within him; was all to end thus, so foolishly and so soon? The dull sound of battering came up from below.

'Let Miss Cochran try,' suggested the Prince. 'I think it is rather skill than strength which is needed.' And O'Sullivan relinquished his place to the girl. He was very pale, and Strickland had obvious difficulty in keeping the candle upright.

'Isobel, Isobel, can ye no' stir it?' exclaimed Lady Easterhall, wringing her old hands.

The girl's slender fingers were striving with the boss of carved woodwork which concealed the spring. 'O God!' she whispered, and shut her eyes. 'Is there no other hiding-place—' Ewen was beginning in desperation when, with a loud grinding noise, the panel ran back, revealing a dark wall and the first few steps of a winding stair which plunged steeply downwards.

'Quick!' said O'Sullivan, seizing Strickland by the arm. 'You first, to light the stair. Now, your Highness!' The Prince stepped through the aperture and O'Sullivan himself followed. But Ewen lingered a moment on the threshold of safety.

'Madam,' he said earnestly to the shaken old lady, 'if I may advise, do not you or Miss Cochran stay a moment longer in this room! To be in your bedchambers retiring for the night, when the soldiers succeed in forcing an entrance, as I fear they will, is the best answer you can make to the charge of entertaining the Prince. Do not, I beg of you, be found here – for he has still to get clear of the house!'

'Ye're richt,' said Lady Easterhall. The frozen terror had left her face now. ' 'Tis you hae had the wits all along, young sir! In wi' ye! Noo, Isobel, pit tae the door – and then let's rin for it!'

Behind Ewen came a grinding and a snap, and he was left in almost complete darkness to find his way as best he could down the stair. Somewhere below he heard echoing steps and cautious voices, so the Prince and his companions were still in the house. There must, indeed, be a passage as well as a stair if one was to emerge into the West Bow right on the other side of it. For him there was no hurry; it was just as well to play rear-guard. He started leisurely to descend, feeling his way by the newel, and hoping that he would never again go through another five minutes like the last.

He had certainly not accomplished more than a dozen steps of the descent when he stopped and stiffened, his heart jumping into his throat. There had suddenly floated down from above an ominous dragging, rasping sound which he had heard too recently not to recognize. It was the panel sliding open again! Had the soldiers found it already? It seemed almost impossible

Tugging at his sword, Ewen half leapt, half stumbled, up the dark twisting stair again, and was met by an oblong of light, barred across its lower half by the replaced writing-table. But, as he was instantly aware, the room, though still brilliantly lit – for there had been no time to extinguish the sconces – was empty, and silent save for the sound of furious battering which came up from below through its closed door. It was clear what had happened. The spring of the secret entrance, damaged perhaps, had failed to catch, and after the hurried departure of the two ladies it had released the panel again . . . and so the first thing to attract the notice of anyone entering the room would be that yawning gap in the wall.

Ewen sprang at the sliding door and tried to push it to again, but on its smooth inner surface there was nothing by which to get sufficient purchase. Closed it must be, at whatever cost, and on whichever side of it he was left. He thrust aside the escritoire, stepped out into the room, and pressed the boss which concealed the spring. The panel obediently returned . . . to within half an inch of its place. By getting hold of a projecting line of carving with his nails, Ewen feverishly contrived to push it completely home, but was instantly aware that it would no longer engage itself securely in whatever mechanism usually kept it fast there – in short that, having first refused to open, it now refused to shut. And if the Prince were not yet clear of the passage down below, if the fastenings of the door into the West Bow, for instance, were rusty from disuse, as well they might be, he would yet be taken.

There was a final crash from below; the door was undoubtedly down and the invaders in the house. If only the existence of the sliding panel could be concealed for a few moments longer! To stand before it sword in hand (as was Ewen's impulse) were only to advertise its presence. He looked round in desperation. Perhaps the corner of the escritoire, pressed well against the line of carving, would eliminate that betraying crack in the woodwork? Yes, the escritoire, was sufficiently heavy to keep the panel in place, and, provided that it was not itself moved away from its position, all might yet be well . . . though not for him, who must now throw himself to the wolves to keep the secret inviolate.

To ensure that the writing-table stayed as he had put it he must be near it, and have a reasonable excuse, too, for his position. The most natural was the best; so, throwing off his hat and cloak, he pulled up a chair, sat down – unfortunately this necessitated his having his back to the door – and, seizing a sheet of paper and a quill, began hastily to write a letter. His heart might be beating faster than usual, but his hand, as he saw with pleasure, was quite steady.

'My dear Aunt Margaret, – I told you in my last Letter of the Victory gain'd—' They were coming up the stairs now, and at the noise of their approach he realized how unnatural it would look to be found writing a letter in the midst of such a disturbance as had been going on below. He let his head sink forward on his arm as if he were overcome by sleep; and so was sitting when a second or two later the door was flung violently open, heavy feet came tumbling in, and there was a triumphant shout of 'Here's one o' them, sir.'

Ewen judged it time to wake. He lifted his head and turned in his chair with a start; and then sprang to his feet in simulated astonishment. '*Soldiers!* What are you doing here?'

There were a sergeant and three men of Lascelles's regiment in Lady Easterhall's drawing-room, and the sergeant advanced resolutely towards the tall gentleman in amber satin. ' 'Tis for us to ask that of you, sir.' Then he stopped, his face light-

ing up with a sort of incredulous joy. 'Lord, it's him himself!'
he exclaimed. 'Call the officer quick, one of ye! Bide where
ye are, sir,' he said with a mixture of triumph and respect. 'If
ye don't stir ye'll not be harmed.'

Ewen saw that the man took him for the Prince – a mistake
well worth encouraging if possible, though it was not very
likely that an officer from the Castle would make the same
mistake. In any case he had no intention of stirring from his
place; as it was he imagined that the crack of the panel was
widening behind his back, and dared not turn his head to
look. What would be the end of this? Edinburgh Castle and
captivity, at the best; perhaps a fate even less agreeable.

Ah, here was the officer pushing eagerly through the soldiers
round the doorway. One glance at the figure in front of the
escritoire and that eagerness was wiped away.

'That is not the Prince, you fool!' he said to the sergeant.
'What was he doing when you came in – did he offer any
resistance?'

Through the sergeant's reply that the gentleman was sitting
at the table and seemed to be asleep, Ewen was striving not to
manifest a surprise which, this time, was perfectly genuine.
For, however he had become part of the marooned garrison of
Edinburgh Castle, his captor was no officer of Lascelles's regiment from that fortress; he was Captain Keith Windham of
the Royal Scots.

Chapter Three

B u t Ewen's own powder, satin and lace were, apparently, as
good a disguise to him, for it was quite clear that Captain
Windham had not recognized in this fine gentleman the tartan-
clad victor of Loch Oich side, nor even his seven days' host –
no, even though he was now looking at his captive more
directly, and saying, with military abruptness: 'You are my
prisoner, sir!'

Ewen drew himself up. 'By what right, if you please?' he
demanded. 'By what right indeed do you break at all into a
private house? The Lord Provost shall know of this tomorrow,'
he went on, with a sudden idea of passing himself off as an
ordinary peaceful burgess. 'The Lord Provost shall know of it,

and will require an explanation from General Guest.'

Alas, his voice, at any rate, was not unfamiliar, like his hair and costume. Captain Windham suddenly strode forward, gave an exclamation, and recoiled a little. 'What! It is *you*, Ardroy! Then I know that the Pretender's son is in this house, for you are one of his aides-de-camp! Sergeant, leave a couple of men here, and search the next floor with the others; I will follow in a moment.'

'Is that your pretext for breaking into an old lady's house at this hour of night?' asked Ewen with a fine show of indignation, as the sergeant withdrew. 'Surely you know the way to Holyrood House, Captain Windham – though in truth it may not be so easy to force an entrance there!'

In spite of his anxiety he was able to view with pleasure Captain Windham's visible annoyance at this speech. 'Mr Cameron,' said the soldier, with a steely light in his eyes, 'I am not to be played with like this! The Pretender's son, with three companions, was seen to enter this house a short while—'

'I am sorry to disappoint you, sir,' broke in Ewen, 'but it was *I* who entered with three companions. As you see, I have just been mistaken anew for the Prince. My three friends have left – yes, those are their wine-glasses on the table – Lady Easterhall has retired, and I was beginning to write a letter when I fell into the doze which your noisy and illegal entry has cut short.'

'I don't believe you,' said Keith starkly, though at the mention of the letter his eyes had strayed for a second to the escritoire – and Ewen immediately wished he had not called attention to it. 'Nor do I believe that our informant mistook you for the Pretender's son; tall though he is, you are much taller. He is somewhere hidden in this house.'

'Tall . . . taller . . .' observed Ewen meditatively. 'Ah, yes, I was forgetting your opportunities of observation at Glenfinnan. I suppose you were able to tell them his exact height at Fort William after you had so craftily given me the slip.'

This effort at provoking an argument about the ethics of that action was unsuccessful, though he could see that his late prisoner did not relish the expression which he had applied to it. But Captain Windham merely repeated, with more emphasis: 'He is somewhere hidden in this house!'

'If so, then perhaps you will have the good fortune to find

and recognize him,' said Ewen with an air of levity. 'Or if not His Royal Highness, one of the other two, perhaps.'

'I have no doubt I shall,' replied Keith shortly. 'Meanwhile – your sword, if you please, Mr Cameron!'

This object Ewen had not the slightest intention of surrendering. But any kind of parley with the enemy gained time, which was the important matter. So, after a long look at the floor, as though seeking counsel there, he put his hand to the hilt, and very slowly drew the small sword from its velvet sheath. But, once the blade was out, his fingers retained their grip.

'After all, I find that I dislike making you an unconditional gift of it,' he announced coolly, while the candlelight played menacingly up and down the steel. 'But I cannot prevent your *taking* it, Captain Windham – if you think it worth the trouble.' And with his free hand he tucked his lace ruffle out of the way.

But, as he had expected – half hoped, yet half feared, for at bottom he was pining for a fight – the Prince's pursuer did not wish to engage either himself or his men in personal conflict while part of the house still remained unexplored. 'I'll deal with you later, Mr Cameron,' he replied curtly, and turned to the soldiers. 'See that the prisoner does not move from that spot, men. I am going to fasten the door.' He went out and, sure enough, could be heard to bolt the door on the outside.

Ewen smiled to himself to think how little he desired to quit his self-chosen position. 'You'll not object to my sitting down, I hope?' he observed politely to his two guardians, and, turning round the chair from which he had risen – casting, too, a quick glance at the panel behind him, still in place – he sat down, facing his jailers, his sword across his knees. Though they had no orders to that effect, he thought it just possible that they might attempt to disarm him, but they showed no sign of such a desire, standing stiffly by the door with their muskets and screwed bayonets, and glancing nervously at him out of the corners of their eyes, mere young north-country English lads, overawed by his dress and his air. Had they not been there, however, he could have decamped through the secret door, and what a charming surprise that would have been for Captain Windham when he returned – Fassefern House the other way round! But on second thoughts Ewen

was obliged to admit to himself that this withdrawal would
not have been feasible in any case, because he could not close
the panel from the inside.

Meanwhile Captain Windham, in pursuit of a prey already
(please God!) out of the snare, was presumably searching Lady
Easterhall's bedchamber, and, a still more delicate matter, Miss
Cochran's. Ewen could not suppose that the task would be to
his liking, and the thought of his opponent's embarrassment
afforded him much pleasure, as he sat there with one silk-
stockinged leg crossed over the other. His ill-temper had gone.
Too young a man to have at all enjoyed the rôle of disapproving
critic forced upon him this evening, with his two elders
covertly sneering at his prudence, and even the Prince amused
at him, he was more than relieved to be free of his ungrateful
part. Events had most amply justified his attitude, and now,
with rising spirits, he was free to try what his wits – and perhaps, in the end, his arm – could accomplish against Captain
Windham and his myrmidons. It was true that, short of getting
himself killed outright, he did not see much prospect of
escaping imprisonment in the Castle, but at any rate he might
first have the satisfaction of a good fight – though it was to
be regretted that he had not his broadsword instead of this
slender court weapon. Still, to get the chance of using it against
what he knew to be overwhelming odds was better than having
to submit to being told that he had an old head on young
shoulders!

Sooner than he had expected he heard returning feet, and
now Captain Windham and he would really come to grips!
It was by this time, he guessed, some twenty minutes since
the Prince had slipped down the stair, and, provided that
there had been no difficulty about exit, he must be almost back
at Holyrood House by this time. But one could not be sure of
that. And in any case Ewen had no mind to have the way he
took discovered. Here, at last, was an opportunity of repaying
to Captain Windham the discomfiture which he had caused
him last August over his expired parole, perhaps even of
wiping out, somehow, the insult of the money which he had
left behind. The young man waited with rather pleasurable
anticipations.

And Captain Windham came in this time, as Ewen knew he
would, with an overcast brow and a set mouth. He was

followed in silence by the sergeant and five men, so that the room now contained nine soldiers in all.

'Ah, I was afraid that you would have no luck,' observed Ewen sympathetically. He was still sitting very much at his ease, despite his drawn sword. 'A pity that you would not believe me. However, you have wasted time.'

Keith Windham shot a quick, annoyed, questioning glance at him, but made no reply. His gaze ran rapidly round Lady Easterhall's drawing-room, but there was in it no article of furniture large enough to afford a hiding-place to a man, and no other visible door. He turned to the two soldiers whom he had left there. 'Has the prisoner made any suspicious movement?'

'He has not moved from yonder chair,' he was assured in a strong Lancashire accent.

'And yet this is the room they were in,' muttered the Englishman to himself, looking at the disordered chairs and the used wine-glasses. After frowning for a moment he started to tap the panelling on his side of the room, a proceeding which made Ewen uneasy. Had they heard up at the Castle of the existence of a secret passage somewhere in this house? It was unpleasantly possible. But when Captain Windham came to the three windows giving on to the Grassmarket he naturally desisted. And the farther side of the room – that where Ewen and his writing-table were situated – faced, obviously, down the close by which the soldiers had entered, so (if the Highlander followed his reasoning correctly) Captain Windham concluded that there was no room there for a hiding-place, and did not trouble to sound the wall.

Ewen, however, judged it time to rise from his chair. 'I told you, Captain Windham, that my friends had gone,' he remarked, brushing some fallen powder off his coat. 'Will you not now take your own departure, and allow an old lady to resume the rest which I suppose you have just further disturbed?'

He saw with satisfaction that the invader (who was, after all a gentleman) did not like that thrust. However, the latter returned it by responding dryly: 'You can render that departure both speedier and quieter, Mr Cameron, by surrendering yourself without resistance.'

'And why, pray, should I be more accommodating than you

were last August?' inquired Ewen with some pertinence.

Keith Windham coloured. 'To bring back the memory of that day, sir, is to remind me that you then put me under a deep obligation, and to make my present task the more odious. But I must carry it out. Your sword, if you please!'

Ewen shrugged his shoulders in the way Miss Cameron condemned as outlandish. 'I had no intention, sir, of reminding you of an obligation which I assure you I had never regarded as one. But why *should* I render your task, as you call it, more pleasant? And why make a task of it at all? The Prince, as you see, is not here, and Generals Guest and Preston will find me a very disappointing substitute.'

Keith Windham came nearer and dropped his voice. His face looked genuinely troubled. 'I wish, Ardroy, for your own sake, that you would let me take you unharmed! Take you I must; you are a chieftain and the Prince's aide-de-camp, as I happen to know. It is the fortune of war, as it was last August, when our positions were reversed. So, for the sake of the courtesy and hospitality which I then received from you—'

'My sorrow!' burst out Ewen. 'Must my past good conduct, as you are pleased to consider it, lead to my undoing now? . . . And I very much doubt whether our positions *are* reversed, and whether any further disturbance – and you have made not a little already – do not bring the guard from the West Bow about your ears. If I must give advice in my turn, it would be to get back to the Castle while yet you can!'

'Thank you,' said Keith with extreme dryness: 'we will. Sergeant, have your men secure the prisoner.'

He stood back a little. Ewen had already decided in the event of a fight to abandon his post by the writing-table, where, on one side at least, he could be taken in flank, and where any shifting of the table itself, highly probable in a struggle, would cause the panel to reveal its secret. (Not that that would greatly matter now.) Immediately the Englishman stepped back, therefore, he darted across the room and ensconced himself in the corner by the nearest window, hastily wrapping his cloak, which he had snatched up for the purpose, round his left arm. His eyes sparkled; he was going to have his fight!

'I am ready,' he remarked cheerfully, seeing the much slower preparations of his assailants. 'Is it to be a charge with the bayonet, or are you going to use the butt, my friends?'

'You'll not use either!' said Keith sharply to his men. 'I do not wish this gentleman injured.'

'Then make him put up his sword, sir,' retorted the sergeant in justifiable indignation. 'Else it's ourselves will be injured, I'm thinking!'

Ewen was about to endorse this opinion when a familiar and most welcome sound came to him through the closed window behind him. No mistaking that strain; and that the soldiers should hear it too he turned a little and dashed his elbow, protected by the curtain, through the nearest pane of glass. In it flowed, wailing and menacing, the Cameron rant: 'Sons of the dogs, come hither, come hither and you shall have flesh . . .'

'I think you had best call off your men altogether, Captain Windham, if they are to save their own skins!' And in the uneasy silence which he had procured Ewen added, with some exultation: 'It is my own clan, the Camerons; they are coming down the West Bow into the Grassmarket. There will not be much left of you, my good fellows, if you so much as scratch me!' And, seeing the effect of his words, he tugged aside the curtain, flung open the partly shattered casement, and called out in Gaelic to the line of kilted figures just emerging from the West Bow.

The long yell of the slogan answered him as he swung quickly back on guard. But there was no need of his sword. Preston-pans had taught the Castle garrison exaggerated terror of those who uttered such cries. The soldiers, the sergeant included, were already huddling towards the door, and Keith Windham was not in time to get between them and the exit. He stamped his foot in fury.

'Do your duty, you dirty cowards!' he shouted, pointing at the figure by the window. But a second heart-shaking yell came up from the Grassmarket: '*Chlanna nan con, thigibh an so, thigibh an so . . .*' Perfectly deaf to their officer's objurgations, the English soldiers were occupied only with the question of which should be first from the room. Keith seized the last fugitive by the collar, but the only result of this appeal to force was that the man, who was very powerful, shook him off, thrust him back with small regard for his rank, and banged the door behind himself. Captain Windham, livid, threw himself upon the handle to pluck it open again – but the knob merely turned in his hand. The violent slam had evidently shot to the bolt on the outside. Hunter and quarry – only now it was hard to know which was which – were equally prisoners.

Ewen, over at the window, laughed aloud; he could not help it. 'You seem always to be unfortunate in your men, Captain Windham,' he remarked, and, shaking the cloak off his left arm, slid his blade back into the scabbard. 'I fear it is I who shall have to ask you for *your* sword. Would you prefer to give it up to me before the guard arrives?'

He got it . . . but not in the fashion which he had expected. Keith, quite beside himself with mortification and rage, had already whipped out his weapon while Ewen, with bent head, was sheathing his own, and now, really blind to the fact that the Highlander was for the moment defenceless and off his guard, Captain Windham sprang furiously at him without warning of any sort. Ewen had no chance to draw again, no space to spring aside, no time for anything but to catch wildly at the blade in the hope of diverting it. At the cost of a badly cut right hand he succeeded in saving himself from being spitted, and the deflected point, sliding through his clutching fingers, went by his hip into the panelling where, both men loosing their hold at the same moment, the weapon stuck for the fraction of a second, and then fell ringing to the floor.

Horrified and sobered, Keith had sprung back: Ewen, after a first instinctive movement to catch him by the throat, had checked himself, and, clasping his bleeding hand tightly with the other, leant back against the wall and looked at him with a mixture of sternness and inquiry. His breath was coming rather quickly, but, compared with his assailant, he was the image of calm.

'My God!' stammered the Englishman, as white as a sheet. 'I never saw . . .' He indicated Ardroy's sheathed sword. 'I might have killed you. . . .' He took a long breath and drew a hand across his eyes. Still looking at him curiously his victim fished out his lace-bordered handkerchief and began to wrap it round his palm, a very inadequate precaution, for in a moment the cambric was crimson.

In another Keith was at his side. 'How deeply is it cut? Let me . . .' And he pulled out his own more solid handkerchief.

'I don't know,' answered Ewen composedly, putting back

his Mechlin ruffle, which had slipped down again. 'Pretty deeply, it seems.' He surrendered his hand. 'Thanks; over mine then – tie it tighter still.'

'Good God, I might have killed you!' said Keith again under his breath as he bandaged and knotted. 'I . . . I lost my temper, but, as Heaven's my witness, I thought you had your sword out.'

'Why, so I had, a moment earlier,' replied Ewen. 'You did not intend murder, then?'

'I deserve that you should think so' murmured the soldier, still very much shaken. 'Perhaps as it is I have disabled you for life.'

Ewen had nearly retorted: 'Why should that trouble you?' but he was so much astonished at the depth of feeling in his enemy's tone that he merely stared at his bent head as he tied the last knot.

'These handkerchiefs are not enough,' said Keith suddenly, relinquishing the wounded hand. He pushed aside the little brass gorget at his neck, untied and unwound his own lace cravat, and bound that over all. Then he stood back.

'You will soon get attention now, Ardroy. Keep your hand up. so. . . . There is my sword.' He made a jerky movement towards the floor, and walking abruptly away to the hearth, stood there with his back turned.

For a moment or two Ewen also stood quite still where he was, looking at that back. That Captain Windham was ashamed of his attack on a practically unarmed man he could understand; he would have had precisely the same scruples in his place, and he would certainly have felt the same rage and humiliation had he been deserted by his followers in so disgraceful a manner (though he could not imagine Highlanders ever acting so). And, observing the dejection revealed in Captain Windham's attitude, where he stood with bowed head and folded arms by the dying fire, and the complete absence in him of any of that mocking irony with which he himself had more than once made acquaintance at Ardroy, Ewen began to feel less vindictive about the incident of the guineas. Captain Windham, being an Englishman, did not understand Highland pride, and had probably never intended any insult at all. And now, with this sudden turning of the tables, he was again a prisoner, made in rather an absurd and ignominious fashion.

Ewen could find it in his heart to be sorry for him. And what would be the advantage of yet another prisoner? The officers taken at Gladsmuir had had to be paroled and sent away. . . .

He picked up the fallen sword, faintly smeared with red along its edges, and went over to the hearth.

'Captain Windham!'

The scarlet-clad figure turned. 'Your Camerons are very tardy!' he said with a bitter intonation. 'Or are those yells all we are to know of them?' It was indeed sufficiently surprising that the rescuers had not entered the house some minutes ago, particularly as the door was broken open.

Ewen listened. 'I think that they are possibly chasing . . . a retreating enemy. But in any case' – he held out Keith's sword – 'I cannot stomach taking advantage of your being left in the lurch by those rascals. Put on your sword again, and I'll convey you safely out of the house.'

A dull flush swept over the English soldier's face. 'You mean that I am to run the gauntlet of those caterans, when they return, under your protection? No; I have been humiliated enough this evening; it would be less galling to go as a prisoner. Keep my sword; 'tis the second of mine you have had, Mr Cameron.'

Yes, he was sore, and no wonder! Ewen decided that he would not even mention the objectionable guineas.

'I cannot hold this sword much longer,' he said lightly, 'having but the one hand at present. – No, the caterans shall not see you at all, Captain Windham, and you shall go alone. Only, for Heaven's sake, be quick, for some of them must soon be here!'

Bewildered, half reluctant, Keith closed his fingers on the hilt held out to him, and Ewen drew him to the escritoire on the right of the hearth. When he pushed it aside the panel behind slid slowly back.

Keith Windham stood before the gap momentarily speechless. 'That, then—' he began at last, thickly.

'Yes, that is the way my friends went. But you can use the same road. It comes out, I understand, in the West Bow; there you will have to trust to chance, but it seems a dark night. Here, take my cloak,' – he went and picked it up – ''twill cover your uniform. And you must have a candle to light you down.'

To these directions and the proffered candlestick and cloak

the baffled hunter paid no heed. 'Your friends!' he said between his teeth. 'The Pretender's son, you mean! He *was* here this evening, then, in this very room!'

'Yes, but he was gone a little time before you entered,' answered Ewen soothingly. 'I was only troubled lest the door should slide open and betray the path he took. But 'tis of no moment now.'

'No, it's of no moment now!' repeated Windham bitterly. Wrath, reluctant admiration, disappointment and concern for what he had so nearly done – and not in fair fight – to the man before him strove openly in his tone as he went on: 'Is this your revenge for—' – he pointed to the swathed right hand – 'and for my outwitting you last August? It's a sharp one, for all that it's generous. . . . Yes, you have fairly outmanœuvred me, Ardroy, with your secret stair and your clansmen so pat to the moment, like a stage play! But I warn you that this mumming will turn to grim earnest some day; there'll be a bloody curtain to the comedy, and you will regret that ever you played a part in it!'

'That depends, does it not, on how many more battles of Gladsmuir we have?' retorted Ewen, with a smile on his lips and a sparkle in his eyes. 'But go – go!' for at last there had come a rush of feet up the stairs, and the rescue party (oblivious of the bolt) were hammering upon the door with cries. He thrust the candlestick and the cloak – the Prince's cloak – into the Englishman's hands, calling out something in Gaelic over his shoulder the while. 'Go – they'll have the door down in another minute!'

He almost pushed Captain Windham into the aperture, pressed the spring, and wedged the returning panel with the table, only a second or two before the unfortunate door of Lady Easterhall's drawing-room fell inwards with a crash, and Cameron kilts plunged over it.

Chapter Four

W A L K I N G home with her father next day up the crowded Canongate after rain, Miss Alison Grant suddenly became aware of a tall Highland officer striding up the street some way ahead. From the occasional glimpses of him, which were all that she was able to obtain in the moving throng, it seemed to be her betrothed; but, if so, he was carrying his right arm in a sling. This was disturbing. Moreover, Ewen, if it were he – and at any rate the officer was a Cameron – was walking at such a pace that Alison and her parent would never overtake him, unless indeed he were on his way to visit them where they lodged in Hyndford's Close, a little beyond the Netherbow.

'Papa,' whispered Alison, 'let us walk quicker; yonder's Ewen, unless I am much mistaken, on his way to wait upon us, and he must not find us from home.'

They quickened their pace, without much visible effect, when lo! their quarry was brought to a standstill by two gentlemen coming downwards who encountered and stopped him.

'Now let us go more slowly, sir,' suggested Alison, dragging at her father's arm. To which Mr Grant, complying said: 'My dear, to be alternately a greyhound and a snail is hard upon a man of my years, nor do I understand why you should be stalking Ardroy in this fashion.'

'Ewen *is* rather like a stag,' thought Alison; 'he carries his head like one. – Papa,' she explained, 'I want to know – I *must* know – why he wears his arm in a sling! Look, now that he has turned a little you can see it plainly. And, you remember, he disappeared so strangely last night.'

And now, crawl as they would, they must pass the three gentlemen, who made way for them instantly, not to turn the lady with her hooped petticoats into the swirling gutter. As Ewen – for it was he – raised his bonnet with his left hand, Alison cast a swift and comprehensive glance over him, though she did not pause for the fraction of a second, but, acknowledging his salutation and those of his companions, went on her way with dignity.

But she walked ever slower and slower, and when she came to the narrow entrance of their close she stopped. Yet even then she did not look back down the Canongate.

'Papa, did you hear, those gentlemen were asking Ewen what had befallen him. I heard something about "disturbance" and "Grassmarket". You saw his hand was all bandaged about. He looked pale, I thought. What can he have been at last night – not fighting a duel, surely!'

'Well, my dear, here he is, so he can tell us – that is, if he is disposed to do so,' observed Mr Grant. 'Good day, Ardroy; were you coming in-bye?'

'I intended it, later on,' replied Ewen, with more truth than tact, 'but—'

'But now you see that you behove to at this moment,' finished Alison, with determination, looking very significantly at his arm; and Ewen, without another word, went obediently up the close with them, secretly admired from above by a well-known Whig lady who happened to be at her window, and who remarked to her maid that the Jacobite Miss lodging overhead had a braw lover, for all he was a wild Hieland-man.

And presently the wild Hielandman was standing in the middle of Mr Grant's parlour, and the Jacobite Miss was declaring that she could shake him, so little could she get out of him. 'They say you can ask anything of a Cameron save butter,' she said indignantly, 'but it's clear that there are other things too you'll never get from them!'

Ewen smiled down at her, screwing up his eyes in the way she loved. He was a little pale, for the pain of his cut hand had kept him wakeful, but he was not ill-pleased with life this afternoon.

'Yes, other people's secrets, to wit,' he said teasingly; and then, feigning to catch himself up: 'My sorrow, have I not the unlucky tongue to mention that word in a woman's hearing! What I have told you, *m'eudail*, is the truth; I had an encounter last night with some of the Castle garrison, and my hand, as I say, was hurt – scratched, that is, as I warrant you have some-times scratched yourself with a needle of a bodkin.'

'The needle's never been threaded whose scratch required as much bandaging as *that*!' retorted Alison, with her eyes on the muffled member in the sling. 'And what was yon I heard as I passed about a disturbance in the Grassmarket?'

'Has she not the ears of a hare?' observed Ewen to Mr Grant. ' 'Tis true, there was a disturbance in the Grassmarket.'

'If that is so, then I'll learn more of it before the day's out,' deduced Alison, with satisfaction. 'And you, sir, that ought to know better, brawling in the town at such an hour! I thought the Prince had summoned you last night. Not that I remarked your absence from the ball,' she added. 'I was quite unaware of it, I assure you, in the society of my cousins of Glen-moriston.'

Ewen looked across at Mr Grant and smiled. 'My dear,' protested the old gentleman, 'an encounter with the Castle garrison can scarce be called brawling. We are, it may be said, at war with them.'

'But are they not all as mild as milk up there now that the Prince has lifted the blockade?' inquired Alison. 'And how could Ewen have met any of them in the Grassmarket? The poor men dare not show their faces there; the place is hotch-ing with Camerons and MacDonalds!'

'Who said I met them in the Grassmarket?' retorted Ewen. 'But never fret, Miss Curiosity; some day I'll be free to tell you where it was.'

'Wherever it was,' said Miss Grant, with decision, 'I'll be bound 'twas you provoked the disturbance!'

Her lover continued to smile at her with real amusement. In a sense there was truth in this last accusation. 'It's a fine character you give me, indeed! I think I'd best be taking my leave until you appreciate me better!' And he put out his left hand to take his bonnet from the table where he had laid it. Something sparkled on the hand as he moved it.

'Who gave you that ring?' exclaimed Alison. 'Nay, that I have a right to know!'

Ewen put his hand behind him. 'No woman, Alison.'

'Then you can tell me who it was. . . . Come, *Eoghain mhóir*, if there be a mystery over the ring also, why, you should not be wearing it for all the world to see!'

'That's true,' said Ardroy, and he relinquished his hand. 'Yes, you can take it off. 'Tis not so plain as it looks, neither. There is a spring beneath.'

'Oh!' breathed Alison, her eyes very wide. The chased gold centre of the ring had moved aside in the midst of the rose diamonds, and it was a tiny miniature of the Prince which she held. 'Ewen, *he* gave you this?'

'I did not steal it, my dear. Yes, he gave it me this morning.'

'For . . . on account of what happened last night?'

Ewen nodded. 'For my prudence. You see, the Prince does not write me down so turbulent as you do.'

There was something like tears in Alison's eyes. 'Prudence? No! It was because you gained that "needle-scratch" for him!'

She kissed the ring, and, taking the strong, passive hand, slipped it on again. 'I will not plague you any more. Does the wound pain you, dearest heart?'

But next day Hector Grant came into possession of the story, more or less correct, which was flying about Edinburgh, and presented his sister with a fine picture of her lover, alone against a score of the Castle redcoats, standing with his back to the secret stair hewing down the foe until his sword broke in his hand, and the Cameron guard rushed in only just in time to save him. And, Alison unveiling this composition to the hero himself at their next meeting, Ewen was constrained in the interests of truth to paint out this flamboyant battle-piece and to substitute a more correct but sufficiently startling scene. Alison certainly found his sober account quite lurid enough.

'And you let the English officer go, after that!' she exclaimed breathlessly. 'But, Ewen dearest, why?'

'For one reason, because 'twas such curst ill luck that his men should run away for the second time!' replied Ewen, settling his silken sling more comfortably.

'For the second time?'

'I have not yet told you who the officer was. Cannot you guess?'

'Surely 'twas not . . . *Captain Windham* . . . here in Edinburgh?'

'It was Captain Windham himself. I have no notion how he got here; it must have been before we took the town. But I was sorry for him, poor man, and it was quite plain that he had no real intention of killing me; indeed he was greatly discomposed over the affair. So you must not lay that to his charge, Alison.'

'And so you *have* met again!' said Alison slowly, her eyes fastened on her lover. ('A great service' . . . 'a bitter grief' . . . This was neither.) 'It was not then because of your foster-father's prophecy that you let him go?'

And now Ewen stared at her. 'Faith, no, darling, for I had clean forgot about it. *Dhé!* It begins to fulfil itself then!'

Bright and cold, or wet and windy, the October days went by in Edinburgh. Ewen's hand healed, and that secret fear which he had mentioned to no one save Dr Cameron, who dressed it, that he would never be able to grip a broadsword

again, passed also. And having waited upon Lady Easterhall
and Miss Cochran a day or two after the fracas to ask how
they did (not that he had omitted to reassure himself of this
on the night itself, before he left) he then, by the old lady's
desire, carried Alison to visit them also. And it is possible that
Miss Cochran envied Miss Grant.

But up at the Castle the days went a great deal more slowly,
particularly for Captain Keith Windham, who had little to do
but to pace the battlements and look down, as he was doing
this morning, when October was almost sped, on that un-
rivalled vista of which he was now heartily sick, and remember all the mortifications, professional as well as personal,
which he had suffered there since the end of August, when he
had made his way thither from Fort William with the news
of the Highland advance. For after the startling tidings of
Cope's avoidance of the rebels, leaving the road open before
them to Edinburgh, Keith, secure but chafing, had endured the
spectacle of vain attempts by the frightened citizens to repair
and man the walls, and to raise a body of volunteers (almost
immediately disbanded lest their lives should be endangered),
and the sight of two regiments of His Majesty's dragoons in
full flight along the Lang Dykes with no man pursuing. Finally,
to complete and symbolize the great scandal and shock of
Cope's lightning defeat, he had with his own eyes seen, struck
defiantly into the outer gate of the Castle, the dirk of the
single Jacobite officer who on that occasion had chased a party
of terrified troopers thither like rabbits to their burrow.

On top of all this had come his own personal humiliation
and disappointment, and of this Ewen Cameron and no other
had been the cause. The soldiers of Lascelles' regiment who
had so shamefully deserted the officer in charge of them had
been severely punished, but this did little to heal the very sore
place in Captain Windham's memory. Sometimes it was only
anger which coloured his recollections of that scene in Lady
Easterhall's house, sometimes it was shame. Sometimes he
wondered if he had not permanently injured Ardroy, and
though, as a loyal subject of King George, he ought no doubt
to have been glad of the possibility, in view of how the hurt
had been inflicted and of the Highlander's subsequent be-
haviour, the idea filled him with a feeling far removed from
satisfaction. And even worse might easily have come of his

onslaught. Keith was inclined to shudder still when he thought of that contingency, and not merely because, with Ewen dead or dying on the floor, he himself would have received short shrift from the Camerons when they broke in.

How nearly he had succeeded in capturing the Prince he supposed he would never know, but there was no doubt that it was Ardroy who had destroyed whatever chance he might have had. Chosen as Keith had been to lead the flying raid that evening because he was the only officer in the Castle who had seen Charles Edward Stuart face to face, he could then have blessed Fate for having sent him to Glenfinnan. Thus, he had reflected as they marched stealthily down the close, does profit come out of the unpleasant. Already he saw his name in every news sheets as the captor of the Pretender's son. . . . Alas, he had merely come anew into collison with the same stubborn and generous character, and once again, though their positions this time had seemed to be reversed, he had had the worst of it. And on this occasion the Highlander had shown him a new and unsuspected side of himself, for it was Ardroy who had played with *him*, sitting so coolly in front of that table on which hung the secret. God! if he had only guessed.

And so Keith had come back empty-handed, with the knowledge that but for Ardroy's quixotry he would not have come back at all. Huddled in his enemy's own cloak (for its real ownership, luckily for his peace of mind, he never discovered), pushed ignominiously to safety down the very passage by which his quarry had eluded him, he had been ever since weighed down by a debt which was wellnigh a grievance. There were times when he almost regretted that he had not remained and been made prisoner . . . and always times when he asked himself why Ewen Cameron had acted as he did. He was sure that he himself would not have been so foolish. The days of chivalry were over; one did not go about in this century behaving like the knights in the old romances. An enemy was an enemy – at least to a professional soldier – and it was one's business to treat him as such.

The cursed part of it was that people who were insane enough to behave as Ardroy had behaved somehow attained a position of superiority which was distinctly galling. And galling also was it to realize, as Keith Windham suddenly did at this moment, how much time he spent in speculating what that curious young man might be doing down there in the city spread out like a map. . . . Strange that he had not at first recognized him that night – extraordinarily handsome Ardroy had looked, and devilish cool he had kept, too, in a tight place! . . . Fool that he was, he was at it again. Keith turned from the battlements, glad of a diversion, for he had become aware of the approach of a wheeled chair, which he knew to contain the aged but spirited form of General Preston.

General George Preston, deputy-governor of Edinburgh Castle since 1715, to whom, old and infirm though he was, it was likely that his Hanoverian Majesty owed it that that fortress had not been surrendered to the invaders, was a veteran of Marlborough's wars, bearing in fact souvenirs of Ramillies which had ever since affected his health and his prospects of promotion. He was eighty-six years of age, even older than General Guest (now, since Cope's flight, commander-in-chief); but whereas that warrior had scarcely left his quarters since he had removed for safety into the Castle, Preston, during the more strenuous days of the 'blockade', had caused himself to be wheeled round in a chair every two hours to supervise and encourage. Since Colonel Philip Windham, Keith's father, had also fought under Marlborough, Keith had on one occasion asked the old soldier some questions about the great Duke's battles, and found Preston very ready to hold forth on them, and in particular on that bloody fight of Malplaquet, where he had commanded the Cameronian regiment. And Keith remembered suddenly that the Scottish friend of his father's after whom he himself was named had met his death at Malplaquet, and spoke to the old soldier about that misty John Keith of whom he knew so little.

'Aye,' said the General, a Perthshire man himself, 'I wondered that ye should bear a Scots name in front of an English, Captain Windham. I suppose yon Keith will have been in a Scottish regiment, but I don't mind of him. 'Tis thirty-six years syne, ye ken – a lang time, more than your hale life-time, young man.'

So John Keith, who had fallen on a Flanders battlefield nearly forty years before, became more misty than ever. But Captain Windham's pre-natal connection with a Scot of Malplaquet had interested old Preston in him, and he announced an intention of reporting on the zeal and vigilance which the officer of the Royals had displayed in the defence of the Castle.

From his chair the old General beckoned to that officer now, and sent his servant out of hearing.

'Captain Windham, a word in your ear!' And, as Keith stooped, he said gleefully: ' 'Tis a good word, if ever there was one. I've reason to believe that Edinburgh will be free of these Highland pests the morn!'

Keith gave an exclamation. 'They are evacuating the city, sir?'

The veteran chuckled. 'They intend marching for England, whence I pray not a man of 'em will return alive. The news has just come in by a sure hand, but I had jaloused it already. In a day or two ye'll not see a plaid between Greyfriars and the Nor' Loch!'

General Preston's sure hand had carried perfectly correct tidings. Against the wishes and the instincts of the Chiefs, Prince Charles was about to march into England, believing that he would thus rally to his standard those cautious English Jacobites on whose promised support he built such large hopes, and many others too, who had made no promises, but who would surely declare for him when he appeared in person to lead them against their alien ruler.

And early on the morning of the first of November Ewen took his farewell of Alison in Hyndford's Close. Lochiel's regiment, like the bulk of the army, was already assembled at Dalkeith; for since Prestonpans the Prince had never quartered troops in the city to any great extent, and he himself was already gone. But Ewen, in order to be with his own men in this strange country to which they were bound, had resigned his position as aide-de-camp, had remained behind in order to bring away the Cameron guard, who would presently march out of Edinburgh with colours flying and the pipes playing.

But here there was no martial display, only a knowledge that this, and not the farewell at Ardroy in August, was the real parting. Ewen was setting off today for something much more portentous than a mere rendezvous – armed invasion. Yet some unspoken instinct made them both try to be very matter-of-fact, especially Alison.

'Here is a sprig of oak for your bonnet, Ewen – you'll be wearing your clan badge now, I'm thinking. I picked it yesterday.' And she fastened beside the eagle's feathers a little bunch of sere leaves. 'And see, I have made you a new cockade . . . I doubt you'll get your clothes mended properly. England's a dour place, I'm sure. Oh, I wish you were not crossing the Border!'

'Nothing venture, nothing win,' replied Ewen tritely, looking down at his bonnet, about which her fingers were busy. 'I doubt, for my part, that those oak leaves will bide long on their stalks, Alison, but you may be sure I'll wear them as long as they do. And the cockade – 'tis a very fine one, my dear – I'll bring back to you somehow. Or maybe you'll get your first sight of it again in London!'

'I wonder will you meet Captain Windham anywhere in England?' said Alison.

'How that fellow runs in your head, my darling! I vow I shall soon be jealous of him. And I marching away and leaving him here in the Castle – for I suppose he is there still. Make him my compliments if you should meet him before setting out for Ardroy,' said Ewen, smiling. For to Ardroy were his betrothed and her father retiring in a day or two.

'Ewen,' said the girl seriously, taking him by the sword-belt that crossed his breast, 'will you not tell me something? Was there ever a danger that, from the injury Captain Windham did you, you might never have had the full use of your hand again?'

'Why, what put that notion into your head?'

'A word you let fall once, and an expression on Dr Cameron's face one day when I mentioned the hurt to him.'

'For a day or two Archie did think it might be so,' conceded her lover rather unwillingly. 'And I feared it myself for longer than that, and was in a fine fright about it, as you may imagine. – But Alison,' he added quickly, as, exclaiming, 'Oh, my poor darling!' she laid her head against him, 'you are not to cast that up against Captain Windham. It was I that took hold of his blade, as I told you, and I am sure that he never meant—'

'No, no,' cried Alison, lifting her head, 'you mistake me. No, I am glad of what you tell me, because that hurt he did you is perhaps the fulfilment of the "bitter grief" which Angus

said that he should cause you . . . only happily it is averted,'
she added, taking his right hand and looking earnestly at the
two red puckered seams across palm and fingers. 'For that
would have caused you bitter grief, Ewen, my darling.' She
covered the scars with her own soft little hands, held the
captive hand to her breast, and went on, eagerly pursuing
her exegesis. 'Indeed, if for a time you believed that you would
be disabled always – how dare you have kept that from me? –
he has already caused you great grief . . . and so, that part is
over, and now he will only do you a service!'

But Ewen, laughing and touched, caught her to him with
his other arm.

'The best service Captain Windham can do is never to let
me see his face again, or I may remember how angry I was
with him when I found his letter and his guineas that night
at Fassefern. Nor do I think he'll want to see mine, for in his
soul he was not best pleased, I'll undertake, at being so lightly
let off the other evening and shown down the very secret stair
he could not find. – But now, *mo chridhe*, do not let us talk of
the tiresome fellow any more. . . .'

And five minutes later, when Hector Grant in his French
uniform appeared at the door, they had forgotten everything
except that they were parting.

'Come, Ardroy, you'll be left behind,' he called gaily. 'Dry
your tears, Alison, and let him go; we've eight good miles to
cover.'

'I was not greeting, never think it,' said Alison as she was
released. 'But oh, I'm wishing sore I could come with you
two!'

'Indeed, I wish you could,' said Hector. 'For I doubt the
English ladies cannot dance the reel.'

Alison looked from her brother to her lover and back again.
She might not have been crying, but there was little gaiety in
her. 'There'll be more than dancing over the Border, Hector!'

'There'll be better than dancing, you mean, my lass,' said
Hector Grant, and his left hand fell meaningly on his sword-
hilt. 'I suppose I may take a kiss of her, Ardroy?'

The Ebb

'Then all went to wreck.'
— *The Lyon in Morning*

Chapter One

T H E R E was a bitter wind sweeping across the Beauly Firth, and Inverness on the farther shore lay shivering under a leaden sky. The Kessock ferry had to tug at his oars, although he carried but one passenger, a gaunt, broad-shouldered young man, fully armed, who sat looking across at the little town with rather harassed blue eyes.

Four months – four months and a week over – for today was the seventh of March – since, full of hope and determination, the Prince's army had set out on the road to England. Of what avail those hopes? England had not risen for the Stuarts, had not stirred. And yet, just when it seemed that, if the invaders had put their fortunes to the touch and pushed on, they might have gained a kingdom, they found themselves turning their backs on their goal and trailing home again over the Border. Little more than forty days had been spent on the other side, and, save for the rear-guard action near Penrith, the sword had not left its sheath there. The invasion had been a failure.

Yet, in spite of weariness and heartburnings, the little army had at least recrossed Esk in safety – except those of it so mistakenly left to garrison Carlisle – and many were not sorry to be back on Scottish soil. But to have retreated once more after beating Hawley at Falkirk in January, even though the bad weather had hindered pursuit and prevented a more decisive victory, to have left Stirling, after failing to take it, in such haste and disorder that the withdrawal had been more like a rout, what name best befitted that strategy? For gradually all the Lowlands had been occupied in their rear, and there was a slow tide setting northwards after them which one day might be slow no longer.

The Prince, maddened at the decision to withdraw north, which was against his every instinct, had been told that the daily desertions were so great as to leave no choice, that the only course was to master the forts in the north, keep together a force until the spring, and then increase it to fighting strength. But had the desertions been so extensive? It was hard to judge, yet, from his own experience, Ardroy would not have said so. Still, there were other difficulties, other divisions; there was the preponderating influence of the Irish favourites, who always had the Prince's ear because they always fell in with his opinions; there was the growing ill-feeling between him and his able but hot-tempered general-in-chief, so acute that Ewen had with his own ears heard Charles Edward charge Lord George Murray behind his back with treachery. Yet Lochiel had been for withdrawal, and whatever Lochiel did was right in Ewen's eyes. He was wondering today whether the Chief were still of the same opinion; he had not seen him for over a fortnight.

The ferryman's voice broke in on his passenger's reflections. ' 'Tis all much changed in Inverness now, sir, and for the better.' Evidently, like most of the inhabitants, he was Jacobite at heart. 'To think that only two weeks ago I ferried Lord Loudoun and the Lord President and the Chief of Macleod over in this very boat, and all their troops crossing helter-skelter too, to get away from the Prince. . . . You'll be yourself, perhaps, from chasing after Lord Loudoun yonder?' he added tentatively.

'Yes,' answered Ewen, his eyes still fixed on Inverness, 'I am from Lord Cromarty's force.'

The reason why the Earl of Loudoun, commanding the district for the Government, had evacuated Inverness without a battle, was really due to the somewhat ludicrous failure of his attempt to seize the person of the Prince when, in mid-February, the latter was the guest of Lady Mackintosh at Moy Hall. Conceiving the idea of surprising him there, the Earl had set out secretly at night with a force of fifteen hundred men for that purpose. But timely warning having been sent from Inverness, the Prince slipped out of Moy Hall, and the whole of Lord Loudoun's force was thrown into confusion, and a part of it into headless flight, by the ruse of Donald Fraser, the Moy blacksmith, and four of Lady Mackintosh's Highland servants, who, by firing off their pieces in the dark and calling to imaginary regiments to come up re-enacted the comedy of High Bridge on an even more piquant scale. Not only was the Earl obliged to return ignominiously to Inverness, but the desertions from his Highland companies consequent upon this affair were so great that he thought it better to await Cumberland's advance among the Whig clans of Ross and Cromarty, to which he and his force accordingly retired; and Prince Charles's army had entered Inverness without a blow.

The water lapped the sides of the ferryboat impatiently. The sky looked full of snow, and nearly as dark as on the day of Falkirk, while the wind was even colder than Ewen remembered it as they had plodded over Shap Fell in the December retreat from England. In Cæsar's time, as he used to read in his boyhood, armies went into winter quarters. But all *their* marching and fighting had been done in the severest season of the year, in autumn and winter; and who knew what awaited them in the not less cruel rigours of a Highland spring? For Cumberland, he knew, had been at Aberdeen since the end of February.

Ewen frowned, and his thoughts went back to the somewhat comic warfare from which he had just been recalled. For when Lord Cromarty had been sent with a Jacobite force over the Moray Firth after Lord Loudoun, the latter, retreating farther north into Sutherland, established himself at Dornoch on the other side of the deep-winding firth of that name, which Cromarty, having no boats, could not cross. But directly Cromarty attempted to go round by the head of the firth Lord Loudoun sent his men across by ferry to Tain, on the Ross-shire side, once more; and when Lord Cromarty returned to Ross, Lord Loudoun recalled his followers to Dornoch. And thus a vexatious and absurd game of catch as catch can had been going on, and might go on for ever unless the Prince could send another detachment to hold Tain. No, Ewen was not sorry that Lochiel had recalled him.

He pulled his bonnet with the draggled eagle's feathers and the soiled cockade farther down on his brows, and wrapped his plaid round him, for they were now in the icy middle of the firth. The ferryman babbled on, telling him for the most part things he knew already; how, for instance, when the Prince had had the castle here blown up after its surrender, an unfortunate French engineer had been blown up with it. It was useless to ask the man what he really wanted to know, how Miss Alison Grant did over there in Inverness, Alison on whom he had not set eyes since Hector and he had said farewell to her last All Hallows in Edinburgh. It was a question whether they three would ever meet again, for Hector had been one of the officers left behind as part of the ill-fated garrison of Carlisle, and since the thirtieth of December he had been a prisoner in English hands. How Alison was bearing this ill news Ewen could only guess; it was all the heavier for her too, because her father was in France, having been despatched thither on a mission by the Prince directly after Falkirk.

Ewen knew that Alison and his aunt had come to Inverness in the hopes of seeing him, immediately on the news of the town's surrender to the Highland army on 18 February, but as it was before their arrival that Ewen himself had been sent off with Lord Cromarty's composite force, the meeting had not taken place. Miss Cameron, as a letter had since told him, had thought it best on that to return to Ardroy, but, feeling sure that sooner or later Ewen's duties would bring him to Inverness, she had left Alison there in the care of Lady Ogilvy, whose husband, with his regiment, was on the other side of the Spey. And now Lochiel had recalled Ewen – but only to accompany him on another enterprise. Of his approaching return Ewen had told Alison in a letter which he had despatched yesterday by Lachlan, but he had not told her how brief his stay would be, nor had he broached the project which was in his own mind – the determination which had been growing there since the retreat northward.

But, as he thought of what that was, the harassed look went out of his eyes, and he became deafer than ever to the ferryman's chatter.

At the guardhouse by the bridge over the Ness Ewen stopped to inquire where Lady Ogilvy was to be found, for he was not sure of her lodging, and as he was talking to the officer there, he heard a youthful voice behind him asking exactly the same question in Gaelic.

Ewen turned quickly, for he knew that voice. There in the entry stood a half-shy, half-excited boy of fifteen, who had never been in a town before – young Angus. Neil MacMartin's eldest son. His face lit up, and he darted forward. 'Letters, Mac 'ic Ailein!' And out of an old sporran too big for him he produced two, none the better for their sojourn in that receptacle.

With a smile and a kind word his master took them. One was from Miss Cameron to himself, the other, addressed to Miss Alison Grant at Ardroy, in an unknown and foreign-seeming hand, had been redirected by his aunt to Inverness. He put them both in his pocket, gave the lad money to procure himself food and lodging and a new pair of brogues to go home in, told him where to find his father and not to return to Ardroy without seeing him again, and himself set off in haste for Lady Ogilvy's lodging.

But Angus Og, footsore and hungry though he was, seeing his young chieftain quite unaccompanied, pattered at a little distance behind him with all the air of a bodyguard, his head full of wild plans for joining his father and uncle in this place of many houses instead of returning to Slochd nan Eun. If they were in Mac 'ic Ailein's tail why not he?

Young Lady Ogilvy lodged in one of the larger houses at the lower end of Kirk Street, and as Ewen passed the many-paned projecting window on the ground floor he caught sight of a blue ribbon confining dark curls. After that he was not much conscious of being admitted, or of anything until he found its wearer in his arms.

'Oh, my darling! . . . You were expecting me – Lachlan brought you my letter?'

Alison nodded, holding very fast to him, her eyes closed like one surrendered to ecstasy. Much as they had to say to one another, for a time neither said it; it was enough merely to be together again after the months of strain and waiting and endurance and disillusioned hopes. But when they had their fill of looking at each other they began to talk.

'I knew that you would come back to Inverness,' said Alison happily. They were both sitting on the window seat now. And she added, with all her old gaiety: 'If Lochiel would permit so forward an act, I would kiss him for having recalled you from Lord Cromarty's force.'

'But he has not recalled me in order to stay in Inverness, darling – at least not for more than a couple of days. He and Keppoch are shortly going with reinforcements to the siege of Fort William, and I go too.'

All the peace and content was dashed out of Alison's face. 'Oh, Ewen . . . and I thought you would be staying here!' She bit her lip and the tears came into her eyes.

Her hand was in Ewen's, and he sat a moment silent, looking down with some intentness at his ring upon it. 'But we shall have two days together, *m'eudail*. And . . . do you not think those two days are long enough . . . that the time has come . . . to change this ring of my mother's for another?'

The colour ran over Alison's face and her hand made a movement as if to withdraw itself. 'Oh, my dear,' she said rather breathlessly, 'not when my father is absent – not till he comes back! And not when . . . when one does not know what will befall next!'

'But, my heart,' said Ewen quietly, 'that is just why I want to make you my wife. Do you not see that? Why, you should have been mine these six months. I have waited even longer than I had thought to wait, and God knows that was long enough.' And as Alison said nothing, but looked down, twisting her ring, he went on, suppressing a little sigh: 'There are many reasons why we should be wed without further loss of time, and these two days that we have now seem designed for that. Our marriage could easily be arranged in the time; Mr Hay, the Episcopal minister of Inverness, is, I believe, in the town; Lochiel would take your father's place. And I could carry you back to Ardroy, as its mistress, when we start for Fort William . . . Alison dear love, say Yes!'

He was very gentle as he pleaded, for she seemed oddly reluctant, considering that they had been formally contracted since last July, and should indeed have been married in the autumn. She even mentioned Hector and his perilous situation, rather tentatively, as a reason for delay; but Ewen told her that her brother's prospects were ten times better than those of most who wore the white cockade, for he held a French commission, and could not be treated otherwise than as a prisoner-of-war. And finally Alison said that she would ask Lady Ogilvy's opinion.

Ewen tried not to be hurt. Since he had not the mistaken conviction of some young men that he knew all about women, even Alison's feelings were sometimes a mystery to him. He longed to say: '*I* have not a French commission, Alison,' and leave her to draw a conclusion which might get the better of her hesitancy, but it would have been cruel. And as he looked at her in perplexity he remembered a commission of another kind, and put his hand into his pocket.

'When I saw you, Alison, everything else went out of my head. But here is a letter I should have given you ere this; forgive me. It was sent to you at Ardroy, and Aunt Margaret despatched one of the MacMartin lads hither with it; and meeting me by the bridge just now he gave it to me for you. It is from France, I think.'

'I do not know the hand,' said Alison, studying the super-scription, and finally breaking the seal. Ewen looked out of the window, but he did not see any of the passers-by.

Suddenly there was an exclamation from the girl beside him on the window seat. He turned; her face was drained of colour.

'My father . . . Ewen, Ewen, I must go at once – he is very ill . . . dying, they think. Oh, read!'

Horrified, Ewen read a hasty French letter, already more than two weeks old, which said that M. Grant, on the point of leaving France again, had been taken seriously ill at Havre-de-Grâce; the writer, apparently a recent French acquaintance of his, appealed to Mlle. Grant to sail for France at once, if she wanted to see her father alive – not that the state of M. Grant at the moment was desperate, but because the doctor held out small hope of ultimate recovery.

Alison had sprung to her feet, and clasping and unclasping her hands was walking up and down the room.

'Ewen, Ewen, what if I am not in time! My dearest, dearest father, ill and quite alone over there – no Hector anywhere near him now! I must go at once. I heard Lady Ogilvy say that there was a French vessel in port here due to sail for France in a day or two; I could go in that. Perhaps the captain could be persuaded to sail earlier . . .'

In contrast to her restlessness, Ewen was standing quite still by the window.

'Ewen,' she began again, 'help me! Will you make inquiries

of the captain of the ship? I think she is for St Maloes, but
that would serve; I could post on into Normandy. Will you
find out the captain now – this afternoon? . . . Ewen, what
ails you?'

For her lover was gazing at her with an expression which
was quite new to her.

'I am deeply sorry to hear this ill news of Mr Grant,' he said
in a low voice, and seemed to find a difficulty in speaking,
'– more sorry than I have words for. But, Alison, what of
me?'

'You would not wish to keep me back, surely?'

'What do you think?' asked the young man rather grimly.
'But I will not – no, it would not be right. I will let you go, but
only as my wife. You'll marry me tomorrow, Alison!'

There was no pleading about him now. He moved a step or
two nearer, having to keep a tight hold on himself neither to
frighten her nor to let slip a word against this other claim
which, much as he respected it, was coming in once more to
sweep her away from him, when he had waited so long.
Whatever might be read on his face, his actions were perfectly
gentle.

And Alison came to him, the tears running down her cheeks,
and put her two hands in his. 'Yes, Ewen, I am ready. Heart's
darling, I wish it, too; you must not think I am unwilling. . . .
And you said that you would carry me off by force if I were,'
she added, laughing a little hysterically, as he folded her once
again in his arms.

So next day they were married in the little Episcopal meet-
ing-house of Inverness. Only a very few people were present,
but the Prince was among them: not the light-hearted adventurer of the escapade in Edinburgh in which the bridegroom
had played so belauded a part, but a young man who looked
what the last three months had made him, soured and dis-
trustful. Yet he gave them a glimpse of his old charming
smile after the ceremony, when he kissed the bride and wished
them both happiness.

'I would I were venerable enough to give you my blessing,
my friends,' he said, 'since 'tis all I have to give; but I think I
am somewhat the junior of your husband, Lady Ardroy; and
in any case, how could I bestow my benediction upon a bride-

groom who has the bad taste to be so much taller than his future King!'

'But you know that I am at your feet, my Prince,' said Ewen, smiling, and he kissed once more the hand which he had kissed that night at Holyrood.

Last of all Lochiel, grave and gentle, who had given Alison away, kissed her too, and said: 'Ewen is a very fortunate man, my dear; but I think you are to be congratulated also.'

For their brief wedded life a little house which Mr Grant had hired the previous summer had been hastily prepared; it was bare almost to penury, a tent for a night or two, meet shelter for those who must part so soon. And Ewen had no gift ready for his bride – save one. When they came home he put on her middle finger the ring which the Prince had given him in Edinburgh.

Next day was theirs to play at housekeeping, and they were a great deal more gay over it than Jeanie Wishart, Alison's woman, who went about her work perpetually murmuring: 'Puir young things!' In the afternoon, since the March sun had come out to look at them, they wandered among the Islands and gazed down at Ness, hurrying past, broad and clear and shallow, to the firth. That evening they had thought to spend alone by their own fireside; yet nothing would serve Lady Ogilvy save to give a supper for the new-married pair, and Lady Ardroy, in a rose-coloured gown, was toasted by not a few who would never drink a pledge again; and all the Jacobite songs were sung . . . but not, somehow, that only too appropriate, 'Oh, this is my departing time, for here nae longer maun I stay,' with which gatherings were wont to conclude.

Yet Ewen and Alison sat by their fire after all, sat there until the last peat crumbled, and it began to grow cold; but Alison, as once before, was warm in the Cameron tartan, for Ewen had wrapped it round her knees over her pretty gown. He sat at her feet, looking very long and large, the firelight, while it lasted, playing on the shining golden brown of his hair, accentuating too the faint hollow in his cheek, the slight suggestion of a line between the brows which the last two months had set there.

'Ewen, I want to tell you something.' Alison hesitated and

a tinge of colour stole over her face. 'Do you know, *m'eudail*, that you talk in your sleep?'

He looked up at her surprised. 'Do I? No, dearest, I did not know. Did I talk much – to disturb you?'

She shook her head. Ewen seemed to turn over this information for a moment. 'I believe,' he said thoughtfully, 'that as a boy I used to do it sometimes, so Aunt Margaret said, but I thought that I had outgrown it. What did I talk of – you, sweetheart, I'll warrant?'

'No,' said Alison, smiling down upon him. 'Not a word of your wife. You seemed to think that you were speaking to someone of whom she may well be jealous; and what is more, when I spoke to you, thinking for a moment that you were awake, you answered quite sensibly.'

'Jealous!' exclaimed Ewen, turning his clear, candid gaze full upon her. 'My little white love, there's no one in this world of whom you have occasion to be jealous, nor ever has been. Do not pretend to be ignorant of where my heart is kept!' He took her clasped hands, opened them gently, and kissed the palms. 'The space is small,' he said, looking critically at it, 'but, such as the heart is, all of it lies *there*.'

Alison enveloped him in a warm, sweet smile, and slid the hands round his neck. 'All? No; there's a corner you have kept for someone else, and in it you have set up a little shrine, as the Papists do, for your saint – for Lochiel. But I am not jealous,' she added very softly. 'I understand.'

Ewen gave her a look, put his own hands over those clasped round his neck, and dropped his head on to her knee in silence. After a while she put her cheek against the thick, warm waves of his hair. Joy and apprehension had so clasped hands about Alison Cameron this day that it was hard to know which was the stronger.

But in the night she knew. The icy fingers of foreboding seemed gripped about her heart. Not even Ewen's quiet, unhurried breathing beside her, not even the touch of his hand, over which her fingers stole in search of comfort, could reassure her; his nearness but made the pain the sharper. Oh, to have him hers only to lose him so soon! But her father – alone, dying, over the seas! She reached out and lit a candle, that she might look once more at the husband she was leaving for her father's sake, for God knew whether she should ever see him asleep beside her again. It was not the seas alone which were about to sunder them. . . .

Ewen was sleeping so soundly, too, so quietly; and he looked as young and untroubled as the boy she had known five years ago in Paris. There was no sign on his face, in its rather austere repose, of the trouble which had forced its way through his unconscious lips last night. Alison had not told him by the fire, that on their bridal night he had uttered protests, bewildered questionings, against that double retreat in which he had shared. 'Must we go back, Lochiel – must we go back?'

She gazed at him a long time, until for tears she could see him no longer, and, blowing out the light, lay and sobbed under her breath. She thought she should die of her unhappiness; she almost wished that she might; yet she sobbed quietly lest she should wake Ewen to unhappiness also. But quite suddenly, though he had not stirred, she heard his voice in the darkness; and then she was in his arms, and he was comforting her in their own Highland tongue, with all its soft endearments and little words of love. And there at last she fell asleep.

But Ewen stayed awake until the grudging March daylight crept into the little room where he lay wide-eyed, with Alison's dark curls on his heart, and within it a chilly sword that turned and turned. He would never hold her thus again; he was sure of it.

The morning was very cold, and when he took Alison to the French brig a little snow was falling; the gang-plank was slippery too with rime. He carried her bodily over it, and down to the cabin which she would share with Jean Wishart.

There under the low beams Alison's courage broke at last. Clinging to him convulsively she said, in a voice that was not hers, that he must come with her; that she could not go without him – she could not! He must come too, and then he would be safe . . .

Ewen turned even paler than she. 'My darling, my heart's darling, you don't mean that!'

Alison swayed, her eyes closed. Alarmed, he put her on a seat against the bulkhead, and, kneeling by her, began to chafe her hands. Soon they clenched in his, and she opened her eyes, dark pools of sorrow, and said firmly through colourless lips:

'No, no, I did not mean it! I know that you cannot come. Will you . . . can you forget what I said, Ewen?'

'It is forgotten. It was not you who spoke,' he answered, trying to keep his own voice steady as he knelt there, holding her hands very tightly. There was a trampling sound on deck; how long had they for all the thousand, thousand things that remained to say? There was no time to say even one. He bent his head and pressed his lips passionately upon the hands he held. Anguish though it was to lose her, it was better that she should go. For since he had urged her to marry him that he might take her back to Ardroy he saw with different eyes. The future looked blacker than he had realized; away in Ross he had not known of the desperate want of money, even of food, the gradually thinning ranks. He knew of these now, and saw even Cumberland's delay at Aberdeen in a sinister light, as if the Hanoverian commander knew that the fates were working on his side and that there was no need for haste. . . .

Above him Alison's voice said suddenly: 'Ewen . . . Ewen, why do you not say: "Stay then in Scotland with me – do not go to France yourself!"?'

He was startled; had she read his thoughts? 'Why, my darling,' he answered as readily as he could, 'because your father needs you so sorely.'

Her voice sank still lower. 'There is another reason, too – do not deny it! You think that I am safer away!'

And Ewen did not answer.

'And you gave me this ring – the Prince's ring – not only as a wedding gift, but because you feared that one day . . . soon . . . it might be taken from you!'

After a pause he said: 'Partly, perhaps.'

'Then . . . I cannot leave you, even for my father,' said Alison, and sprang up. 'I must stay in Scotland, beside you. I am your wife. Take me back to the quay – Ewen – tell Mrs Wishart . . .'

But Ewen, on his feet too, caught her in his arms. 'No, darling, no! Think of your father, whom you may never see again. And, love of my heart' – he tried to make his voice light – 'you cannot come besieging Fort William with me! When we have beaten Cumberland, as we beat Cope and Hawley, I will come to France and fetch you home to Ardroy.'

'When we have beaten Cumberland.' Alison looked up into

her husband's eyes with a moist insistent question in her own. But he did not answer the question, though he knew very well what it was, for he said gently: 'How can one see into the future, darling? One can only . . . do one's duty.'

Even as he uttered that rigorous word there came a knock at the cabin door, and a gruff French voice announced that they would be casting off in another minute or two, and that if Monsieur wished to land he must be quick.

So the sword slid down between them. Ewen's grasp tightened.

'Alison, white love, rose of my heart, we are one for ever now! You will know, I think, what befalls me.'

Her face was hidden on his breast, so close that he could not even kiss it. 'Darling, darling, let me go . . .' he whispered. But it was rather a question, he felt, whether he could ever unloose his own clasp and cast his heart from him. And men were running about shouting overhead; the hawser was coming inboard . . .

Suddenly Alison lifted her face, and it was almost transfigured. 'Yes, I shall know . . . for I think you will come back to me. God keeping you.' She took her arms from his shoulders; he bent to her lips for the kiss that first turned his heart to water and then ran through it like wine, loosed his hold of her, and walked straight out of the cabin without another word or look. With the same unchecked movement he crossed the gang-plank from the deck, as if he could not trust himself to remain the moment or so longer that it would take the sailors to cast off the second hawser.

But on the quay he turned, wishing they would be quick, and make it impossible for him to leap on board again, though the plank was now withdrawn, and be carried off with Alison. And at last, after an eternity which was all to short, the end of the rope splashed into the water. More sails went up; the distance began to widen. Alison was going from him.

He stood there motionless, long after the brig had left the shore, watching her move to the waters of the firth. The sparse snowflakes whirled relentlessly against him, but they melted as soon as they came to rest, as brief in their stay as his two days' happiness.

From the quay Ewen went straight to Lochiel's headquarters and reported himself for duty. Two hours later his body was

marching out of Inverness in the van of the Cameron reinforcements. Where his soul was he hardly knew.

Chapter Two

To rid the Great Glen of both its obnoxious English forts was
an enterprise which highly commended itself to those clans
whom they chiefly incommoded, the Camerons and the Glengarry and Keppoch MacDonalds. There had been jubilation
among these when, on 5 March, Fort Augustus had surrendered
after two days' siege, and what artillery the besiegers possessed
was free to be turned against Fort William.

But Fort William, between Inverlochy Castle and the little
town of Maryburgh, was not so accommodating at its fellow.
For one thing, it was in a better position to defend itself, since
sloops of war could come up Loch Linnhe to revictual it, even
though the Highlanders held the narrows at Corran. It had a
garrison of five hundred men, both regulars and Argyll militia,
plenty of guns, and, after the middle of March, that zealous
officer Captain Carolina Scott to assist Major-General Campbell
in the defence. Already, by the time that Ewen arrived with
Lochiel and the reinforcements, there had been some severe
skirmishes, and the Highlanders had fought an engagement with
the soldiers from the fort and the sailors from the *Baltimore*
and *Serpent* sloops, in which the latter succeeded in landing
and destroying the ferry-house and several small villages on
the Ardgour side. On this the Camerons ensconced themselves
at Corpach, where Loch Linnhe bends to its junction with
Loch Eil, and there beat off an armed flotilla of boats with such
success that the *Baltimore* was ordered thither to open fire
and cover a landing. But the Highlanders' position was so good
that the bombardment made no impression, and Captain How
had to withdraw baffled.

Ewen was with these adventurers at Corpach, enjoying himself and finding in conflict an anodyne for his thoughts; it made
the blood run pleasantly and enabled him to forget Alison for
an hour or so. But the ordinary business of the siege was less
stimulating, since he had nothing to do with the artillery under
Stapleton and Grant and their Franco-Irish gunners, and the
only chance of hand-to-hand fighting lay in repelling the con-

stant raids of the garrison and trying to protect the unfortunate dwellers in the countryside who suffered by them. He seemed to himself to live in a series of disconnected scenes, sometimes here in Lochaber, where Ben Nevis, thickly capped with snow, looked down impartially on assailants and defenders alike, sometimes back in Inverness, going through every moment of those short two days with Alison. But no one who did not observe him constantly and closely could have guessed this. Lochiel, who knew him well and did observe him closely, gave him as much to do as possible.

But it was certainly not Lochiel who enjoined on him the feat which brought his share in the siege to an abrupt end.

It was a fine morning in the latter half of March, blown through with a gusty wind. Brigadier Stapleton, having got some mortars into position on one of the little eminences about half a mile from the fort, had started to shell it from that point, and the fort was replying. Since its fire was directed towards destroying the hostile batteries, there was no great danger from it to those not serving the guns, and the Highlanders had no doubt grown a little careless, which might account for the fact that near the crest of another hillock, about a quarter of a mile away from Stapleton's mortars and the same distance as they from Fort William, Lochiel and Keppoch were standing unconcernedly in the midst of a little group of Camerons and MacDonalds. Below them, on the slope that looked towards the fort, a half-ruined stone wall hinted at a by-gone attempt at cultivation or enclosure. The two chiefs were interested in some rather suspicious activities on board the *Baltimore* sloop, visible at anchor in the loch beyond the counterscarp and bastions of the fort.

'I vow it seems like another raid preparing,' said Alexander MacDonald. 'Do you look, Lochiel.'

He passed the Cameron his spyglass. Ewen, who was sitting comfortably in the heather at a few yards' distance, nearer the battery, rested his elbows on his knees and shaded his eyes the better to see also, his brain at these words busy with a vision of a possibly gratified desire for what he considered real fighting.

Suddenly, as it were with half an eye, he became aware of

something unusual in the fort, where, a mere eight hundred yards away, movements were perfectly visible. Surely the defenders had altered the position of one of their six-pounders . . . could they be intending . . . Lochiel standing there with the glass to his eye looking at the sloop was fully exposed to their view . . .

In a second Ewen was on his feet, shouting a warning, but as he sprang came the flash and the roar. 'God!' he cried in agony, and with another bound was up on the crest of the hillock, his arms wide. Could one man's body suffice?

There was a crash as the shot pitched into the ruined wall on the slope below, breaking and scattering the big rough stones in all directions. Ewen never saw what struck him, but at the moment of impact, which seemed to drive his soul from his body, he had just time to think: 'It is for *him*! Alison, forgive me . . .' Then he went into darkness.

When he came out of it again he found himself lying on the farther slope in the midst of a group of people, with his head on someone's arm, and hands unfastening his coat. A voice said: 'No, the head wound is only slight; 'tis here on the breast that the large stone must have struck him.'

Ewen tried to get his own voice. It was difficult, and the world heaved. 'Is . . . Lochiel safe?'

Archibald Cameron, kneeling beside him, looked up for a second. 'He is holding you at the moment, dear lad. No – lie still!' He went on with his examination.

But Ewen disobediently turned his swimming head a little, and saw that he was indeed in Lochiel's hold, so Lochiel must be unharmed. Why then had he his other hand over his eyes? Puzzled but content, he shut his own again.

When next he thought much about his surroundings he was lying in the same place, wrapped in a plaid, with Lachlan squatting near, gazing at him with anguished eyes. Over the level top of Ben Nevis clouds, as white as the snow which crowned it, were hurrying against the blue. It came back to Ewen that he had heard Archie say that he was greatly bruised, but that no bones seemed broken, and no internal injury, he hoped inflicted; so, after speaking a word or two of reassurance to his foster-brother, he relapsed into his state of happy content, with pain every time he drew a breath and a violent headache. But Lochiel was safe.

Presently he felt his hand taken, and there was Lochiel himself kneeling by him, and Lachlan on the other side removing himself respectfully to a distance.

'Ewen, Ewen,' said the well-beloved voice, with trouble in it, 'you should not have done it!'

Ewen gave him a radiant smile. He felt neither penitence nor any need for it.

'I saw . . . what was going to happen,' he observed.

'I do not think that anything would have reached me. No one was struck but you, who deliberately threw yourself in the way of the fragments, and one of Keppoch's gillies, slightly. If you had been killed on my behalf—' Lochiel left the sentence unfinished, and glanced down at the cuff of his coat, there was a stain on it.

Ewen's eyes had followed his. 'Do not say that you are hurt after all!' he exclaimed in a tone of horror.

'It is your own blood, Ewen. Your head was not much cut, Archie says. But oh, my child, if I had had your death too at my door, when there is so much that I must answer for!'

And the young man saw that his Chief was moved – more deeply moved than he had ever seen him; but, being still stupid from the blow on the head, he thought: 'Why does he say that . . . whose death is at his door?' And he lay looking with a mixture of affection and perplexity at the kinsman who was still as much his pattern of all that was noble, wise and generous as when he himself had been a boy under his tutelage. Then the fort fired one of its twelve-pounders at the battery, and through the din Lochiel told him that a litter had been sent for to take him to Glen Nevis House, where he should see him again later.

Soon after, therefore, four of his men carried Ewen to that house of Alexander Cameron's at the opening of the glen which Lochiel and Keppoch had made their headquarters; and he heard the voice of the Nevis, telling of the heights from which it had descended; and a little later, when that had faded from his hearing, a less agreeable one, Lowland and educated, saying how disgraceful it was that a peaceful writer could not go a mile from Maryburgh to visit a client without being seized by cattle-thieves; that indeed the said thieves could do no less than send him back under escort and safe-conduct. And here the indignant speaker's gaze must have fallen upon the litter with its burden, for his next remark was: 'What have we here – another of ye killed? I'm rejoiced to see it!'

Ewen felt constrained to deny this imputation. 'I am not in the least killed,' he rejoined with annoyance, opening his eyes to find himself almost at the door of Glen Nevis House, and to see, in the midst of the group of rather shamefaced Highlanders, Mr Chalmers, the Whig notary of Maryburgh, whom he knew and who knew him. The lawyer gave an exclamation.

'Gude sakes, 'tis Mr Ewen Cameron of Ardroy! I'm unco sorry to see you in this condition – and in such company, Ardroy!'

'Why, what other company do you suppose I should be in?' asked Ewen, and shut his eyes again and heard no more of Mr Chalmers and his grievances. But that chance meeting was to mean a great deal to him afterwards.

What meant more to him at the moment, however, was that Dr Cameron kept him in bed longer than he had anticipated, and he had not been on his legs again for more than a day or two when the siege of Fort William was suddenly abandoned. The defenders were too resolute, the besiegers unfortunate, and their artillery not sufficiently powerful; and in the night of 3 April, after spiking their remaining cannon, the attacking force withdrew. And, since they were in their own land of Lochaber, and it was seed-time or past it, Lochiel and Keppoch gave permission to their men to go home for a few days. So Ewen and his little force returned to Ardroy, and he saw Loch na h-Iolaire again, and caused Neil to row him upon it, for it was too cold for a swim; in the middle of which voyage he was struck by a sudden suspicion, and, landing on the islet, examined it for traces of the heron. There were none; and the nest, up at the top of the tallest pine tree, must long have been uninhabited, for the winds had blown it nearly all away.

Shortly afterwards Lachlan had a singularly unpleasant interview with his chieftain, in which, upbraided with the most direct disobedience, he replied that his concern for the being he loved best on earth was even stronger than his wish to obey him; after which, in a dramatic but perfectly sincere manner, he drew his dirk and said that rather than Mac 'ic Ailein should look at him with such anger he would plunge it into his own heart. In the end Ewen was constrained to forgive him, after pointing out how little his disobedience had availed. There were more herons than one in Lochaber.

And other officers than Captain Windham in King George's army, he might have added. His twice-held prisoner had indeed passed from his thoughts these many weeks; the question of the slaughtered heron necessarily brought him back there for a moment, but without any permanence. Ewen did not anticipate another meeting with him, for were Angus's prophecy going to be fulfilled to the letter, they would surely have encountered each other in the confusion of Falkirk fight, where the second battalion of the Royals had – until it fled – faced the Camerons across the ravine. No; that two meetings should come to pass out of the five predicted was quite a reasonable achievement of the old *taibhsear*.

And then one afternoon, when he was absorbed in thoughts of Alison, with all the final suddenness of the expected came a panting messenger from Achnacarry, with a scrawl in Lochiel's writing: 'Gather your men and march at once. Cumberland is moving. God send we reach Inverness in time!'

A bad dream is sometimes only a dream to the sleeper, he may know it to be such, and tell himself so. But this, though it held some of the elements of nightmare, was no dream; it was reality, this tramping of a tired and half-starved army through the night in a hopeless attempt to surprise the Duke of Cumberland's camp – hopeless because it was plain that they would never get to Nairn before daylight now. Aide-de-camp after aide-de-camp, officer after officer, had come riding past to the head of the column of Highlanders and Atholl men to urge Lord George Murray to halt, for the rear could not keep up. And yet, thought Ewen rather scornfully, they had not just marched more than fifty miles over mountainous country in two days, as most of Clan Cameron had.

It was by this feat of endurance and speed that Lochiel and his men had reached Inverness the previous evening, to learn, to their dismay, that Cumberland had been allowed to cross the Spey unopposed. Despite fatigue they had made a brief halt in the town and had proceeded to Culloden House, whither the Prince had gone earlier in the day. A warm welcome had been theirs, for he was becoming alarmed at their non-appearance, the more so that by no means all his scattered forces were yet returned from the various enterprises on which they had been despatched. Cromarty, the Macgregors and the Mackinnons were still north of the Moray Firth, no one knew where, and Keppoch had not yet appeared, nor the Frasers, nor Cluny Macpherson and his men. Today, since early morning, the whole army had been drawn up on the chosen ground on Drumossie Moor, in the belief that Cumberland would advance that day and attempt to reach Inverness. But the hours went by and the enemy did not appear, and then the cravings of hunger began to be felt, for all the food which had passed any man's lips that day was a single biscuit served out at noon. And at last it was clear that, 15 April being his birthday, Cumberland was remaining at Nairn to allow his troops fitly to celebrate it. The Prince's hungry forces therefore withdrew from the moor again to the vicinity of Duncan Forbes's mansion.

It was known that Lord George Murray had not liked the ground chosen for their stand, and Brigadier Stapleton and Colonel Ker of Graden, the ablest staff officers the Prince possessed, had crossed the water of Nairn that morning to seek for a better. They reported that the boggy, hilly ground there was much more suitable than the open moor for receiving the Hanoverian attack, since it was almost impossible for cavalry and artillery, and the foot might perhaps be tempted into some pass where they could be fallen upon and annihilated. On the other hand, it was urged that, if the Highlanders withdrew over the stream into the hills, Cumberland would almost certainly slip by them to Inverness, seize the baggage and stores and starve them out. The matter was still unsettled when, at an informal council of officers in the afternoon, someone (Ewen was not clear who) had proposed to surprise the Hanoverian camp by a night attack. Most of the soldiers there, it was thought, would be more or less drunk after the festivities of the birthday. Lord George Murray and the Prince were both found to be in favour of the idea; moreover, owing to the scandalous neglect of the commissariat shown by Hay of Restalrig, who had succeeded Murray of Broughton as secretary, there was not a crumb of food for the men next day. Objections to the plan there were indeed: the distance – a good

ten miles – the danger of a spy's carrying the news to the
English camp, the absence of so many contingents. But the
arrival of Keppoch with two hundred MacDonalds when the
meeting was in progress clinched the matter, and the night
attack was resolved upon.

The decision had purposely been kept from the men themselves, and it was with remorseful knowledge of the futility of
their preparations that Ewen had watched his own little company choosing the driest spots on the heathery hillside for a
night's repose, making a fire and rolling themselves supperless
in their plaids to seek in sleep a palliative for the gnawing
hunger which possessed them. Perhaps it would have been
better if the rank and file had been told what was afoot, for
by the time planned for the start, seven o'clock, it was found
that hundreds of them had stolen off in search of food. And to
the mounted officers sent out in the utmost haste to beat them
up and bring them back – no easy task – many had replied
that the officers might shoot them if they pleased, but go back
they would not until they had had meat. The Prince was urged
to give up the plan, but he refused; and as those who had
remained were assembled, the word had been given to march
off.

It was an excellent night for a surprise, dark and misty; but
it was also very favourable for tired and hungry men to drop
unobserved out of the ranks, and many of them did so. Ewen
was as tired and hungry as anyone else, but he shut his mouth
and plodded on like an automaton at the head of his company.
Lochiel was in front, and where Lochiel went he followed as
a matter of course. And close on his heels came Neil and
Lachlan, of the same mind regarding him.

Although Lord George had never consented actually to stop,
he had been obliged to march slower and slower in consequence of the messages from the rear; but now at last there
came a halt, and a prolonged one. The Duke of Perth rode past,
and presently Hay of Restalrig. Discussion was evidently going
forward in the van. And meanwhile the unwished-for light
was growing in the east, not yet daybreak, but its harbinger.
Faces began to be distinct, and haggard faces they were.

And here came back one of the Mackintosh guides, the same
who, not long before, had brought the order to attack with the
sword only. Before he spoke to him Ewen guessed what orders

he brought now. They were to retrace their steps; the surprise was being abandoned. Too much time had been lost on the way, and to attack in daylight would be madness. All the nightmare effort had been for nothing – for worse than nothing . . .

Between five and six of that cold, grey morning Ewen found himself once more before the gates of Culloden House. Men were dropping where they stood; some, he knew, were lying worn out along the roadside. He was in no better case himself; in some ways, indeed, in a worse, for it was not three weeks since he had left his bed after his experience at Fort William. But in anger and desperation he despatched Neil and Lachlan, who still seemed capable of movement, to Inverness with orders to get food for their comrades if they had to steal it. It was all he could do, and when he got inside the house he sat down exhausted in the hall, and fell asleep with his head on a table. He was hardly conscious of the stir a little later, when the Prince arrived, tired, dispirited and sore from the complaints which he could not avoid hearing. But from scraps of talk about him (for the place was full of officers in the same plight as himself) Ewen's weary brain did receive the welcome impression that they would at least have some hours to rest and recuperate – and later, please Heaven, to get some food – for Cumberland was evidently not going to attack today.

He was dreaming that he was at home, and sitting down to a good meal, when he felt someone shaking him, and, raising his head, saw one of his own cousins from Appin, Ian Stewart.

'What is it?' he asked stupidly.

'A straggler has just come in with news that some troops are advancing from Nairn. He did not know whether it was the main body or only skirmishers . . .'

Ewen dragged himself to his feet. All round the hall others were doing the same, but some would require more to rouse them than a mere rumour. It was broad daylight; a clock near marked nine o'clock. 'It cannot be the main body – the attack!' he said incredulously. 'There was no sign of general movement at Nairn; the camp fires were burning – we could see them four miles away. However, the truth can soon be discovered.'

The weary-faced Appin lad shrugged his shoulders. 'It will not be very easy to make sure,' he said. 'FitzJames's Horse is all dispersed after fugitives and food. I tell you, Ardroy, I do not much care which it is, if only I can get an hour's sleep.'

'I must find Lochiel,' said Ewen. He had no idea where he was – a sufficient comment on his own state – but was told that he was upstairs with the Prince, who, on coming in, had thrown himself just as he was upon his bed. Half dizzy with sleep and hunger. Ewen went up the wide staircase, hearing everywhere voices discussing the report, and arguing and wondering what was to be done, and declaring that the speakers disbelieved the news – because they desired to disbelieve it.

When he reached the landing the door of the Prince's bed-chamber opened, and Lord George Murray and Ker of Graden came out together, the latter looking very grim, Lord George plainly in a rage. They went down the stairs to the encumbered hall, Lord George calling for his aides-de-camp. The door mean-while had been left ajar; loud voices came through it, and Ewen had a glimpse of the Prince, sitting on the edge of his bed, still booted, with Sir Thomas Sheridan, his old tutor, be-side him. He was speaking, not to him, but to someone invisible.

'I tell you,' his voice came sharply, edged with fatigue and obstinacy, 'I tell you the English will be seized with panic when they come to close quarters. They cannot face my High-landers in the charge, 'twill be again as it was at Gladsmuir and—'

Then the door shut behind Lochiel, coming slowly out. He did not see the young man waiting for him, and on his tired, unguarded face Ewen could read the most profound dis-couragement.

As he crossed the landing Ewen took a couple of strides after him, laying hold of his plaid, and the Chief stopped.

'Is it true, Donald?'

'I suppose so,' answered Lochiel quietly. 'At any rate we must take up our positions at once.'

'Over the water of Nairn, then, I hope?'

'No. The Prince is immovable on that point. We are to take our stand on our old positions of yesterday on the moor.'

'When you and Lord George disapprove? – It's the doing, no doubt, of the same men who were for it yesterday, those who have nothing to lose, the French and Irish officers!'

Lochiel glanced over his shoulder. 'Don't speak so loud,

Ewen. But you are right – may God forgive them!'

'May God – reward them!' said Ewen savagely. 'We are to march our companies back to the moor then?'

'Yes. And we and Atholl are to be on the right wing today.'

Ewen was surprised, the MacDonalds always claiming and being conceded this privilege. But he did not seek the reason for the change, and followed his Chief in silence down the stairs. The confusion in the hall had increased, and yet some officers were still lying on the floor without stirring, so spent were they.

'Find me Dungallon and Torcastle,' said Lochiel. 'By the way, have you had anything to eat, Ewen, since noon yesterday?'

'Have you, which is more to the point?' asked Ewen.

Lochiel smiled and shook his head. 'But fortunately a little bread and whisky was discovered for the Prince.'

Ewen found Ludovic Cameron of Torcastle, the Chief's uncle, and Cameron of Dungallon, major of the regiment, and himself went out in a shower of sleet to rouse his men, having in several cases to pull them up from the ground. He had got them into some kind of stupefied order when he saw Lochiel and Dungallon come by. A body of MacDonalds was collecting near, and as the two Camerons passed – Ewen scarcely realized it then, but he remembered it afterwards – there were muttered words and a black look or two.

But he himself was thinking bitterly: 'I wonder are we all fey? We had the advantage of a good natural barrier, the Spey, and we let Cumberland cross it like walking over a burn. Now we might put the Nairn water between him and us – and we will not!' An insistent question suddenly leapt up in his heart; he looked round, and by good fortune Lochiel came by again, alone. Ewen intercepted and stopped him.

'For God's sake, one moment!' He drew his Chief a little apart towards the high wall which separated the house from the parks. 'If the day should go against us, Lochiel, if we have all to take to the heather—'

'Yes?' said his cousin gravely, not repudiating the possibility.

'Where will you make for? Give us a rendezvous – give me one, at all events!'

'Why, my dear boy, I shall make for Achnacarry.'

'But that is just where you would be sought for by the Elector's troops!'

'Yet I must be where the clan can find me,' said the Chief. 'Loch Arkaig is the best rallying point. 'Tis not easy neither to come at it suddenly in force because there is always the Lochy to ford. And if I were strictly sought for in person, there are plenty of skulking places round Achnacarry, as you know.'

'But none beyond the wit of man to discover, Donald – and most of them known to too many.'

'Of the clan, perhaps, yes. But you do not imagine, surely, that any of them would be betrayed by a Cameron! Moreover, Archie came on a new one the other day when we were there; he showed it to me. Truly I do not think the wit of man could find that unaided, and no one knows of it but he and I. So set your mind at rest, dear lad.' He took a step or two away. 'I'll tell you too, Ewen.'

The young man's face, which had become a little wistful, lit up. 'Oh, Donald . . .'

'Listen,' said Lochiel, dropping his voice, and coming closer to the wall. 'Half-way up the southern slope of Beinn Bhreac, about a hundred paces to the right of the little waterfall. . . .'

And Ewen, listening eagerly, heard of an overhanging birch tree whose old roots grasped like hinges an apparently immovable block of stone, which could be moved if one knew just where to push it, and of a cave, long disused, which Dr Cameron had found behind it – a place whose existence could never be suspected. And there, if hard pressed . . .

'Yes, surely there you would be safe!' said Ewen with satisfaction. 'That is a thousand times better than any of the old places. I thank you for telling me; I shall not forget.'

'Whom should I tell if not you, my dear Ewen,' said his Chief, laying his hand for a moment on his shoulder. 'You have always been to me—' More he did not say, for Dungallon was at his elbow, urgently summoning him. But perhaps, also, he could not.

Ewen pulled his bonnet lower on his brows, and, bending his head against the sleety blast, set his face with the rest towards the fatal stretch of moorland, the last earthly landscape that many a man there would ever see. But over that possibility he was not troubling himself; he was wondering whether it were possible to be much hungrier, and what his foster-brothers would do when they returned and found him gone into battle

without them. And like a litany he repeated to himself, to be
sure that he remembered them aright, the directions Mac
Dhomhnuill Duibh had given him: 'Half-way up the southern
slope of Beinn Bhreac, about a hundred paces to the right of
the waterfall . . .'

Just as they were all taking up their positions a gleam of sun
shot through the heavy, hurrying clouds, and fell bright upon
the moving tartans, Stewart and Cameron, Fraser, Mackintosh,
Maclean and MacDonald, lighting too the distant hills of Ross
across the firth, whence Cromarty came not, and the high
ground over the Nairn water on the other hand, where Cluny
Macpherson was hurrying towards them with his clan, to
arrive too late. Then the gleam went out, and the wind howled
anew in the faces of those who should spend themselves to
death unavailingly, and those who should hold back for a
grudge; it fluttered plaid and tugged at eagle's feather and
whipped about him the cloak of the young man for whom the
flower of the North stood here to be slain; and faint upon it,
too, came now and then the kettledrums of Cumberland's
advance.

Chapter Three

ONCE more Keith Windham – but he was Major Windham
now, and on General Hawley's staff – was riding towards
Lochaber. This time, however, he was thankful to find himself
so occupied, for it was a boon to get away from what Inverness
had become since the Duke of Cumberland's victory a couple
of weeks ago – a little town crammed with suffering and
despair, and with men who not only gloated over the suffering
but who did their best to intensify it by neglect. One could
not pass the horrible overcrowded little prison under the
bridge without hearing pitiful voices always crying out for
water. And as for last Sunday's causeless procession of those
poor wretches, in their shirts or less, the wounded too, carried
by their comrades, simply to be jeered at – well, Major Windham, feigning twinges from his wound of Fontenoy, had withdrawn, sick with disgust, from the neighbourhood of the
uproariously laughing Hawley.

And not only was he enjoying a respite, if only of a few

days, from what was so repugnant to him, but he had been chosen by the Duke himself to carry a despatch to the Earl of Albemarle at Perth. It seemed that the Duke remembered a certain little incident at Fontenoy. General Hawley, relinquishing his aide-de-camp for the mission had slapped him on the shoulder and wished him good luck. The errand seemed to promise transference to the Duke's own staff; and, if that should occur, it meant real advancement at last, and when Cumberland returned to Flanders, a return with him.

So Keith was in better spirits than he had been for the last week. Surely the end of this horrid Scottish business was approaching for him! Falkirk – a bitter memory – was more than avenged, for the late victory on the moor of Culloden could not have been completer – he only wished he could get out of his mind some of the details of its completion. But there was this to be said for ruthless methods of suppression, that they were the sooner finished with.

To tell truth, Major Windham's immediate situation was also exercising his mind a good deal. Wade's road from Fort Augustus to Dalwhinnie and Perth ran over the steep Corryarrick Pass into Badenoch, and he had been told that somewhere in the neighbourhood of the Pass he would find a military post under a certain Major Guthrie of Campbell's regiment, in which bivouac he proposed to spend the night. (There had been a time last August when Sir John Cope with all his force dared not risk crossing the Corryarrick; it was different now.) Keith had first, of course, to get to Fort Augustus, and had set out from Inverness with that intention; but about half-way there, just before the road reared itself from the levels of White-bridge to climb to its highest elevation, he had been inexplicably tempted by a track which followed a stream up a valley to the left, and, on an impulse which now seemed to him insane, had decided to pursue this rather than the main road. His Highland orderly, a Mackay from Lord Reay's country, only too pleased, like all his race, to get off a high road, even though he was riding a shod horse, jumped at the suggestion, averring, in his not always ready English, that he knew the track to be a shorter way to the Corryarrick road. So they had ridden up that tempting corridor.

It was a most unwise proceeding. At first all had gone well, but by this time it was clear to Keith that he and his orderly, if not lost, were within measurable distance of becoming so. The original track had ceased, the stream had divided and they knew not which branch to follow; and either only seemed to take them higher and higher towards its source. Bare and menacing, the mountain-sides closed in more and more straitly upon the foolhardy travellers. The Highlander was of use as a pioneer, but Keith had expected him to be a guide, whereas it soon appeared that he had no qualifications for the post, never having been in these parts before, despite his confident assertion of an hour ago. Every now and then they were obliged to lead their horses, and they were continually making detours to avoid boggy ground. Keith trudged on silent with annoyance at his own folly, his orderly voluble in assurances that 'herself' need not be alarmed; there were worse places than this in Sutherland, yet Dougal the son of Dougal had never lost himself.

It was hard to believe that it was the first of May, so cold was it; not only were the surrounding mountains capped with snow, but it lay in all the creases of the northern slopes to quite a low level. There were even patches not far above the route which the travellers were painfully making out for themselves. And it was actually a pocket of snow in a sort of over-hanging hollow some way off to their left, a little above them, which drew Keith's eyes in that direction. Then he saw, to his surprise, that there was a figure with a plaid drawn over its head sitting in the hollow – a woman, apparently.

He called Mackay's attention to it at once. 'Ask her if she can tell us the best way to the Corryarrick road.'

The Highlander shouted out something in his own tongue, but there was no answer, and the woman huddled in her plaid, which completely hid her face, did not move. 'She will pe asleep, whateffer,' observed Mackay. '*A bhean!* – woman, woman!'

But another thought had struck the Englishman. Tossing the reins of his horse to Mackay, he strode up to the hollow where the woman sat, and stooping, laid a hand on her shoulder. For any warmth that struck through the tartan he might as well have touched the rock against which she leant. He gave an exclamation, and, after a moment, drew the folds of the plaid a little apart.

If the young woman who sat crouched within it, stiff now,

like the year-old child in her arms, knew the way anywhere, it was not to the Pass of Corryarrick. There was a little wreath of half-melted snow in a cranny near her head; it was no whiter than her face. The upper half of her body was almost naked, for she had stripped herself to wrap all she could round the little bundle which she was still clasping tightly to her breast. But it was only a bundle now, with one tiny, rigid hand emerging to show what it had been.

Keith removed his three-cornered hat, and signed to Mackay to leave the horses and come.

'The poor woman is dead,' he said in a hushed voice, '– has been dead for some time. Can she have met with an accident?'

'I think she will haf peen starfed,' said his orderly, looking at the pinched face. 'I haf heard that there are many women wandering in the hills of Lochaber and Badenoch, and there iss no food and it hass been fery cold.'

'But why should she have gone wandering like this, with her child, too?'

The Mackay turned surprised eyes upon him. 'Because you English from Fort William will haf burnt her house and perhaps killed her man,' he replied bluntly. 'Then she wass going trying to find shelter for herself and the wean. . . . And now there iss no one to streak her and to lay the platter of salt on her preast. It iss a pity.'

He, too, with the innate reverence of his race for the dead, was standing bareheaded.

'I wish we could bury them,' said Keith. But it was out of the question; they had neither the implements nor the time: indeed, but for the food that they carried, and their horses, the same end might almost be awaiting them in these solitudes. So Mackay replaced the plaid, and they went silently back to the horses and continued their journey.

'You English' – we English – have done this; we whose boast it has always been that we do not war with women and children; we English whose vengeance (Keith had realized it ere this) is edged by the remembrance of past panic, of the disgrace of Prestonpans and Falkirk and invasion. He went on his way with a sensation of being branded.

Yes, he had been too true a prophet. The comedy *had* turned grim and bloody earnest. And, despite relief and natural exhilaration at victory – of which there was not much left in him now – despite the liberation of his native country from a menace which she affected to despise, but which in the end had terrified her, despite the vindication, at last, of the worth of trained troops, Keith Windham could say with all his heart: 'Would God we were back in the days of farce!' Yes, even in the days when last he was in Lochaber, for the very mortification of the rout at High Bridge last summer and of his subsequent captivity had been easier to bear than the feeling that he belonged now to a band of executioners – was indeed closely connected with the most brutal of them all. He had been gratified when Hawley, on his arrival at Edinburgh, had, on Preston's recommendation, chosen him to fill a vacancy on his staff; but during the last two weeks he had come to loathe the position. Yet his ambitious regard for his own career forbade him to damage it by asking permission to resign his post; indeed, had he taken such a remarkable step, he would not now be on his way to Perth, having turned his back for a while on what had so sickened him.

Another half-hour passed, and the memories which had been sweeping like dark clouds over Keith's mind began to give way to a real sensation of alarm, not so much for his personal safety as for the carrying out of his mission. Suppose they did not find their way before nightfall out of this accursed maze into which he had so blindly ventured! He consulted anew with Mackay, and they resolved to abandon the line which they had been taking, and try instead to find a way over a spur on their right, for the mountain which sent it forth was neither craggy nor strewn with scree, and the slope of the spur was such that it was even possible to make use of their horses. At the worst its summit would give them a view, and they might then be able to strike out a better route for themselves.

As Keith was putting his foot in the stirrup, Dougal Mackay caught his arm and said excitedly: 'I wass hearing a shout sir!'

'I heard nothing,' responded Major Windham, listening. 'Where did it come from?'

The orderly pointed ahead. 'The men that shouted will pe round the other side of this *beinn*. Let uss make haste, sir!'

Praying that the Highlander was not mistaken Keith scrambled into the saddle, and his horse began to strain up the slope. He himself could hear nothing but the melancholy notes of a disturbed plover, which was wheeling not far above their heads, and he cursed the bird for drowning more distant sounds. Then, sharp through the mournful cry, there did come a sound, the crack of a shot – of two shots – and the mountains re-echoed with it.

For a moment both Keith and his orderly instinctively checked their horses; then Keith struck spurs into his, and in a few minutes the panting beast had carried him to the top of the shoulder . . . and he had his view.

Directly before him rose another mountain-side, much greener than the rest, and this greenness extended downwards into the almost level depression between it and the slope whose summit he had now reached. Below him, in this narrow upland valley, stood a small group of rough huts for use when the cattle were driven up to the summer pasture, and in front of these was drawn up a body of redcoats, to whom a mounted officer was shouting orders. On the ground near the entrance of the largest shieling lay a motionless Highlander. The shots thus explained themselves; the soldiers were at their usual work, and Keith had ridden into the midst of it. He felt weariness and disgust, but he needed direction too badly not to be glad to meet with those who could give it. Presumably the detachment was from the post on Wade's road, and the officer might even be Major Guthrie himself. Hoping that the worst was now over, he rode slowly down the hillside through the bloomless heather, unnoticed by the group below.

The fern-thatched roof of one of the shielings had already been fired, and from its first cracklings Keith realized with distaste that the butchery was not yet finished. Three or four scarlet-clad figures came out of the hut before which the dead man lay, half carrying, half dragging another Highlander, alive, but evidently wounded. The officer pointed, and they followed the usual summary method in such cases, and, after planting him against the dry-stone wall of the building itself, withdrew, leaving him face to face with the firing-party. But apparently their victim could not stand unsupported, for a moment or so after they had retired he slid to one knee and then to the ground.

'Detestable!' said Major Windham to himself. He had recognized the tartan now – the one of all others that he would never mistake, for he had worn it himself – the Cameron. But that did not surprise him. The doomed Highlander was now struggling to his feet again; he gained them unaided, and, steadying himself with one hand against the wall behind him, stood once more upright, so tall that his head was well above the edge of the low thatch. Now Keith was near enough to see the lower end of a dirty bandage round his left thigh, and the whole of another on his sword arm, for all that he had upon him was a kilt and a ragged shirt. And—

'Good God!' exclaimed the Englishman aloud; and, calling out at the top of his voice: 'Stop! stop!' he drove the spurs into his horse, came slithering down the last part of the slope, raced towards the shieling, leapt off, holding up his hand – but all faces were now turned towards him – ran in between the already levelled musket and Ewen Cameron.

Ewen alone had not seen him. His face was the colour of the wall behind him; his eyes were half closed, his teeth set in his lower lip, and it was plain that only his force of will was keeping him upright there. A tiny trickle of blood was beginning to course down his bare leg. And even the blind instinct to face death standing could keep him there no longer; for the second time he swayed, and the wounded leg gave way under him again. But this time Keith's arms caught him as he sank.

Oblivious of the stupefaction which had descended upon the soldiers, and of the more than stupefaction manifested by the officer behind them, Keith lowered that dead weight to the ground and knelt beside it. In Ardroy's gaunt face a line of white showed under the closed lids, and Keith's hand pressed on the torn shirt found a heartbeat so faint that he thought: 'He was dying when they dragged him out, the brutes!' Perhaps he had not been in time after all. He remembered that there was brandy in his holster, and looked up with an idea of summoning Mackay.

But by this time the officer had ridden up, and was there a pace or two away, towering over the pair by the wall.

'Am I tae tak ye for a surgeon, sir?' he inquired in a strong Lowland accent, and in a tone compounded of hot rage and cold. 'If sae, an' ye'll hae the kindness tae shift yersel' oot o' the way for a meenut, there'll be nae further need o' yer sairvices!'

Keith laid Ewen's head down on the grass, and, standing up,

regarded the rider, a neat, fair-complexioned Scot about five-and-forty, with little light eyes under sandy brows.

'Major Guthrie, I think?' he suggested, and saluted him. 'I am Major Keith Windham of the Royals, on General Hawley's staff, and now on my way with despatches from His Royal Highness to Perth.'

'I care little if ye hae despatches frae God Himsel'!' retorted Major Guthrie with increasing fury. 'And this isna Perth . . . Hand awa frae yon wa' – unless ye've a fancy tae be shot tae!'

But Keith did not move. 'This is not a common Highlander, sir,' he said, as calmly as he could. 'He is an officer, despite his dress.' For officers, as Major Guthrie must know, were not shot in cold blood – now.

'What's that tae me?' inquired Guthrie. He turned. 'Here, ye sumphs, pit him up afore the wa' again!'

Two of the men made an undecided move forwards, but the sight of this other officer of equal rank standing so resolutely in front of the prostrate Highlander daunted them.

'But listen, Major Guthrie,' pleaded Keith, keeping a tight hold upon his own rapidly rising temper and disgust, 'this gentleman is really of more than ordinary importance, for he was at one time aide-de-camp to the Pretender's son, and he is Lochiel's near kinsman – some kind of cousin, I think. You surely would not—'

'Lochiel's near kinsman, did ye say?' interrupted Guthrie, bending down a little. 'Hoo is he called?'

'Cameron of Ardroy, a captain in Lochiel's regiment. I am sure,' went on Keith, eager to follow up the impression which Lochiel's name appeared to have made, 'I am sure you will recognize, Major, that the Duke would not wish him to be shot out of hand like this!'

'Indeed I'm obliged tae ye, Major Somebody or ither, for sae kindly instructing His Royal Highness's wishes tae me,' retorted the Lowlander, but he bent still farther from the saddle, and gazed down for a moment at what was lying so still by the wall – at the dirty, bloodstained, half-clothed figure which Keith had last seen so gallant in powder and satin, cool, smiling and triumphant. The plea he had offered – the only plea that he could think of – was it going to save Ewen Cameron from lying there stiller yet? He tried to read Guthrie's intentions on his face, but all that he could see there was its innate mean-ness and cruelty.

The saddle creaked as the rider came upright again. He looked down at Keith himself now with eyes that seemed to hold a flickering light.

'This is God's truth ye're tellin' me, that yon' – he pointed contemptuously – 'is Lochiel's cousin?'

'Yes, on my honour as an officer.'

'And may I speir hoo ye ken it?'

'Because I have met him before. I assure you, sir, that if they knew at Inverness—'

'This is nae mair Inverness than it is Perth, Major – Keith! I'm actin' here on my ain authority, and if yon lousy rebel lying there had the Duke's ain protection on him I wudna regard it if I thocht fit. Still and on, I'm weel aware that as Lochiel's near kinsman he may be of mair value alive than deid – we shall see of hoo much in a day or two. . . . Aye, I doot they'll be wishing they had him at Inverness!'

'But you cannot send him all the way to Inverness,' pro-tested Keith, rather alarmed. 'He is evidently badly wounded – ill. . . .' He dropped on one knee beside Ewen again.

Guthrie gave a short laugh. 'Did I say I was gaun to? Ye maun tak me for a fule, Major. Findin's keepin', as they say. – But deil kens,' he added, suddenly dismounting, 'hoo I'm tae transport the man even to my ain camp the nicht; I've naething tae carry him on, and I dinna jalouse—' Here he too came and stooped over the unconscious figure. 'Aye, *he's* no' for sittin' a horse, that's plain. I'm thinkin' I'll e'en hae to leave him here till the morn, and send doun a party wi' a litter. There's ane thing,' he added coolly, raising himself with a shrug of his shoulders, 'he'll no' rin awa', and there's naebody left aboot the place. Aye, that's what I'll dae.'

'You are going to leave him here alone all night, in this state?' exclaimed Keith, loosing the almost pulseless wrist.

Guthrie stared angrily at him. 'Upon my soul, Major! Are ye expectin' a spital on Ben Loy? For a man on Hawley's staff ye're unco tender tae a rebel! If I canna tak the prisoner wi' me I've nae choice but leave him here . . . unless ye'd prefer me tae blaw his harns oot after a'. It's nane too late for it yet, ye ken.' And he laid a hand on one of his own pistols.

'No, you are quite right, sir,' said Keith hastily, almost humbly. 'I see that you can do nothing else but leave him till the morning.'

'Sergeant,' called out Major Guthrie, 'pit the prisoner ben the hoose again, and dinna fire yon shieling. Noo, Major Keith, in payment for the guid turn ye've done me, I'll hae the pleasure of offerin' ye hospeetality for the nicht, and settin' ye on the richt road for Perth, which we're no' on the noo, ye ken!'

'I am much beholden to you, sir,' replied Keith stiffly. 'But I am not aware of having laid you under any obligation.'

Guthrie raised his sandy eyebrows. 'Are ye no'? Aweel, ye may be richt; we'll see, we'll see. – Aye, sergeant, fire the lave o' them; we mauna leave ony bield for the rebels.'

The thatch of the next shieling, going up with a roar, lit sharply the uniforms of the men who, roughly enough, lifted Ardroy from the ground, and, staggering a little, for he was no light weight, disappeared with him round the corner of the miserable little dwelling. Biting his lip, Keith watched them go; and then Mackay brought up his horse, restive at the flames. The men came out again.

'Well, Major, are ye no' satisfied?' asked Guthrie, already back in the saddle.

Satisfied? No. But he was on such dangerous ground; this man's mercy, if so it could be called, was like a bog; at any moment there might be no more foothold. A little more pressing for better treatment, and he would have Ardroy shot out of mere spite; Keith was sure of it. But – left alone, scarcely breathing . . . and in what condition *had* Ewen been left in there?

'I'll ride after you in a moment, sir,' he said. 'You see, I am under a sort of obligation to this young Cameron. I'll just go in and leave him my brandy-flask.'

Really Major Guthrie of Campbell's regiment had the most unpleasant eyes he had ever encountered! 'As ye will, sir,' he returned. 'I doot he'll no' be able tae thank ye. But I advise ye no' tae be ower lang wi' him, for I canna wait, and 'tis for me tae warn ye this time that the Duke'll no' be verra pleased if ye lose the way tae Perth again.' He turned his horse; Keith took the flask out of his holster, said a word to Mackay, and went round to the door of the shieling.

It was Neil MacMartin who lay shot not far from the entrance; Keith recognized him instantly. No doubt it was only over his dead body that they had been able to get at his wounded foster-brother. Inside the tiny place it was so dark that for a moment Keith could hardly see anything; then, by a sudden red glow from without, he distinguished Ewen's body in the far corner, on a heap of something which proved to be dried fern and heather. The soldiers had flung him back there with little regard for his wounds or for the coming of night. But there was a plaid lying in a heap on the floor; Keith picked this up and spread it over him. Ardroy was still senseless, but when Keith tried to arrange him more comfortably he moaned; yet it was only the faintest trickle of brandy which the Englishman could get down his throat. He desisted finally, for fear of choking him, and closed his cold, nerveless hand round the flask instead. Looking about he saw not a trace of food nor even of water, though there was an overturned bowl on the floor; he hurried out with this to the burn which he had noticed, filled it and placed it within reach. But it seemed rather a mockery, now that the only hand which might have held it to Ewen Cameron's lips was lifeless outside. Had he done Ardroy a kindness after all in saving him from the volley?

Mackay was in the doorway. 'The redcoats iss all gone, Major. I am not seeing them now.'

Keith jumped up. His duty came before an enemy's plight, whatever were his feelings towards that enemy. He could do no more.

The leaping flames outside had died down to mere incandescence, and the dead man and the senseless were left in possession of the darkening hollow where the burn's voice, babbling on in protest or unconcern, was now the only sound to break the silence.

Chapter Four

'WEEL, sir, and was yer *frien'* able tae thank ye?' inquired Major Guthrie when the Englishman overtook him at the end of the little column as it wound along the mountain-side. Keith said No, that he had not yet recovered his senses.

' 'Tis tae be hoped he'll hae gotten them again when I send for him,' commented the Lowlander. 'He'll no' be o' muckle use else. But are ye sure, Major, that he kens whaur Lochiel is the noo?'

'How do I know what he knows? And use – of what use do you expect him to be?' asked Keith shortly.

'What use?' Guthrie reined up. 'Losh, man, dinna ye ken there's a thousand punds on Lochiel's heid, that he's likely skulking somewhere round Achnacarry or Loch Arkaig, and that tae ken his hiding-place wad be half-way tae the apprehension o' the man himsel'! Gin ye come frae Inverness ye canna be ignorant o' that! – And why for else did ye lay sic a stress upon you rebel bein' sib tae Lochiel, if ye didna mean that he wad be o' use tae us in that capacity?'

Keith sat his horse like a statue, and stared at the speaker with feelings which slowly whitened his own cheek. 'Is it possible you imagine that I thought Ewen Cameron, a Highlander and a gentleman, would turn informer against his own Chief?'

'Then for what ither reason,' retorted Guthrie, 'when ye came wi' yer damned interference, did ye insist on his kinship wi' Lochiel, and imply that he kenned o' his whereaboots?'

'I never implied such a thing!' burst out Keith indignantly. 'Not for a moment! You must most strangely have mistaken me, Major Guthrie. And if Cameron of Ardroy did know, he would never dream of betraying his knowledge!'

'Ah,' commented Guthrie, surveying him slowly. 'Then it's no' worth the fash o' sendin' for him the morn.' And smiling crookedly he touched his horse with his heel, and moved on again after his men.

But Keith Windham remained behind on the mountain path, almost stunned with disgust. That he should be thought capable of suggesting such a reason for sparing Ewen Cameron's life! This then was the cause of Major Guthrie's change of intention at the mention of Lochiel's name, the meaning of his reference to the 'good turn' which Major Windham had done him! Keith's impulse was to leave the very path which Guthrie's horse had trodden. But he could not gratify this desire; he was dependent on Guthrie's guidance. Besides, Ardroy lay helpless and utterly alone in the hut; he had not saved him yet. Great heavens, what line was he to take to that end now?

He moved on slowly after the Lowlander, who took no notice of him. On the narrow path they were obliged to ride in single file, but soon the track, descending to a lower level, joined a wider one, and here the Major waited for him to come abreast.

'Since your object in hinderin' the execution a while syne wasna zeal for His Majesty's sairvice, as I thocht,' he observed, 'ye maun gie me leave to say, Major . . . I didn'a richtly get yer name – that I find yer conduct unco strange.'

'I am fully prepared to answer to my superiors for my conduct, sir,' replied Keith very stiffly. 'As I told you just now, I am under an obligation to that young Cameron such as any soldier may owe to an enemy without dishonour. He spared my life when it was his for the taking, and as his prisoner last year I received very different treatment from that which we are now giving to ours!'

'Ah, sae ye were his prisoner?' repeated Guthrie, fixing his little ferret eyes upon him. 'When micht that hae been?'

'It was after the affair at High Bridge last summer,' answered Keith shortly.

'High Bridge!' A light seemed to dawn on Guthrie's face – not a pleasant light. 'What, it's *you* that lost the twa companies of Sinclair's there, along wi' Scott last August – ye'll be Major Windrum then?'

'Windham,' corrected Keith, still more shortly.

'Ou aye, Windham. Tae think I didna ken the man I was gangin' wi', me that's aye been ettlin' tae meet ye, for I mind hearin' ye were pit on Hawley's staff after yon tuilzie – ha, ha! Aye, I mind hearin' that verra weel. – Nae offence meant, Major Windham' – for Keith expression was distinctly stormy – 'we all hae oor meelitary misfortunes . . . but we dinna a' get promoted for them! – And ye were sayin' yon rebel made ye prisoner. What did he dae wi' ye?'

'He accepted my parole,' said the Englishman between his teeth.

'And let ye gang?'

'No. I was at his house for some days, and afterwards accompanied him to Glenfinnan.'

'Ye seem tae hae been chief wi' him! And whaur was this hoose of his, if ye please?'

'Can that be of any moment to you, sir?' retorted Keith, goaded by this interrogatory.

'Dod! I should think sae! It's o' moment tae me tae ken hoo far it lay frae Lochiel's ain hoose of Achnacarry.'

'Well, that I am afraid I cannot tell you,' replied Keith sourly. 'I was never at Achnacarry, and I have no knowledge of the neighbourhood. I am not a Scotsman.'

'Fine I ken that! But e'en a Southron has lugs tae his heid, and ye maun hae heard tell the name o' the district whaur yon rebel's hoose was situate? If ye canna tell me that I'll be forced tae think—' He broke off with a grin.

'And what, pray, will you be forced to think?' demanded Keith, surveying him from under his lids.

'Aweel, I suld think ye could jalouse that,' was Guthrie's reply. 'Come noo, Major, ye can surely mind some landmark or ither?'

It was no use fencing any more. 'Mr Cameron's house was near a little lake called the Eagle's Lake, in the mountains some way to the north of Loch Arkaig.'

'Ah, thank ye, Major Windham, for the effort,' said Guthrie with another grin. 'I hae a map in the camp. . . . And syne ye couldna be pairted frae yer rebel frien', but gaed wi' him to Glenfinnan tae see the ploy there?'

'Do you suppose I went willingly? I have told you that I was his prisoner.'

'But ye were at Glenfinnan wi' him, and that's o' moment too, for nae doot ye'd see him an' Lochiel thegither. Did ye no'?'

'Once or twice.'

'And hoo did they seem – on intimate terms wi' ane anither?'

'I was not concerned to spy upon them,' retorted Keith, who had an instant picture of the Chief as he had once seen him, with an affectionate hand on Ewen's shoulder, a picture he was not going to pass on. 'I have told you that they were cousins.'

'Aye, ye tellt me that. But ilka Highlander is cousin tae twenty mair.' They rode on for perhaps a moment in silence, and then Guthrie began again. 'See here, Major Windham, what the de'il's the gude o' tellin' me the Cameron's this and that, and syne, when ye've hindered me frae shootin' him as he desairves, tae begin makin' oot he's naething o' the sort? I suppose ye'll say noo he wasna aide-de-camp tae the Pretender's son neither?'

'I am not in the habit of telling lies,' replied Keith. 'He was aide-de-camp to the Pretender's son, at least when the Highland army occupied Edinburgh, and that, as I said, and say still, is an excellent reason for not shooting him out of hand.'

'Ye met him in Enbra, then?'

'I did.'

'As an enemy or a frien'?'

'As an enemy, of course.' Keith was having to keep a tight hold of himself. 'Yet there again he put me under an obligation.' And at Guthrie's expression he was unable to resist adding: 'But I dare warrant the recognition of an obligation is no part of your creed, sir.'

Guthrie met this thrust instantly. 'And me that gleg the noo tae allow mine tae ye! Fie, Major! But as a plain soldier I'm thinkin' there's ower muckle obleegation atween you and yer Cameron; ye're gey frien'ly wi' him for an enemy, rinnin' in like that when ye micht hae gotten a ball in yer ain wame. But since ye assure me he'll no' tell what he kens aboot Lochiel, he maun e'en bide in yon shieling and rot there, for it's no' worth a brass bodle tae bring him in.'

Keith's heart sank at these words. Yet he could not bring himself to assert that Ardroy would impart his knowledge (if he had any), for he was certain that he would rather die than do such a thing. Yet somehow he *must* be got out of that desolate place.

He summoned up all his own powers of dissimulation.

'You are quite mistaken, Major Guthrie,' he said carelessly. 'I am not a friend of Mr Cameron's in the sense that you imply, and I should be as glad as anyone to hear of Lochiel's capture – if it would advance His Majesty's affairs in this kingdom.' He added this qualifying clause to salve his own conscience, since Lochiel's capture was about the last he would rejoice at. But he had to say something worse than this, and he did it with loathing, and a hesitation which perhaps served him better than he knew, fidgeting meanwhile with his horse's reins. 'You know, sir, that although I am sure

Mr Cameron would never answer a direct question, he might perhaps drop . . . inadvertently drop . . . some hint or other – and I presume you have a certain measure of knowledge and might find a hint valuable – I mean that it might, by good luck, complete your information. At least I should think that it would be worth your while to bring him into camp on the chance of it.'

It sounded to him so desperately feeble a bait that it was surely to no purpose that he had soiled his lips with its utterance. Yet Guthrie appeared to respond to the suggestion with surprising alacrity.

'Drap a hint,' he said meditatively, rubbing his chin. 'Aye, maybe. Thank ye for the notion, Major; I'll e'en think it ower. I could aiblins drap a hint mysel'.' And they rode on in silence for a few minutes after that, Keith not knowing whether he more detested himself or the man beside him.

But by the time that they came in sight of the little river Tarff, which they must ford before they could get up to the Corryarrick road, Major Guthrie was busy weaving what he evidently considered a highly diverting explanation of his companion's interest in 'yon rebel', which he now refused to attribute to the alleged 'obligation' under which Major Windham professed to labour. 'I see it a',' he chuckled; 'he had a bonny sister, and she was kind tae ye, Major – kind as yon ither lass of a Cameron was kind to the Pretender's son. Or a wife maybe? Oot wi' it, ye sly dog—' And for a moment or two he gave rein to a fancy so coarse that Keith, no Puritan himself, yet innately fastidious, longed to shut his mouth.

'And that's how ye repaid his hospitality, Major,' finished the humorist as they splashed through the Tarff. ' 'Tis a guilty conscience, not gratitude, garred ye save him!'

After that he reverted to the subject of his companion's staff appointment, which seemed to possess a sort of fascination for him, and tapped a very galling and indeed insulting vein of pleasantry in regard to it. And Keith, who would not have endured a quarter of this insolence from anyone else in the world, no, not from the Duke of Cumberland himself, swallowed it because he knew that Ewen Cameron's life hung on this man's pleasure. First of all his companion supposed that General Hawley did not know what a viper he was cherishing in his bosom, in the shape of an officer who possessed a weakness for rebels which could certainly not be attributed to that commander himself; of this Keith took no notice, so Major Guthrie passed on to affect to find something mightily amusing in the distinction of staff rank having been bestowed on a man who had run away at the first shot of the campaign. He actually used the expression, but at once safeguarded himself by adding, with a laugh: 'Nae offence, my dear Major! I ken weel the twa companies o' Sinclair's just spat and gied ower, and you and Scott could dae nae less but gang wi' them – 'twas yer duty.' But after a moment he added with a chuckle: 'Forbye ye rinned farther than the rest, I've heard!'

Ardroy or no Ardroy, this was too much. Keith reined up. Yet, since it seemed deliberate provocation, he kept surprisingly cool. 'Major Guthrie, I'd have you know I do not take such insinuations from any man alive! If you know so much about me, you must know also that Captain Scott sent me back to fetch reinforcements from Fort Augustus.'

Guthrie, pulling up too, smote himself upon the thigh. 'Aye, I micht ha' kent it! Forgie me, Major Windham – yon was a pleasantry. I aye likit ma joke!'

'Allow me to say, then, that I do not share your taste,' riposted Keith, with a brow like thunder. 'If we were not both on active service at the moment—'

'Ye'd gar me draw, eh? Dinna be that hot, man! 'Twas an ill joke, I confess, and I ask yer pardon for it,' said Guthrie, with complete good humour. 'See, yonder's the camp, and ye're gaun tae sup wi' me.'

Keith wished with all his heart that he were not. But he felt, rightly or wrongly, that he must preserve a certain measure of amenity in his relations with the arbiter of Ardroy's fate, and, though it seemed to him that he had never done anything more repugnant (except make his recent speech about the possibility of Ewen's dropping a hint) he affected a demeanour modelled in some remote degree upon his companion's, and insincerely declared that he was foolish not to see that Major Guthrie was joking, and that he bore him no ill-will for his jest.

What baffled him was the reason for the ill-will which he could hardly doubt that Guthrie bore *him*. Was it because he had hindered the shooting of a rebel? But, according to his own showing, Major Guthrie hoped to find the rebel more useful alive than dead.

It was certainly no deprivation to the Englishman when he discovered, on arriving at Guthrie's camp athwart the road, some miles from the top of the pass, that he was not to share the commanding officer's tent. Finding, as he now did, that the distance from the mountain-side where he had come upon the soldiers was not so great as he had feared, he would much have preferred to push on over the pass to Meallgarva, but his horse and his orderly's were too obviously in need of rest for this to be prudent, and when he was offered a vacant bed in another tent (for it appeared that the captain of the company had gone to Fort Augustus for the night) his worst apprehensions were relieved. The lieutenant, indeed, who made a third at the meal which he was nevertheless obliged to share with Guthrie, was of a different stamp entirely, an open-faced lad from the Tweed named Paton, whom Keith at once suspected of disliking his major very heartily.

On the plea that he must make an early start, the guest afterwards excused himself from playing cards with Guthrie and his subaltern, and withdrew to Lieutenant Paton's tent. Once there, however, he made no attempt to undress, but flung himself on the camp bed and lay staring at the lantern on the tent-pole. A few miles away on the other side of the Tarff the man whom he had tried so hard to save lay dying, perhaps, for want of food and care. What Guthrie's real intentions were about fetching him in tomorrow he, probably of set purpose, had not allowed his visitor to know. And the question rather was, would Ewen Cameron be alive at all in the morning – he seemed at so low an ebb, and the nights were still so cold. Do what Keith would he could not get him out of his head. It was useless to tell himself that he had, alas, witnessed worse episodes; that it was the fortune of war; that he was womanish to be so much distracted by the thought of an enemy's situation. He had been that enemy's guest; he had seen his domestic circumstances, met his future wife, knew what his very furniture looked like. Was not all that even more of a tie than that double debt which he felt he owed him? His instincts were stronger than his judgment, and when, an hour or so later, Lieutenant Paton slipped quietly through the flap of the tent, he rose up and abruptly addressed him.

'Mr Paton, you look as if you had the natural sentiments of humanity still left in you. Can you tell me where I could procure some food, and if possible some dressings, for that unfortunate rebel left alone upon the mountain-side, about whom you heard at supper?'

The young man looked considerably taken aback, as well he might. 'But how would you propose, sir, to get them to him? And the Major, I thought, spoke of fetching him into camp tomorrow.'

'I am not at all sure that he will, however,' replied Keith. 'And even if he does I fear he may fetch in a corpse. If I can get some food and wine I propose to take them to him myself; I think I can find the way back without difficulty, and my orderly is a Highlander.' And as Lieutenant Paton looked still more astonished, he added: 'You must not think me a mere philanthropist, Mr Paton. I owe the man in that hut a good deal, and I cannot endure the thought of having turned my back upon him in such a plight. In any case, I should be making an early start for Dalwhinnie. Is there any cottage in this neighbourhood where I could buy bread?'

'No, but I could procure you some in the camp, sir,' said the boy quite eagerly. 'And, as for dressings, you are welcome to tear up a shirt of mine. I . . . I confess I don't like these extreme measures, even with rebels, and I should be very glad to help you.'

'You'll not get into trouble, eh?'

'Not tonight, at any rate, sir; the Major is in bed by now. And tomorrow, if it is discovered, I can say that you ordered me to do it, and that I dared not dispute the orders of a staff officer.'

Chapter Five

AND thus it was that a few hours later Major Windham started back to Beinn Laoigh again with bread and meat and wine, and an orderly who plainly thought him mad. Lieutenant Paton had seen them clear of the camp, whose commander was fortunately wrapped in slumber. Keith would not need to pass its sentries on his return, for the track up from the Tarff joined the road to the pass on the farther side of it.

He found that he had noted the position of the shieling hut better than he could have hoped, considering the disagreeable preoccupation of his mind during the ride thence with Major Guthrie, and by good chance there was a moon not much past the full. In her cold light the mountains looked inexpressibly lonely and remote as Keith rode up the sheep track to the pasture where the harmless little shelters had stood. A faint exhausted smoke yet lifted itself from one or two of the blackened ruins. The stream was chanting its changeless little song, and in the moonlight Neil MacMartin still lay on guard outside the broken door of the one unburnt shieling. Keith bent over him as he passed; he was stiffening already in the plaid which was his only garment. And Ardroy?

Taking from Mackay the lantern which he had brought for the purpose, and the food and wine, Keith went rather apprehensively into the dark, low-roofed place. Except that he had flung his left arm clear, its occupant was lying as he had left him, long and quiet under the tartan covering; his eyes were closed and he did not look very different from his dead foster-brother outside. But as the light fell on his face he moved a little and faintly said some words in Gaelic, among which Keith thought he heard Lachlan's name. He stooped over him.

'Ardroy,' he said gently, and laid a hand on the arm emerging from the tattered shirt-sleeve.

At the touch Ewen opened his eyes. But all that he saw, evidently, in the lantern-light, was the bright scarlet uniform above him. 'What, again!' he said, with an accent of profound weariness. 'Shoot me in here, then; I cannot stand. Have you not . . . a pistol?'

Keith set the lantern on the floor and knelt down by him. 'Ardroy, don't you know me – Windham of the Royals? I am not come for that, but to help you if I can.'

The dried fern rustled as the wounded man turned his head a little. Very hollow in their orbits, but blue as Keith remembered them, his eyes stared up full of unbelief. '*Windham!*' he said at last, feebly; 'no, it's not possible. You are . . . someone else.'

'No,' said Keith, wondering how clear his mind might be, 'it is really Windham, come to help you.' He was searching meanwhile for the flask of brandy which he had left, and finding it slipped down, untouched, among the sprigs of heather, he wetted Ewen's lips with a little of the spirit.

'Yes, it *is* Windham,' said Ewen to himself. His eyes had never left his visitor's face. 'But . . . there were other soldiers here before . . . they took me out to shoot . . . I think I must have . . . swooned. Then I was . . . back in this place. . . . I do not know why. . . . Are you sure you . . . have not orders to . . . take me out again?'

'Good God, no!' said Keith. 'I have nothing to do with shooting; I am alone, carrying despatches. Tell me, you are wounded – how severely?'

'My right arm . . . that is nothing much. . . . This thigh . . . badly. I cannot . . . move myself.'

'And what of food?' queried Keith. 'I do not see any here – but I have brought some with me.' He began to get it out. 'Are you not hungry?'

'Not now,' answered Ewen. 'I was once . . . Captain Windham,' he went on, apparently gathering together what forces he had, 'your coming . . . this charity . . . I cannot . . .'

'Do not try!' put in Keith quickly. 'Not hungry? How long, then, is it since you have eaten?'

'Eaten!' said the Highlander, and what might be interpreted as a smile dawned on his bony face. 'There is no food . . . in these hills. I have had nothing but water . . . for three days . . . I think. . . . That is why Lachlan has gone . . . to try . . .' The words tailed off as the spark of astonishment and animation in him went out quite suddenly, leaving his face the mask it had been when Keith entered.

Three days! No wonder that he was weak. Keith threw the water out of the bowl, poured some wine into it, and lifting Ewen's head from the bracken held it to his lips. 'Drink this!' he commanded, and had to say it two or three times before Ewen obeyed.

'But this is wine, Lachlan,' he murmured confusedly. 'How did you come by wine?' Then his eyes turned on Keith as if he recognized him again, and the recognition was only a source of bewilderment.

Keith meanwhile was breaking bread into the wine. He knew that one must not give a starving man too much food at first. But the fugitive, far from being ravenous, seemed to find it difficult to swallow the sops which were put to his lips. Keith, however, persevered, and even added some meat to the bread, and patiently fed him with that, till Ewen intimated that he could eat no more. Keith's next intention was then announced.

'Now I am going to dress your wounds, if they need it,' he said. 'You'll permit me?'

'*Permit* you!' repeated Ewen, gazing at him with a renewal of his former wonder.

Keith took the bowl, and went out for water. The moon was hidden behind a bank of cloud, but a planet hung like a great flower over one of the black mountain-tops. The grazing horses lifted their heads inquiringly, and Mackay, sitting propped against the shieling wall, scrambled sleepily to his feet.

'No, I am not going on yet. Get me that torn linen from my saddle-bag.'

To his surprise, when he went back into the hut after even so momentary an absence, Ewen had fallen asleep, perhaps as the result of eating after so long a fast. Keith decided not to rouse him, and waited. But five minutes saw the end of the snatch of feverish slumber, for Ardroy woke with a little cry and some remark about the English artillery which showed that he had been back at Culloden Moor. However, he knew Keith instantly, and when the Englishman began to unbandage his wounded sword arm, murmured: 'That was a bayonet-thrust.'

The arm had indeed been transfixed, and looked very swollen and painful, but, as far as Keith could judge, gave no particular cause for anxiety. He washed the wound, and as he bound it up again saw clearly in the rays of the lantern, which for greater convenience he had set upon an old stool that he had found, a curious white seam on the palm of the hand; another ran across the fingers. He wondered for a moment what they were; then he guessed.

But when he came round and unbandaged Ewen's thigh – and miserably enough was it bandaged – and found there a deep gash, in no satisfactory state, he was somewhat horrified. This injury called for a surgeon, and he nearly said so; but, reddening, checked himself, recalling the deliberate denial of care to the Jacobite wounded at Inverness, and the actual removal of their instruments from the few of their own surgeons imprisoned with them. Would Ewen Cameron get real attention in Major Guthrie's hands?

He glanced at him, lying with his eyes shut and his hands gripped together on his breast, but making neither sound nor movement, and wondered whether he were hurting him intolerably, and what he should do if he went off into another of those long swoons, and thereupon finished his task as quickly as he could and had recourse to the brandy flask once more. And then he sat down at the bottom of the rough bed – for the heather and fern was spread on a rude wooden framework standing about a foot from the floor – and gazed at him with a furrowed brow. The lantern on the stool beside him revealed the Highlander's pallor and exhaustion to the full, but, though his eyes were closed, and he lay quiet for a considerable time, he was not asleep, for he suddenly opened them, and said:

'I cannot understand; did you know that I was here, Captain Windham . . . or is it chance that has brought you . . . so opportunely?'

'It was chance the first time – for this is the second time that I have been here,' replied Keith. 'I will tell you about it. I was on my way this afternoon from Inverness to Perth when some impulse made me attempt a very foolish short cut among the mountains. I think now that it must have been the finger of Fate pushing me, for thus I came upon this place just a moment or two before they dragged you out and set you against the wall . . . only just in time, in fact. I protested and argued with the officer in charge – a Major Guthrie, who has a camp on the Corryarrick road up there – and was fortunately able to prevent his shooting you in cold blood.' And as Ewen gave a little exclamation, he hurried on in order not to give him time to ask (should he think of it) how he had accomplished this feat. 'But he intends – at least I think he intends – to send a party in the morning and take you prisoner; and indeed, brute though he is, I hope that he will do so, for otherwise what will become of you, alone here?'

But Ewen left that question unanswered, and was equally far from asking on what ground he had been spared. The fact itself seemed enough for him, for he was trying agitatedly to raise himself a little. 'It was you . . . though I saw no one . . .

you saved my life, then!' he exclaimed rather incoherently. 'And now . . . is it possible that you have come back *again* . . . out of your way. Captain Windham, this debt . . . this more than kindness . . .' He struggled to go on, but between emotion, weakness and recent pain it was more than he could do, and seeing him almost on the point of breaking down Keith stopped him quickly.

'For God's sake don't talk of debts, Ardroy – or, if you must, remember what I owe you! See, you are horribly weak; could you not eat a little more now?'

Ewen nodded, not trusting himself to speak, and put out a shaky left hand, apparently to show that he could feed himself. And while he nibbled in a rather half-hearted way at the slice of bread and meat which Keith put into it, Major Windham himself wandered slowly about the hovel. The ashes of last summer's fires lay white in the middle of the floor, and through the hole in the roof which was the only outlet for the smoke a star looked in as it passed.

It seemed to Keith that before he went on his way he must tell Ardroy the means he had used to save him. Surely there was nothing blameworthy or unnatural in his having revealed who Ewen was, when he stood between him and imminent death? But from telling him the reason which Guthrie supposed or feigned to suppose lay at the back of his action, the Lowlander had mentally shied away like a nervous horse, the whole subject so horribly distasteful to him. Moreover, it was not Guthrie who had suggested that Cameron of Ardroy might 'inadvertently drop a hint'. How *could* he tell Ewen that he had said that about him?

He turned round, miserably undecided. Ewen had finished his pretence at a meal, and his eyes were fixed on his visitor. Keith had a sudden access of panic, he was sure that the Jacobite was going to ask him on what plea he had stopped his execution. He would put a question to him instead.

'How did you get so far with a wound like that?' he asked, coming back to his former place, and sitting down again. 'You had Neil MacMartin to help you, I suppose? You mentioned Lachlan, too, just now.'

He had not anticipated more than a brief reply, but Ewen, once started, told him the whole story – not indeed, with any superfluity of words, and slowly, with pauses here and there.

But the narrative was quite connected, though the speaker gave a certain dreamy impression of having half forgotten his listener, and of going on as if he were living his experiences over again rather than narrating them.

It appeared that he had received both his wounds in that desperate charge into which the clans of the right wing had broken, maddened by the cruel artillery pounding which they had endured, a charge so furious that it had pierced and scattered the English front line of regiments, only to dash itself to pieces – on the bayonets of Sempill's behind them. At the second and severer injury he fell, and was unable to get to his feet again, for it seemed as if a muscle had been severed in his thigh, and he was besides losing blood very fast. Only the devotion of one of his followers got him away from the heap of dead and wounded strewn about like seaweed along the front of the second line; this man, powerful and unhurt, tied up the gash as best he could, and succeeded in carrying his chieftain a little out of the carnage, but in doing so he was shot dead, and once more Ewen was on the ground among the fallen. This time he was lying among the dead and wounded of the Atholl men, with none of his own clan to succour him, and here a strange – and yet ultimately a lucky – mischance befell him. For a wounded Stewart, half crazed no doubt by a terrible cut on the head, crawled to him where he lay across his dead clansman and, cursing him for one of the Campbells who had taken them in flank, dealt him a furious blow on the forehead with the butt of a pistol. The result for Ewen was hours of unconsciousness, during which he was stripped by some redcoats who would certainly have finished him off had they not thought him dead already. He came to his senses in the very early morning, naked, and stiff with cold, but so thirsty that he contrived to drag himself as far as the little burn which crossed the end of the English line in the direction of their own. There, almost in the stream, and unconscious again, Lachlan and his brother, who had been searching for him since evening, almost miraculously found him.

His foster-brothers carried him to a farm-house on the moor, where, indeed, he was not the only wounded fugitive, but by noon that day, fearing (and with good reason) a search and a massacre, they somehow procured an old worn-out horse, and taking turns to ride it and to hold him on its back, succeeded in crossing the Water of Nairn and gaining the slopes of the Monadhliath Mountains. What happened then Ewen was not quite clear about; between pain, loss of blood, and exposure he was always more or less fevered, but he remembered an eternity of effort and of going on. At last the old horse fell dead; for a whole day Neil and Lachlan carried him between them till, weakened by want of food, they could get him no farther, and had taken shelter on Beinn Laoigh because the shieling hut at least gave him a roof from the cold and the rain. They did not know of Guthrie's camp on the Corryarrick road, which indeed was pitched after they got to Beinn Laoigh; in any case, they could not entirely avoid the road, for it would have to be crossed somewhere if they were ever to get back to Ardroy. But in these lonely mountains they were really faced with starvation, and Lachlan had at last been forced to go out scouting for food, and must either have gone far afield or have met with disaster, for he had been gone since the day before.

'But if he still breathes,' finished Ewen, 'I know that he will return; and if he is in time perhaps he can contrive to get me away to some other hiding-place before the soldiers come for me tomorrow. But in any case, Captain Windham – no, I see that it is Major – I am not likely to forget this extraordinary charity of yours . . . nor your intervention yesterday. . . . Was it yesterday?' he added rather vaguely.

'Yes, since it must now be after midnight. The tartans attracted my notice first,' said Keith, 'and then, by great good fortune, I looked again, and recognized you.'

'This is Neil's kilt that I have on,' said Ewen with a faint smile. 'There was not a stitch of my own left upon me. . . . You wore the philabeg too, once . . . it seems a long time ago. . . . But I do not think,' he went on, rather feverishly talkative now, 'that you would have recognized me the day before, with a two weeks' beard on me. It happened, however, that I had made poor Neil shave me as best he could with his *sgian*.'

'That was good fortune, too,' agreed Keith. 'Certainly I should not have known you bearded.'

'And it is because I had been shaved that I am alive now?' Ewen gave a little laugh. 'Do you know, Windham, that before ever I met you old Angus, my foster-father – you re-

member him? – predicted that our lives would cross . . . I
think he said five times. And this is . . . I can't count. . . .
How many times have we met already?'

'The old man predicted five meetings!' exclaimed Keith.
struck. 'How strange! This is the third . . . yes, the third
time we have met. If he is right, then we shall meet again, and
more than once. I hope it may be in happier circumstances.'

'And that I can thank you more fitly,' murmured Ewen.
Last time . . . do you remember the house in the Grassmarket? . . . You told me the comedy would end some day,
and the players be sorry they ever took part in it.'

Keith nodded. It was not the first time in the last twelve
hours that he had remembered the house in the Grassmarket.

'But I, for one, do not regret it,' went on Ewen, with a
touch of defiance. 'Not for myself, that is. I would do it again.
Yet there is poor Neil outside, killed defending me . . . and
so many others on that horrible moor. . . . You were there,
I suppose?'

'I was there,' said Keith. 'But *my* hands are clean of the
blood of massacre!' he added almost fiercely. 'If I could have
stopped— We'd best not speak of it. But your cause is lost,
Ardroy, and I suppose you know it. It only remains for you to
escape the consequences, if you can.'

'I do not seem to be in very good trim for doing that,' said
Ewen, and again he gave the shadow of a smile. 'But, since we
speak so frankly, I cannot think that our cause is lost while the
Prince and Lochiel remain at large. We may be scattered,
but— The Prince has not been captured, has he?' he asked
sharply, having evidently seen the change which the mention,
not of the Prince but of Lochiel, had brought to Keith's
face.

'No, no, nor is it known where he is.'

'Thank God! And Lochiel?'

Keith shrank inwardly. Now it was coming. His momentary
hesitation had a cruel effect on Ewen, who dragged himself to
his elbow. 'Windham,' he said hoarsely and imploringly,
'surely he's not . . . what have you heard? . . . My God, don't
keep me in suspense like this! If he's captured tell me!'

'You mistake me,' said Keith, nearly as hoarsely. 'He has
not been captured. . . . I am sorry if I misled you.'

Ewen had relapsed again, and put a hand over his eyes. It was fairly clear that his Chief's fate was even more to him than that of his Prince. And now that odious information must be imparted.

Keith tried to gain a little time first. 'But Lochiel was wounded in the battle. Did you know that?'

Ewen removed his hand. 'Yes, and have thanked God for it, since it caused him to be early carried off the field.'

'You saw him fall?'

'No, but afterwards we met with some of the clan, and got news of him.'

'That must have been a great relief to you,' murmured the Englishman. Suddenly he was possessed with a desire to find out how much Ewen knew about Lochiel. Half of him hoped that he knew very little – why, he could not have said – but the other half thought: If he knows a certain amount, Guthrie will take better care of him. 'But you can have had no news of your Chief since then?' he hazarded.

'No,' answered the Highlander. 'There has been no opportunity.'

Keith looked at him nervously. Ardroy was lying gazing upwards; perhaps he could see that peering star. Would it be possible to advise him, if he found himself in Major Guthrie's custody, to pretend to have definite knowledge of Lochiel's whereabouts, even though that were not the case? Dare he suggest such a thing? It was not one-half as offensive as what he had already suggested to Guthrie!

Ewen himself broke the silence. 'Since we speak as friends,' he said, his eyes travelling to the open doorway '– and how could I regard you as an enemy after this? – I may tell you that I have, none the less, the consolation of knowing where Lochiel is at this moment – God bless him and keep him safe!'

Keith's mouth felt suddenly dry. His unspoken question was answered, and the frankness of the acknowledgment rather took his breath away. Yet certainly, if Ardroy was as frank with Guthrie it might serve him well.

'You know where Lochiel is?' he half stammered.

Ewen shut his eyes and smiled, an almost happy smile. 'I think he is where (please God) he will never be found by any redcoat.'

'You mean that he has gone overseas?' asked Keith, almost without thinking.

Ardroy's eyes opened quickly, and for a second, as he looked up at the speaker, there was a startled expression in them. 'You are not expecting me to tell you—'

'No, no,' broke in Keith, very hastily indeed. 'Of course not! But I should be glad if he were so gone, for on my soul there is none of your leaders whom I should be so sorry to see captured.'

Yet with the words he got up and went to the doorway. Yes, Ardroy *had* the secret; and he wished, somehow, that he had not. The moment could no longer be postponed when he must tell him of his conversation with Guthrie, were it only to put him on his guard. Bitterly as he was ashamed, it must be done.

He stood in the doorway a moment, choosing the words in which he should do it, and they were hatefully hard to choose. Hateful, too, was it to leave Ardroy here helpless, but there was no alternative, since he could not possibly take him with him. Yet if Lachlan returned, and in time, and especially if he returned with assistance, he might be able to get his foster-brother away somewhere. Then Ewen Cameron would never fall into Guthrie's hands. In that case what use to torment him with prospects of an interrogatory which might never take place, and which could only be very short?

No; it was mere cowardice to invent excuses for silence; he must do it. He came back very slowly to the pallet.

'I must tell you—' he began in a low voice, and then stopped. Ewen's lashes were lying on his sunken cheek, and did not lift at the address. It was plain that he had fallen anew into one of those sudden exhausted little slumbers, and had not heard even the sentence which was to herald Keith's confession. It would be unnecessarily cruel to rouse him in order to make it. One must wait until he woke naturally, as he had done from the last of these dozes.

Keith took the lantern off the stool and sat down there. And soon the wounded man's sleep became full of disjointed scraps of talk, mostly incoherent; at one time he seemed to think that he was out after the deer on the hills with Lachlan; then he half woke up and muttered: 'But it's we that are the deer now,' and immediately fell into another doze in which he murmured the name of Alison. Gradually, however, his slumber grew more sound; he ceased to mutter and to make little restless movements, and in about five minutes he was in the deep sleep of real repose, which he had not known, perhaps, for many nights – a sleep to make a watcher thankful.

But Keith Windham, frowning, sat watching it with his chin on his hand, conscious that his time was growing very short, that it was light outside, and almost light in this dusky hovel, and that the pool of lantern-shine on the uneven earth floor looked strange and sickly there. He glanced at his watch. No, indeed, he ought not to delay any longer. He took up and blew out the lantern, went outside and roused Mackay, washed the bowl and, filling it with water, placed it and the rest of the food and wine within reach.

His movements had not roused the sleeper in the least. For the last time Keith stooped over him and slipped a hand round his wrist. He knew nothing of medicine, but undoubtedly the beat there was stronger. It would be criminal to wake Ardroy merely in order to tell him something unpleasant. There came to the soldier a momentary idea of scribbling a warning on a page of his pocket-book and leaving this on the sleeper's breast; but it was quite possible that the first person to read such a document would be Guthrie himself.

He rearranged the plaid carefully, and stood for a moment longer looking at the fugitive where he lay at his feet, his head sunk in the dried fern. And he remembered the hut at Kinlochiel last summer, where he had done much the same thing. He had talked somewhat earlier on that occasion, had he not, of obligation and repayment; well, he had more than repaid. Ewen Cameron owed him his life – owed it him, very likely, twice over. Yet Keith was conscious again that no thought of obligation had drawn him to dash in front of those muskets yesterday, nor had the idea of a debt really brought him back now. What then? . . . Absurd! He was a man who prided himself on being unencumbered with friends. Moreover, Ewen Cameron was an enemy.

It was strange, then, with what reluctance, with what half-hopes, half-apprehensions, he got into the saddle and rode away under the paling stars, leaving his enemy to rescue or capture; very strange, since that enemy was likewise a rebel, that he should so greatly have desired the former.

'Your Debtor, Ewen Cameron'

'So in this snare which holds me and appals me,
Where honour hardly lives nor loves remain . . .'
—H. BELLOC. *On Battersea Bridge.*

Chapter One

T H E mist shrouded every mountain-top, sagging downwards in some places like the roof of a tent, and in others, where a perpetual draught blew down a corrie, streaming out like smoke. How different from last week, when, cold as it was up there, the top of the Corryarrick Pass had presented to Major Windham's eyes a view from Badenoch to the hills of Skye. Today, recrossing it, and looking back, he could hardly distinguish through the greyish-white blanket more than three or four of its many traverses winding away below him.

But here, on the lower levels of the mountain road, where it prepared to debouch into that which ran along the Great Glen, this clogging mist had become a fine and most penetrating rain, bedewing every inch of the rider's cloak and uniform, the edges of his wig, his very eyebrows and lashes, and insinuating itself down his collar. Major Windham did not know which was the more objectionable form of moisture, and wished it were late enough in the day to cease exposing himself to either, and to put up for the night at Fort Augustus, which he should reach in another twenty minutes or so. But it was still too early for that, and, bearer as he was of a despatch from Lord Albemarle to the Duke of Cumberland, he must push on beyond Fort Augustus before nightfall; must, indeed, reach the only halting-place between that spot and Inverness, the tiny inn known, from Wade's occupation of it when he was making the road, as the General's Hut. However, he intended to stop at Fort Augustus to bait the horses – and to make an inquiry.

It was six days since he had left Guthrie's camp, and he was not altogether surprised today to find it gone, but, to judge from the litter lying about, only recently gone. There was, therefore, no one to give him news of Ardroy, but he was sure that, if the Jacobite had been made prisoner, he would have been sent or taken to Fort Augustus, and he could get news of him there.

That night in the shieling, just a week ago, seemed to Keith much farther off than that, and the emotions he had known than to have lost their edge. 'Gad, what a fit of philanthropy I had on me that day!' he reflected. If 'Hangman' Hawley came to know of it how he would sneer at him, and the rest of the staff, too. Luckily they would not know. So consoling himself, and cursing the rain anew, he came to Fort Augustus, or rather to what remained of it. Its Highland captors who, during their attack upon it, had partially demolished the new fort, had, on the summons to face Cumberland, blown up and fired most of the residue. A small temporary garrison had been sent there after the victory to secure the abandoned stronghold for the Government; but it had now been taken possession of by a larger force in the shape of the Earl of Loudoun's regiment, under the Earl himself, and eighteen 'independent companies'. These had only marched in a few hours before, in consequence of which influx the whole place was in a state of great turmoil.

There was so little accommodation in the ruined fort that a small village of tents was being erected in the meadows by the mouth of the Tarff, and between the confusion of camp-pitching and the fact that nearly everyone whom he encountered was a newcomer, Keith found it difficult to discover who was or had been responsible for prisoners sent in before Lord Loudoun's arrival. He did, however, elicit the information that Major Guthrie's detachment was now somewhere on the road between Fort Augustus and Inverness. And at last, though he did not succeed in seeing anybody directly responsible, he was told that a wounded Cameron, said to be the head of one of the cadet branches of the clan, had been captured the previous week and sent in by that very detachment, and that he had been given proper care and was progressing favourably.

That was all Keith wanted to know for the moment, and he delayed no longer. A certain vague disquiet which had teased him during the past week about Guthrie's possible treatment of his prisoner was allayed. For the rest, he had already made his plans about Ardroy. It was at Inverness, with Cumberland, that he could really do Ewen service, especially if the Duke did take him on to his personal staff. To His Royal Highness he could then represent what he owed to the captured rebel, and, before he himself returned with the Commander-in-Chief to Flanders, he might very well have the satisfaction of knowing that the object of his 'philanthropy' had been set at liberty.

As he turned away from Fort Augustus, where the vista of Loch Ness was completely blotted out in rain, and addressed himself to the long steep climb up the Inverness road, Keith's thoughts went back to the Earl of Albermarle in Perth, craving like himself to get overseas once more – whence, though colonel of the Coldstream Guards, he had come to serve as a volunteer under Cumberland. His lordship, who had, moreover, greatly preferred commanding the front line in the recent battle to his present post with the Hessian troops in Perth, had lamented his situation quite openly to Cumberland's messenger; he detested Scotland, he announced, and had fears, from a sentence in the despatch which that messenger had delivered to him, that he might be appointed to succeed Hawley in this uncongenial country. Having thus, somewhat unwisely, betrayed his sentiments to Major Windham, he was more or less obliged to beg his discretion, in promising which Keith had revealed his own fellow-feeling about the North. When they parted, therefore, Lord Albermarle had observed with much graciousness that if this horrid fate of succeeding General Hawley should overtake him, he would not forget Major Windham, though he supposed that the latter might not then be in Scotland for him to remember. No; Keith, though grateful for his lordship's goodwill, distinctly hoped that he would not. He trusted to be by then in a dryer climate and a country less afflicted with steep roads . . . less afflicted also with punitive measures, though, since Perth was not Inverness, he was not so much dominated by those painful impressions of brutality as he had been a week ago.

The greater part of the lengthy and tiresome ascent from the level of Loch Ness was now over, and Keith and Dougal Mackay found themselves again more or less in the region of mist, but on a flat stretch of road with a strip of moorland on one hand. Water glimmered ahead on the left: it was little Loch Tarff, its charms dimmed by the weather. Keith just noticed its presence, tightened his reins, and, trotting forward on the welcome level, continued his dreams about the future.

Twenty-five yards farther, and these were brought abruptly to a close. Without the slightest warning there was a sharp report on his right, and a bullet sped in front of him, so close that it frightened his horse. Himself considerably startled too, he tried simultaneously to soothe the beast and to tug out a pistol from his holster. Meanwhile, Dougal Mackay, with great promptitude and loud Gaelic cries, was urging his more docile steed over the heather towards a boulder which he evidently suspected of harbouring the marksman.

As soon as he could get his horse under control Keith also made over the strip of moorland, and arrived in time to see a wild, tattered, tartan-clad figure, with a musket in its hands, slide down from the top of the boulder, drop on to hands and knees among the heather and bogmyrtle, and begin to wriggle away like a snake. Major Windham levelled his pistol and fired, somewhat at random, for his horse was still plunging; and the Highlander collapsed and lay still. Keith trotted towards him; the man had already abandoned his musket and lay in a heap on his side. The Englishman was just going to dismount when shouts from Dougal Mackay, who had ridden round the boulder, stayed him. 'Do not pe going near him, sir; the man will not pe hit whateffer!' And as this statement coincided with Keith's own impression that his bullet had gone wide, he stayed in the saddle and covered the would-be assassin with his other pistol, while Mackay, who certainly did not lack courage slid off his own horse and came running.

And it was even as Mackay had said. At the sound of the feet swishing through the heather the heap of dirty tartan lying there was suddenly, with one bound, a living figure which, leaping up dirk in hand, rushed straight, not at the dismounted orderly, but at the officer on the horse. Had Keith not had his pistol ready he could hardly have saved himself, mounted though he was, from a deadly thrust. The man was at his horse's head when he fired. . . . This time he did not miss; he could not. . . .

'I suppose I have blown his head to pieces,' he said next moment, with a slightly shaken laugh.

'Inteet, I will pe thinking so,' replied Mackay, on his knees in the heather. 'But it will be pest to make sure.' And he put his hand to his own dirk.

'No, no!' commanded Keith, as he bent from the saddle for somehow the idea of stabbing a dead man, even a potential murderer, was repugnant to him. 'It is not necessary; he was killed instantly.'

There could be small doubt of that. One side of the Highlander's bearded face was all blackened by the explosion, and as he lay there, his eyes wide and fixed, the blood ran backwards through his scorched and tangled hair like a brook among water-weeds. The ball had struck high up on the brow. It came to Keith with a sense of shock that the very torn and faded philabeg which he wore was of the Cameron tartan. He was sorry. . . .

Deterred, unwillingly, from the use of his dirk, the zealous Mackay next inquired whether he should not put the cateran's body over his horse and bring him to Inverness, so that, dead or alive, he could be hanged at the Cross there as a warning.

'No, leave him, poor devil,' said Keith, turning his horse. 'No need for that; he has paid the price already. Let him lie.' He felt curiously little resentment, and wondered at the fact.

Dougal Mackay, however, was not going to leave the musket lying too.

'Ta *gunna* – she is Sassenach,' he announced, examining it.

'Take it, then,' said Keith. 'Come, we must get on to the General's Hut before this mist grows thicker.'

So they rode away, leaving the baffled assailant staring into vacancy, his dirk still gripped in his hand, and under his head the heather in flower before its time.

Once more the road mounted; then fell by a long steep gradient. The General's Hut, a small and very unpretentious hostelry, of the kind known as a 'creel house', was at Boleskine, down on its lower levels, and before Keith reached it he could see that its outbuildings were occupied by soldiers. They were probably Major Guthrie's detachment. Indeed, as he dismounted, a uniformed figure which he knew came round the corner of the inn, but it stopped dead on seeing him, then, with no further sign of recognition, turned abruptly and disappeared again. It was Lieutenant Paton.

So these *were* Guthrie's men, and he could hear more of

Ardroy. But he would have preferred to hear it from Paton rather than from Guthrie, and wished that he had been quick enough to stop that young man.

The first person whom Keith saw when he entered the dirty little parlour was Guthrie himself – or rather, the back of him – just sitting down to table.

'Come awa', Foster, is that you?' he called out. 'Quick noo; the brose is getting cauld.' Receiving no response he turned round. 'Dod! 'tis Major Windham!'

Keith came forward perforce. 'Good evening, Major Guthrie. Yes, I am on my way back to Inverness.'

'Back frae Perth, eh?' commented Guthrie. 'By the high road this time, then, I'm thinkin'. Sit ye doun, Major, and Luckie whate'er she ca's hersel' shall bring anither cover. Ah, here comes Foster – let me present Captain Foster of ma regiment tae ye, Major Windham. Whaur's yon lang-leggit birkie of a Paton?'

'Not coming to supper, sir,' replied Captain Foster, saluting the new arrival. 'He begs you to excuse him; he has a letter to write, or he is feeling indisposed – I forget which.'

'Indeed!' said Guthrie, raising his sandy eyebrows. 'He was well enough and free o' correspondence a while syne. However, it's an ill wind— Ye ken the rest. Major Windham can hae his place and his meat.'

Keith sat down, with as good a grace as he could command, at the rough, clothless table. This Foster was presumably the officer whose bed he had occupied in the camp, a man more of Guthrie's stamp than of Paton's, but better mannered. Lieutenant Paton's absence, coupled with his abrupt disappearance, was significant, but why should the young man not wish to meet Major Keith Windham? Perhaps because the latter had got him into trouble after all over his 'philanthropy'.

Between the three the talk ran on general topics, and it was not until the meal was half over that Guthrie suddenly said:

'Weel, Major, I brocht in yer Cameron frien' after ye left.'

Keith murmured that he was glad to hear it.

'But I got little for ma pains,' continued Guthrie, pouring himself out a glass of wine – only his second, for, to Keith's surprise, he appeared to be an abstemious man. He set down the bottle and looked hard at the Englishman. 'But ye yersel' were nae luckier, it seems.'

Keith returned his look. 'I am afraid that I do not understand.'

'Ye see, I ken ye went back tae the sheiling yon nicht.'

'Yes, I imagined that you would discover it,' said Keith coolly. 'I trust that you received my message of apology for departing without taking leave of you?'

'Yer message of apology!' repeated Major Guthrie. 'Ha, ha! Unfortunately ye didn't apologize for the right offence! Ye suld hae apologized for stealing a march on me ahint ma back. 'Twas a pawky notion, yon, was it no', Captain Foster?'

'I must repeat that I am completely in the dark as to your meaning, Major Guthrie!' said Keith in growing irritation.

'Isna he the innocent man! But I forgive ye, Major – since ye gained naething by gangin' back.'

'*Gained!*' ejaculated Keith. 'What do you mean, sir? I did not go back to the shieling to gain anything. I went—'

'Aye, I ken what ye said ye gaed for,' interrupted Guthrie with a wink. ' 'Twas devilish canny, as I said, and deceived the rebel himsel' for a while. All yon ride in the nicht juist tae tak' him food and dress his wounds! And when ye were there tendin' him sae kindly ye never speired aboot Lochiel and what he kennt o' him, and whaur the chief micht be hidin', did ye? – Never deny it, Major, for the rebel didna when I pit it tae him!'

'You devil!' exclaimed Keith, springing up. 'What did you say to him about me?'

Guthrie kept his seat, and pulled down Captain Foster, who, murmuring 'Gentlemen, gentlemen!' had risen too. 'Nae need tae be sae disturbel'd, Captain Foster; I'm na. That's for them that hae uneasy consciences. What did I say tae him? Why, I tellt him the truth, Major Windham: why ye set such store on saving his life, and how ye thocht he might be persuaded tae "drap a hint" aboot Lochiel. Forbye he didna believe that at first.'

Keith caught his breath. 'You told him those lies . . . to his face . . . and he believed . . .' He could get no farther.

'Lies, were they?' asked Guthrie, leaning over the table. 'Ye ne'er advised me tae bring him into camp tae "complete ma knowledge"? Eh, I hae ye there fine! Awheel, I did my best, Major Windham; nane can dae mair. But I doot he has the laugh of us, the callant, for he tellt me naething, either by hints or ony ither gait, a' the time I had him in ma care. So I e'en sent him wi' a bit report tae Fort Augustus, and there he is the noo, as ye may have heard, if ye speired news o' him when ye came by.'

Keith had turned very white. 'I might have known that you would play some dirty trick or other!' he said, and flung straight out of the room.

Fool, unspeakable fool that he was not to have foreseen something of this kind with a man of Guthrie's stamp! He *had* had moments of uneasiness at the thought of Ardroy's probable interview with him, but he had never anticipated anything quite so base as this. 'Take me to Lieutenant Paton at once!' he said peremptorily to the first soldier he came across.

The man led him towards a barn looming through the mist at a little distance. The door was ajar, and Keith went in, to see a dimly lit space with trusses of straw laid down in rows for the men, and at one end three horses, his own among them, with a soldier watering them. The young lieutenant, his hands behind his back, was watching the process. Keith went straight up to him.

'Can I have a word with you alone, Mr Paton?'

The young man stiffened and flushed; then, with obvious reluctance, ordered the soldier out. And when the man with his clanging buckets had left the building, Paton stood rather nervously smoothing the flank of one of the horses – not at all anxious to talk.

'Mr Paton,' said Keith without preamble, 'what devil's work went on in your camp over the prisoner from Ben Loy?' And then, at sight of the look on Paton's face, he cried out: 'Good God, man, do you think that I had a hand in it, and is that why you would not break bread with me?'

Lieutenant Paton looked at the ground. 'I . . . indeed I found it hard to believe that you could act so, when you seemed so concerned for the prisoner, but—'

'In Heaven's name, let us have this out!' cried Keith. 'What did Major Guthrie say to Mr Cameron? He appears to have tried to make him believe an infamous thing of me – that I went back to the shieling that night merely in order to get information out of him! Surely he did not succeed in making

him think so – even if he succeeded with you . . . Answer
me, if you please!'

The younger man seemed very ill at ease. 'I cannot say, sir,
what Mr Cameron believed about you in the end. He certainly
refused, and indignantly, to believe it at first.'

'He *cannot* have believed it!' said Keith passionately. ' "In
the end"? How long, then, did Major Guthrie have him in his
custody?'

'He kept him for twenty-four hours, sir – in order to see if
he would make any disclosures about Lochiel.' And Lieutenant
Paton added, in a very dry tone, turning away and busying
himself with a horse's head tall: 'A course which it seems that
you advised.'

Keith gave a sound like a groan. 'Did the Major tell Mr
Cameron that also?'

Paton nodded. 'Yes, he did – and more, too: whether true
or not I have no means of judging.'

Keith had the sensation that the barn, or something less
material, was closing in round him. This honest boy, too—
'Look here, Mr Paton, I will be frank with you. I was so
desperately afraid that Ardroy would be left to die in that
shieling that I did suggest to Major Guthrie that it might be of
advantage to bring him into camp, thought I knew that he
would have his trouble for nothing. Though I unfortunately
recommended that course I was perfectly certain that Mr
Cameron would not give the slightest inkling of any knowledge that he might have.'

'No, it was plain from the beginning that he would not,'
said the young man, 'and that was why . . .' He broke off.
'If Mr Cameron is a friend of yours it is a good thing that
you were not in our camp that morning . . . or no, perhaps
a misfortune, because you might have succeeded in stopping it
sooner. I could not.'

'Succeeded in stopping what?' asked Keith. Then the inner
flavour of some of Guthrie's recent words began to be apparent
to him. He caught Paton by the arm. 'You surely do not mean
that Major Guthrie resorted to – violent measures? It's impossible!'

Thus captured, the young soldier turned and faced him.
'Reassure yourself, sir,' he said quickly, seeing the horror and
disgust on his companion's face. 'He could not carry them out;

the prisoner was in no state for it. He could only threaten, and . . . question.'

'He threatened to shoot him after all?'

'No, not to shoot him, to flog him.' And as Keith gave an exclamation and loosed his hold, Paton added: 'And he went very near doing it, too.'

'Threatened to flog him! Mr Paton, you are jesting!' said Keith incredulously. 'Flog a badly wounded prisoner, and a gentleman – a chieftain – to boot!'

'I am not jesting, sir; I wish I were. But I am thankful to say that it was not carried out. - Now, if you will excuse me, Major Windham, I must be about my duties.' His tone indicated that he would be glad to leave a distasteful subject.

But Keith made a movement to bar his passage. 'Mr. Paton, forgive my insistence, but your duties must wait a little. You cannot leave the matter there! For my own sake I must know what was said to Mr Cameron. You see how nearly it concerns my honour. I implore you to try to recall everything that passed!'

Reluctantly the young man yielded. 'Very well, sir; but I had best speak to the sergeant to ensure that we are not disturbed, for this barn is the men's quarters.'

He went out to give an order. Hardly knowing what he did, Keith turned to his horse, busy pulling hay from the rack, and looked him over to see that Mackay had rubbed him down properly. Threatened with flogging – Ewen Cameron!

Paton came back, closed the door and brought up a couple of pails, which he inverted and suggested as seats. 'You must be tired, Major, after your long ride, and I am afraid that this will be a bit of a sederunt.' So Keith sat down in the stall to hear what his ill-omened suggestion had brought on the man whom he had saved.

Chapter Two

IT appeared that Major Guthrie, on learning next morning of Major Windham's departure on his errand of mercy, had been not only exceedingly angry, but suspicious as well – 'or at least,' said Paton, 'he declared that he was suspicious' – and sent off a party almost immediately to fetch in the wounded rebel from the shieling. About a couple of hours later they returned, carrying him on a litter, which they deposited outside their commander's tent, where Paton happened to be at the moment. Guthrie immediately went out to him, and said – the narrator remembered his first words exactly – 'Well, my fine fellow, and so you know where Lochiel is like to be skulking!' The prisoner replied by asking whether Major Guthrie thought he should tell him if he did? Major Guthrie retorted, with a grin, that he knew it was the thing to begin with a little bluster of the sort, but that they had better get to business without wasting time. 'And he added, sir,' said the young soldier, looking away, ' "I know that you know; Major Windham says so." '

Keith had put his hand over his eyes. 'Yes; go on,' he said after a moment.

'This was plainly rather a blow to Mr Cameron,' continued Paton. 'I saw the blood rush to his face. "*What* did you say?" he asked. The Major replied that you, sir, being a loyal subject of King George, were just as eager to secure Lochiel as himself, which was the reason why you had very properly stopped him from having the prisoner shot. To that Mr Cameron replied, short and sharp, "I don't believe it!" The Major affected to misunderstand this, and . . . well, sir, he said a good many things incriminating you in the affair, twisting what you had, perhaps said . . .'

'Try, for God's sake, to remember what those things were,' begged Keith miserably, without looking up.

The young man paused a moment, evidently trying to remember accurately.

'First, I think, he told Mr Cameron that you had said he was Cameron of Ardroy, Lochiel's cousin, and had had you as his prisoner after the affair at High Bridge, and he added: "I doubt he wanted to get even with you for that!" And to make his assertion more credible he asked Mr Cameron how otherwise he should have known who he was, since he took him for a gillie when he had him up against the shieling wall. And the Major went on to say that for the news of Mr Cameron's identity he was grateful to you, but not so grateful when he found that you had stolen a march on him by sneaking back to the shieling by night in order to get information out of the prisoner before he could. But at that Mr Cameron tried to raise himself on the litter, and burst out, "That's a lie!" And then the Major silenced him by what I can only suppose was an arrow drawn at a venture, since you . . . I don't suppose that you . . .' Paton began to stumble.

'Let me have it!' said Keith, looking up this time.

'He said, "And so he never speired about Lochiel . . . where he was . . . if yu kenned where he was?"'

Keith stared at the narrator half dazed. 'How did he know that . . . he *could* not have known it!'

'As I say, it seemed to silence Mr Cameron altogether,' continued Paton, glancing at him with a sort of pity. 'He looked quite dizzy as he dropped back on the litter. But the Major laughed. And he went on, in that bantering way he has: "I hope you did not tell him, for I want you to tell *me*. Did you tell him?" The rebel took no notice of this question; he had shut his eyes. It was as I looked at him then, sir, and saw the effect which that question had had on him, that I first began, I confess, to have doubts of your good faith.'

'You had cause,' answered Keith with a groan. 'I did ask him about Lochiel – in all innocence. My God, what he must think of me!' He took his head between his hands. 'Go on!'

'Finding that Mr Cameron was silent,' resumed Paton. 'Major Guthrie went nearer and said something, I do not exactly remember what, about dropping a hint inadvertently with regard to Lochiel's hiding-place, which it was easy to do, he said, and which he should give the prisoner every opportunity of doing, keeping him there, indeed, until he did. He kept harping for a while on this question of dropping a hint, and he brought you even into that, for he said that it was your suggestion, that you had advised him to bring the rebel into camp and watch him well for that purpose. . . . And from what you have just told me, sir, it seems that that was true.'

Paton paused; but Keith, his head between his hands, said nothing; he was beyond it. This was what came of doing evil in order to accomplish good!

'Still Mr Cameron took no notice,' pursued Paton, 'even when the Major went on to say in so many words that you had betrayed him – Mr Cameron – and had then ridden off, leaving him the dirty work to do. Then he changed his tone, and said: "But I shall not flinch from it; 'tis my duty. Do you know, Mr Cameron of Ardroy, how we deal with folk that have valuable information and will not part with it?" At that the prisoner did open his eyes, and said with a good deal of contempt that, from what he had seen of the Major, he could very well guess.

'The Major at that bent over him and gripped him by the nearer arm. He may not have observed that it was bandaged – I cannot say – and repeated: "Ah, you can quite imagine, can you? D'you think you'll like it?" Mr Cameron did not answer; perhaps he could not, for he was biting his lip, and I saw the sweat come out on his brow. Major Guthrie let go and stood up again, and said that a flogging with belts would soon loosen his tongue; and that did rouse Mr Cameron, for he coloured hotly and said he thought the Major forgot that he was a gentleman. But the Major replied with a chuckle that he looked so little like one at present that it was easy to assume that he was not. Then he asked him whether he intended to save himself from this unpleasant experience, as he easily could do; Mr Cameron's look was sufficient answer to that. So, to my horror, the Major sent for the drummers and ordered a tent to be struck, in order to have the pole available to tie him up to.'

'This is intolerable!' exclaimed Keith, starting up. 'Stop! I had rather not—' He pulled himself together. 'No, I have got to hear it. Go on!'

'I assure you that I did not enjoy it,' said the young officer, 'for I thought that the matter was going through. They lifted Mr Cameron off the litter; he could not stand, it appeared, owing to the wound in his thigh, and the men were obliged to support him. But the Major said to him that he would not be able to fall this time, as he had done yesterday, because we had ropes here. . . . I myself, who would willingly have interfered before, sir, had there been any chance of being listened to, now took the Major by the arm and told him plainly that he would kill the prisoner if he was so barbarous as to have him flogged in his present condition. But he shook me off, and said, when everything was ready (except Mr Cameron himself, who was still held up there, facing him, as white as you please, but perfectly unyielding and defiant): "Now, before you make acquaintance with His Majesty's leather, will you tell me what you know about Lochiel?" And the rebel, with his eyes blazing, said, in a sudden access of fury: "Not if you cut me to pieces!"

'Well, sir, though I am convinced that the Major was not acting a part and merely threatening, but that he really meant to go through with the horrid business, I think it must have come to him then that, if he did, he would have Mr Cameron dead on his hands, as I had warned him, and there would be an end to that source of information. (It is possible, too, that he thought he might be called to account for it afterwards.) And even the men were looking uneasy and murmuring a little. So he said that he would postpone the flogging until the afternoon. He had the prisoner carried into his own tent, not much, I fear, the better for this scene; and in his tent Mr Cameron was all the rest of the day and the night. I do not know what passed in there, for whenever I made an effort to go in, I was stopped; but I am sure the Major questioned him pretty continuously. He still spoke of the flogging taking place, but it never did. Next morning I was not surprised to hear that the prisoner seemed worse, and in a fever, so that the Major resolved to be rid of him, and sent him to Fort Augustus. I was heartily glad, for his own sake, to see Mr Cameron taken away. And at Fort Augustus he must have had care, or he would not be alive now, which he is, for I asked news of him yesterday, as we came by. But that I should be ashamed to meet him, I would fain have seen him to ask his pardon.'

Paton's voice ceased; in the silence one of the horses near them stamped and blew out its nostrils. Keith, standing there very still, released his own tightly gripped elbows.

'Mr Paton, I thank you most heartily for your frankness. I, too, am ashamed – with much more cause than you, I think – yet I am going back to Fort Augustus to see Mr Cameron.'

'Back to Fort Augustus – tonight!' said Paton, rather startled.

'Yes, tonight. My horse,' he glanced at that animal, 'can still carry me so far – a matter of ten or twelve miles, is it not? I intended to lie here the night, and to start about six o'clock tomorrow morning for Inverness. I shall lie at Fort Augustus instead, and start proportionately earlier, that is all. I must find my orderly at once, but I shall not take him back with me.'

Paton said no more, and they went out of the barn together, by which evacuation the waiting soldiers outside, huddled against its wall for shelter, were enabled to enter their sleeping-place. While the surprised Mackay resaddled his officer's horse, Keith strode back to the inn parlour. But just outside, where he could hear Guthrie's voice in conversation, he paused. If he meant to get back to Fort Augustus he must not enter Guthrie's presence first; the fury and resentment which possessed him could have but one result – a quarrel with the Lowlander. Moreover, Lieutenant Paton might suffer for his communicativeness. Clenching his hands, Keith turned away from temptation.

But there was one last question to ask.

'Mr Paton,' he said in a low voice as his horse was brought towards him, 'have you any notion why Major Guthrie hates me so, for it is plain that he does?'

And to his surprise the young man answered, in a voice equally low:

'I have a very good notion why, sir. He had had great hopes of securing that post on General Hawley's staff which was eventually given to you. Your obtaining it was a very sore point with him, because he thought his claims superior to those of an officer who – who . . .' Paton hesitated.

'Yes, I understand,' said Keith, his mouth tightening. 'Who had lost one of the companies at High Bridge.' Guthrie's sneers on that fatal ride were explained now. 'So that was my offence!' he said under his breath, as he swung into the saddle. 'And this is how he has avenged himself!'

The wind had risen greatly in the last hour, and the rain was no longer a fine, almost caressing, drizzle; it beat upon the rider as he urged his horse back along the lower levels with a vehemence which predicted real difficulty in proceeding when he should reach the higher. But he did not notice it.

There could not be the slightest doubt that Ewen Cameron must believe him to have acted in a manner unspeakably treacherous and vile. From the deadly success of Guthrie's 'arrow at a venture', as Paton had rightly called it, he must even think that his visitor had gone straight back from tending him in the shieling to Guthrie's camp with the news that he had succeeded in gaining the fugitive's confidence, and had ascertained that he did know of Lochiel's hiding-place. It was an absolutely intolerable thought, and nothing, nothing should stop him until he had seen Ardroy and assured him of his innocence – neither the rising storm nor fatigue, nor the possible danger in riding thus alone at night (though to that, despite the afternoon's attempt on his life, he gave scarcely a thought), nor Lord Albemarle's despatch. It was a mercy that this contained, as he knew, nothing of urgency, nothing but a mere expression of compliments, and that he could therefore retrace his steps consistently with his military obligations. In any case, the letter would reach Inverness no later than if he had spent the night at the General's Hut, so on that score at least his mind was at rest.

It was certainly the only score on which it was. The more Keith thought of the situation, the more it horrified him. Why, good God, Ardroy might even imagine that the infamous proposal of flogging, which turned him hot to think of, came from *him*! Guthrie was evidently quite capable of stating that it had, and though Paton had not reported him as having done so in his hearing, who knew what had been said, what had been done, during the rest of the twenty-four hours in Guthrie's tent? He was utterly without scruple, and Ardroy completely helpless.

Yet even now Keith could hardly blame himself for his total absence of suspicion that Guthrie might be tempted to do more than question his prisoner . . . rather closely perhaps. No, he told himself again and again, he could not have guessed to what he was delivering up Ardroy. A prisoner-of-war – above all, an officer – in a Christian country and a civilized century stood in no danger of such proceedings. It was true that there had been barbarity after the battle, barbarity which had sickened him, but there had never been any suggestion of deliberately torturing prisoners in order to extract information. (For Major Lockhart of Cholmondeley's regiment, Captain Carolina Scott of Guise's, and Captain Ferguson of H.M.S. *Furness* – all Scots, too – had still to win their spurs in this field.)

Keith was up on the higher levels now, where the wind was really savage, and the rain stung like missiles. It seemed as though the elements desired to oppose his return. But his thoughts ran ahead of him to Fort Augustus. Would there be difficulty in getting access to the prisoner? There might be some, but an officer on Hawley's staff, riding on the Duke's business, would be hard to gainsay. If necessary he should approach the Earl of Loudoun himself. And in what state should he find Ardroy? What sort of a captivity had been his now that he was out of that scoundrel Guthrie's clutches? Remembrances of Inverness, very sinister remembrances, kept floating into his mind. No, it would be different here; and, as Paton had pointed out, they must have taken good care of the Highlander, or he would hardly be alive now, judging from his state a week ago – a state which must have been, which evidently had been, rendered even more precarious by Guthrie's damnable proceedings. On Guthrie himself he hardly dared allow his mind to dwell; but there could not be another like him at Fort Augustus!

And when he had got access to Ardroy? Surely it would not be difficult to convince him that it was Major Guthrie's almost incredible spite and jealousy which had wrought this mischief, that nothing in the world had been farther from his own thoughts than the belief that Ewen would betray his Chief? Yes, but unfortunately, though he could deny everything else (save the mere fact of having been forced to establish Ardroy's identity) he could not deny that most unlucky suggestion to which, in desperation, he had been reduced on the hillside. Oh, if only he had not shirked telling Ewen Cameron of it that night in the shieling! Better, far better, to have faced a measure of shame on that occasion than to have left in Major Guthrie's hands a weapon capable of working this havoc!

For Guthrie, it was clear, had, in his calculated spite, struck at him through Ewen and at Ewen through him. He had evidently *wished* the Highlander to believe himself betrayed. Did he then think the ties between them so close when they were only . . . What were they then? Was it really only philanthropy, as Keith had assured himself a few hours ago, which had sent him back to the shieling that night? It was certainly not philanthropy which was driving him to Fort August now.

At nine o'clock, wet and buffeted, he was back in the lines of Loudoun's camp, still humming with life. Mentioning that he was on the staff he asked, as he had asked that afternoon, to see the officer in charge of prisoners there. Once again there was an obstacle; this time it appeared that the officer, a certain Captain Greening, was closeted with Lord Loudoun, who was very busy, and not to be disturbed save for a matter of great importance.

Keith still retained enough sense of proportion to realize that a private inquiry after the well-being of a rebel prisoner was not likely to wear that aspect in the eyes of Cope's late adjutant-general. However, perhaps he could arrive at seeing Ardroy without the consent of Captain Greening, so he said to his informant, the officer of the guard:

'I wish to see a certain Mr Ewen Cameron of Ardroy, who lies here a prisoner. He was taken last week not far from the Corryarrick Pass. Do you think this would be possible without deranging Captain Greening?'

'Cameron of Ardroy?' said the lieutenant with an accent of enlightenment. 'Oh, have you come from Inverness about the question of Lochiel's capture, sir? Then you'll be glad to hear that we have got the necessary information at last.'

Keith's heart gave a great twist – foolishly, surely! 'Ah, from whom?'

'Why, from him – from Cameron of Ardroy, naturally. We knew that he had it.'

This time Keith's heart did not twist – it seemed to die in his breast. 'Got it from him – from *him*!' he faltered with cold lips. 'When?'

'Last night, I believe,' answered the lieutenant carelessly, pulling his cloak closer to him. 'But I fear that I cannot give you permission to visit him, sir, and as Captain Greening is—'

But to his surprise the staff officer was gripping him hard by the arm. 'Tell me, in God's name, what means you used? Ardroy would never—' He seemed unable to finish.

'Means? I really don't know,' replied the lieutenant, still more surprised. 'I should be obliged if you would let go my arm, sir! I have nothing to do with the prisoners. Perhaps this Cameron was promised his liberty or something of the sort – but on my soul! I don't know . . . or care,' he muttered under his breath, rubbing his arm as Keith released it.

'Promised!' cried Keith in a tempest of fury and horror. 'No, he has been tortured into it! – that is the only possible explanation of his giving that information – if it be true that he has done so. My God, what has this campaign reduced men to! Take me to Lord Loudoun at once!'

'I cannot, sir,' protested the lieutenant. 'He has given the strictest orders—'

'Take me to him at once,' repeated Keith in a dangerous

voice; and the young officer, probably thinking that the safest way to deal with a superior who seemed off his balance was to humour him, shrugged his shoulders, and began to lead him in the rain between the tents.

Last night! That meant, then, that for nearly a week they had been trying . . . and had succeeded at last in wresting the secret from a man badly wounded, ill from starvation, and now, perhaps, dying – dying as much of a broken heart as from their usage of him. It was with that unbearable picture of Ewen Cameron in his mind that, after parleys with sentries of which he heard nothing. Keith stepped into the Earl of Loudoun's presence without any clear idea of what he was going to do there.

He found himself in a large, well-furnished tent, with a brazier burning in one corner, and, round a table, several officers of various ranks (most of them, like the Earl himself, wearing tartan), was announced as an officer of the staff from Inverness, and, duly saluting, gave his name and regiment.

The Earl of Loudoun – more Lowland Scot than Highlander in his appearance – looked less annoyed at the interruption that might have been expected; indeed his air showed that he supposed the intruder to be the bearer of some tidings of importance from headquarters.

'You are on His Royal Highness's staff, Major Windham?' he asked.

'On General Hawley's, my Lord,' replied Keith. 'I am on my way back to Inverness from Perth, and I have ventured to ask for this interview because—'

'You have not a despatch for me from the Duke, then – or from General Hawley?'

'No, my Lord. I have but seized this opportunity of appealing to your Lordship on behalf of a prisoner here' – the Earl's homely, blunt-featured face changed – 'who, if he has really made any disclosures, can only have done so under violent measures, taken unknown to your Lordship, and I—'

'What is all this about a prisoner?' interrupted Loudoun, frowning. 'You mean to say, Major Windham, that you are here on a purely private matter, when I especially gave orders— Who admitted you to me under false pretences?'

But the officer of the guard had discreetly vanished.

'Is it a purely private matter, my Lord,' retorted Keith hotly,

'that a badly wounded Highland gentleman should be tortured
into giving information against his own Chief? It seems to me
a matter affecting the good name of the whole army. I only
hope that I have been misinformed, and that no such disclosures have been dragged from him.'

'Have you come here, sir,' asked Lord Loudoun with increasing displeasure, 'and on no one's authority but your own to
dictate to me on the treatment of prisoners?'

'No, indeed my Lord,' replied Keith, making an effort to be
properly deferential. 'I have come, on the contrary, because I
feel sure that your Lordship—'

'If you want news of any prisoner,' interrupted his Lordship with a wave of the hand, 'you must wait until Captain
Greening here is at liberty. Meanwhile you will perhaps have
the goodness to remember that I only marched in to Fort
Augustus this morning, and am still so pressed with business
that I see small chance of sleep tonight if I am to be interrupted
in this manner.'

It was a dismissal: less harsh than at one moment seemed
likely, but proving to Keith that he had gained nothing. He
tried another tack.

'My Lord, give me permission then, I implore you, to visit
the prisoner in question, Mr Ewen Cameron of Ardroy.'

Loudoun's eyebrows went up. 'Is there anyone of that name
confined here, Captain Greening?' he asked in an annoyed
voice, turning to a fair, rather womanish-looking young man
on his left.

Captain Greening smiled a peculiar little smile. 'Oh, yes, my
Lord; he has been here nearly a week. Major Windham has
already made inquiries for him once today, so I hear – when
he passed on his way to Inverness this afternoon. I was out of
camp at the time.'

'What!' exclaimed the Earl, looking from the officer to
Keith in astonishment. 'Major Windham has been through
Fort Augustus once already today? This is very singular!
Instead of your questioning me, Major Windham, I will ask
you to explain your own conduct. Kindly tell me on what
errand you originally left headquarters?'

Keith saw a possible gulf opening for himself now. But he
was too passionately indignant to care much. 'I have been to
Perth, my Lord, with a despatch from His Royal Highness to

Lord Albemarle. I was on my way back to Inverness today
when I heard that Cameron of Ardroy—'

'Leave Cameron of Ardroy out of it, if you please!' said
Lord Loudoun in growing anger. 'What I want, Major Wind-
ham, is some explanation of your own extraordinary be-
haviour. I gather that you are now on your way back from
Perth. Are you carrying despatches from Lord Albermarle to
His Royal Highness, or are you empty-handed?'

'I have a letter, of no particular moment, from Lord
Albemarle to the Duke,' replied Keith more warily.

'You have, at any rate, a despatch, sir. You have passed this
place already on your way to Inverness, carrying it. Some
hours later you are back again, making fresh inquiries about
a rebel. Had you confided your despatch to another hand in
the interval?'

'No, my Lord,' confessed Keith. 'Knowing that the matter
was not urgent, and that it was impossible for me to reach
Inverness tonight, I resolved to lie at the General's Hut. There
I heard something which determined me to have more reliable
news of Mr Cameron of Ardroy, to whom I owe it that I am
alive at all today. Instead of going to bed at the General's Hut
I rode back here, and whether I start from Boleskine at six or
from Fort Augustus at half-past four, Lord Albemarle's letter
will reach His Royal Highness's hands at exactly the same
hour.'

'You seem to have a strangely easy idea of your military
duties, Major Windham,' commented Lord Loudoun, drumming on the table. 'May I ask how long you have borne His
Majesty's commission?'

'Twelve years,' answered Keith curtly.

'And in all those years you have not learnt the sacredness of
a despatch! You are entrusted with one to the Commander-
in-Chief, and you take upon yourself to turn back in order to
assure yourself of the welfare of a rebel prisoner! – Is it true
that this man has made a disclosure?' he asked suddenly of
Captain Greening.

'Quite true, my Lord,' responded the fair young officer. 'I
have notes of it here; it was one of the matters which I desired
to bring to your Lordship's notice. It relates to Lochiel's
hiding-place near Loch Arkaig, and will prove of the greatest
service in your Lordship's future operations.'

At that reply all thoughts of his own situation abandoned Keith; he was caught up again in a wave of fury and shame. 'My God!' he cried, striding forward, his eyes fixed on Captain Greening, 'are there devils here too? You have tortured him into it . . . never deny it, I'll not believe you! As well be in a camp of Red Indians or African savages! Inverness was bad enough, with its prisons stuffed with purposely neglected wounded; then that man Guthrie, and now—'

Lord Loudoun sprang up, very threatening of aspect. 'Major Windham, may I ask you to remember where you are! I'll not be spoken to in such a manner!'

'I was not addressing you, my Lord,' said Keith fiercely. 'I know that you only reached Fort Augustus this morning. You are not responsible for what has been going on – God knows what it was – before you came. But this officer here—'

'Be silent, sir!' shouted the Earl of Loudoun. 'Neither will I have aspersions cast on officers now under my command . . . and by a member of General Hawley's staff, too! Are your own hands so clean, pray? You do not deserve that I should reply to your insinuations, but – Captain Greening, *was* this information got from the Cameron prisoner by unlawful means?'

'No, my Lord, I assure you that it was not. He gave it . . . voluntarily.' But again there was that little smile.

'There, you hear, sir!' said the Earl. 'Your charges—'

'I don't believe it,' said Keith in the same moment. 'I will not believe it until I hear it from Ardroy himself.'

And at that Lord Loudoun completely lost his temper. 'God's name, am I to suffer you to browbeat me in my own tent? – you, who have just behaved in a manner unpardonable in a soldier! Major Windham, I place you under arrest for insubordination. You will kindly give up your sword!'

It was as if a douche of cold water had descended on Keith's head. His left hand went to his sword-hilt. 'Insubordination, my Lord? No, I protest!'

'Very well, it shall be for neglect of duty, then,' said the Earl, still very angry. 'Lord Albemarle's despatch is in truth not safe with a man who can go twenty miles out of his way while carrying it. I shall send it on by one of my own aides-de-camp tonight. Give it up at once, if you do not wish to be searched. Captain Munro, call a guard!'

Like rain upon a bonfire, the cold douche had, after a temporary extinction, only inflamed Keith Windham's rage. He unhooked his sword, scabbard and all, and flung it at Loudoun's feet, saying that he was glad to be rid of it. By this time – seeing too that the falling weapon had nearly caught his Lordship on the toes – every officer in the tent was rushing towards him. 'Reassure yourselves, gentlemen,' said Keith, laughing angrily, and, opening his uniform, took out Lord Albemarle's despatch and tendered it to the nearest. Then, without more ado, he followed the guard out into the rain, his last memory, as he left the lighted tent, not of Lord Loudoun's affronted, angry face, but of Captain Greening's, with that sly, secretly amused smile round his girlish mouth.

Chapter Three

T H E early morning bugle, close at hand, woke Keith Windham with a start. He had had little sleep during the night, and was all the deeper buried now. Where was he? He stared round the tent – an unfamiliar one. Then he remembered.

And all that endless day he sat in his canvas prison and did little else save remember. For the first time in his life he was in the midst of camp routine without a share in it – with no right to a share in it. No sword hung upon the tent-pole, and a sentry paced outside whose business was not to keep intruders out, but him in.

Had he not still been sustained by rage he might have felt more dejection than he did. The rage was not against Lord Loudoun, to whose severity he could not deny some justification, nor was it on his own account; it was against the effeminate Captain Greening and other persons unknown. Not for a moment did he believe that officer's half-sniggering asseveration of voluntary betrayal on the part of Ewen Cameron . . . though at times the other alternative haunted him so horribly that he almost wished he could believe it. Far better to have let Ardroy go down riddled by bullets on the mountain-side than to have saved him for agony and dishonour; far better had he *not* come upon him in time!

And where *was* Ardroy? Unable to make personal investigations. Keith could not well ask the soldier who brought him his meals. And, even if he discovered, even if he were allowed an interview with the prisoner – very improbable now – was he so sure that he himself wanted it? Could he bear to see the Highlander again, in the state which must be his by now?

His own plight seemed negligible in comparison. He thought of it, indeed, but only with a sort of dull wonder. Up till now his own advancement had been for him the one star in a grey heaven. Now the heaven was black and there was no star at all.

A rainy yellow sunset was smearing the sky when the flap of the tent was pulled aside and an officer came in – a very stiff young aide-de-camp.

'I am to inform you, sir,' he said, 'that as this tent is required tonight a room has been prepared for you in the fort. And Major-General Lord Loudoun supposes that rather than be marched through the camp under escort, you will agree to make no attempt to escape *en route*, in which case I am to conduct you there now myself.'

'His Lordship is extremely considerate,' replied Keith. 'I am only surprised that he is willing to rely on my word. But no doubt he is aware that I should hardly better my situation by deserting.'

'Then if you will kindly follow me,' said the aide-de-camp still more stiffly, 'I will lead you to the fort.'

But, for all his own sarcastic words, for all the absence of an escort, Keith did not enjoy that short journey very much. Everyone whom they met, either among the tents or on the brief stretch of muddy road, must know why he went thus without a sword and whither he was going; and it was with some instinct of avoiding their scrutiny that he tried to lag behind two lieutenants of independent companies, who were strolling ahead of him deep in talk. It was impossible, however, not to overtake them in the end; and, as he and his escort drew nearer, scraps of their conversation floated backwards to the Englishman's ears bearing, so he thought, the word 'Cameron'. Instantly he strained his ears to catch more; perhaps they were discussing Ardroy. As he drew still nearer he found that he was mistaken, but that one officer must be concluding an account of his experiences in a scouting party from which he had recently returned.

'. . . The same everywhere by Loch Lochy; and there's not

a doubt the rebels are much more numerous in that neighbourhood than we had any notion of – Camerons and Mac-
Donalds, too. 'Tis thought they even contemplate making a
stand in a few days' time. His Lordship will be sending out a
fresh reconnaissance . . .'

Here they passed the speaker, and the rest was lost; but
what he had heard did not particularly interest Major Windham. Only one Cameron was in his mind at present.

And now they were at the shell of the fort, where the remains of the burnt-out buildings within the enceinte hardly
looked as if they could afford any accommodation at all.

'I suppose,' said Keith carelessly to his guide, 'that the rebel
prisoners, if you have any, are confined here?'

'Yes. But you must not think, sir,' explained the ever-
correct aide-de-camp, 'that Lord Loudoun has any wish to put
your case on a level with theirs. We are indeed short of tents,
and you will not, I believe, find the room assigned to you in
the fort any less comfortable.'

Keith thanked him for the assurance, but he was not really
listening. Ewen Cameron was somewhere in this half-ruined
enclosure.

His new quarters turned out to be bare, but not more so,
certainly, than the tent. In the night, tossing on the camp bed,
he made up his mind that if it proved impossible to obtain
access to Ardroy in person, he would at least contrive to get
a letter smuggled in to him somehow. Surely he could find a
venal sentry or jailer. He wondered what his own custodian
was like, for on arrival, being much absorbed in his own
thoughts, he had only received an impression of someone
stout and middle-aged.

Morning and breakfast revealed him; a sergeant who might
have been a well-to-do sufferer from gout, so painfully did he
hobble in with the meal. Talkative upon encouragement, and
apologetic for his bodily shortcomings, he explained that his
lameness was due to a wound in the foot received when Fort
Augustus was besieged by the Highlanders, he being a sergeant
of Guise's regiment, three companies of which then held it.
When they surrendered and marched out, he was left behind.
'And though I looked to have my throat cut, sir, by the wild
MacDonalds and what not, I was very well treated, and my
wound cared for. Is this what you wish for breakfast, sir?'

'I am not in a position to exercise much choice,' said Keith. 'You know that Lord Loudoun has put me under arrest?'

The stout sergeant seemed shocked at this blunt reference to an unfortunate fact. 'If I may presume on your being English, sir, same as I am myself—'

'You may,' replied Keith.

'I would say, sir, that it don't seem right that a Scotchman should be able—' But there he stopped, aware no doubt that he was about to make a remark even blunter.

Keith could not help smiling. 'I think, my friend, that we had better not pursue that subject. May I ask whether it is by a delicate attention of the authorities that you have been detailed to wait upon me?'

'No, sir; I only come to the fort yesterday, the corporal that was here before having gone off duty sick; and me not being capable of much at present with this foot, I was told off in his place.'

'Are the ordinary prisoners – the rebels, I mean – in your charge?'

'Yes, sir, so I find; though there's only a few, picked up in the last week. Them's in the rooms below, the dungeons as we call 'em – all but a young man as has been kept by himself at the top of this very building; he's been ill, I understand.'

Small doubt who that was. 'You have seen this young man already, I suppose, Sergeant,' asked Keith, making no attempt to begin his breakfast. 'How did he seem? I am interested in him.'

'Indeed, sir! Well, he looks in but a poor way, and seems very melancholy like.'

'You do not know . . . you have not heard – anything particular about his previous treatment?' asked Keith, his heart suddenly beating hard. 'You have not heard, for instance, that . . . that forcible measures have been used to wring certain information out of him?'

'Lord, no, sir! Have they so? Yes, 'tis true he looks as though something of the sort might have happened to him, but I put it down to his having been ill with his wound.'

Keith had turned away his face. 'Do you mean,' he said after a moment, 'that he is actually in this very corner of the fort?'

'Yes, sir; a-top of you, as it were. 'Tis the least damaged

portion, and even at that there's some holes in it. You know them Highlanders used near twenty barrels of powder a-blowing of this place up. – Have you all you want, sir?'

'By the way,' said Keith, as his attendant was hobbling out, 'do not tell the young man – Mr Cameron of Ardroy – that I was asking about him.'

'No, sir, I won't mention of it. Mr Cameron, is that his name now? Why, 'twas a Dr Cameron dressed my foot; a very kind gentleman he was, too.'

Keith's breakfast was totally cold before he began it, and when the sergeant appeared again he opened his campaign at once. His guardian proved much less obdurate than he had feared. Obdurate indeed he was not; it was quite natural caution on his own behalf which withheld him from acceding sooner to Major Windham's request to be taken up to see the rebel prisoner 'up a-top of him'. It was fortunate for Keith's case that Sergeant Mullins was unaware of the close connection between that prisoner and the English Major's arrest; he believed the latter to be suffering merely for hot words to General Lord Loudoun, cause unknown. The fact of Keith's being a fellow-countryman went for something, as did also the remembrance of the Highlanders' good treatment of himself. Finally he yielded, on condition that he chose his own time for letting the sequestered officer out of his room, and that Major Windham gave him his word of honour not to take any steps to help the rebel to escape. Keith promised without difficulty that he would not even speak of such a thing; it was the past, and not the future, which was more likely to engage his tongue.

So about six o'clock in the evening he followed his limping guide up the stair and found himself standing, with real dread in his heart, outside a door which the sergeant unlocked, saying to an unseen occupant:

'I have brought someone to see you, Mr Cameron.'

The room was light and airy – rather too airy, for one wall had in it a good-sized breach, across which a piece of canvas had been stretched in an attempt to keep out rain and wind. Facing the door was a semicircular embrasure pierced with three narrow windows, and having a stone seat running round it. And on the floor of this embrasure, on some sort of a pallet, with his back propped against the seat, his legs stretched out in front of him, and his eyes fixed on the slit of window opposite him (though from his position on the floor he could not have seen anything but a strip of sky) Ewen Cameron was sitting motionless. He did not turn his head or even move his eyes when the door opened and closed again; and Keith stood equally motionless, staring at a haggard and unshaven profile which he found difficulty in recognizing.

At last he took a few steps forward. Ewen turned his head indifferently . . . and then was as suddenly frozen as one who looks on Medusa. There was a long shivering pause.

'Why are you here . . . *Judas?*'

Half prepared though he was, Keith felt slashed across the face. He caught his breath.

'If I were that, I should not be here,' he answered unsteadily. 'I have come . . . I came directly I had news of you, to explain . . . to put right if I could . . .' But the words died on his lips; it seemed a mockery to talk of putting anything right now.

'To *explain!*' repeated Ewen with an indescribable intonation. 'To explain why you told your confederate Major Guthrie everything you knew about me, to explain why you came back that night and fooled me, why you urged him to tear from me what I knew, having first made sure that I knew it – it needs no explanation! You wanted to pay off old scores – Edinburgh, Loch Oich side. Be content, you have done it – you have more than done it!'

'Ardroy, no, no, as God's my witness,' struck in Keith desperately, 'I had no such thought!' But he was not heeded, for Ewen tore on hoarsely:

'Since you desired so greatly to be even with me for a moment of triumph, could you not have let me be shot, and watched it? Or was that not sufficient for you because I did not know that you were there? . . . Oh, if God would but give me back that moment against the shieling wall, and allow it to finish as it was meant to! Then I should not be today what you have made me – a worse traitor than you are yourself!'

After that there was silence. What use in talking of his good faith and his charitable intentions when they had resulted in this! For it was true then – Ardroy *had* given the information. Indeed the fact was written on his haunted face.

But at last Keith said, in a scarcely audible voice and with his eyes on the floor: 'What did they . . . do to you?'

There was no answer, and, looking up, he saw that the wounded man's outburst had exhausted him; breathing fast, he had put his head back against the edge of the seat behind him, and his eyes were half shut. His appearance was so ghastly that Keith went forward and seized a bowl of water from the floor beside him.

But a shaking hand came up to keep him off, and he hesitated. 'What, are you trying to act *that night* over again?' asked Ewen bitterly. And Keith stood there helpless, his fingers tightening on the bowl. Was this anguished hostility utterly to defeat him?

The Highlander looked as if he had not slept for nights and nights; his eyes, naturally rather deep-set, were fearfully sunk, and glittered with a feverish brilliance. All his courtesy, all his self-command, his usual rather gentle address, every quality which Keith had observed and carelessly admired in him, seemed obliterated by the event which had brought him almost to breaking-point. 'Will you not go?' he gasped out, clenching his hands; 'will you not go now that you are satisfied?'

Keith put down the bowl; the action seemed symbolic. 'Ardroy, if you would only listen for a moment!' he pleaded. 'Indeed it is not as you think! I never betrayed you – I would as soon betray my own brother! There has been a horrible—'

'Why must I endure this, too, after all the rest?' broke out Ewen violently. 'You cannot make a fool of me again, Major Windham! Have a little pity at the last, and leave me!'

'No, for your own sake you *must* hear me!' urged Keith. 'It is Major Guthrie who is respon—'

But Ewen Cameron, with a face like stone (save that no stone image ever had eyes like that), had put his hands over his ears.

It was hopeless then! Baffled, Keith slowly turned and went to the door. He had wrecked his own career to no purpose. . . . But it was not of that catastrophe which he thought as, having rapped to be let out, he stood there with bent head. He was not even conscious of resentment at the more than taunts which had been flung at him, for it was he who had brought the man who uttered them to this pass.

He knocked again, louder; but the sergeant must have gone away, possibly to keep watch below. It came to Keith dimly, like a shape seen through fog, that Ardroy and he had once before been locked in together. . . . Then he was aware that the half-prostrate man on the floor had moved a little, that he was leaning on his left hand, and that those glittering blue eyes were on him again.

'Cannot you get out?' There was impatience in the icy voice.

'No, for I also am locked in,' answered Keith very low.

'*You* – the informer!'

Keith swallowed hard. 'I am a prisoner . . . like you.' But the words would hardly come.

'Why?'

'For neglect of duty,' replied Keith wearily. 'For turning back while carrying a despatch.'

'So you cannot even serve your own side faithfully!' observed Ewen with contempt.

Keith turned a little whiter and gripped the handle of the locked door. For an instant the flame of his hot temper flickered, only to subside among the ashes. 'No,' he answered after a moment; 'no, so it seems. I have disgraced myself. as well as ruining you. . . . The jailer must have gone away, I am afraid, and I cannot relieve you of my presence until he returns.'

'It is of no moment,' replied Ewen coldly, and he shifted himself a trifle so as to look at his visitor no longer, and propped his head on his clenched fist. The plaid in which he was partly wrapped had slipped from his shoulders when he put his hands up to his ears, and there was now nothing to hide his torn and dirty shirt – which, after all, was only of a piece with the general neglect of his person. The only evidence of care or cleanliness was the fresh bandage round his sword-arm. . . . 'So that has been recently dressed,' thought Keith, 'and he can use it. . . . That must be the plaid which I spread over him in the shieling. He was a very different man then. . . .'

He was surprised, after another appreciable silence, to find himself being addressed again, though not looked at.

'Why did you turn back?'

'What is the use of telling you – you will not believe me! Indeed I wonder whether you believe me when I say that I am under arrest; that might be a lie also.'

He had at least succeeded in gaining Ardroy's attention, for the latter dropped his arm and once again looked across the room at him. 'I should like to know why you turned back?' he repeated, without comment on the reply which he had drawn forth.

Yes, that at all event he should hear! Keith left the door, where there was no sound of Sergeant Mullins's approach.

'Cannot you guess? I came because of you – because, a dozen miles beyond here, on my way back to Inverness, I learnt both of the abominable way in which you had been treated in Guthrie's camp, and of the manner in which that scoundrel had twisted my words and my actions in order to misrepresent me to you. It was the night before last; it was late, but I resaddled and came back at once – neglecting my duty, Lord Loudoun said. I rode back in the greatest haste to see you, I was in such apprehension about you. When I got here I heard that you—' Ewen drew his breath sharply, and the sentence was not finished. 'I insisted on seeing Lord Loudoun at once, and when I was told that you had . . . had made disclosures of your own free will, I demanded to see you. I said that I would never believe that unless you told me so yourself. Then there was a scene of some violence, and I had to give up my sword and my despatch – and I suppose that in a few days my commission will go the same road. Should I have acted so – so madly against my own interests if I had been what you think me? . . . But I am forgetting; you will say that this is false also, though every officer in Fort Augustus should tell you that it is true!'

Ewen had put his head down on his updrawn right knee. A shaft of sunlight, striking through one of the narrow windows, fell across its auburn disorder. And, looking with something more painful than pity at the utter desolation of his aspect, Keith thought that life could scarcely hold anything more terrible for a gallant man than to feel himself at once a traitor and betrayed. But betrayed he had not been! If only he could be brought to see that!

And perhaps Ewen was being brought to it, for from his huddled figure there came a long sigh, and, after another silence, words which sounded as though they were wrung from his very heart:

'I wish to God that I could trust you again!'

Chapter Four

K E I T H ventured nearer. 'Why is it so difficult? You trusted me that night.' His own voice was not much less moved than the Highlander's. 'I am not changed; it is circumstances which have brought about this horrible situation.'

The head stirred, but did not raise itself. 'Yes . . . that night I thought you . . . generous, kind, charitable beyond anything that could be imagined. . . . It was not what I should have expected from you. Afterwards I saw what a simpleton I was to think you could have done all that for me without some very good reason . . . for by that time next day I had learnt what that reason was.'

'Is it fair, is it just,' pleaded Keith, 'to believe what a brute, and my enemy, said of me behind my back rather than to judge me by my own actions, Ardroy?'

'You were . . . too humane,' said the voice dully. 'And you did ask me about Lochiel . . .'

'And must I have had an ill motive behind my humanity, as you call it? You cannot say I pressed you for information about your Chief!'

'But you found out that I had it!'

It was so difficult to answer this that Keith did not attempt it. 'What motive, then,' he urged, 'brought me hastening back here, into disgrace, into complete ruin, perhaps? Is there nothing in your own heart to tell you? When you hear that I have been broke for neglecting my duty and offending my superior officer on your behalf, Ardroy, will you still think that I betrayed you to Major Guthrie?'

Ewen raised his ravaged face. 'Will you swear to me on your word of honour that you never told him that I knew Lochiel's hiding-place?'

'I do most solemnly swear it, on my honour as a gentleman. I never saw Guthrie again till the day before yesterday.'

'And will you swear, too, that you had not *already* suggested to him that I knew it, and would tell?' asked Ewen, narrowing his eyes.

'No, I never suggested that,' answered Keith, with a steady mien but a sinking heart. Nothing but the naked truth would avail now . . . and yet its nakedness might prove too ugly. 'I am going to tell you exactly what I did suggest.'

'You will not swear it – I thought as much!'

'No, I will not swear until I have made clear to you what I am swearing to. – Yes, you must listen, Ardroy; 'tis as much for your own sake as for mine!' He dragged forward a stool for himself. 'Go back to that scene on the mountain – if you can remember it. Do you think it was easy for me to find weapons to save you with? When I rushed in and caught you as you sank down by the wall, when I stood between you and the firing-party, with that scoundrel cursing me and ordering me out of the way and telling the men to set you up there again, I had to snatch at anything, *anything* to stop your execution. I told Guthrie who you were – too important to shoot out of hand like that. Afterwards he asserted that I had implied that you, as Lochiel's kinsman, would give information about him. As God sees us, such an impossible notion never entered my head, and I said that you would never do it. It was as we were riding away; so he replied, that devil: "Then it is not worth my while to fetch him into camp tomorrow; he can rot there in the hut for all I care!" And I saw that you would rot there unless I could persuade him to send for you. Being at my wits' end I made a most disastrous suggestion, and said, loathing myself the while for saying it, that it might perhaps be worth his while to fetch you into camp on the chance of your . . . of your dropping some hint by inadvertence. And he—'

Ewen had given a sharp exclamation. 'You said that – you did say that! It was true, then, what he told me! God! And how much more?'

'No more,' said Keith, wincing. 'No more, on my soul. And I only said that to hoodwink him into sending for you. You cannot think that I—'

'You advised him to take me for that reason!' interrupted

Ewen, dropping out every word, while his eyes, which had softened, began to turn to ice again. 'And, when you came back that night, you never told me what you had done. Is not that . . . somewhat difficult to explain?'

'No,' said Keith with a sigh, 'it is easy. I was ashamed to tell you – that is the explanation . . . and yet I only made the suggestion because your life, so it seemed to me, was in the balance. When at last I had brought myself to the point of confession you had fallen into the sleep in which I left you. If I had guessed— But of what use is regret now! And, Ardroy, you cannot imagine that I really thought that you would . . . or that anyone would try by force to . . .' He suddenly covered his eyes with his hand.

And presently he heard the Highlander say, in a strange, dry, reflective tone: 'Yes, it ill becomes me to accuse another man of treachery.' And then, even more quietly: 'You say you did not believe it when they told you that I had made a disclosure . . . voluntarily. I ought to thank you for that.'

The tired voice seemed for the moment empty of emotion; and yet it wrung Keith's heart as its frenzied reproaches had not. He uncovered his eyes. 'Nor do I believe it now,' he said vehemently. 'If it is true that they have got your secret from you, then I know that they must have . . . half killed you first.'

'No,' said Ardroy in the same dull tone, 'they have not laid a finger on me here. . . . Yet I have told them what Major Guthrie nearly flogged me to get from me.'

If Keith had seen a visitant from the dead he could not have stared more wildly. 'That's impossible!' he stammered. 'I don't believe it – you don't know what you are saying!'

Ewen's lip twisted a little. 'Why, by your own admission you said that I might drop a hint inadvertently!' The shaft went visibly deep. 'Forgive me!' he exclaimed hastily. 'It is true – I think I do not know what I am saying!'

'Oh, let it pass,' said Keith, recovering himself. 'Only, in God's name, tell me what happened!'

Ewen shut his eyes. 'It is quite simple, after all. It seems that I still at times talk in my sleep, as I used when a boy. I was warned of it, not so very . . . not so very long ago.' He paused; Keith gave a stifled ejaculation, and had time to taste the immensity of his own relief. This then, was the explanation of what had been to him so inexplicable – or else so abhorrent. Under his breath he murmured: 'Thank God!'

But Ewen, his eyes open now, and fixed on the other side of the room, was going on.

'When I was first brought here I was too ill and feverish to realize what they wanted of me. Afterwards, when I knew well enough (since they openly asked me for it so often, and it was what Major Guthrie had wanted too) and when I felt that the secret might slip from me in sleep, because it was so perpetually in my mind, I resolved never to allow myself to go to sleep except when I was alone. But I so seldom was alone. At first I thought, very foolishly, that this was from care of me; then I discovered the real reason, for I think they must have been hoping for this result from the first. Perhaps I talked when I was in Guthrie's hands; I do not know. But, for all my endeavours,' he gave a dreary smile, 'it seems that one *must* sleep some time or other. And the fifth night – two nights ago – I could hold out no longer, and being left by myself I went to sleep . . . and slept a long time, soundly. I had thought that I was safe, that I should wake if anyone came in.' Ewen stopped. 'I ought to have cut my tongue out before I did it. . . . And I would have died for him – died for him!' His head went down on his knee again.

'Good God!' murmured Keith to himself. The methods that he feared might not have been used, but those which had been were pretty vile. And though their victim had neither given the information voluntarily – not, at least, in the true meaning of the word – nor had had it dragged out of him by violence, his distress was not less terrible. Yet surely—

'Ardroy,' he said quickly, and touched him on the shoulder, 'are you not leaping too hastily to conclusions? No doubt you may have said *something* about your secret, since it was so much on your mind, but that in your sleep you could have given any precise information about it I cannot believe. Granted you were told that you had – perhaps in hopes that you would really betray yourself – why did you believe it. and give yourself all this torment?'

Ewen raised his head, and out of his sunken, dark-rimmed eyes gave Keith a look which wavered away from him as if undecided, and then came back to his face and stayed there.

Despair sat in those blue windows, but behind despair could be caught now a glimpse of a more natural craving for sympathy which had not been there before.

'Because,' he answered, his hand gripping hard the plaid over his legs, 'they had written down every word I said – every word. In the morning they read it over to me. Of course I denied that it was correct . . . but there it all was – the secret that only I and one other besides Lochiel himself knew. Never having seen the actual spot myself I had learnt the directions off by heart; 'Twas the last thing I did before the battle.' He shuddered violently, and once more dropped his head on to his knee. 'O God, that ever I was brought away from Drumossie Moor!'

'Devils!' said Keith under his breath, 'cold-blooded devils!' But who had first suggested that Ardroy should be watched? He sprang up, and began to pace distractedly about the room; but that thought could not be so shaken off. Yet a rather stinging consolation dawned on him: since the prisoner had acknowledged to him, what he had denied to his inquisitors, that the information was correct, he must trust him again – he must indeed, for he had thus put it in his power to go and betray him afresh.

'You'll tell me, I suppose,' began Ewen's dragging voice again, 'that a man cannot be expected to control his tongue in sleep, and it is true; he cannot. But they will keep that part out, and Lochiel, all the clan, will hear that I gave the information of my own free will. Is not that what you have been told already?' And as Keith, unable to deny this, did not answer, Ewen went on with passion: 'However it was done, it has been done; I have betrayed my Chief, and he will know it. . . . If I were only sure that it would kill me outright, I would crawl to the breach there and throw myself down. I wish I had done it two nights ago!'

From the camp, where a drum was idly thudding, there came the sound of cheering, and the broken room where this agony beat its wings in vain was flooded with warm light as the sun began to slip down to the sea behind the hills of Morven, miles away. And Keith remembered, with wonder at his obtuseness, that he had once decided that Ewen Cameron was probably a very impassive person. . . .

What was he to say? For indeed the result of Ardroy's disclosure might very well be just the same for Lochiel as if he had made it when in full possession of his senses. One argument, however, leapt unbidden to Keith's lips: his Chief would never believe that Ardroy had willingly betrayed him. Would Ardroy believe such a thing of him, he asked.

But Ewen shook his head, uncomforted. 'Lochiel would not have allowed himself to go to sleep – I did.'

'But you must have gone to sleep sooner or later!' expostulated Keith. 'Lochiel himself would have done the same, for no human being can go very long without sleep.'

'How do you know?' asked Ewen listlessly. 'I cannot sleep now when I wish to . . . when it is of no moment if I do.'

Keith looked at him in concern. That admission explained a good deal in his appearance. If this continued he might go out of his mind, and yet one was so powerless to help him; for indeed, as Ardroy had said, what was done, was done. He began to pace the room again.

Suddenly he stopped and swung round. Perhaps he was not so impotent to help after all. Somehow that idle drum, still beating out there, with its suggestion of march and movement, had revived a memory only twenty-fours hours old.

'Listen to me, Ardroy,' he said quickly, coming back and sitting down again. 'But tell me first: you would only expect Lochiel to take to this refuge, would you not, if he were skulking, as the phrase goes here, not if he had a considerable body of followers with him?'

'No,' admitted Ewen, looking faintly surprised. 'Only if he were alone, or nearly so. But he is alone, or at the best he can have but a handful with him.'

'It is there that I think you are wrong,' retorted Keith. 'Though that may have been the case at first, it is evidently so no longer. That is what I overheard yesterday.'

And he told him, word for word, what had fallen from the officer who had been scouting down the Glen. Ardroy listened with the look of a drowning man sighting a distant spar.

'My God, if only that is true! No, if the clan has rallied somewhat he would not be in hiding. Yet, after a skirmish, or if he were surprised—'

'But consider,' urged Keith, 'that, if they are so numerous, only an attack in force would be possible, and Lochiel could hardly be surprised by that: he would have scouts posted, surely. And after a skirmish, supposing the results unfavourable to him, he would probably withdraw altogether with his men, not go to earth in the neighbourhood. If the place is searched, believe me, it will be found empty!'

The eagerness with which Ewen hung upon his words was pathetic to witness.

'You are not,' he asked painfully, 'inventing this story . . . out of compassion?'

'No, no; I heard it exactly as I have hold it to you, and I can see no reason why the speaker's statement should not have been true.'

(And, whether true or no, he thought, it will have served a very good purpose if it prevents this too tightly stretched string from snapping altogether.)

Ewen draw a long breath and passed his hand over his eyes as if to wipe out a sight which was too much there. Then his head sank back against the edge of the seat behind him, his hand fell away, and Keith saw that he had fainted, or as near it as made little difference. He supposed that his attentions would be permitted now, and, grabbing up the bowl, dashed some of the water in the Highlander's face; then, putting his arms round him, succeeded in shifting him so that he could lay him flat upon the pallet.

But Ardroy was not gone far. In a moment or two he raised a hand to his head as he lay there, and murmured something about a ray of hope. Then his eyes opened, and looking straight up into Keith's face as he bent over him he said clearly, but with a catch of the breath: 'Forgive me – if you can!'

'I have so much to be forgiven myself,' answered Keith, looking down unhappily at the dirty, haggard wreck of his 'young Achilles', 'that I can scarce resent what you, of all people, have thought of me. Oh, Ardroy, what a curst tangle it has been! – Are you well like that – your wounded leg . . . ?'

The blue eyes held on to him. 'You have not answered my question. If you could forgive me for so wronging you . . . I know I have said unpardonable things to you . . . you who saved my life!'

Keith took into his own the hand he had scarred. 'Forgotten – if you will forget what I said of you?'

'But what have I to forget?' asked Ewen, and he suddenly bit his lip to keep it steady. 'I think I have to remember! And indeed, indeed, Windham, I did not doubt you lightly! I fought against it; but it all fitted together so devilishly . . . and I was not sound in mind or body. And now – selfish wretch that I am – if you are broke through what you have done for me!'

But it seemed as if it were a third person who fancied himself in more imminent danger of that fate, for Ardroy had got no farther when there were hasty, hobbling steps outside the door, a fumbling with the lock, and there stood Sergeant Mullins, much flustered.

'If you please, Major,' he said, sadly out of breath, 'will you come away at once? I misdoubt you'll be found up here if you stay a minute longer, for I saw Lord Loudoun's aide-de-camp coming along the road – and I shall be sent packing without the pension that's been promised me!'

'Go – quickly, Windham,' said Ewen earnestly. 'It will do *you* no good, either, to be found up here.'

There was nothing for it. 'Yes, I'm coming, Sergeant. – We cannot undo the past, Ardroy, but for God's sake try to torment yourself less about a calamity which may never befall – a certain person.'

Ewen looked up at him with a faint, forlorn smile. 'And *your* calamity?' he asked.

'I must endeavour to take my own advice,' said his visitor rather grimly. 'I shall try to see you again if possible . . . that is, if you . . .' he hesitated.

Ewen's left hand reached up and gripped his wrist. 'You say the past cannot be undone. There are some hours in it which I am glad I can never lose again – that night in the shieling, now I know that you were . . . what at the time I thought you!'

Three minutes after Keith had got back to his quarters the correct aide-de-camp appeared to announce to him that he would be taken to Inverness under escort early next morning, as he had been sent for from headquarters. Keith shrugged his shoulders. That meant a court-martial, in all probability, and the loss of his commission. But at any rate the sacrifice was not all in vain, for he had cleared himself, in Ewen Cameron's eyes, of charges far worse than any court-martial could bring against him.

All evening he thought of Ardroy up there, destitute in body and tormented in mind – though less tormented, fortunately, by the time he had left him. . . . Yet why, he asked himself, should he care what Ardroy was suffering, now that he had cleared his account with him? Was it because he had somehow become responsible for him by snatching him from death? God knew.

But that, he supposed, was why, when Mullins hobbled in with his supper, he handed the sergeant a sheet of paper.

'I want you to take this to Mr Cameron tonight, Sergeant. Read it, and you can satisfy yourself that it contains nothing which it should not.'

The note briefly said that the writer would not be able to see the recipient again, since he was obliged to go to Inverness next morning, but that he would go thither with a mind vastly more at peace than he had come; and would go even more cheerfully if he were permitted to leave with the sergeant a sum of money sufficient to provide for the captive's immediate needs in the way of food and clothes. 'You can repay it at your convenience,' Keith had added, 'but, if you will not accept this loan, I shall depart feeling that you have not truly forgiven me.'

As he expected, Sergeant Mullins made no bones about delivering a missive when he had connived at a much more serious breach of discipline. But when, on his return, he handed his letter back to Keith, the Englishman's heart fell, until he saw that Ardroy, having no writing materials of his own, had used the back of it for his reply. And thereon was scrawled with a blunt pencil of the sergeant's these words:

'If there is any Justice on Earth, you should not only be reinstated but advanc'd at Inverness. I pray you to inform me, if you can, of what happens. I accept your Loan with Gratitude; it is for me to ask your Forgiveness still. Perhaps I shall sleep tonight. – Your Debtor, EWEN CAMERON.'

Keith at any rate slept, though he was rather bitterly amused at the idea of being given advancement by the Duke of Cumberland because he had got himself into a scrape for the sake of a rebel. The cause of his dereliction of duty would be the chief count in his probable disgrace.

Chapter Five

IT was raining hard, and blowing too, and rain and wind kept up a constant siege of the inadequate canvas stretched over the breach in Ewen's place of confinement, the drops pattering against it like small shot. Ewen himself, shaved and wearing a clean shirt, but the same disreputable kilt, was sitting on the seat which ran round the embrasure, to which, with some difficulty, he could now hoist himself. His object in so doing was to see out, but this morning there was little to see when he had got there.

Ten days had passed since his momentous interview with Major Windham, ten days of wearing, grinding suspense. Every hour, almost, he had expected to learn of Lochiel's capture. But, as day followed day, and nothing of the sort occurred, nor, from what Sergeant Mullins told him, was any attempt being made against Achnacarry, the spar of hope which his visitor had flung to him began to have more sustaining qualities. It did look as if Windham's information were correct, and that the clan was known to be in such force that it was not a mere question of hunting down the wounded Chief, of plucking him out of the refuge whose secret was a secret no longer. For the comfort of that thought he had to thank the generosity of an enemy whom he had accused to his face of an infamous action.

Major Windham had always been something of an enigma to Ewen, and the depth of the concern which he had shown the other day still surprised him. That he had personally attracted the English soldier would never have occurred to him. Apart from wishing to clear himself of the charge of treachery, Major Windham, he supposed, felt a somewhat exaggerated sense of obligation for having been allowed to go free in Edinburgh – though indeed some men might have resented that clemency, and there had been a time when Guthrie's insinuations had driven Ewen to the belief that this was so. Yet now the remembrance of the night in the shieling hut was no longer a draught of poison, but what it had been at the time, that cup of cold water which holds a double blessing.

But it was strange how accurate had been his foster-father's prophecy, that the man to whom the heron would bring him should alike do him a great service and cause him bitter grief. Both predictions had been fulfilled; and by the same act on Major Windham's part.

Ewen himself seemed to have been forgotten by the authorities. The same military surgeon came from time to time and grumblingly dressed his wounds, but, though rough and quite devoid of consideration, he was tolerably skilful, and the patient's own splendid physique was doing the rest, now that he had proper care and that his mind was a little more at ease. Old Mullins, mindful alike of a substantial *douceur* from Major Windham and of his own good treatment by the Highlanders, looked after him to the best of his ability, particularly when he discovered him to be Dr Cameron's cousin. He still boggled, however, at procuring the captive entirely new clothes (for how, he said, should he account to Captain Greening for having the money to pay for them), but he brought him better food than was provided, a couple of clean shirts and a second blanket, and shaved him every other day. But Captain Greening, whom Ewen loathed, he thought, even more than he had loathed the brute Guthrie, never came near him now. He had got what he wanted, presumably, and troubled no more about the prisoner whom at one time he had had so assiduously watched.

The outcome of those horrible days and nights remained deeply branded on Ewen's soul: he was a traitor, if an unconscious and most unwilling one; but the actual memory of them, and of the twenty-four hours in Guthrie's hands, he was now beginning, with the natural instinct of a healthy mind, to put behind him. And with the slight relaxation of tension due to Major Windham's suggestion and the inactivity of the authorities – due also to the wild hope which sometimes visited him, that Lochiel was no longer near Achnacarry at all, and that they knew it – he was beginning to feel the pressure of captivity, and would spend hours peering hungrily through the narrow slits of windows. Even if, as today, he could see little for the rain and mist, he could always smell the blessed air, and he now screwed himself into a still more uncomfortable position in an endeavour to get as much of this as possible. Yes, the rain, as he thought, was stopping; the wind was blowing it away. Often, on such a morning, on the braes above Loch na h-Iolaire—

Several people seemed to be coming quickly up the stairs. The surgeon and others? Ewen turned his head. No; when the door was unlocked and flung open there came in three officers all unknown to him. The foremost was of high rank, and Ewen after a second's astonishment, realized that he could be none other than the Earl of Loudoun himself.

Sitting there, he instinctively stiffened. With the opening of the door the wind had swooped through the breach in the wall, and even the Earl's dark, heavy tartans fluttered for a moment. There was a sheet of paper in his hand, and he wore a look of great annoyance.

'Mr Cameron,' he said, like a man too much pressed for time to indulge in any preamble, 'when you gave us this information about Lochiel's hiding-place a couple of weeks since,' he tapped the paper, 'why did you name as the spot on a mountain-side which does not exist anywhere near Loch Arkaig?'

Ewen's heart gave a bound so sudden and violent that he thought it must suffocate him. What did Lord Loudoun mean? He stared at him breathlessly.

'Come, sir,' said the Earl impatiently, 'do not play the innocent! On 7 May you gave Captain Greening a detailed account of a cave on a mountain-side which Lochiel would be apt to use in an emergency, how its whereabouts could be recognized, its concealed opening found, and the rest. The mountain, according to you, was called Ben Loy. But you made a slip – or something more intentional – for guides who know the district well declare that there is no mountain of that name in the neighbourhood, though it is true that there is a Glen Loy farther down the Lochy, but much too far to serve as a convenient refuge from Achnacarry. This makes nonsense of your information.' His voice was warm with a sense of injury. 'The mistake has only been discovered in the nick of time. . . . Why, what's wrong with you man?'

For Ewen, with an exclamation, had leant forward and buried his face in his hands. Was it possible that this rebel tongue had, all unknown to himself and to his inquisitor, undone so much of the harm it had wrought? And how had he not realized it himself?

Lord Loudoun much mistook the cause of his emotion. 'The slip can easily be repaired, Mr Cameron,' he said impatiently.

'You cannot possibly have meant any of the heights of Glen Loy – none of which, moreover, appears to be called Ben Loy. It must be one of the other names I have on this paper. – Come, my time is precious! I am about to set out for Achnacarry to-day.' And as Ewen, really too much overcome by his 'slip' to pay much attention to these adjurations, still remained with his face hidden, a new note crept into the Earl's voice. 'You are not, I hope, indulging in scruples *now*, Mr Cameron? 'Tis too late for that; nor is it any manner of use to withhold a part when you have told us so much. We shall know the place when we come upon it.'

Ewen raised his head at last and looked at him, but still dizzily. '*Withhold!*' he said. 'Is it possible, Lord Loudoun, that you do not know how such information as you have was extracted from me?'

'Extracted from you!' repeated the Earl. 'Why, you gave it of your own free will when you were asked for it; I have Captain Greening's word for that.'

'My own free will! Did Captain Greening tell your Lordship that he had me watched and questioned day and night for nearly a week, hoping that I should tell him in my sleep, as at last I did, unknowingly? While I had life in my body he should never have got it otherwise!' And, seeing clearly from Loudoun's face that this was indeed news to him, Ewen went on with more heat: 'Whatever lies you were told by your English underlings, how dare you, my Lord, believe that a Cameron would ever willingly betray Mac Dhomhnuill Duibh?'

'Go and see if you cannot find Captain Greening this time, and bring him here,' said the Earl to one of the officers. He took a turn up and down, his hands behind his back, looking very much disturbed.

'I had no idea of this; 'tis a method which should never have been used,' he muttered after a moment. It was evident that he entirely believed the prisoner's assertion. 'But you must admit, Mr Cameron,' he went on mildly, 'that I am not to blame for it, seeing that I was not here at the time. And, as to believing that you made the disclosure willingly, I confess that I ought to have remembered – since I have the honour to be one myself – that a Highland gentleman does not willingly betray his Chief.'

Yet, having elicited this *amende*, Ewen said nothing, his

racial distrust of a Campbell inclining him to wait for what was to come next.

'I cannot pretend, however,' began the Earl again, 'that I am sorry to possess this information, since I am a soldier, and must obey orders. In accordance with these, I set out today with two thousand men for Loch Arkaig and Achnacarry.' He gave time for this news to sink in. 'But Mr Cameron, though our clans have unfortunately been at enmity in the past, that shall not prevent me from treating Lochiel, when he is in my hands, with all the regard due to his position and merit.'

'As his kinsman,' replied Ewen to this, 'I thank your Lordship for the intention, even though I trust that you may never have the chance of carrying it out.' Why had the Campbell become thus smooth-spoken, and was it true that he was going with so overwhelmingly large a force against Lochiel?

Before Lord Loudoun could offer any further remarks, Captain Greening came in, apologizing that he should have been sought for twice, and evidently ignorant of what was in store for him. The Earl cut short his excuses.

'Why did you assure me, Captain Greening, that the information about Lochiel obtained from Mr Cameron of Ardroy here was given of his own free will? Mr Cameron tells me that, as the result of unceasing persecution on your part, it was dragged out of him in sleep, which is a very different matter!'

Somehow Captain Greening, while appearing to have his eyes fixed respectfully on his superior, contrived to shoot a glance of a very different nature at Ewen.

'If your Lordship believes that story,' he said with a scarcely believed sneer, 'it does credit to your Lordship's nobility of disposition – as well as to Mr Cameron's powers of invention! Sleep! As if he could have given all that detail in his sleep! But the tale may serve to patch the hole in his reputation, though I'll wager he was no more asleep than you or I!'

'You are a pretty consummate scoundrel, are you not!' observed Ewen softly.

'Yet, whether he was asleep or awake, my Lord,' went on Greening quickly, 'I submit that what I said was perfectly correct – no force of any kind was used. I certainly had no intention of misleading your Lordship on that point, when you asked me that question in order to satisfy . . . a somewhat indiscreet inquirer after Mr Cameron.'

But Lord Loudoun, frowning heavily, declined to be drawn into a side issue. 'It was playing with words, sir, to call information thus given "voluntary". I am very much displeased at the means employed. And even so, as might have been foreseen, the matter was bungled, for the information itself, on which you led me to rely, is not complete!'

'Not complete!' stammered Greening, flushing. 'My Lord—'

'No, sir, it is not complete – and only now, within an hour or so of setting out for the neighbourhood, has its insufficiency been discovered! The guide, who knows that district well, swears that there is no mountain of the name of Ben Loy anywhere near. And Ben Loy is the name you have written here.'

Captain Greening almost snatched the paper from the Earl's hand, and ran his eyes feverishly over it.

'My Lord, the guide is perhaps mis—'

'I tell you that he knows that part of the country like the palm of his hand,' interrupted Lord Loudoun angrily. 'It might, he says, be any of the three mountains whose names are written below. But how can I hope to surprise Lochiel if I have to go searching every brae-side near Loch Arkaig for this cave? And I tell you further, Captain Greening, that this ridiculous wrong name, occurring thus, gives me very much to doubt whether the whole description be not the product of . . . of a dream, or of imagination – whether this cave near a waterfall is to be found on any mountain-side whatever, be the mountain called what it may!'

In the extremely mortified silence which ensued on Captain Greening's part at this, Ewen saw his opportunity.

'I was wondering,' he observed mockingly, 'how long your Lordship would be before you discovered the real value of Captain Greening's dirty work!'

'Do not believe him, my Lord,' urged Greening, his light, womanish voice roughened by rage and disappointment. 'If I cannot answer for the name of the mountain, I can, by God, for the rest! Had you seen the prisoner's face when I read over to him next morning what he had told me, you would know that his description was accurate enough. It is only a question of finding out which mountain he had in mind, and if your Lordship will give me half an hour or so with him—'

Lord Loudoun turned on him. 'You have mismanaged this business quite enough,' he snapped. 'I do not desire you, Captain Greening, to meddle with it any further. Nor is Mr Cameron asleep now.'

There was that in Captain Greening's expression as he turned away, biting his lip, which suggested that he would not consider that state necessary for his purpose.

Ewen shut his eyes and leant his head against the wall. The Earl and his two officers were talking together in low voices, and he longed for them to go away and leave him to turn over, as if it were a grain of gold out of a muddy river, the thought of this wonderful and saving slip of the tongue. He could not understand how he came to have stumbled so mercifully; was it because in his illness he fancied himself at times back in the shieling on that mountain which was, he believed called Beinn Laoigh, the calf's mountain? That he had not himself noticed the mistake in the name when Captain Greening read over to him, next morning, what he was pleased to call his deposition, he could, after all, understand; the horror of the accuracy of the rest had too much swamped his soul. He tried now to calculate how much security was given back to the secret place by his happy blunder, but it was not easy.

Then he heard a movement to the door. Thank God, they had done with him! No, feet were approaching him again. He opened his eyes and saw Lord Loudoun standing looking out through one of the narrow windows only a few feet away. Save for him, the room was empty, though the door remained ajar. Evidently the Earl desired a measure of privacy.

'I am very sorry about your treatment, Mr Cameron,' he began, his eyes still fixed on the narrow slit. 'It has been an unfortunate business.'

'Which, my Lord,' asked Ewen coolly, 'my treatment or the information which proves to be worthless?'

'I referred, naturally, to your treatment,' said Lord Loudoun with dignity (but Ewen did not feel so sure). 'However, you must admit that I may fairly consider the other affair a . . . disappointment. As a soldier, with my duty to carry out, I must avail myself of any weapon to my hand.'

'Evidently,' commented his prisoner. 'Even of one which is not very clean!'

Lord Loudoun sighed. 'Alas, one cannot always choose. You

yourself, Mr Cameron, had no choice in the matter of your disclosure, and are therefore in no sense to blame. . . . I should wish everyone to know that,' he added graciously, turning round and looking down at him.

'Then our wishes coincide, my Lord, which is gratifying,' observed Ardroy. 'And is it to discuss with me some means of compassing this end that your Lordship is good enough to spare time for this interview now?'

Although Lord Loudoun could not possibly have been insensitive to the irony of this query, it apparently suited him to ignore it. In fact he sat down upon the stone bench, on the opposite side of the embrasure.

'Chance made your revelation incomplete, Mr Cameron,' he said, giving him a rather curious look. 'Yet, if the missing link in the chain *had* been there, the same . . . blamelessness would have covered it.'

Ewen, his eyes fixed upon him, said something under his breath and gripped the edge of the seat. But the Earl went on meaningly: 'There is still time for the true name of that mountain to have been . . . *spoken by you in your sleep*!'

And still his captive merely looked at him; yet Lord Loudoun evidently enjoyed his gaze so little that his own seemed to be caught by the breach in the wall, and stayed there.

'This room appears a very insecure place of confinement,' he murmured. 'Has that thought never occurred to you?'

Ewen was still looking at him. 'I cannot walk, much less climb, my Lord.'

'But with a little help from outside, a little connivance,' suggested the Earl, gazing at the breach. 'Sentries, I am afraid, are sometimes both venal and careless . . . especially when the commander is away. But I dare say the negligence would be overlooked at headquarters, in view of the – the exceptional circumstances.' There was a little silence as he turned his head and at last looked the Highlander in the face again. 'Is it useless to hope that you will see reason, Mr Cameron?'

'*Reason!*' exclaimed Ewen. Contempt had warmed to rage by this time. 'Treason is what you mean, you false Campbell!' With difficulty he shuffled himself along the seat to a greater distance. 'I wish I had the use of both my legs! I like ill at any time to sit upon the same seat with a son of Diarmaid, and to sit near one who after all that fine talk tries to bribe me to betray my Chief, who offers me my liberty as the price of his—' And he somehow dragged himself to his feet, and stood clutching at the corner of the wall, breathless with anger and effort.

Lord Loudoun, his smile completely vanished, was on his feet too, as flushed as his prisoner was pale. 'You *have* betrayed him, Cameron – what use to take that tone? You might as well complete the disclosure . . . and if your pride will not stomach the gift, I'll not offer you your liberty in exchange. I had already made you an offer which would mend your self-esteem, not hurt it. Here's another: tell me what is the real name of that mountain and I'll engage that Lochiel shall never know who told us of the cave upon it!'

'And I'm to rely on nothing but a Campbell's word for that!' cried Ewen, still at white heat, but sinking down again on the seat despite himself. 'No, thank you, my Lord; the security's not good enough! Nor am I going to tell you the name on any security, so you were best not waste your time.'

'Then,' said the Earl, and there was a new and dangerous note in his voice, 'I warn you that Cameron of Lochiel will have the mortification of knowing that it was a Cameron who betrayed him. But I repeat that if you give it to me—'

'There is one place the name of which I feel at liberty to give you,' interrupted Ewen, half closing his eyes, in which the light of battle was gleaming. 'I think I should be doing my Chief no harm if I told you the way—' He paused as if un-certain, after all, whether to go on, and Greening and the two other officers, who, hearing voices raised had reappeared in the doorway, pressed quickly forward.

Lord Loudoun fell into the trap. 'The way to where?' he asked eagerly.

'The way to Moy,' answered Ewen, and the glint in his eyes was plain to see now. 'To Moy in Lochaber – there *is* a place of that name there. Though whether you will encounter a second Donald Fraser too I don't know.'

Lord Loudoun gave a stifled exclamation and grew very red. Consternation overcame his officers. The too-famous 'rout of Moy', as Ewen had well guessed, was not mentioned in the Earl's hearing. But the Earl was the first to recover himself.

'You are not only insolent but foolish, Mr Cameron. When

Lochiel falls into my hands I shall not now be inclined to keep silence on the subject of his refuge, whether he is found in it or no, and it will depend upon me whether he is told that you made your disclosure about it involuntarily, as you declare that you did, or of your own free will.'

And thus did the Earl of Loudoun, a not ill-natured nor inhumane man, who in calmer moments would have been ashamed of such an impulse, threaten to use a calumny which he knew to be such in order to bring a captive foe to heel. The merest sign of pleading on the Cameron's part and he would have relented. But nothing was farther from Ardroy's mind than pleading. All he craved, in his wrath, was a fresh weapon with which to draw blood. He found it.

'But you may not capture Lochiel at all,' he said with an appearance of carelessness. 'He may have followed your Lordship's example when, after your amusing performances on the Dornoch Firth, you ran away from your captured troops and sought safety in Skye. Only,' he added venomously, 'in my Chief's case, it will be *after* the battle, not, as in yours, John Campbell, *before* it!'

The effect on Lord Loudoun, who was no coward, of this really undeserved interpretation of his misfortunes was all that Ewen could have wished. His hand clenched on his sword-hilt. 'By God, sir, if we were . . . elsewhere . . . I'd make you pay for that!'

And alike from him, fourth earl of his line, representative peer of Scotland and royal aide-de-camp, and from the defiant, ragged young man on the seat before him, with his French training and his natural courtesy (which an Englishman had not long ago thought almost excessive), there slipped for a moment the whole cloak of eighteenth-century civilization, and they were merely two Highlanders, heirs of an age-long feud, waiting to spring at each other, dirk in hand, amongst the heather. The metamorphosis lasted but a second or two, and they were themselves again, but John Campbell had had his answer; he knew better now the temper with which he had to deal than to expect an appeal for mercy, much less the revelation he coveted.

'I am only sorry that your future is not likely to allow of your giving me satisfaction for that insult, Mr Cameron,' he said grimly, and turned his back upon him. 'Captain Greening, you will have the prisoner removed from this room to some securer place of confinement. But bear in mind, if you please, that he is not to be ill-treated.' And, without another look behind him, he left the room. Nor was his going devoid of dignity.

As the hated Diarmaid tartan vanished Ewen's whole body relaxed against the wall. But he soon became aware that Captain Greening had stayed behind, and was standing there in Loudoun's place addressing him, his delicate features contorted with rage.

'If I had only guessed, you dirty cattle-thief, that you had fooled me after all! It would not have taken a fortnight to get the real name out of you somehow!' His teeth ground together. 'Perhaps in the dungeons you'll learn at least to keep a civil tongue in your head, as long as it is on your shoulders.' He flung away towards the door, then turned again. 'Yes, smile while you can! "Not to be ill-treated", eh? We'll see about that when the Earl is gone, my fine Highlander!'

As the door slammed behind his guardian the contemptuous smile died off Ewen's face, and, lowering himself with some difficulty from the stone bench, he lay down on the pallet below and pulled his plaid over his head. Now that the clash of the interview was over he felt shaken and sick. A great consolation had indeed emerged from it, but even that consolation could do little for him against the immediate anguish of knowing that the hounds were on the trail at last, and the quarry perhaps unsuspecting. How could Lochiel escape so large a force? He and his few hundreds would be surrounded as in a net; he would be killed or captured even if he did not take to the cave on Beinn Bhreac. And, if he did, chance might always lead the pursuers straight to it. Could Ewen in that hour have sent a message to Lochiel he would willingly have bought the privilege not merely by his own death – that went without saying – but by a death in any manner protracted and horrible. Yet no suffering could buy that chance; there was nothing to do but lie there helpless, at the lowest ebb of dejection, and hear from the camp the drums and bugles of departure.

At last came evening, and Mullins with food and water.

'Is there any news, Sergeant?' asked Ewen, raising himself.

'Yes, sir, His Royal Highness the Duke's expected here tomorrow with nine regiments of foot and some horse. And

Captain Greening ain't in charge of prisoners no longer; his
Lordship saw to that before he left – seems he was annoyed
with the Captain about something or other. I can't say as I'm
sorry. But I'm afraid, Mr Cameron, you're going to be moved
from here tomorrow, and put in one of them nasty places
they call the dungeons, though they ain't scarcely that, so to
speak, and—'

Ewen cut short the bulletin. 'You can put me in my grave
for all I care at present. It's the expedition to Loch Arkaig I
want news of. Is there *none*?'

'No, sir, how could there be, so soon? – Bless me, how wild
you look. Have you kin in those parts?'

'More than kin,' said Ewen brokenly. 'My heart and my
honour . . . O God, send a mist, a storm – send someone to
warn him!'

Next day Cumberland and his ten regiments marched in
from Inverness. But of this great stir Ewen heard nothing. He
was down in a damp little cell under the ford, with fever once
more in his blood, fighting a desire to knock his head against
the wall. The old sergeant, who still had charge of him, could
tell him nothing of what he wanted to know, save that there
was a report of great burnings going on down the Glen, and
quantities of cattle driven off.

So Ewen had to endure the suspense as best he might until
the following morning, when a light suddenly streamed through
the open door, and a kilted figure was roughly pushed down
the steps by a couple of redcoats. But in the short-lived radiance
Ewen had recognized the tartan of his own clan.

'Who is it – are you from Loch Arkaig?' he asked hoarsely,
raising himself on his heap of straw.

'Aye, Alexander Cameron from Murlaggan,' answered the
newcomer. 'My sorrow, but it is dark in here! Who are you –
a Cameron also?'

Ewen dragged himself to one knee. 'Lochiel . . . Lochiel –
is he safe? Tell me quickly, for God's sake!'

The Cameron groped his way to the corner. 'Yes, God be
praised! There was but a handful of us captured; the rest
scattered while the redcoats were fording the river of Lochy. –
There, honest man, sure that's good news, not bad!'

For – the first time in his grown life – Ewen was shaken by

uncontrollable sobs, by a thankfulness which tore at his heart like a grief. Alexander Cameron sat down by him in the straw, seeming very well to understand his emotion, and told him more fully the story of what had happened: how the Argyll militia with Lord Loudoun had at first been mistaken for a body of MacDonald reinforcements which were expected, but distinguished in time by the red crosses on their bonnets; how the Camerons had thought of disputing the passage over Lochy, but realizing the overwhelming force of the enemy, had withdrawn swiftly along the northern shore of Loch Arkaig, so that by the time the latter got to the neighbourhood of Achnacarry the Chief must have been well on his way to the wild country at the head of the loch, where they would never pursue him. But the burnings and pillagings had begun already, and one could guess only too well the heavy measure of vengeance which was going to be meted out in Lochaber.

The two men lay close together that night under one plaid for warmth, and Ewen at last knew a dreamless sleep. Not only had Lochiel escaped, but he was not likely ever to hear now that the secret of the cave by the waterfall had been partly betrayed; nor, if he had left the district altogether, would he be tempted to make use of it in the future. The horror was lifted.

Chapter Six

I T was the seventeenth of July, and Keith Windham in his quarters at Inverness was turning over an official letter which had just come to him from Fort Augustus. It was, he saw, in the handwriting of Sir Everard Faulkner, Cumberland's secretary, and as he looked at it hope whispered to him that it might portend the lifting the cloud under which he had lived for the last two months. And, not to silence that voice too soon, he left the letter unopened for a minute or two, and sat staring at it.

His case had never come before a court-martial; it had been privately dealt with by Hawley and the Duke. Three things had combined to save him from being cashiered; the fact that Cumberland was graciously pleased to set his conduct at Fontenoy against his present lapse, that Lord Albemarle had written some words of appreciation of him in that despatch

which Keith had never delivered, and that Hawley had regarded, and succeeded in making Cumberland regard, Lord
Loudoun's action in putting his staff-officer under arrest as high-
handed, and to be resented. 'I can't understand your conduct,
Windham,' he had said angrily to his erring subordinate, 'but
I'm damned if I'll stand Lord Loudoun's!' Hawley chafed all
the more because he knew his own star to be on the decline;
and thus military jealousy played no small part in saving Keith
from complete disaster.

But all was over, naturally, with his chance of being
appointed to Cumberland's staff, nor could Hawley keep him
on his, even for the short time that should elapse before he
resigned his own none-too-fortunate command. Although Major
Windham's might be regarded as a mere technical offence –
and even Cumberland, severe as he was showing himself in
matters of discipline, did not seem to regard it as more – Lord
Loudoun's treatment of it had given it so much publicity that
for appearances' sake the defaulter had to be punished. Keith
had hoped that he might escape from Scotland by being sent
back to his own battalion of the Royals, now in Kent, or that
perhaps he would be attached to the second, just proceeding
to Perth; but he was offered instead a vacancy in Battereau's
regiment, which was to remain behind with Blakeney's
when the bulk of the army should move with Cumberland to Fort Augustus. He was, in short, put on the shelf;
but he was very plainly shown that it was a choice between
accepting this position or sending in his papers altogether.
He might indeed count himself extremely lucky that he
had escaped being broke, and so the Duke himself had told
him.

The last week in May, therefore, had found him left behind
in Inverness, no longer the centre of military activity now
that Cumberland was gone, but rather a depôt for prisoners,
entailing on the two regiments remaining in the town duties
which were both dull and – to Keith Windham at least – hateful. But the shelf has an uncommonly sobering effect upon a
hot-tempered and ambitious man, and it did not require two
months of it to bring reflection to Major Windham. Before
they were half over he was viewing his own irregular conduct
in a much more critical light, and from cursing his impetuosity
he had come to marvelling at his folly. Saving Ewen Cameron's

life he did not for an instant regret; he would have done the
same again without a moment's hesitation, nor did he regret
his return to the shieling in the guise of the Good Samaritan;
but to have dashed in that manner back to Fort Augustus
while carrying a despatch, still more to have thrust himself
into Lord Loudoun's presence and almost to have brawled
there – was it any wonder that he had found himself under
arrest? Prudence could not undo the past, but it might modify
the future, and he therefore set himself to practise this virtue
in Inverness, much as it went against the grain. Warned by
the fate of an officer who was court-martialled for having
shown the wretched captives there some kindness, he did not
go out of his way to emulate him, nor did his old wound
again furnish a pretext for his withdrawal from scenes which
he disliked. If the officers of Battereau's had known him
previously they would have thought him remarkably changed.
General Blakeney, a hard man, had no fault to find with
Hawley's disgraced staff-officer.

The first fruit of this new prudence had been Keith's abstention, not only from writing to Ewen Cameron, but even from
sending him a direct message. He had sent instead by an
acquaintance in Bligh's regiment, when it proceeded to Fort
Augustus, a verbal recommendation to Sergeant Mullins to be
faithful to the 'commission' which he had given him, in the
hope that the sergeant would, besides obeying this injunction,
pass on unsolicited to Ardroy the scanty news of himself
which his messenger was instructed to add. A man under a
cloud could not, he felt, afford to compromise himself still
further in the matter of open friendship with a rebel – though
to Cumberland and Hawley he had vigorously denied any such
relations with Ewen Cameron. Made wary by his experiences
with Guthrie, and afraid of giving a handle against Ewen, he
had merely urged in defence of his own conduct a not unnatural anxiety about a Scottish acquaintance – the name, of
course, he had been unable to withhold – who had shown him
hospitality and kindness *before* the raising of the standard of
rebellion. It was disingenuous, but in the absence of close
questioning the version had served its purpose.

And as the weeks went by he had not only made no attempt
to communicate in any way with the captive Jacobite, but
was careful never to inquire for him by name whenever an

officer came from Fort Augustus, whence indisposition (induced, so they asserted, by their melancholy surroundings)
was always bringing a few. Yet, as the clearing out of Lochaber
and Babenoch proceeded, he did his best always to ascertain
what prisoners were arriving at Inverness for transhipment to
England, but he never found Ewen Cameron's name among
them. And at last, since he felt sure that the latter would never
have been kept until July at Fort Augustus, he came to the
conclusion that he must have overlooked his name in the lists,
and that he had been shipped off from Inverness without his
knowledge – unless he had been despatched by land from Fort
Augustus to Edinburgh. Keith hoped indeed that the latter
course had been taken, for he knew something of the horrible
condition in which the prisoners were kept in the ships, packed
together like cattle with nothing to lie upon but the stones
and earth of the ballast. He was sorry, very sorry, that he had
not been able to see Ardroy once more, but it was the fortune
of war; and there was no denying the fact, once recognized,
that this young man, to whom he had been so unusually
attracted, had brought him nothing but ill-luck.

The letter, its seal broken at last, merely said that His Royal
Highness the Duke of Cumberland commanded Major Windham's attendance without delay at Fort Augustus. Now Cumberland, as Keith knew, was on the very eve of departure for
England; the summons must evidently have some connection
with that fact, and it was full of the most hopeful speculations
that he went at once to procure leave of absence from his
colonel.

And when, some five hours later, he came down the descent
to Loch Ness, he could not but remember the last time that he
had ridden into Fort Augustus, on that wet night in May, on
fire with indignation and disgust. Well, he had learnt his lesson
now!

Since Cumberland's advent, Fort Augustus had naturally
become an armed camp of a much greater size; there were
hundreds of tents pitched by the Tarff, and besides these, the
women's quarters, the horse lines of the dragoon regiment of
Kingston's horse, and quantities of cattle and ponies driven in
from the ravaged countryside. As had been foreshadowed, the
Earl of Albemarle, who had already been there for some time,

was to succeed the Duke as commander-in-chief on the latter's departure tomorrow. Remembering his lamentations at Perth in May, Keith wondered whether his Lordship were more reconciled to the prospect now.

But the Duke sending for *him* at this juncture – it *must* mean something to his own advantage.

He asked, as he had been instructed to do, for Sir Everard Faulkner, and found the ex-banker, ex-ambassador to Constantinople and patron of Voltaire at a table in a tent, very busy writing.

'Good afternoon, Major Windham,' said he, looking up. 'You have made good speed hither, which is commendable.'

'So your letter bade me, sir.'

'Yes,' said Sir Everard, laying down his pen. 'I sent for you by His Royal Highness's recommendation, to request your assistance on a certain matter of importance to His Majesty's Government. If you can give it, you will lay not only me, but the Duke also, under a considerable obligation.'

'If you will tell me what the matter is . . .' murmured Keith, amazed. To be able to lay Cumberland under an obligation was a chance not to be made light of, but he could not for the life of him imagine how he had it in his power to do so unlikely a thing.

'I have for some time,' proceeded Sir Everard, fingering the sheets before him, 'been collecting evidence against such prisoners in Inverness and elsewhere as are to be sent to England in order to take their trials. Yesterday I received a letter from the Lord Justice Clerk in Edinburgh transmitting a copy of the Duke of Newcastle's order that prisoners are to set out as soon as may be, and that particular care is to be taken that the witnesses sent to give evidence against them should be able to prove' – he took up a paper and read from it – ' "that they had seen the prisoners do some hostile act on the part of the rebels, or marching with the rebel army" You appreciate that point, of course?'

'Certainly,' agreed Keith. 'But surely there is no lack of such evidence?'

'No, in most cases there is not,' replied the secretary. 'But – to come to the point – we have here in Fort Augustus a prisoner of some importance, who is most undoubtedly guilty of overt acts of hostility in this late unnatural rebellion, but to my chagrin (and His Royal Highness's) I cannot put my hand on any person who actually saw him commit such acts, though there must be numbers who witnessed them – not even on anyone who observed him in the company of the rebels. There is indeed a probability – but only a probability – that if he is sent to Fort William he may be identified by someone or other as having taken part in the attack upon it in the spring, for it is pretty certain that he was there with Cameron of Lochiel. The prisoner's name, by the way,' he added, with a carelessness too complete to be quite natural, 'is also Cameron – Ewen Cameron of Ardroy.'

There was a silence in the tent. 'So he *is* still here!' said Keith under his breath. 'And that is why you have sent for me, Sir Everard; because you think that I can supply the evidence which will bring Cameron of Ardroy to the scaffold?' He checked himself, and added, in a studiously expressionless tone: 'Why, to what do you suppose that I can witness against him?'

Deceived perhaps by the manner of his last words, Sir Everard referred complacently to his notes.

'I understand that you can testify to his taking you prisoner by force on the outbreak of hostilities at High Bridge in Lochaber. That in itself would be more than sufficient, but it seems that you also encountered him in Edinburgh, and can therefore bear witness to his being in the Pretender's son's so-called army.'

Keith stared at Sir Everard Faulkner's wig, which was awry, with dismay in his soul. Surely Ardroy could not have been so mad as to have admitted these facts – which *he* had so carefully suppressed – to anyone at Fort Augustus! 'Who told you these details, sir – not that I admit their truth?'

'Major Guthrie of Campbell's regiment was so obliging as to mention to me the service which you could render to the Government in this matter. And he had the facts, it seems, from you yourself, shortly after the victory on Culloden Moor. Release from your duties at Inverness,' pursued Sir Everard amiably, 'can easily be obtained, Major Windham, and no expense would be incurred by you for your journey to Carlisle; it would be defrayed . . .'

But Keith was not listening; he was wishing that he had Guthrie in some private spot with a couple of swords between them – no, better, one horsewhip! This was his crowning piece of malevolence!

Sir Everard stopped short in his beguiling recital, which had reached the assurance that the Duke would not forget the service which the hearer was about to render. 'What is the matter, Major Windham?' he inquired. 'You seem discomposed. Has Major Guthrie misinformed me?'

Keith did not answer that question. 'Why does not Major Guthrie go as witness himself?' he asked in a half-choked voice.

'Because he cannot testify to overt acts, as you can,' explained Sir Everard. 'It is true that he captured Cameron of Ardroy, badly wounded – and there is no room for doubt when he took those wounds – but a jury might not convict on that evidence alone, whereas you, Major Windham—'

'Whereas mine – supposing it to be what you say – would successfully hang him?' finished Keith, looking straight at the secretary.

Sir Everard nodded with a gratified expression. 'You would have the satisfaction of rendering that service to His Majesty, and at the same time – if you'll permit me to be frank, Major Windham – of purging yourself of any suspicion of undue tenderness towards the rebels. I fancy,' he added with an air of finesse, 'that the accusation arose in connection with this very man, Ewen Cameron, did it not? You see how triumphantly you could clear your honour of any such aspersions.' And Sir Everard smiled good-humouredly.

'My honour must be in a sad case, sir,' said Keith, 'if to act hangman to a man who spared my own life will cleanse it! I am obliged to you for your solicitude, but I must beg to decline. Had it been some other rebel I might perhaps have been able to gratify you, but against Cameron of Ardroy I cannot and will not give evidence. I will therefore wish you good day.' He bowed and turned to go, inwardly seething.

'Stop, stop!' cried Sir Everard, jumping up; but it was not his summons which stayed Keith (in whose head at that moment was some wild idea of going to search for Major Guthrie), but the fact that he almost collided with a stout young officer of exalted rank just coming through the aperture of the tent. Keith hastily drew back, came to attention, and saluted respectfully, for it was Cumberland himself.

The Duke took no notice of him, but went straight over to

his secretary. There had come in with him another stout officer of high rank, twenty years or so his senior, in whom Keith recognized the Earl of Albermarle. The couple of aides-de-camp who followed posted themselves just inside the tent door.

'I hope you have completed those damned tiresome notes about evidence, Faulkner,' said the Prince rather fretfully, 'for there are a thousand and one matters to be attended to before tomorrow, and Lord Albemarle also desires some talk with you.'

'All are in order, your Royal Highness,' responded Sir Everard deferentially, 'save the case of Cameron of Ardroy, for which we shall have to rely on evidence at Fort William. With your permission, my Lord,' he turned to the Earl of Albemarle, 'I will speak to your secretary about it.'

'But have you not summoned Major Windham from Inverness, as I bade you?' exclaimed the Duke. 'You told me yourself that his testimony would be invaluable. Why the devil didn't you send for him?'

'Your Royal Highness's commands were obeyed to the letter,' responded Sir Everard with some stiffness. 'But it seems that Major Windham has scruples about giving his testimony – as he can explain in person to your Royal Highness, since he is present.'

Cumberland swung round his bulk with an alertness which showed his five-and-twenty years. He glanced at Keith, standing motionless at the side of the tent. 'Won't give it – scruples? Nonsense! You must have misunderstood him, Faulkner. Write a line to Major-General Blakeney at once, informing him that Major Windham is seconded, as he sets out with me for England tomorrow. Now, Major, you see how easy it is to leave your new regiment, so no difficulty remains, eh?'

Keith's head went round. Advancement at last – and good-bye to Scotland! But his heart was cold. There was a condition to this favour impossible of fulfilment.

He came forward a little. 'If the honour your Royal Highness designs to do me,' he said in a very low voice, 'depends upon my giving evidence against Cameron of Ardroy, I must beg leave, with the greatest respect, to decline it. But if it is without such a condition, your Royal Highness has no more grateful servant.'

'Condition, sir – what do you mean?' demanded the Prince sharply. 'Are you trying to bargain with me?

'Indeed, no, your Royal Highness. I thought,' ventured Keith, still very respectfully, 'that it was rather the other way about . . . But I was no doubt mistaken.'

The pale, prominent eyes stared at him a moment, and their owner gave vent to what in any other but a scion of royalty would have been termed a snort. 'Indeed you are mistaken, sir! I do not bargain with officers under my command; I give them orders. Be ready to start for Edinburgh tomorrow with the rest of my staff at the time I design to leave Fort Augustus. In England leave will be given you for the purpose of attending the trial of this rebel at Carlisle, whenever it shall take place. After that you will rejoin my staff and accompany me – or follow me, as the case may be – to the Continent. It is part of the duty of a commander-in-chief, gentlemen,' went on the Duke, addressing the remainder of the company, 'to remember and reward individual merit, and Major Windham's gallantry at Fontenoy has not passed from my mind, although I have not until now been able to recompense it as it deserves.'

The aides-de-camp, Sir Everard and even Lord Albemarle expressed in murmurs or in dumb show their appreciation of His Royal Highness's gracious good memory. As for Keith, he was conscious of an almost physical nausea, so sickened was he by the unblushing hypocrisy of the bribe – it was nothing less. He looked at the ground as he answered.

'Your Royal Highness overwhelms me, and I hope to show my gratitude by always doing my duty – which is no more than I did at Fontenoy. But there are private reasons why I can not give evidence against Cameron of Ardroy; I am too much in his debt for services rendered in the past. I appeal therefore to your Highness's generosity to spare me so odious a task.'

The Duke frowned. 'You forget, I think, Major Windham, with what kind of men we are dealing – bloody and unnatural rebels, who have to be exterminated like vermin – like vermin, sir! Here is a chance of getting rid of one rat the more, and you ask that your private sentiments shall be allowed to excuse you from that duty! No, Major Windham, I tell you that they shall not!'

Keith drew himself up, and this time he met Cumberland's gaze full.

'I would beg leave to say to your Royal Highness, speaking as a soldier to the most distinguished soldier in Britain, that it is no part of military duty, even in the crushing of a rebellion, to play the informer.'

The faces of the aides-de-camp, one of them a most elegant young man, expressed the kind of shock produced on a refined mind by an exhibition of bad taste, Lord Albemarle shook his head and put his hand over his mouth, but Sir Everard Faulkner's demonstration of horror could not be seen, since he was behind his royal master, and the latter had almost visibly swollen in size.

'What, you damned impertinent dog, are you to tell *me* what is a soldier's duty!' he got out. 'Why, this is mutiny!'

'Nothing is farther from my thoughts,' replied Keith quietly and firmly. 'Give me any order that a soldier may fitly execute and your Royal Highness will soon see that. But I have been accustomed to meet the enemies of my country in the field, and not in the dock.' And as the Duke was still incoherent from fury and incredulity he repeated: 'With the utmost respect, I must decline to give evidence in this case.'

'Damn your respect, sir!' shouted the Commander-in-Chief, finding his tongue again. 'You're little better than a rebel yourself! A soldier – any soldier – under my command does what he is ordered, or I'll know the reason why!' He stamped his royal foot. 'By Heaven, you *shall* go to Carlisle, if I have to send you there under guard! But you need not flatter yourself that there will be any vacancy for you on my staff after this. Now, will you go willingly, or must the provost-marshal take you?'

Keith measured his princely and well-fed opponent, the adulated victor, the bloodstained executioner. He was tolerably certain that the Duke, for all his powers, could not force him to give evidence, and that this talk of sending him to Carlisle by force was only a threat. But he knew that civilians, at all events, could be subpœnaed as witnesses, and was not too sure of his own ultimate position. He brought out therefore a new and unexpected weapon.

'If my presence should be constrained at the trial, I must take leave to observe to your Royal Highness that I shall then be obliged to give the whole of my testimony – how Mr Cameron spared my life when he had me at his mercy after the disaster at High Bridge last summer, and how, in Edinburgh, he saved me from the hands of the Cameron guard and gave me my liberty when I was abandoned by the soldiers with me and trapped. Since those facts would undoubtedly have some influence on an English jury, I cannot think that I should prove an altogether satisfactory witness for the Crown.'

The victor of Culloden stood a moment stupefied with rage. When he could command his voice he turned to his secretary. 'Is this true, Faulkner, what this – mutineer says?' (For indeed, owing to Keith's calculated reticence at Inverness, it was news to him.) To Sir Everard's reply that he did not know, the Duke returned furiously: 'It's your business to know, you blockhead!' and after that the storm was loosed on Keith, and a flood of most unprincely invective it was. The names he was called, however, passed him by without really wounding him much. They were nothing compared to those he would have called himself had he sold Ardroy's life as the price of his own advancement.

But it was pretty clear that he had finally consummated his own ruin, and when he heard the angry voice declaring its owner's regret that he had overlooked his previous ill-conduct with regard to this misbegotten rebel, Keith fully expected the Duke to add that he intended to break him for his present. Perhaps that would come later; for the moment the Duke contented himself with requesting him, in language more suggestive of the guard-room than the palace, to take his ——— face where he would never see it again. 'And you need not think,' he finished, out of breath, 'that you will save the rascally rebel who has suborned you from your duty; there are plenty other witnesses who will see to it that he hangs!'

But that Keith did not believe, or the Duke and Sir Everard would not have been so eager to secure his evidence. And as, at last, he saluted and rather dizzily left the tent where he had completed the wreck of his ambitions, it was resentment which burnt in him more fiercely than any other emotion. That it should be supposed that anyone – even a Prince of the blood – could bribe him into an action which revolted him!

Late as it was, he would much have preferred to start back to Inverness that evening, but his horse had to be considered. And, while he was seeing that the beast was being properly looked after, he was surprised to find himself accosted by an

elegant young officer whom he recognized as one of the two
aides-de-camp present at the recent scene.

'Major Windham, is it not? General Lord Albemarle requests
that you will not leave the camp without further orders, and
that you will wait upon him at some time after His Royal
Highness's departure tomorrow.'

'Do you mean, sir,' asked Keith bluntly, 'that I am to consider myself under arrest?'

'Oh, my dear Major, by no means!' answered the young man,
greatly shocked. 'On the contrary! His Lordship – but I am
being prodigious indiscreet – recognized in you, it seems, an
acquaintance, so do not fail to wait upon him tomorrow.'

'I will do so,' said Keith. 'Meanwhile, can you tell me if a
certain Major Guthrie of Campbell's regiment is in camp?'

'Major Guthrie – la, sir, I've not the pleasure of his acquaintance. But stay, part of Campbell's regiment marched the day
before yesterday for Badenoch, so it is like the Major is gone
with them.'

'If it be a question of further burnings and floggings, I am
sure he will be gone with them,' commented Keith. 'Perhaps
it is as well. . . . Tell his Lordship that I will certainly obey
his commands tomorrow.'

Once again he spent a night at Fort Augustus after a clash
with authority. But this time it was a collision with a much
more devastating force than Lord Loudoun. Cumberland was
not likely to forget or forgive. And Keith felt quite reckless,
and glad to be rid of the prudence which had shackled him
since May. He had no more to lose now. If he could have
shaken the life out of Guthrie it would have been some consolation. From Lord Albemarle's message it did not seem as if
he were going to be relieved of his commission after all; but,
if he were, then, by God, he would get at Guthrie somehow,
and challenge him!

When Cumberland first came to Fort Augustus he had been
housed in a 'neat bower' which was specially constructed for
him, and Lieutenant-General Lord Albemarle evidently preferred this abode of his predecessor's to a tent. It was there,
at any rate, that he received Major Windham next afternoon
when the racket of the Duke's departure was over.

William Anne Keppel, second Earl of Albemarle, the son of

King William's Dutch favourite, was at this time forty-two years of age, but his portly habit of body made him look older. Plain as well as stout, he gave the impression of a kind but easily flustered nature.

'We met at Perth, did we not, Major Windham?' he asked, and as Keith bowed and assented the Earl said pleasantly: 'I should like a few minutes' conversation with you. You can leave us, Captain Ferrers.'

And when the elegant aide-de-camp had withdrawn, Albemarle, pacing up and down with short steps, his hands behind his broad back, began: 'I must say that I am very sorry, Major Windham, that you felt constrained to take up such an attitude towards His Royal Highness yesterday.'

'So am I, my Lord,' returned the culprit, with truth. 'But I had no choice. I hope your Lordship is not going to renew the same request, for there are some things which a man cannot do, and one of those is, to help hang a man who has spared his own life.'

'Is that so – the prisoner in question spared your life?' asked Albemarle with an appearance of surprise, though, thought Keith, unless he had not been listening he must have learnt that fact yesterday. 'Surely you did not make that clear to His Royal Highness, who is as remarkable for clemency as for just severity!'

Keith looked at him askance; was my Lord Albemarle joking or sincere?

'No, Major Windham,' went on the new Commander-in-Chief, 'I do not intend to renew the request, for I should not presume to flatter myself that I could succeed where one with so much stronger a claim on your obedience has failed. Your revealing this fact alters matters; I sympathize with your scrupulosity, and so must the excellent Prince have done had you but presented the case fairly to him. A pity, Major Windham!'

Keith inclined his head, but said nothing. A grim amusement possessed him, and he could not imagine why Lord Albemarle should be at pains to make this elaborate pretence.

'His Royal Highness's zeal has been wonderful,' pursued the Earl. He sighed, sat down, and began to drum his fingers on the table beside him. 'How I am expected to replace him I do not know. He has indeed accomplished most of his great task, but I am left with part of it still upon my hands – the capturing of the Pretender's son, if indeed he has escaped the last search party of fifteen hundred men sent out from here and from Fort William three days ago. . . . And again, I fear that relations with the Scottish authorities may be sadly difficult. *L'Ecosse est ma bête*, Major Windham, as I think I said to you before, on a certain occasion when I was very indiscreet. Had I then had an indiscreet listener I might have harmed myself by my imprudence.' He stopped drumming and looked up. 'I shall see what I can do for you, Major Windham,' he concluded, with a suddenness which took Keith's breath away.

'Your Lordship . . .' he stammered, and found no more words. Albemarle smiled.

The opportunity may shortly present itself of employing you. I must see. Meanwhile I wish you to remain here; I will arrange that with Major-General Blakeney and your colonel.'

And Keith murmured he knew not what. It seemed impossible that at Perth he should have made an impression so deep as to lead to this; and in a moment it appeared that there was another factor in the case, for Lord Albemarle, fidgeting with the sand-box on the table, revealed it.

'Years ago,' he said reflectively, 'when I was a younger man, I used to know a lady – the most beautiful, I think, whom I have ever met in my life. Perhaps you can guess whom I mean? . . . I did not know when you brought me the despatch at Perth, Major Windham, that Lady Stowe was your mother; I have learnt it since. It would give me pleasure to extend to her son a trifle of help at a crisis in his fortunes. – No, say no more about it, Windham; 'tis but the payment of a debt to Beauty, who allowed unreproved worship at her shrine!'

And he raised his eyes to the roof of the neat bower, apparently absorbed in sentimental retrospect, while Keith, startled, grateful, yet sardonically amused, tried to picture this plain· and unwieldy Anglo-Dutch peer paying his devoirs to a lady who had almost certainly made game of him behind his back. Or had she found him useful, like Lord Orkney, who, when Keith was a mere boy, had promised the pair of colours in the Royal Scots which had saved his mother so much trouble and expense – and had deprived him of any choice in the matter of a regiment.

But the adorer in question at this moment had now brought his eyes to the ordinary level again.

'You are not like the Countess, Major Windham,' he observed.

'My Lord, I am only too well aware of that. My half-brother Aveling resembles her much more closely. He is a very handsome youth.'

'I must make Lord Aveling's acquaintance some day,' said the Earl rising. 'Commend me meanwhile to Lady Stowe.'

'I shall not fail to do so, my Lord,' replied Keith, preparing to withdraw, but hesitating. Yes, this unlooked-for and melting mood was certainly that in which to proffer his request. 'Your Lordship's extreme generosity towards a disgraced man,' he went on, 'emboldens me to ask a small favour, which is, that I may see Cameron of Ardroy once before he goes south to his trial – giving my most sacred word of honour that nothing shall pass between us relative to escape. I desire only to say farewell to him, and your Lordship, who has shown yourself so sensible of my obligation towards him—'

'Yes, yes,' interrupted his Lordship, putting up a plump hand. 'Yes, before he goes you shall see him, I promise you, Major Windham. But not at present – not at present,' he added, as if he felt that the line of his complaisance must be drawn somewhere. 'Send me in Captain Ferrers, if you please, as you go out.'

So Keith left, meditating on the hopeful change in his outlook. It was strange that Lord Albemarle did not fear Cumberland's wrath, if the Duke ever learnt of the favour shown to a man under his extremest displeasure. If it was solely for the sake of the beautiful Countess of Stowe that his Lordship was braving this possibility, the situation was still more ironical, for Keith knew well that his mother would not feel any particular gratitude for this clemency towards her elder son. She would rather that some special token of favour had fallen on the head of his young half-brother, who had no need of it.

The next few days went slowly by, and Keith began to wonder whether Lord Albemarle's lenity were not going to end in nothing but the assurance to him of an idle existence at Fort Augustus. He was glad, however, to be there, for he could fairly well assure himself that Ardroy was not taken away without his knowledge. Inquiries revealed the fact that old Sergeant Mullins was no longer his jailer, but Keith got speech with his successor, a Scot, and learnt that Ewen was to be taken on the twenty-fifth of the month to Fort William to be identified. On the morning of the twenty-fourth, fearing to wait any longer, he sought out the exquisite Captain Ferrers and begged him to recall to Lord Albemarle's mind his promise that he should see the prisoner before departure; and in the afternoon was duly handed a signed order permitting an interview.

Chapter Seven

In thinking of Ewen, Keith had always pictured him where last he had seen him, in the upper room, light and wind-blown, and when he was conducted to the regions under the remains of the fort, he realized with something approaching dismay that Ardroy's quarters had not been changed for the better. And as the door was opened, and he saw before him, down a few steps, a sort of cellar which seemed darker than it really was, and which smelt of damp, he was horrified, though in reality, the fort being of quite recent construction, its 'dungeons' were not nearly as noisome as their name suggested.

There was one small grated window, high up, and under this Ewen was sitting on a stool with his back to the door, reading, though there hardly appeared sufficient light for it. He did not turn his head. 'Is that supper already, Corporal?' he asked. 'What time is it then?'

'No, Mr Cameron, nae supper, but an officer tae veesit ye. – Hae a care o' yon steps, sir!'

But Ewen had turned on his stool, had seen who his visitor was, and was getting to his feet. He clashed as he moved, for he was in irons.

'Windham!' he exclaimed with an accent of surprise and pleasure. 'This is very good of you! Where have you come from?'

And as Keith, distressed by everything, the darkness, the want of accommodation and the chains, stood rooted, Ewen, with more jangling, limped towards him, holding out a fettered hand. He was blanched by two months of semi-darkness, worn down by illness and insufficient food to the framework of himself, but he was shaven and respectably clothed, and he had all his old erectness of poise.

Keith took the proffered hand. 'How long have you had *those* on?' was his first question.

'These irons? Only for a few days. They have just come off a man imprisoned for a short time with me who had the distinction of helping the Prince to escape when he was in Skye, MacDonald of Kingsburgh, and when he was carried to Edinburgh they put them on me. I was flattered, not having the same qualification for them. Sit down, Major, on the stool he had, which still remains to me – or take mine, if you consider that less treasonable. Faith, no, I suppose Kingsburgh, who was never "out", is less of a rebel than I.' He laughed, shuffled to a corner, and came back with another stool. 'Now tell me how you came here, and what your situation is now? Mullins gave me some news of you – very scanty – in May. Are you quit of the cloud you drew upon yourself for my sake?'

'It is of yourself that we must speak,' said Keith, hoarsely, thrown off his balance by this unaffected cheerfulness, and deeply ashamed, all at once, of the cowardly 'prudence' which had left Ardroy without a letter. 'Sit down; you should not stand, I am sure. How goes your wound?'

Rather stiffly, Ewen sat down. 'Quite healed, though the leg is weak. However, I am to ride thirty miles tomorrow, for I go to Fort William to be identified, thence to Carlisle for trial – by what means of transport I do not know.'

'You think that you will be identified by this man at Fort William?'

'Man? There is more than one; indeed there'll be a measure of jealousy, I'm thinking, who shall travel to Carlisle on my affair at the expense of the Government. – Why, I vow it never occurred to me before that *you* might go, Windham, and save me the journey to Fort William; for you can identify me, none better!'

Keith winced. 'Don't jest,' he said in a sombre voice; 'don't jest on such a theme, I beg of you. And, Ardroy,' he added earnestly, 'I doubt whether the authorities here really place very much reliance on this testimony from Fort William, or they would not have—' He pulled up, biting his lip, for he had no intention of speaking of his encounter with Cumberland. Though he had no cause for shame, he was ashamed; moreover he did not wish to parade his own self-abnegation.

In the dim light, momentarily becoming to Keith, however, a little less dim, the prisoner looked at him with those clear eyes of his. Then, with a jangle, he laid his bony hand on the Englishman's wrist. 'My sorrow, I believe my jest went near the truth! They did want you to go as a witness against me – was not that what you were about to say? Why, then, did you not comply?'

Keith turned on him almost savagely. 'How dare you ask me that, Ewen Cameron! Do you think I baulked Guthrie only to go in cold blood and bring you to the scaffold myself? Are you like the Duke, that you can fancy I would do such a thing for any consideration on earth . . . and witness moreover to acts by which I had been the gainer?'

'I beg your pardon,' said Ewen mildly. 'In truth I was not thinking of the implications of what I said. But, Windham,' he went on anxiously, 'has not your refusal involved you once more in Cumberland's displeasure? I'm sure it has!'

'No, no,' said Keith mendaciously. 'He was angry, but he has not punished me further. He could not force me to be a witness; and Lord Albemarle has subsequently shown me some favour, and holds out hopes of employing me, which is why I am here at Fort Augustus. As far as I am concerned, therefore, good may yet come out of evil. – But, tell me, to what does this evidence at Fort William amount?'

But Ewen replied by another question. 'What was the bribe which Cumberland offered you to give evidence against me?'

'Bribe!' exclaimed Keith, rather over-hastily. 'I said nothing about a bribe. I want to hear about these witnesses at Fort William.'

'But I want to know what you have sacrificed for my sake? Or perhaps it would be truer to say, for the sake of your own self-respect? Cumberland did offer you something, did he not?'

'Nothing of consequence,' answered Keith carelessly.

'You will not tell me what it was? Then I know that it was something which you coveted. I seem fated to bring you misfortune, Windham,' said the Highlander rather sadly. 'And yet I never really wished you other than well.'

'But I have brought you even more,' said Keith; 'and indeed

I wished you well, too.' His eyes were on the heap of straw in the corner which constituted Ewen's bed. 'If I had not ridden by the shieling hut that day, you would be lying quietly among the mountains of your own land and not – not about to set out for the chance, at least, of a death far away, and . . . and much less merciful. I should like to hear you say that you for-give me for that.'

'Forgive you for saving my life!' exclaimed Ewen. 'My dear Windham, you are really absurd! Don't, for God's sake, go recalling the crazy things I said to you at our last meeting! You must remember that I was nearly out of my senses then.'

'I know that, and I have never given them another thought, I assure you. But there is a count,' said Keith rather hesitatingly, 'on which you must find it hard to forgive me – suffering of the mind for which I must always hold myself in a measure responsible. You know to what I refer.'

Ewen looked down at the floor. 'I had some dark days, it is true. . . . Yes, they were very dark . . . but not so dark after your return. You gave me hope; and above all you gave me back that night in the hut.' He smiled. 'I often think of it. I think of it when I hear very different stories of the English. And I suppose you know that nothing came of my betrayal – they never even searched the place for Lochiel, I believe. And, moreover' – he suddenly looked almost boyishly elated and mischievous – 'by some wonderful mischance I never gave the name of the mountain where the secret place was. In my sleep I presented them with the name of Ben Loy, where you came upon me, and they did not discover the error until too late.'

Keith put his hand on the speaker's knee. 'I heard at Inver-ness, to my satisfaction, that Lochiel had escaped capture. Then that is all over, and your mind at rest; I am thankful.'

Ewen looked grave again. 'No, it cannot be at rest until I am sure that Lochiel knows the truth.'

'But why should he ever hear anything at all about the matter?'

'And I have thought that at my trial,' went on Ewen with-out taking notice of the interruption, 'I may get the chance of publicly denying that I gave the information knowingly. And then I believe that I could die in peace.'

Keith withdrew his hand. 'Why do you make so sure of your condemnation?' he asked almost irritably. 'Of what real worth is the testimony of persons who imagine that they saw you during a siege? No one could swear to you out of so many Camerons!'

'You think we are all as alike as sheep?' queried Ewen, looking amused. 'But I had at least one hand-to-hand conflict with the Argyll militia, and another day I encountered a writer of Maryburgh with whom I had had dealings; he knew me at once, and will be only too glad to give evidence against me; I cannot think how they have not got hold of it already. – No, Windham, 'tis better to face the truth; once I reach Fort William I am certainly for Carlisle, and with such good evidence against me I have small chance of acquittal. I have known that for the last ten days; though naturally I have not acquainted the authorities with the excellent case they are like to have.'

And to this Keith found nothing to say. It was strange, it was alarming, to feel, as by this time he did, how strongly their intimacy had progressed in two months of absence and, on his side, of deliberate abstention from communication – like the roots of two trees growing secretly towards each other in darkness. But it was so; and now the roots must be severed.

'I hear that some of the prisoners at Inverness intend to swear that they were forced out,' he remarked after a silence.

'I dare say that may be true of some of them,' replied Ewen with composure. 'But you are not suggesting that I should employ that plea, are you?'

'I know too well that you would not,' returned his visitor, and then murmured something about transportation as a possible alternative to a worse fate.

'Transportation!' exclaimed the Highlander. 'To be sent to work in the plantations oversea as an indentured servant! I'd far liefer be hanged and quartered!'

Keith sighed heavily. 'Yes, I have brought you nothing but harm. I would give my right hand to save you – and I can do nothing!'

Ewen twisted round on his stool. 'How can you say that? Who knows what the want of your evidence at Carlisle may mean to me? For there is always a chance that the witnesses at Fort William may have left or died.'

'You have just said that once you reached Fort William there was no chance of escaping Carlisle. I am not a child,

Ardroy!' retorted Keith, glowering at him in his own pain.

'Neither am I,' replied Ewen with a sudden smile. 'Do not, therefore, talk about wishing in vain to give your right hand for my sake, for I strongly suspect that you have already given what means as much or more to you.'

Keith got up, that the speaker might not see in his face how near this guess went to the truth. 'Even in my refusal to witness against you,' he said gloomily, 'I begin to think that I acted like a fool. For, as I told His Royal Highness, if he sent me to Carlisle by force, as he threatened to do, nothing should have prevented my testifying also to your granting me my life in Lochaber and my liberty in Edinburgh. I have thought since that, on that score, it might have been better to agree to go. . . . But now, I could not have done it!' he added.

Ewen smiled up at him with a look that was almost affection, and laid his manacled hand on his cuff. 'I almost wish that you had consented, so that we might meet again. For, if old Angus is right, this is our last meeting – I have counted them many times. And, indeed, I do not see how it could be otherwise. So' – his voice was very gentle – 'we cannot bring each other misfortune any more.'

The words knocked sharply at Keith's heart. And how young the speaker looked, for all his half-starved air; a boy going to extinction, while he, only four years his senior, felt as if he were middle-aged. (But no, at their last meeting, when he had trembled before him, Ewen had not been a boy.)

'Is there nothing I can do for you?' he asked painfully. 'Do your kindred know of your situation; I suppose so?'

'I am not sure if my aunt knows. If she does, she has no doubt tried to communicate with my wife in France, but—'

'Your wife! Then you—'

'Yes. Miss Grant and I were married at Inverness in March. She is in France with her sick father, and since the battle I have been unable to write to her, so that, unless my aunt has contrived to do so, she may not know whether I am alive or dead. If you would write to her, Windham – you remember her, no doubt – that would indeed be a kindness. Will you?'

'Certainly, if you wish it,' answered Keith, though he did

not like the prospect. 'But,' he went on with a little hesitation, 'why do you not write yourself, and I would use my best endeavours that the letter should reach her.'

'I cannot write,' said Ewen. 'They will not allow me the materials; I have often tried to come by them. You must tell her of me, if you will; and I particularly charge you not to omit how you saved my life and visited me, and . . . and all the rest that you have done,' he concluded a trifle unsteadily. 'That is a last command, Windham.'

But Keith had drawn a pencil from his pocket. 'You had a book in your hand when I came in; can you not tear out a blank page and write upon that? I promise you that, if I compass it, no eye shall see the letter but your wife's.'

'A book?' queried Ewen. 'Ah, yes, but 'tis only a little Gaelic psalter which I contrived to get hold of. However—' He took it out of his pocket, remarking that the pages were but small, and, carefully tearing out the fly-leaf, accepted the proffered pencil. Keith, unable to withdraw as he would have wished, walked slowly up and down the narrow place with bent head. 'I have saved him for this!' was still the burden of his thoughts. Had Ardroy been shot that day he would have known little about it; he was barely conscious. It would have been over in a moment, and it would have been a man's death, too. Now . . . he shuddered to think of the alternative, purposely prolonged and horrible, the death of an animal in the shambles. He hoped with all his heart that Alison Cameron, away in France, did not know, and would never hear, the details of the English sentence for treason.

Ewen did not write much, for there was not a great deal of space on his paper. He read it over very composedly and signed his name. Then he folded the letter, stooped his head and put his lips to it. Keith turned his back, but the distance between them was so small that he knew that the writer, after that, had buried his face in his hands.

Ah, if only he had listened to him on that evening last summer, which now seemed such centuries ago, he would not now be giving up his love, as well as his life and lands!

But there was a clashing behind him; Ewen was getting to his feet. 'I beg your pardon for keeping you waiting so long. Since you are so good I think that I should like to send my wife also the only remembrance that I can send. Have you a knife, and can you trust me with it? – or better still, will you cut off a piece of this for her?'

He indicated his hair, and coming closer, bent his head. So Keith, with a rather blunt penknife, and not particularly good eyesight at the moment, sawed off a little lock on his temple.

'Women like such things,' said the young man half apologetically as Keith, his mouth tight shut, wrapped the trophy in his handkerchief. 'And the more of which one can cheat Carlisle gate the better.' He spoke quite lightly and calmly, but his little letter, which he gave Keith the moment after, had been so tightly held in his hand that it was marked with his nail-prints. 'I have written the direction upon it,' he went on, watching the Englishman put it carefully away. 'Perhaps I may be able to write to her once more from Carlisle, but who knows? And the messenger might not be trustworthy, whereas I know you are. – Now, Windham, there is another matter. The money you so generously left for my use—'

'For God's sake don't think of that now!' cried Keith, quite distracted.

'But I must! Miss Cameron, if I can communicate with her, which may be allowed at Carlisle—'

'Will you waste time over a few guineas? In Heaven's name, take them as a gift – cannot you see that it would be kinder to me?'

Ewen evidently saw; he could hardly fail to see it. 'Very well, then I will; and thank you for the gift. After all, I took a greater at your hands on Beinn Laoigh. And do you remember the money you left as payment for my clothes at Fassefern House? My sorrow, but I was angry with you! I threw it away into the bushes, and Clanranald's and Keppoch's men hunted for it all night, so I heard afterwards.' His tone suddenly changed. 'Do you mean to leave this penknife here – is that a gift, too?'

He pointed to that object, lying where Keith had laid it down on one of the stools in order to have both hands free to wrap up the lock of hair. The Englishman hesitated, looking from it to the prisoner, and read, plain to see in his eyes, the value which he would set on even so small and blunt a weapon tomorrow. For a moment he was tempted, against honour and duty.

'Why did you put me in mind of it?' he asked reproachfully

'I had indeed honestly forgotten it, and had I so left it, you could have taken it with you tomorrow? . . . But I gave Lord Albemarle my word not to help you in any way to escape . . .'

Ewen instantly picked up the penknife, shut it, and held it out to him. 'Take it. They are sure, too, to search me before I go tomorrow. Come,' he still held it out, 'you have sacrificed enough for me; your honour you shall not sacrifice!'

As Keith reluctantly took the knife from the shackled hand he had a shock as if a lightning flash had stabbed asunder the sky above him and shown him something he had never seen – never wished to see – before. The barren and solitary path which he had marked out for himself through life was *not* the best. Here was a man who would never willingly fail friend or lover, much less play them false. Now, at this their last meeting, when friendship with him was a thing impossible of realization, he knew that he would have asked nothing better – he who never wished for a friend.

Like a lightning flash too in its speed the revelation was over. Mechanically he put the penknife away, and Ewen limped the few paces back to his stool. 'Come and sit down again, Windham,' he said, 'for once more you cannot get out if you wish to. And there is a matter about which I have long been curious. Why do you bear a Scots name – if I may ask without indiscretion? Have you perhaps Scottish kin?'

Keith, sitting down beside him again, shook his head. 'There's not a soul of my blood north of Tweed. But my father, who was a soldier also, had once a Scottish friend, killed at Malplaquet before I was born, for whom he must have had a great affection, since he gave me his name.'

They looked at each other, and the shadowy dead Scot of Marlborough's war seemed, to his namesake at least, to assume the shape of a symbol or a prophecy. Keith shivered suddenly.

'I can hardly hope,' said the Jacobite, 'that you will care to name your son after me when I have ended . . . not on a battlefield . . . but I should like to feel that you will remember sometimes, not me, but what you did for me. For whereas you think but poorly of your fellow-men and yourself – or am I wrong? – you act, Keith Windham, very much otherwise!'

Moved and startled, Keith dropped his gaze and stared between his knees at the floor. Yes, they might have been friends: they were meant to be friends – Ardroy felt that too, did he?

'I . . . in truth I do not well know what I think,' he murmured; 'and as for my actions, why, I seem to have failed on every side. – But one thing I do know,' he went on with a touch of defiance, 'and that is, that I do not believe in your Highland second sight. Who can say that we shall not meet again – and you a free man?'

Ewen looked hard at him a moment. Outside the jangling of keys could be heard coming nearer. 'I wish very much that I could think so too,' he answered simply, as he rose to his feet with a corresponding clashing. And again the strange constriction in his throat betrayed Keith into irritation.

'Are you so superstitious, Ardroy, that you'll read into an old man's maunderings a menace that was never there? Did your foster-father say a word about death in his precious prophecy? I warrant he did not!'

Ewen smiled. 'My dear Windham, at bottom I believe as little in the two sights as you. But surely 'tis not superstition to realize that I am at least threatened with that fate. Yet who knows? If it pass me by, and we ever meet again in this world, then maybe I'll have more time to thank you fitly for all you have done and given up for me. Yet I do thank you now, from my heart – my inmost heart!'

He held out his fettered hands, and Keith as he took them was hardly capable of speech.

'I have failed in everything,' he muttered. 'But your letter – I promise you it shall go by a safe hand. I . . . I . . .' The door, opening, recalled him to an Englishman's last obligation, the suppression of emotion before witnesses. 'Tomorrow,' he said, loosing his grasp, and in a tolerably composed voice, 'tomorrow you will at least be out of this dismal place and free of those irons.'

'Aye, will he,' commented the jailer in the doorway. 'And riding a braw horse forbye!'

'I doubt I'll make much show as a horseman,' replied Ewen. 'I fear I shall fall off.'

'Ye're no' like tae hae the chance, Mr Cameron,' replied the man dryly. 'Ye'll be tied on. – Noo, sir, if ye please.'

'What time is he to start?' asked Keith.

'Sax o' the clock.' The keys jingled impatiently.

Keith took a resolve. But he did not put it into words. All he said was 'Good-bye,' and, for fear of being totally unmanned, stole only the most cursory glance at the pale, gravely smiling face under the rather untidy auburn hair.

But Ewen held out his hand again. '*Beannachd leat*, as we say in the Erse. "Blessing go with you; may a straight path be before you, and a happy end to your journey"!'

Without answering Keith wrung the hand and went quickly up the steps past the jailer and into the passage. He was hardly there before the heavy door clanged to between him and his last meeting with Ewen Cameron.

'A peety,' said the jailer reflectively, taking the key from the lock, 'a peety yon muckle young man behoves to hae a rope aboot his thrapple. But there, wha will tae Cupar maun tae Cupar . . . Yon's the way up, sir.'

At twenty minutes to seven next morning Keith Windham, having propped himself up on one elbow in his camp bed, was staring with incredulous and remorseful eyes at the watch which he had just drawn from beneath his pillow. That he should not wake in time to catch a final glimpse of Ardroy as he rode away had never occurred to him; the question last night had rather been whether he should ever get to sleep . . .

Well, evidently old Angus MacMartin's fates were determined that he should not see Ewen Cameron again. And after all, he thought, trying to stifle regret, did I really desire to see him carried away, bound upon a horse, by Kingston's dragoons?

When he was dressed he went to the door of the tent, which opened towards Loch Ness, and looked out. It was a beautiful, fresh morning, and the loch was smiling up at the flanking hills. Even the ruins of the fort, rearing themselves against that brightness, looked less blackened in the sunshine. But for Keith those gutted buildings held nothing now; and the busy camp around him was empty, too. How far on the road were they got by this time, and were the troopers riding too fast . . . ?

He dropped the flap of the tent and, going over to the table, took out from the breast of his uniform the handkerchief with the curl of hair and the scrap of a letter, and sealed them up carefully in a little packet, first copying down the address and scrupulously averting his eyes from the rest of the torn fly-leaf in doing so. Then, wondering how soon and in what manner he should find an opportunity of fulfilling his trust,

he sat on, staring at the packet, now directed in his own hand
to Mrs Ewen Cameron at an address in Havre-de-Grâce.

What was it that Ardroy had wished him yesterday – a
straight path and a happy end to his journey. Ewen's own path
seemed straighter than his, now, but the end to which it led?
Keith had a sudden horrible vision, corollary of those which
had haunted him in the night. He pressed his hands over his
eyes and bade it begone, bade himself be as little perturbed at
the prospect as Ewen himself had been yesterday – Ewen who
would certainly go cheerfully and courageously to that ghastly
business, but who, had it not been for his interference, might
be lying now unmutilated under the turf of Ben Loy, with only
the plovers and the curlews to disturb his rest.

Keith suddenly got up and began to pace restlessly to and
fro, his head on his breast. He was finding his self-defensive
philosophy of a very meagre assistance now. If he were again
the child he had been, the child who every night at his nurse's
knee asked so simply and naturally for what he desired, it
would have been easy to utter the prayer in his heart. But of
what use such supplication to the Power whose only concern
with the world was that He had set it a-rolling? Yet it was
some time before he came to a standstill, and, with a heavy
sigh, replaced in his breast the little packet for Ewen Cameron's
wife; with this for consolation in his mind, that he who was
riding southward was not yet condemned, and that till the
sentence was spoken his case was not hopeless.

All that afternoon there came marching wearily back to
Fort Augustus, in a woeful state of fatigue and rags, the various
units of the fifteen hundred men whom Cumberland had sent
out in his last battue for Prince Charles nearly a fortnight before. They had met with no success whatever.

At nine o'clock that evening Keith, to his surprise, received
a summons from Lord Albemarle, and found him heated and
discomposed.

' 'Tis a most extraordinary and vexatious thing,' declared
the Earl, pacing up and down his quarters with his heavy tread.
'It seems as though the Pretender's son must have broken
through the chain of sentry posts round Clanranalds' country,
and yet I can scarce believe it, they were so close together. I
shall make a fresh effort, with fresh men; these poor fellows

are quite worn out with their exertions. For my part, Major Windham, I declare that to capture that young man, source of all our woes, I should with infinite pleasure walk barefoot from Pole to Pole!'

Had Lord Albemarle but known, no such heroic pilgrimage was required of him; a ten-mile expedition that night to a certain cave in Glenmoriston would have been sufficient.

'Your Lordship's zeal is common knowledge,' murmured Keith, wondering what the Commander-in-Chief wanted him for. 'If it could only be crowned with success. . . .'

'Aye, if only it could! One report says,' continued the Earl, going to a table and turning over some papers, 'that the Pretender's son is in Badenoch on his way to the east coast; another that he has gone north to Caithness. Some say he is still in Morar and Knoidart; and the very latest of all declares that he has gone back to the Long Island – as you know they call that chain of islands from South Uist to Lewis. It is distracting!'

It was; but Keith could not think why he should have been summoned to hear this truth.

'Why, bless my soul,' said Albemarle, as if he had read his thought, 'I am so prodigiously put about that I have forgotten, I believe, to tell you, Major Windham, that you are one of the officers whom I design to employ in my new effort.'

'My Lord!' ejaculated Keith, flushing.

'Yes, I intend to send you without delay to the neighbourhood of Arisaig, not because I think that the young man is there at the moment, though one report says so, but because I think it not unlikely he may try in the end to escape from the very spot where he landed last July.'

'Your Lordship is really too good,' stammered Keith, rather overcome. 'If the most active vigilance—'

'Yes,' cut in Albemarle, 'I depend upon you to show that, Major Windham. Your future is in your own hands, and my reputation, too. For reasons upon which I touched the other day, it is you whom I am sending to what I cannot but consider the most likely spot for securing the person of the arch-rebel. The day that you bring him back a prisoner your difference with His Royal Highness will be no more remembered against you. And perhaps I, too,' added the Earl with a sigh, 'shall be able to leave this most distasteful country.'

'I assure your Lordship,' said Keith with a beating heart, 'that failure shall not be due to any want of exertion on my part. Your generous selection of me for this expedition overwhelms me with gratitude, and whether I secure the prize or no I shall be your Lordship's lifelong debtor for the opportunity.'

Lord Albemarle nodded, pleased as one who knows that he confers a benefit. 'You will march at daybreak with a hundred men. I do not say that you are to station yourself exclusively at this Loch nan – on my soul, I cannot pronounce its outlandish name. Dispose your men as you think best. My secretary is preparing a few notes for your guidance. The devil of it is, however,' confessed the harassed commander in a further burst of confidence, 'that these informations, when one receives them, are always a se'nnight or two out of date.' And, after adding a few more recommendations as to Keith's conduct, he said kindly: 'Now go and get some sleep, Windham – and good luck to your endeavours!'

Keith went out as one who walks on air. A chance at last – the greatest, if only he could seize it! So the day which had taken from him something which he felt that he had never really possessed had brought him . . . no, not compensation for the loss, for that, perhaps, he could never have, but opportunity to do more than purge his disgrace – to make himself the most envied man in the three kingdoms.

V

The Heron's Flight is Ended

'Hereafter, in a better world than this,
I shall desire more love and knowledge of you.'
—SHAKESPEARE

Chapter One

IT was fortunate for Ewen that the sorrel horse on which he
was tied had easy paces, and that the troopers did not ride fast;
fortunate too that his arms had been bound to his sides and
not behind his back, as had at first been proposed when, limping badly, and shielding his eyes against the unaccustomed
daylight, he was brought out into the courtyard of the fort to
be mounted. For by midday so many hours in the saddle, under
a July sun, were making heavy demands on a man come
straight from close confinement and not long recovered of a
severe wound.

But from Ewen's spirit a much heavier toll was being exacted;
not by the prospect of the death which was in all likelihood
awaiting him, not even by the remembrance of his lost Alison
but by the pain which was actually tearing at him now, this
taking leave of what he loved better than life, the lakes and
mountains of his home. This was the real death, and he kept
his lips locked lest he should cry out at its sharpness.

The picture which had been tormenting Keith Windham he
could look at without undue shrinking; or rather, he did not
trouble to look at it any more now. Like the man who had
saved him, he could not avoid the thought that Guthrie's musket
balls had been more merciful, but the choice had not lain in
his hands; and for the last two months if had been more important to try to keep his equanimity day after day in the cold
and darkness of his prison than to think what he should do or
feel when he came to stand in the hangman's cart. And the
parting with Alison was over; and because he had known that
the kiss in the cabin of the brig might be their last, it had held

the solemnity which had enwrapped their hurried marriage and the bridal night whose memory was holy to him. Alison had been his, though for so brief a space; and one day, as he firmly believed, they would meet again. But Beinn Tigh . . . would he ever see again, in *that* world, his beloved sentinel of the stars?

Ever since its peak had appeared, all flushed by the morning sun, as they began to ride by Loch Oich, he had kept his eyes hungrily upon it, praying that the horses might go slower, or that one might cast a shoe; watching it like a lover as it revealed more of its shapeliness and dominated the shoulder, between it and the loch, behind which, as they went farther, it would inevitably sink. And Loch na h-Iolaire, *his* loch, away behind there, invisible, secluded by its own mountains! If only he could get free of these cords, swim the water between, climb those intervening miles of scree and heather, and see the Eagle's Lake once more! No, never again; neither in this world nor the next. For Loch na h-Iolaire was not like Alison and him; it had not a soul free of time and space. Loch na h-Iolaire existed over there, only there, on that one spot of earth, and in all the fields of heaven there would be no lake so lovely, and in heaven the grey mists would never swoop down on one who ambushed the deer.

At Laggan-ach-drum they had halted and rested and eaten. It was Glengarry's country, yet on the border of the Cameron, and Ardroy was known there; but in the burnt and ravaged clachan there seemed to be no man left, and no risk of a rescue. The troopers of Kingston's Horse had shown themselves rough but not unkindly, and the sergeant, probably thinking that unless they gave the prisoner some attention they would hardly get him to Fort William at the end of the day, had him unfastened and taken off the sorrel and set down amongst them by the roadside with food and drink. But they were very careful of him, tying his ankles together, and putting a cord from one wrist to the belt of the next man. And Ewen had eaten and drunk in silence, looking at the sunlit desolation. *This* was what had been done in the Glen . . . done in all the country-side . . .

A young girl had passed once or twice to a half-burnt croft carrying a bucket of water, and presently the sergeant, wanting some for the horses, called to ask where the water came from, since here they were no longer by a lake-side. Setting down the heavy bucket, she came and stood before him, looking on the troopers with eyes like coals, and only once at their prisoner. (But the softness of the evening was in them then.) The sergeant, without harshness, put his question, but the girl shook her head, and Ewen knew that she had not the English. Already he had seen a sight that set his heart beating, for as she stooped to put down the bucket he had caught a glimpse of the black handle of a *sgian dubh* in her bosom.

'Shall I ask her for you?' he suggested to the sergeant, and, hardly waiting for the answer, he spoke rapidly to her in Gaelic, putting the question about water indeed, but adding at the end of it: 'Try to give me your knife when I am on the horse again – if you have another for yourself!'

The girl gave him a glance of comprehension, and turned away to show where to fetch the water; and the sergeant had no inkling that another question besides his had been put and answered. He even threw a word of thanks to the interpreter.

But while they were tying Ewen on again the girl came among them, as if curiosity had brought her to see the sight, and heedless of the jests which she did not understand, slipped nearer and nearer among the horses until she seemed to be jostled against the sorrel's shoulder. And Ewen felt the little knife, warm from its hiding-place, slide into his right stocking; it was only with an effort that he kept his eyes averted and seemed unaware of her presence. But he turned his head as they rode away, and saw her standing at gaze with her hands joined, as though she were praying.

That was an hour agone and more. How he should ever get at, much less use, the blade against his leg he had no idea, seeing that his arms were immovably pinioned, but to know it there made a world of difference. His thoughts reverted to Major Windham, to that interview yesterday. They might have been friends had Fate willed it otherwise; indeed he could not but think of him already as a friend, and with wonder at what he had done for him. But why had Angus's heron brought them together to so little purpose, to meet, and meet, and then to part for ever, as they had met at first, 'by the side of water' – Loch Oich and Loch Ness? Yet he owed his life to one of those encounters; there was no possible doubt of that. But it was still a mystery to him why the Englishman should have cared so much for his fate as to wreck his own career over it. He had really behaved to Loudoun and (as far as he could make out) to Cumberland – all honour to him for it – as if he were fey. And he had seemed at the outset of their acquaintance of so mocking a temper, so lightly contemptuous as scarcely even to be hostile. One saw him with different eyes now.

But Keith Windham was swept from his thoughts again, as he realized afresh that he was going for the last time along Loch Lochy side. It was bright pain to look at it, but Ewen looked greedily, trying to burn those high green slopes for ever on his memory, to be imaged there as long as that memory itself was undissolved. There was the steep corries and the wall shutting out his home. What though the house of Ardroy were ashes now, like Achnacarry and a score of others, there were things the marauders could not touch, things dearer even than the old house – the sweeps of fern and heather, the hundred little burns sliding and tinkling among stones and mosses, the dark pine trees, the birches stepping delicately down the torrent side, the mist and the wind, the very mountain air itself. But these, though they would remain were not for him any more.

And then Ewen bit his lip hard, for, to his horror, his eyes had begun to fill, and, since he could not move a hand, all that was left was to bow his head and pray desperately that the troopers on either side might not observe his weakness. But they were just then absorbed in heartfelt complaints at the detour which they were obliged to make on his account, instead of setting out with the rest of Kingston's Horse, in two days' time for Edinburgh; and Ewen quickly swallowed the salt upon his lips, thinking: 'Since I am so little of a man, I must fix my mind on something else.' Yet here, in this dear and familiar neighbourhood, he could think of nothing else but what was before his eyes; and his eyes told him now that the radiance of the morning was gone, and that clouds were coming up the Glen from the south-west, from Loch Linnhe, with that rapidity which he knew so well of old. In an hour it would very likely be raining hard; in less, for beyond the Loch Arkaig break he could see that it was raining.

Here he was, looking just as intently at the hills as before!

So he shut his eyes, afraid lest moisture should spring into them again; and also a little because the waters of Loch Lochy, still bright, despite the advancing clouds, were beginning queerly to dazzle him. And when his eyes were shut he realized with increasing clearness that physically too he was nearing the boundary-line of endurance. He had wondered himself how he should ever accomplish the thirty-mile ride, but the problem had not troubled him much, and the untying and rest at Laggan had been a relief. Now – and they still had a long way to go – it was astonishing how the sea of faintness seemed to be gaining upon him. He reopened his eyes as he felt himself give a great lurch in the saddle.

'Hold up!' said the trooper who had the reins. 'Were ye asleep?'

Ewen shook his head. But what curious specks were floating over the darkening landscape! He fixed his eyes on his horse's ears; but once or twice the whole head of the animal disappeared from his sight altogether; and the second time that this phenomenon occurred he felt a grip on his arm, and found the soldier on the other side looking at him curiously. However, the man released him, saying nothing, and Ewen, mute also, tried to straighten himself in the saddle, and looked ahead in the direction of Ben Nevis, since perhaps it was a mistake to look at anything close at hand. The mountain's top was veiled. The last time that he had seen it . . . with Lochiel . . .

But that memory had poison in it now. Oh, to have speech with Lochiel once before he went hence! Ewen set his teeth, as waves of faintness and of mental pain broke on him together. If he could only say to Donald . . .

And there followed on that, surprisingly, a period in which he thought he was speaking to Lochiel; but it must have been by some waterfall – the waterfall near the hiding-place, perhaps – and through the noise of the rushing water he could not make Lochiel hear what he was saying to him. He tried and tried . . . Then all at once someone was holding him round the body, and a voice called out, miles away, yet close: 'He was near off that time, Sergeant!'

Ewen left the waterfall and became conscious, to his astonishment, that they were away from Lochy and within full sight of Ben Nevis and all his brethren. Also that the whole escort had stopped. Landscape and horses then whirled violently round. His head fell on a trooper's shoulder.

'The prisoner's swounding, Sergeant! What are we to do?'

Swearing under his breath, the sergeant brought his horse alongside. 'Shamming? No, he ain't shamming. Here,' he brought out something from his holster, 'give him a drink of his own Highland whisky – nasty stuff it is!'

They held up Ewen's head and put the spirit to his lips. It revived him a little, and he tried to say something, but he himself did not know what it was. The sergeant eyed him doubtfully.

'I'll tell you what,' he remarked to his men, 'we'll untie his arms – not his feet, mind you – and maybe then he can help himself by taking a hold of the mane. Can ye do that?'

Ewen nodded, too sick and dizzy to realize what possibilities would thus be put within his reach.

The dragoons unfastened the cords round his arms and body, gave him some more spirit, rubbed his cramped arms, and in a little while he was able to do what the sergeant suggested; and presently, he leaning hard upon the sorrel's crest, his fingers twined in the mane, they were going slowly down the moorland slope towards the Spean. Ewen felt less faint now, after the whisky and the release of his arms; the fine misty rain which had now set in was refreshing, too, so, although the landscape showed a disposition to swim at times, he could certainly keep in the saddle – indeed, how could he fall off, he thought, with this rope passing from ankle to ankle beneath the horse's belly? And he began to think about High Bridge, still unseen, which they were approaching, and of the part which it had played in this great and ill-fated adventure – and in his own private fortunes, too. For down there the first spark of revolt had flashed out; down there Keith Windham had been turned back by MacDonald of Tiendrish and his men; and because he had been turned back, Ewen himself was alive today, and not mouldering by Neil MacMartin's side on Beinn Laoigh.

But he was none the less on his way to death, and there was no one to stay the redcoats from passing High Bridge now. Tiendrish, marked for the scaffold, lay already in Edinburgh Castle, Keppoch, his chief, slept with his broken heart among the heather on Culloden Moor; Lochiel was a wounded outlaw with a price on his head. The gods had taken rigorous dues from all who had been concerned in the doings of that August day here by the Spean. Yes, strangely enough, even from Keith Windham, who was on the other side. They had made him pay for having dared to show compassion to those whom they pursued. It was singular.

Unconsciously Ewen was back in the dungeon again, seeing the Englishman's troubled face, hearing his voice as it asked him why he had put him in mind of the forgotten penknife . . .

And then Keith Windham's face and voice were blotted out in an instant by a thought which made him draw a long breath and clutch the sorrel's mane almost convulsively. He had something better than a blunt penknife on his person at this very moment, and now, now that his arms were untied, he could perhaps get it into his hand. For the last hour he had completely forgotten the girl's *sgian* in his stocking; and indeed, until recently it might as well not have been there. But now, if he could draw it out unobserved . . .

And then? Rags of a wild, a desperate plan began to flutter before his eyes. And only here, by the Spean, could the plan be put into execution, because, High Bridge once crossed, it was all open moorland to Fort William. Only by the Spean, racing along between its steep, thickly wooded banks, was there a chance of shelter, if one could gain it. It was a mad scheme, and would very likely result in his being shot dead, but, if they stopped at the little change-house on the other side of the Spean, as they surely would, he would risk that. Better to die by a bullet than by the rope and the knife. How his body would carry out the orders of his brain he did not know; very ill, probably, to judge from his late experiences. Yet, as he hastily plotted out what he would do, and every moment was carried nearer to High Bridge, Ewen had an illusory feeling of vigour; but he knew that he must not show it. On the contrary, his present partially unbound condition being due to his recent only too real faintness, he must continue to simulate what for the moment he no longer felt. If only the faintness did not come on again in earnest!

Here was the Spean in its ravine, and here the narrow bridge reared on its two arches, its central pier rising from a large rock in the river-bed. They clattered over it, three abreast. The bridge was invisible, as Ewen knew, when one was fairly up the other side, because the approach was at so sharp an angle, and the trees so thick. And as they went up that steep approach the trees seemed even thicker than he remembered them. If Spean did not save him, nothing could.

The change-house came into view above them, a little low building by the side of the road, and for a moment the prisoner knew an agonizing doubt whether the escort were going to halt there after all. Yes, thank God, they were! Indeed, it would have been remarkable had they passed it.

The moment the troopers stopped it was evident how little they considered that their prisoner needed guarding now; it was very different from the care which they had bestowed in this particular at Laggan. Drink was brought out; nearly all swung off their horses, and broke into jests and laughter among themselves. Ewen's all but collapse of a few miles back, his real and evident exhaustion now, served him as nothing else could have done. Realizing this, he let himself slide slowly farther over his horse's neck as though he could scarcely sit in the saddle at all; and in fact this manœuvre called for but little dissimulation.

And at that point the trooper who had charge of his reins, a young man, not so boisterous as the others, was apparently smitten with compassion. His own half-finished chopin in his hand, he looked up at the drooping figure. 'You'd be the better of another drink, eh? Shall I fetch you one?'

Not quite sure whether this solicitude was to his advantage, Ewen intimated that he would be glad of a cup of water. The dragoon finished his draught, tossed the reins to one of his fellows, and sauntered off. But the other man was too careless or too much occupied to catch the reins, and they swung forward below the sorrel's head, free. This was a piece of quite unforeseen good luck. Ewen's head sank right on to his horse's crest; already his right hand, apparently dangling helpless, had slipped the little black knife out of his stocking; now he was able unsuspected to reach the rope round his right ankle. . . . Five seconds, and it was cut through, and the next instant his horse was snorting and rearing from a violent prick with the steel. The dismounted men near scattered involuntarily; Ewen reached forward, caught a rein, turned the horse, and, before the startled troopers in the least realized what was happening, was racing down the slope and had disappeared in the thick fringe of trees about the bridge.

The sorrel was so maddened that to slip off before he reached the bridge, as he intended, was going to be a matter of difficulty, if not of danger. But it had to be done; he threw himself across the saddle and did it. As he reached ground he staggered and fell, wrenching his damaged thigh, but the horse continued its wild career across the bridge and up the farther slope as he had designed. Ewen had but a second or two in which to pick himself up and lurch into the thick undergrowth at the gorge ere the first of a stream of cursing horsemen came tearing down the slope. But, as he hoped, having heard hoof-beats on the bridge, they all went straight over it in pursuit of the now vanished horse, never dreaming that it was riderless.

Once they were over Ewen, cut away the trailing rope from his other ankle, pocketed it and started to plunge on as fast as he could among the birch and rowan trees, the moss-covered stones and the undergrowth of Spean side. He was fairly sure that he was invisible from above, though not, perhaps, from the other side, if and when the troopers returned. But the farther from the bridge the better. His breath came in gasps, the jar of throwing himself off the horse had caused him great pain and made him lamer than ever, and at last he was forced to go forward on his hands and knees, dragging his injured leg after him. But as he went he thought how hopeless it was; how the dragoons would soon overtake the horse, or see from a distance that he was no longer on its back, and, returning, would search along the river-bank and find him. And he could not possibly go much farther, weak and out of condition as he was, with the sweat pouring off him, and Spean below seeming to make a noise much louder than its diminished summer clamour.

Thus crawling he finally came up against a huge green boulder, and the obstacle daunted him. He would stop here . . . just round the farther side. He dragged himself round somehow, and saw that what he had thought to be one stone was two, leaning together. He tried to creep into the dark hollow between them, a place like the tomb, but it was too narrow for his breadth of shoulder. So he sank down by it, and lay there with his cheek to the damp mould, and wondered whether he were dying. Louder and louder roared the Spean below, and he somehow was tossing in its stream. Then at least he could die in Scotland after all. Best not to struggle

. . . best to think that he was in Alison's arms. She would know how spent he was . . . and how cold . . . The brawling of the river died away into darkness.

Chapter Two

W H E N Ewen came fully to himself again it was night, the pale Highland summer night; he could not guess the hour. He had not been discovered, then! He lay listening; there was no sound anywhere save the rushing of the river below him, nothing to tell him whether the troopers had returned or no. But now was undoubtedly the time to quit his lair and get back over the bridge and along the short but dangerous stretch of high road, until he could leave it and make for the river Lochy. When he had forded Lochy and was on the other side of the Great Glen he would be safer.

Alas, the next few minutes implanted in him a horrible doubt whether he would ever ford Lochy, seeing that between the swimming head of exhaustion and the twist which he had given his damaged leg in throwing himself off the horse he could scarcely even stand, much less walk. And although the people up at the change-house, almost within call were, unless they had been removed, of a Cameron sept, he dared not risk attracting their attention, for a double reason: soldiers, his own escort or others from Fort William, might very well halt there. And to shelter him would probably in any case be disastrous to the poor folk themselves.

His prospects did not seem too bright. All his hope was that he might feel more vigorous after a little more of this not very comfortable rest. Huddled together on his side under the lee of the boulder, to get what shelter he could from the soft, misty rain which he felt rather than saw, he said a prayer and fell into the sleep of the worn-out.

He was wakened by a strange, sharp noise above him, and the sensation of something warm and damp passing over his face. Stiff and bewildered, he opened his eyes and saw in the now undoubted, though misty daylight, the author of these two phenomena, an agitated sheep-dog, of a breed unknown to him. As he raised himself on an elbow the dog gave another excited bark, and immediately darted away up the tree-grown bank.

So numbed and exhausted was the fugitive that it took him a few seconds to realize that he was discovered. But by whom? Not by soldiers, certainly; nor could that be the dog from the change-house. He dragged himself into a sitting posture, got his back against the boulder, pulled the little black knife, his only resource, from his stocking, and waited.

Feet were coming down the steep bank, and soon two men could be seen plunging through the birch and alder, shouting to each other in an unfamiliar accent; in front of them plunged and capered the sheep-dog, with its tail held high, and Ewen heard a loud hearty voice saying: 'Clivver lass – aye, good bitch th'art indeed! See-ye, yon's rebel, Jan!' He reflected: 'I can kill the dog, but what good would that do me? Moreover, I have no wish to.' And as the intelligent creature came bounding right up to him, wagging a friendly tail, and apparently proud of his accomplishment in having found him, he held out his left hand in invitation. The dog sniffed once, and then licked it.

'See thon!' cried the former voice. 'Dang it, see Lassie so freendly and all!'

'Yet you had best not come too near!' called Ewen threateningly. 'I am armed!' He raised his right hand.

The larger of the men, pushing through an alder bush, instantly lifted a stout cudgel. 'If thou harmst t' bitch— Coom here, Lassie!'

'No, I will not harm her,' said Ewen, fending off the dog's demonstrations with his other arm. 'But call her off; I owe her no gratitude.'

'For foindin' thee, thou meanst,' supplied Lassie's owner. 'Aye, thou'st the fellow that gie t' sogers the slip yesterday; we heerd all aboot thee oop at t' little hoose yonder. Eh, but thou'rt a reet smart lad!' There was genuine admiration in his tone. ' 'Twere smart ti hide thee here, so near an' all, 'stead o' gooin' ower t' brig – eh, Jan?'

'Main smart,' agreed the smaller man. 'Too smart fur th' redcoats, Ah lay!'

The smart lad, very grim in the face, and rather grey to boot, sat there against his boulder with the *sgian* clutched to his breast, point outwards, and eyed the two men with a desperate attention, as they stood a little way higher up amid the tangle of bushes, stones and protruding tree roots, and looked at him. They had the appearance of well-to-do farmers, particularly the larger, who was a tremendously burly and powerful man with a good-tempered but masterful expression. The smaller was of a more weazened type, and older.

'See-thee, young man,' said the burly stranger suddenly, ' 'tis no manner o' use ti deny that thou'rt one of these danged Highland rebels, seein' we's heerd all the tale oop yonder.'

Ewen's breath came quickly. 'But I'll not be retaken without resistance!'

'Who says we be gooin' ti taake thee? Happen we've summit else ti moind. Coom here, Lassie, wilt thou! Dunnot be so freendly tiv a chap wi' a knife in his hand!'

'I tell you the dog has nothing to fear from me,' repeated Ewen. 'See then!' And on a sudden impulse he planted the *sgian* in the damp soil beside him and left it sticking there.

'Ah, that's reet, yoong man – that's jannock!' exclaimed the large stranger in evident approval and relief. 'Happen we can 'ev some clack together noo. Hoo dost thou rackon ti get away fra this tod's den o' thine?'

Here, quite suddenly, the little man began to giggle. 'He, he! maakes me laugh to think of it – t' sogers chasing reet away ower t' brig and Lord knaws wheer beyond! They nivver coom back, so t' folk oop yonder tells.'

'Aye, a good tale to tell when we gan back ower Tyne,' agreed the large man, shaking gently with a more subdued mirth. And as Ewen, for his part, realized that the reference to Tyne must mean that the strangers were English, though he could not imagine what they were doing in Lochaber, this large one burst into a great rumbling upheaval of laughter, causing the sheep-dog to bark in sympathy.

'Quiet, lass!' commanded her master, making a grab at her. 'Thy new freend here has no wish for thy noise, Ah'll lay.' He looked straight at the fugitive sitting there. 'Hadn't thee best get thee gone, lad, before 'tis onny loighter?' he asked.

Was the man playing with him, or was he genuinely friendly? Ewen's heart gave a great bound. A momentary mist passed before his eyes. When it cleared the large man was stooping over him, a bottle in his hand.

'Thoo'rt nigh clemmed, lad, or ma name's not Robert Fosdyke. Here's 't stuff for thee – ree Nantes. Tak' a good soop of it!'

The fiery spirit ran like lightning through Ewen's cramped limbs. 'Why . . . why do you treat me so kindly?' he gasped, half stupid between the brandy and astonishment, as he returned the bottle. 'You are English, are you not? Why do you not give me up?'

Mr Fosdyke, who had now seated himself on a large stone near, struck his knee with some vehemence. 'Ah'll tell thee whoy! First, because t' bitch here foond thee and took ti thee, and thou didna stick yon knife o' thine intiv her – but Ah'd 'ev driven in thy skool if thou hadst . . . second, because thou'rt a sharp lad and a bold one, too; and last because Ah've seen and heerd tell o' things yonder at Fort Augustus, wheer we went ti buy cattle, that Ah 'evn't loiked at all. No, Ah didn't loike what Ah heerd of goings on. – Aye, and foorthly, t' cattle was woorth danged little when we'd gotten 'em: all t' best were sold awready.'

Ewen knew what cattle they would be; the one possession of many a poor Highland home, as well as the herds of the gentry. He remembered now having heard that some of the many thousands collected from Lochaber and Badenoch were sold to English and Lowland dealers. Apparently, then, these men were on their way south through Glencoe and Breadalbane with such as they had bought, and now he knew why once or twice during this conversation he had fancied that he heard sounds of lowing at no great distance.

'I wonder if mine are all gone!' he said half to himself.

'Thou hadst cattle of thy own, lad?' inquired Mr Fosdyke. 'If thou canst see onny o' thine among oors oop there thou shalt have them back again – and that's none so generous as thou medst think, for there's some Ah'd soon give away as drive all t' waay ower t' Border.'

Ewen gave a weak laugh. 'What should I do with cattle now? I cannot get home myself, much less drive cattle there.'

'And whoy canst thou not get home, when thou'st put summut in thy belly?' asked the Yorkshireman.

Ewen told him why he should find it difficult, if not impossible, and why he dared not go to the change-house either.

The farmer pronounced that he was right in the latter course, and then made the astonishing suggestion that 'Jan Prescott here' should run up to the house and bring the fugitive something to eat and drink. 'Dunnot say who 'tis for, Jan; say Ah've a moind ti eat by river, if thou loikes.' And while Jan, with amazing docility, removed the birch twig which he had been twisting between his lips and betook himself up the bank, his companion questioned Ewen further as to the direction of his home.

'T' other soide of t' other river? T' other river's nobbut a couple of moiles away. . . . Tell thee what, lad,' he exclaimed, slapping himself once more, 'Ah'll tak thee as far as t' river on one of t' nags. Happen thou canst sit a horse still?'

'Take me there!' Ewen could only stare in amazement.

'Aye. And when thou'st gotten to this river o' thine, hoo medst thou cross it; happen there's a brig, or ferry?'

'No, there is a ford. The ford by which we all . . .' His voice died away. How long ago it seemed, that elated crossing last August after Glenfinnan!

'And when thou'rt on t' other soide?' pursued Mr Fosdyke.

'I'll reach my home somehow, if I have to crawl there.'

'And who'lt thou foind theer – thy parents?'

'My aunt, who brought me up. My parents are dead.'

'No wife nor childer?'

'My wife is in France.' And why he added: 'We were only married two days before parting,' Ewen did not know.

'Poor lad,' said Mr Fosdyke. 'Whoy didstna stop at home loike a wise man?'

Ewen, his head resting against the boulder, said: 'That I could not do,' his eyes meanwhile fixed on the form of Mr Jan Prescott, already descending the slope with a tankard in his hand and two large bannocks clasped to his person. Mr Fosdyke turned and hailed him, and in another moment Ewen had started upon the bannocks, finding that he was famished, having tasted nothing solid since the halt at Laggan yesterday morning. And while he ate Mr Robert Fosdyke unfolded his intention to his companion, who raised no objection, except to remark: 'Happen thou'lt meet redcoats on t' road.'

'Ah shall say t' lad's a drover o' mine, then.'

'In yon petticoat thing?' queried Mr Prescott, pointing at Ewen's kilt.

'He shall have thy greatcoat ti cover him oop.'

'Ah dunno hoo he'll get intiv it, then,' returned Mr Prescott. 'See ye, Robert, Ah'd sooner he had a horse blanket than split ma coat.'

'He can have t' loan of ma coat then,' said Mr Fosdyke. 'He'll not split that. – Beasts all reet oop there?' he inquired.

'As reet as ivver they'll be,' returned his partner, with gloom.

'Ah knawed as we peed too mooch for them,' growled Mr Fosdyke in a voice like subterranean thunder. 'Goviment notice saays – well, niver moind what, but 'twere main different fra what t' cattle were loike. Hooivver, Ah weren't comin' all the way fra t' other soide o' York for nowt.'

'York?' asked Ewen, with his mouth full, since this information seemed addressed to him. 'You come from York, sir.'

'Fra near-by. Dost thou knaw the toon?'

'No,' said Ewen.

'T' sogers werena takin' thee there yistiday?'

'It was Carlisle that I was going to in the end.'

'Ah!' said Mr Fosdyke comprehendingly. 'But some poor devils are setting oot for York, too, we hear. Thou's best coom along wi' us.' And giving his great laugh he began to embroider his pleasantry.

'Thou doesna loike the notion? Whoy not? York's a foine toon, Ah can tell thee, and more gates tiv it for setting rebels' heads on than Carlisle. Ah lay we have a row o' them ower Micklegate Bar come Christmas. And thou'st not wishful ti add thine?'

Ewen shook the imperilled head in question with a smile.

'No,' agreed Mr Fosdyke, 'best keep it ti lay on t' pillow besoide thy wife's. If she's in France, then thou'rt not a poor man, eh?'

'I am what you call a gentleman,' replied Ewen, 'though I expect that I am poor enough now.'

'If thou'rt a gentleman,' pronounced Mr Fosdyke, 'then thou dost reet ti keep away fra York and Carlisle, aye, and fra Lunnon, too. – Noo, Jan, we'll gan and see aboot t' nags. Thou medst bide here, lad. Come on, Lassie.'

With tramplings and cracklings they were gone, dog and all, and, but for the yet unfinished food and drink, which were putting new life into Ewen, the whole encounter might have been a dream. As he waited there for their return he wondered whether Alison's prayers had sent these good angels, which, to his simple and straightforward faith, seemed quite likely.

Presently the larger of the angels came back and helped him along the slope to the scene of his exploits at the bridge. Here was the satellite Jan with two stout nags, a flea-bitten grey and a black. A long and ample coat (certainly not Mr Prescott's) was provided for the Jacobite. 'If thou wert clothed like a Christian there'd ha' been no need for this,' said Mr Fosdyke with frankness as he helped him into it; and then, the difficulty of getting into the saddle surmounted, Ewen found himself half incredulously riding behind the broad back of his benefactor over the brawling Spean, in his hand a stout cattle goad to assist his steps when he should be on his feet again.

In the two miles before they came to the River Lochy they had the luck to meet no one. There the clouds hung so low that the other side of the Great Glen was scarcely visible. When they came to the ford Ewen pulled up and made to dismount. But Mr Fosdyke caught him by the arm. 'Nay, if thou canst scarce walk on land, Ah doot thou'll walk thruff water! Daisy will tak thee ower. Coom on, mare.'

The two horses splashed placidly through in the mist. On the other side Ewen struggled off, and got out of the coat.

'I cannot possibly recompense you, Mr Fosdyke,' he began, handing it up to him.

'If thou offer me money,' said Mr Fosdyke threateningly, 'danged if Ah don't tak thee back ti wheer Ah foond thee!'

'You can be assured,' said Ewen, smiling, 'for I have none. But in any case, money does not pass between gentlemen for a service like this. I only pray God that you will not suffer for it.'

'Ah'd loike ti see the mon that's going ti mak me,' was the Yorkshireman's reply. 'And Ah feel noo as Ah've got even wi' Goviment in t' matter of t' cattle,' he added with immense satisfaction. 'And thou think'st me a gentleman? Well, Ah'm nobbut a farmer, but Ah'm mooch obliged ti thee for the compliment.' He shook Ewen's hand. 'Good luck ti thee, ma lad. . . . If thou lived a few hoondred moiles nearer, danged if Ah wouldna gie thee a pup o' Lassie's – but thou'rt ower far away, ower far!' He chuckled, caught the bridle of the grey, and the eight hoofs could be heard splashing back through the ford. Then silence settled down again, silence, and the soft folds of mist; and after a moment Ewen, leaning heavily on his goad, began his difficult pilgrimage.

Twenty-four hours later, very nearly at the end of his tether, he was hobbling slowly along the last mile of that distance which ordinarily he would have covered between one meal and the next. So slow and painful had been his progress, and with such frequent halts, that it had been late afternoon before he reached Loch Arkaig. And there he had seen the pitiful charred remains left by vengeance of Lochiel's house of Achnacarry, almost as dear to him as his own. In that neighbourhood above all others he had feared to come on soldiers, but the Campbells in Government pay who had burnt and ravaged here had long ago done their work, and the place was deserted; there was nothing to guard now, and none against whom to hold it. A poor Cameron woman, whose husband had been shot in cold blood as he was working in his little field, had given Ewen shelter for the night. She told him what he expected to hear, that the house of Ardroy had been burnt down by a detachment of redcoats; this she knew because the soldiers had returned that way, and she had heard them boasting how they had left the place in flames. Of Miss Cameron's fate she knew nothing; but then she never saw anyone now that her man was gone; the burnt countryside was nearly depopulated. That Ewen had seen for himself already. And she said with tears, as, thanking her from his soul for her hospitality, he turned away from her door in the morning grey: 'Oh Mac 'ic Ailein, for the Chief and the Chief's kin I'd give the last rag, the last mouthful that's left to me – but I'm asking God why He ever let Prince Tearlach come to Scotland.' And Ewen had no heart to find an answer.

Against his will the question had haunted him as he hobbled on. Just a year ago he had the news of that coming; yes, just a year ago he had sat with Alison by the loch and been happy – too happy perhaps. So his father's house was gone! But all the more was his mind set to reach Ardroy, to find out what had befallen those who had remained behind there: Aunt Margaret first and foremost, the servants, old Angus and his grandchildren, the womenfolk, the fugitives from Drumossie Moor. . . . And here at last he was, going incredibly slowly, and accompanied by a dull pain in the thigh which by this

time seemed an inseparable part of himself, but come to the
spot where, after crossing the Allt Buidhe burn, one used to
discern the chimneys of the house of Ardroy between the pines
of the avenue. Since he knew that he would never see them
thus again, Ewen did not look up, but he thought, as he crossed
the burn on the stepping-stones, nearly overbalancing from
fatigue, that one thing, at least, would be the same, for not
even Cumberland could set fire to Loch na h-Iolaire.

Then, unable for the moment to get farther, he sank down
among the welcoming heather for a rest. That, just coming
into bloom, was unchanged; 'thou art the same and thy years
shall not fail' – other words floated into his head and out again,
as he felt its springy resistance give beneath his body. Then,
half lying there, twisting a tuft round and round the fingers
of one hand for the pleasure of feeling it again, Ewen let his
eyes stray to the spot where his father's house and his had
stood. And so strange were habit and memory that he could
see its roof and chimneys still. He put a hand over his eyes to
rub away the false sight . . . but when he removed it the
chimneys were still there, and from one there floated a wisp
of smoke. . . . Trembling, he dragged himself clumsily to his
feet.

Like a man who dreams the impossible he stood a little later
outside the entrance door of Ardroy. The whole affair was like
a dream; for fire had certainly passed upon the house, and yet
it was unharmed. The lintel, the sides of the stone porch were
blackened with smoke; the ivy was brown and shrivelled, but
not even the woodwork was injured. The house seemed
occupied; the door stood open as on fine days it was wont to
do; but there was not a creature about. Where was Aunt
Margaret?

Slowly Ewen went over the threshold, feeling the stone and
wood like a blind man to make sure that it was real. He could
have kissed it – his house that was not burnt after all. The sun
was pouring into the long room; there was a meal laid on the
table – for Aunt Margaret? Then where was she? The place
was very silent. Perhaps – a horrible notion – strangers held
Ardroy now, enemies. He would rather it were burnt. . . .
But had harm befallen Aunt Margaret? He must find her; shame
on him to be thinking first of the house!

He was giddy with hunger and fatigue, but he had no thought of approaching the table; he left the room and, holding very tightly by the rail, went up the stairs. The door of Miss Cameron's room was a little ajar, so he pushed it gently open, too confused to knock. Where, where was she?

And he stood in the doorway rooted, because, so unexpectedly, everything in that neat, sunny room which he had known from a child was just as he had always known it . . . even to Aunt Margaret herself, sitting there by the window reading a chapter in her big Bible, as she always did before breakfast. The surprise of its usualness after his experiences and his fears almost stunned him, and he remained there motionless, propping himself by the doorpost.

It was odd, however, that Aunt Margaret had not heard him, for she had not used to be deaf. The thought came to Ewen that he was perhaps become a ghost without knowing it, and he seriously considered the idea for a second or two. Then he took a cautious step forward.

'Aunt Margaret!'

He was not a ghost! She heard and looked up . . . it was true that her face was almost frightened . . .

'I have come back!' said Ewen baldly. 'May I . . . may I sit on your bed!'

He crashed on to it rather than sat upon it, hitting his head against the post at the bottom, since all at once he could not see very well.

But Aunt Margaret did not scold him; in fact he perceived, after a little, that she was crying as she sat beside him, and attempting, as if he were a child again, to kiss his head where he had struck it. 'Oh, Ewen, my boy – my darling, darling boy!'

'Then did that poor woman dream that the house was burnt down?' asked Ewen some quarter of an hour later, gazing at Miss Cameron in perplexity, as she planted before him, ensconced as he was in the easy-chair in her bedroom, the last components of a large repast. For allow him to descend and eat downstairs she would not; indeed, after the first questions and emotions were over, she was for hustling him up to the attics and hiding him there. But, Ewen having announced with great firmness that he was too lame to climb a stair that was little better than a ladder, she compromised on her bedchamber for the moment, and, with Marsali's assistance, brought up thither the first really satisfying meal which Ewen had seen for more than three months.

In answer to his question she now began to laugh, though her eyes were still moist. 'The house was set fire to – in a way. Eat, *Eoghain*, for you look starving; and you shall hear the tale of its escape.'

Ewen obeyed her and was told the story. But not yet having, so it seemed to him, the full use of his faculties, he was not quite clear how much of the house's immunity was due to chance, to connivance on the part of the officer commanding the detachment sent to burn it, and to the blandishments of Miss Cameron herself. At any rate, after searching, though not plundering, the house of Ardroy from top to bottom (for whom or what was not quite clear to Ewen, since at that date he was safely a prisoner at Fort Augustus), firing about half the crofts near, collecting what cattle they could lay their hands on, the most having already been sent up into the folds of the mountains, and slaying a dozen or so of Miss Cameron's hens, they had piled wood against the front of the house, with what intention was obvious. It was a moment of great anguish for Miss Cameron. But the soldiers were almost ready to march ere the fuel was lighted. And as they were setting fire to the pine branches and the green ash boughs the officer approached her and said in a low voice: 'Madam, I have carried out my instructions – and it is not my fault if this wood is damp. That's enough, Sergeant; 'twill burn finely. Column, march!'

Directly they were out of sight Miss Cameron and Marsali, the younger maidservants and the old gardener, seizing rakes and brooms and fire-irons, had pulled away the thickly smoking but as yet harmless branches. 'And then I bethought me, Ewen, that 'twould be proper there should be as much smoke as possible, to convince the world, and especially the redcoats, should they take a look back. A house cannot burn, even in a spot so remote as this, without there being some evidence of it in the air. So we made a great pile of all that stuff at a safe distance from the house – and, my grief, the trouble it was to get it to burn! Most of the day we tended it; and a nasty thick reek it made, and a blaze in the end. That's how the house was burnt. . . . What ails you, my bairn?'

But this time Ewen was able hastily to dash the back of his hand over his eyes. He could face her, therefore, unashamed, and reaching out for her hand, put his lips to it in silence.

Chapter Three

NOT infrequently in the past had Miss Margaret Cameron animadverted on the obstinacy which lay hidden (as his temper was hidden) under her nephew's usually gentle speech and ways. And now, at the greatest crisis in his life, when that life itself might hang upon his prudence, poor Miss Cameron was faced in her young relative with a display of this quality which really distracted her.

On that joyful and wonderful morning of his return she had allowed him (she put it so) to retire to his own bed in his own room 'just for the once'; the garrets, the cellar or a bothy on the braeside being designated as his future residences. Ewen did not argue – indeed he was not capable of it; he fell into his bed and slept for fourteen hours without waking.

Once he was there, and so obviously in need of rest and attention, Miss Cameron had not, of course, the heart to turn him out; but she kept a guard of young MacMartins and others round the house ready to give tongue in case of a surprise, and promised herself to banish the returned fugitive to more secluded regions directly he was able to leave his room. But when, after three days, Ewen did so, it was not to retire into this destined seclusion; on the contrary, he began at once to limp about, acquainting himself with what had happened to his tenants in his absence, trying to discover the fate of those who had never returned – among whom was Lachlan Mac-Martin – visiting the nearer crofts in person, and interviewing the inhabitants of the farther at the house. Presently, he said, he would 'take to the heather', perhaps; but, as his aunt could see, he was yet too lame for it; and, as for the garrets or the cellar, he was just as safe in his own bedchamber as in those uncomfortable retreats.

Yielding on this point with what she hoped was the wisdom of the serpent, Miss Cameron then returned to a subject much nearer her heart: Ardroy's departure for France or Holland, which he would attempt, she assumed, as soon as he could hear of a likely vessel and was fit to undertake the journey to the coast.

'France?' queried Ewen, as if he had heard this suggestion for the first time. It was the fifth evening after his return; Miss Cameron was sitting knitting in the long parlour, and he stretched in a chair opposite to her. The windows were closely curtained, and young Angus MacMartin and a still younger brother prowled delightedly in the avenue keeping watch. 'France, Aunt Margaret? What put that into your head?'

Miss Cameron laid down her knitting. 'Because you cannot stay here, Ewen. And France is in my head rather than Holland or Denmark because – well, surely you can guess – because your wife is there.'

Ewen got out of his chair and limped to one of the windows. 'I am not leaving Scotland at present,' he said quietly, and drew aside the curtains. 'We need not therefore discuss the claims of one country over another.'

'You cannot mean to stay here at Ardroy! Ewen, are you daft? And, in the name of the Good Being, don't show yourself at a lighted window like that!'

' 'Tis so light outside that the candles do not carry,' returned her nephew. Indeed but for Miss Cameron's prudence they would not have been sitting thus curtained, but in daylight. 'Moreover no one will come to look for me here; the house has been "burnt",' he went on, using the argument he had already used half a dozen times. And he continued to look out. At least Margaret Cameron thought that he was looking out. In reality he had his eyes shut, that he might not see Alison's face – a vain device, for he saw it all the clearer.

His aunt was silent for a moment, for he had implanted in her mind a most disturbing doubt.

'Well,' she said at last dryly, 'I should think that if Major Windham, to whom you owe so much, knew of this freak of yours, he would regret the sacrifices which he had made in order to save you, when this is the use to which you put your liberty.'

'I think Major Windham would understand,' said Ewen shortly.

'Understand what?'

There was no answer. 'Then I doubt if the ghost of poor Neil, who died for you, or of Lachlan, would understand!'

Ewen turned at that, but stayed where he was. 'Poor Neil indeed; may his share of Paradise be his!' he said in a softened tone. 'And Lachlan, too, if he be dead. Since you speak of my foster-brothers, Aunt Margaret, and reproachfully, then you must know that this is one reason why I do not wish to leave Ardroy, because it shames me to take ship for France myself and desert those others who cannot flee, for whose fate I am responsible. Moreover, I have started the rebuilding of the burnt crofts, and—'

'Trust a man to think that he is the only being who can oversee anything practical! I wonder,' observed Miss Cameron, 'how much of rebuilding and repairs I have not ordered and supervised when you were nothing but a small wild boy, Ewen, falling into the loch and losing yourself on the braes about it!'

He hobbled over to her. 'I know, I know. No laird ever had a better factor than you, Aunt Margaret!'

Miss Cameron's knitting slid to the floor. 'Had! Aye, I'm getting an old wife now, 'tis plain, that you dare not leave the reins to me for a year or so, while you take your head out of the lion's mouth for a while.'

'No, no, you know that's not my thought,' said Ewen, distressed. 'I'd leave Ardroy to you as blithely as I did a year ago – I will so leave it . . . presently.'

'Aye, that you will do presently – but not by your own will. You'll go off from this door as you left Fort Augustus a week ago, tied on a horse again, and your father's house really in flames behind you – and all because you will not listen to advice!'

'You make me out more obstinate than I am,' said Ewen gently. 'Your advice is excellent, Aunt Margaret, but you do not know . . . all the circumstances.'

'That can easily be remedied,' said Miss Cameron with meaning. But to that suggestion Ewen made no reply.

Miss Cameron turned round in her chair, and then got up and faced him. 'Ewen, my dear, what is wrong? What is it that is keeping you from getting out of the country? Surely it is not . . . that there is something amiss between you and Alison?'

Ewen did not meet her eyes. But he shook his head. 'Alison and I—' he began, but never finished. How put into words

what Alison was to him? Moreover, that which was keeping
him back did stand between him and her – at least in his own
soul. 'Some day, perhaps, I will tell you, Aunt Margaret,' he said
quietly. 'But I'd be glad if you would not discuss my departure
just now. – You have dropped your knitting.'

He picked it up for her, and Margaret Cameron stood quite
still, looking up uneasily at the height of him, at his brow
all wrinkled with some pain of whose nature she was quite
ignorant, at the sudden lines round his young mouth. She
ended her survey with a sigh.

'And to think that – since we cannot get a letter to her – the
lassie may be breaking her heart over there, believing that you
are dead!'

Ewen took a step away, with a movement as though to ward
off a blow. Then he translated the movement into a design to
snuff the candles on the table behind him. After a moment
his voice came unsteady and hurt: 'Aunt Margaret, you are
very cruel.' And his hand must have been unsteady, too, for
he snuffed the flame right out.

' 'Tis for your own good,' replied Miss Cameron, winking
hard at the engraving of King James the Third as a young man
over the mantelshelf in front of her. Ewen relighted from
another the candle he had slain, saying nothing, and with the
air of one who does not quite know what he is doing. 'At least,
I'm sure 'tis not for mine,' went on Miss Cameron, and now,
little given to tears as she was, she surreptitiously applied a
corner of a handkerchief to one eye. 'You cannot think that I
want you to go away again . . . and leave the house the . .
the mere shell of emptiness it is when you are not here!'

Ewen looked round and saw the scrap of cambric. In an
instant, despite the pain it cost him, he had knelt down by
her side and was taking her hands into his, and saying how
sorry he was to grieve her, and assuring her that there was
nothing, nothing whatever wrong between him and Alison.

Yet even then he made no promises about departure.

Nor had he made any a week later, when, one hot afternoon, he lay, reflecting deeply, on the bed in his own room,
with his hands behind his head. Although his wounded leg
was already much stronger, it rebelled with effect against un-
remitting use all day, and to Ewen's intense disgust he found

it imperative to spend a portion of the afternoon thus. He regarded this necessity as not only burdensome but disgraceful.

The wind soughed faintly through the pines of the little avenue, and then passed on to ruffle the ivy outside his open window. A little brown, some of them, after their fiery ordeal the topmost of those tough leaves were still there, and made just the same rustling noise as of old. And there Ewen lay, apparently at peace; back in his own room, among his modest possessions, his life and liberty snatched from the enemy, his home unharmed after all, and over the seas his young wife waiting for him in safety, the call of the sword no longer keeping him back from her, since the sword was shattered.

But he was by no means at peace; there was unceasing war in his breast. The way to Alison was barred by a spectre which he could not lay. It was in vain to tell himself that, by God's mercy, his most unwilling lapse at Fort Augustus had done no harm, that no one of his own party knew of it, that it was not even a complete revelation. To his acutely sensitive Highland pride the mere fact of the betrayal of his Chief's trust was agony. Alison could not heal that wound, which, now that Ewen was back again in his old surroundings, almost in his old life, seemed to have broken out bleeding afresh. There was only one man who could draw the poison from it, and Ewen knew neither where he was nor how he could come at him.

And meanwhile his dreams were full of Alison; and a night or two ago he had even seemed to hear her voice in one, asking in so pitiful and faint an accent why he delayed to come to her, now that honour no longer forbade it. She was so lonely . . .

Ewen sighed deeply, and withdrew his hands from beneath his head. The double scar on his right palm caught his eye for an instant. He wondered, not by any means for the first time, whether Windham had heard of his escape; if he had, he would know that he had indeed given him his life – yes, even by his refusal to witness against him, since that was the direct cause of the prisoner's being taken over the Spean, where he had met and seized his great opportunity. To judge by the Englishman's palpable distress at their farewell interview, Windham would be exceedingly glad of the news of his escape. Some day, perhaps he might contrive to get a letter conveyed to his hands.

He would like to tell him in person. But he was never to see him again, so it seemed, for the five meetings were over. Again he counted them: here, at Edinburgh, on Beinn Laoigh, at Fort Augustus. . . . And suddenly his pulse quickened with pleasure – that made four, only four! . . . no, of course, there had been two at Fort Augustus. . . . Yet what (save his own recapture) stood now in the way of their meeting again some day?

But the ivy leaves went on rubbing their hands together, and through the window at the other side of the room came the clucking of Miss Cameron's remaining hens, drowsy sounds both, and Ewen, pondering this question, began to fall asleep. Yes, just before he lost consciousness, there shot through his mind, apparently from nowhere, a last flicker of Angus's prediction of a year ago . . . something about twisted threads . . . a thread of one colour and a thread of another. It had meant nothing at the time and he had totally forgotten it since. Now, between the two worlds of sleep and waking, it not only came back to him, but, with the curious pictorial clarity sometimes vouchsafed in that state, he seemed to see what it meant. Then picture and meaning faded, and he slept.

He slept quietly for a while, and then dreamt that a man had come into the room and was standing looking down at him. Yet somehow he knew that it was not a dream, that there was really someone there. He tried to rouse himself, but could not; and then the man laid a hand on his wrist. And at that, still half in a dream, he began to struggle and to speak.

'Let go my arm, you damned torturer? . . . No, not if you cut me in pieces! . . . Ah, my God, but there's another way . . . another way!'

The hand had left his wrist quickly, and now it was laid on his shoulder, and a voice – Lochiel's voice – said: 'Ewen, wake up. No one is hurting you.'

He woke instantly, crying: 'Donald! Donald!' half sure, all the time, that it was but a dream. Then he caught his breath and lay staring upwards. It was not indeed Lochiel, but it was his brother who stood there, looking down at him with a good deal of attention.

'Archie!' he gasped in the most complete astonishment. 'You here! Why?'

'Don't you think you would be the better of a doctor, my

dear Ewen?' inquired his cousin cheerfully. 'That is why I am here.'

'But there's a price on your head,' protested Ewen. 'You should not, should not have come here!'

Archibald Cameron smiled his gentle, quizzical smile and sat down on the bed. 'I understand from Miss Margaret that you daily affirm the house of Ardroy to be perfectly safe. Moreover, one does not dictate to a physician, my dear boy, how and when he shall visit his patients. I heard how you escaped as you were being carried to Fort William, and I did not believe that it was your body which was found some days after in one of the pools of Spean. (You do know, perhaps, that that is what has been given out at Fort Augustus.) But I guessed that that same body needed attention, so, being yesterday in Glendessary, I made my way hither. Now, let me look at those wounds of yours.'

And, though Ewen protested that these were quite healed and that he was only a trifle lame, Dr Cameron insisted. The extent of the lameness, very patent when he made the young man walk about the room, evidently displeased him.

When you get to France, Ewen, you must have the care of a good surgeon. I greatly fear that an important muscle in the thigh has been severed; but with proper treatment it may reunite again.'

'I suppose you have been talking to Aunt Margaret,' remarked his patient, sitting down upon the bed. 'But, as I have told her I am not going to France – yet. The muscle must reunite at home.'

Archie looked at him keenly. He *had* been talking to Aunt Margaret. 'I am not advising France solely in the interests of your lameness, Ewen.'

'Well I know that! But I shall stay in Scotland for the present.'

'Until you are captured again, I suppose?' said Dr Cameron, crossing one leg over the other and leaning back against the post at the bottom of the bed. 'But I do not know on what grounds you assume that you will have so lucky an escape a second time.'

'Oh, I shall not be captured here,' said Ewen carelessly. 'And when I can walk a little better, I shall very likely take to the heather for a while – like you!' And as Archibald Cameron raised his eyebrows he said with more warmth: 'My God, Archie, I'd rather skulk in sight of Loch na h-Iolaire with nothing but my plaid and a handful of meal, even were there a redcoat behind every whin-bush, than lie in the French King's bed at Versailles!'

'No doubt,' responded his cousin, unmoved. 'And so would I. Yet I shall certainly make for France – if God will – when my tasks here are done. I hope indeed that it may not be for long; who knows but next year may see another and a more successful effort, with support from the French. The Prince—'

'Yes, indeed,' said Ewen eagerly, 'what of the Prince? My last news of him was from a fellow-prisoner at Fort Augustus, MacDonald of Kingsburgh, who, though he is Sleat's factor, brought him to his own house in Skye disguised as the maid-servant of one Miss Flora MacDonald, and was arrested in consequence. I heard much from him, and laughable some of it was, too, for Kingsburgh's wife and daughter seem to have been frightened at the queer figure that His Royal Highness made in his petticoats. But you will have later news of him, Archie?'

'The Prince was at the end of July in Glenmoriston,' said Dr Cameron, 'but he is now, I think, in Chisholm's country, farther north. There is so plainly a Providence watching over him that I have no doubt he will be preserved from his enemies to the end; and it is therefore the duty of his friends to preserve themselves too. Yes, I am going to read you a lecture, *Eoghain mhóir*, so you had better lie down again; I shall not begin until you do.' He waited until Ewen had grumblingly complied, and then began, ticking off the points on his fingers.

'*Imprimis*, you stubborn young man, there is this house, almost miraculously preserved from destruction, and, if you keep clear of it, likely to continue immune. There is your good aunt, who can well continue to look after it, but who, if you are found under its roof, will certainly be driven out of it and very possibly imprisoned. You are not on the list of attainted persons, and you have the advantage at this moment of an official report declaring you drowned. Most of all, have you not someone already in France who is breaking her heart for a sight of you?'

Lying there, Ewen changed colour perceptibly, and it was

only after a moment that he answered: 'There are broken hearts in plenty, Archie, in Lochaber.'

'But I do not see, my dear lad, how they are to be mended by your offering up the fragments of Alison's – and your own.

Ewen uttered a sound like a groan, and, twisting over, buried his face in the pillow; and presently there emerged some muffled words to the effect that he longed to go to Alison, but that . . . and then something wholly unintelligible in which the word 'honour' was alone distinguishable.

Dr Cameron looked down at the back of the uneasy auburn head with the affectionate tolerance which one might display to the caprices of a younger brother. 'No, Ewen, to my mind honour points to your going – aye, and duty and common sense as well. You cannot help your tenants by remaining here; Miss Cameron can now do that much more effectively – so long as you do not compromise her by your presence. You cannot help the Cause of the Prince; you cannot help Lochiel,' – the head gave a sudden movement – 'he is for France with me when the opportunity comes. Another day – that is a different tale; but 'tis likely there will never be another day for you if you persist in remaining here now. . . . And there is another point, which I hope you will pardon me for mentioning: is your wife going to bear you a child, Ewen?'

'How do I know?' answered Ewen in a stifled voice from the pillow. 'Our happiness was so short . . . and I have had no letter.'

'Then, before you throw your life uselessly away,' said Archibald Cameron gravely, 'it is your duty to make sure that there will be a son to follow you here, Mac 'ic Ailein. Do you wish your ghost to see strangers at Ardroy?'

No Highlander could ever affect to disregard that argument, and Ewen remained silent.

'And Alison – do you suppose that she found her wedded happiness any longer or more satisfying than you did? God knows, my dear Ewen, I hold that neither wife, children, nor home should stand in a man's way when duty and loyalty call him – for, as you know, I have turned my back on all mine – but when duty and loyalty are silent, then he does very wrong if he neglects those ties of nature.'

And on that Archibald Cameron, conceiving that he had

preached long enough, got up from the bed. Ewen was still lying with his face hidden: was there something on his mind, as Miss Cameron affirmed? The doctor went and looked out of the far window, and saw the lady in question scattering meal to her hens.

'Archie,' came from the bed after a moment or two, 'if I go, it is only on one condition, which you can grant.'

'I?' said Dr Cameron, turning round, rather surprised. Ewen had raised himself on to an elbow. He looked oddly pale and strained. 'What is the condition, *ille?*'

'That I see Lochiel first.' And over his fair skin there swept a wave of red.

It occurred to Dr Archibald then how strange it was that Ewen, for all his intense devotion, had not yet asked news of his kinsman and Chief. But he looked doubtful. 'I am afraid that would be difficult, because you are both disabled; you cannot travel to him, nor he to you.'

'Yes, I had thought of that,' said Ewen, now quite pale again. 'But I must contrive it somehow.' And as Archie was silent, reflecting, he added, with a sharp note in his voice, 'Is there any other reason why I should not?'

'Of course not – save that you will meet in France, please God.'

'That will not serve. I must see him before I leave Scotland. I know that he is no longer in Lochaber.' The short phrases were jerked out; even more so the last one: 'Archie, where is he?

'He—' Archie was beginning, when unfortunately he heard Miss Cameron calling to him from below, possibly uttering a warning of some kind. He turned sharply to the window and never finished. But on Ewen the effect was of a man who has second thoughts about answering a question, and is not only mute, but turns his back upon the questioner.

In his present state of mind, it was quite enough, and next moment, to his visitor's amazement, he had thrown himself off the bed with such violence that he staggered. 'I knew it!' he exclaimed hoarsely. 'You will not tell me where he is because you have heard what I did at Fort Augustus – because Lochiel has heard it. I am not to be trusted! That is why you came, I believe – why you want me gone at any price from Scotland!' And as Archibald Cameron, already swung round again from the window, stared at him in consternation, Ewen added, clenching his hands, 'I'll not go! I'll not be got rid of like that! I'll get myself killed here in Lochaber . . . the only thing I can do in expiation.' And with that he sank down on the side of bed and hid face in his hands.

Dr Cameron hastily left the window, but before his amazement allowed him words, Ewen was adding, in a strangled voice: 'You are quite right, from your point of view, neither to let me see him nor to tell me where he is. But, Archie, I swear to you by my father's memory that I did not do it willingly! How can he believe that of me!'

His cousin stooped and put a hand on his shoulder. 'Ewen,' he said with great gentleness, 'I have not the least notion what you are talking about. What did you do at Fort Augustus? Nothing, I'd stake my soul, that your father's son need ever be ashamed of. You would have let yourself be "cut in pieces" first, eh? I was just on the point of telling you where Lochiel was; he is in Badenoch, hiding in a hut on Ben Alder with Macpherson of Cluny. Now,' he sat down and slipped his arm completely along the bowed shoulders, 'will you tell me what is on your mind, and why you must see him?'

Chapter Four

THINKING it over afterwards, Ewen knew why it had been such a comfort to tell Archie; it was that Dr Cameron seemed to understand so well what he had suffered that he never tried to belittle the cause of it. Instead of attempting to minimize this he said that he would have felt exactly the same had such a terrible mischance befallen him. Only how could Ewen at any stage have imagined that Donald, if he heard of his lapse, would ever believe that he had made a disclosure willingly?

'I blame you for that, my poor Ewen,' he said, shaking his head. 'You must surely have known that he would as soon suspect me as you, who have been like an elder son to him, who so nearly threw away your life for him at Fort William. . . . I think that's the worst part of your confession, but as you say that I am not to suppress anything I must tell him that too, though it will hurt him.'

Ewen raised his colourless face, to which, however, a measure of tranquillity had already returned. 'I am sorry for that; but you must not keep back a word. Tell him how I allowed myself to fall asleep when I suspicioned it might be dangerous; tell him that I insulted Lord Loudoun somewhat unworthily – he would not have done that – tell him everything. You are only a proxy, you know, Archie – though a very satisfactory one,' he added gratefully. 'There's no other man save Lochiel that I could have told. Dhé, but I feel as if Ben Nevis had been lifted off me!'

Archibald Cameron gave his arm a little pressure. 'Now 'tis my turn to make a confession to you. When I first came into this room I found myself emulating that Captain Greening of yours – whom, by the way, I should rejoice to meet on some good lonely brae, with a precipice near by. But, like your talking, my dear lad, my overhearing was accidental.'

'Do you mean that I was saying things in my sleep again? Archie, this is intolerable!'

'You bade me loose your arm when I touched you, and spoke of preferring to be "cut to pieces" and of "another way". You have just told me what that 'other way' was. Ewen, what was the first way, and who took it with you? You have not told me everything, after all.'

The young man was looking on the floor, and there was colour enough in his face now. 'I do not very much wish to revive that memory. . . . But if you must know, I was near being flogged by order of the Lowland officer who captured me. He had been going to shoot me first – I'll tell you of that anon. It was because he wanted . . . what they wanted and got at Fort Augustus. – No, do not look so horrified, Archie; he did not carry it out (though I'll admit I believed he was going to). It was only a threat.'

'Then, if it was only a threat,' remarked Dr Cameron, looking at him closely, 'why did you call me a "damned torturer" when I touched you?'

'I . . . Really, Archie, I cannot be responsible for everything I say in my sleep. I apologize, but if you were worth your salt you would give me some drug to cure me of the cursed habit!'

'I'm afraid the drug does not exist, my dear boy. When your mind is at peace you will not do it any more. And don't you think that it would conduce to that state if you told me why you called me so unpleasant a name?'

Ewen gave him a little shake. '*Mo thruaigh*, Archie Cameron,' he said with vivacity, 'I begin to think it was because you merit it with this persistence of yours! If I said that, I suppose I must have been remembering that when one has had a bayonet through one's arm not long before, it is conveniently sensitive, that is all. But after a few experiments, Major Guthrie found that it was not sensitive enough. They knew better how to do things at Fort Augustus.'

Archibald Cameron still gazed at him, compressing his lips. 'So the Lowlander tried "experiments" did he? And do you still consider yourself a traitor, Ewen? I'd give you a rather different name, and so, I fancy, will Lochiel.'

'But I don't mean you to tell Lochiel *that!* No, Archie that was not confession – you got it out of me unfairly!'

'Unfortunately you made me promise to tell him everything,' retorted his cousin, smiling. 'To turn to another aspect of this matter, then,' for Ewen was really looking unhappy, 'it was, I suppose, to this Major Guthrie with a fancy for experiments that you were betrayed by the English officer who was your prisoner here – I might also say your guest – last August. I hope that he did not go so far as to take part in these proceedings, too? – Bless us, what is wrong now?'

For this partial change of topic had proved far from soothing. With a sharp exclamation Ewen had go up from the bed.

'Good God, Archie, how did you hear that story? It's not true – Major Wndham did not betray me – he saved me!'

'Did he? Well, I'd far liefer hear that than the other thing. But that was what Lachlan MacMartin told us, when he came hotfoot to us at Achnacarry at the beginning of May.'

'Lachlan – *Lachlan* went to Achnacarry!' exclaimed Ewen in amazement.

'Yes, he appeared there one day nearly crazy with rage and remorse because you had been captured while he had left you in order to get food. He wanted Donald to march against Fort Augustus and deliver you.'

Ewen had begun to limp distractedly about the room. 'I did not know that. But, great heavens, what a story to get abroad about Major Windham! Archie, he saved my life at the last minute; I was actually up against the wall before the firing-party when he dashed in between at the risk of his own. I should not be here now for you to bully but for him. It is true that,

I, too, God forgive me, was deluded enough for a short time to think this goodness calculated treachery, but at least I did not spread it abroad. And that is only part of what he has done and given up for me.' He gave his cousin a sketch of the rest. 'I cannot think how Lachlan got such a mistaken notion into his head, for he was not there when I was found and taken, and he can hardly have met with that scoundrel Guthrie, who is capable of any lie.'

'What has become of Lachlan – is he here at Ardroy?'

'No, he has never returned, and no one knows anything of him; he has undoubtedly been either captured or killed, and much more probably killed, I fear. But I wish he had not spread this slander; 'tis at least to be hoped that no word of it reaches poor Windham!'

'I like to see in you, Ewen,' said his cousin, 'the same concern for another man's honour as for your own. But you know the Erse proverb, "A lie goes but on one leg." '

'Like me,' commented Ewen with a smile. 'Yet you think that in France I may go on two again?'

'You will certainly have a better chance of it. Then I may tell Lochiel, when I get back to Badenoch, that you consent to be reasonable?'

'Yes, thanks to you, I will go – since he is going. But I must wait a chance of getting off.'

'There's a chance now,' said his cousin quickly; 'but you must start for the coast tomorrow.'

'Tomorrow!' Ewen's face fell. 'So soon!' His glance swept round the room and lingered for a moment on the heathery distances visible through the window. 'Very well,' he said with a little sigh. 'Tell me what I must do – no,' he caught himself up, 'first tell me a little about Donald. Those wounds of his, are they healed? Archie, I hope due care is being taken of him on Ben Alder?'

'You look as if you think I ought not to have left him,' said Dr Cameron, smiling. 'But he has had Sir Stuart Threipland of Edinburgh with him, and the wounds are healing, though slowly. And I assure you that I have been too busy following Mercury of late to pay much attention to Æsculapius; I have been to and fro in Lochaber and Moidart a great deal more regularly than the post. More by token I am become a sort of banker. For I suppose you did not hear in your captivity, Ewen, that at the beginning of May two French ships landed six barrels of gold – forty thousand louis d'or – in Moidart for the Prince; and with some ado, owing to the reluctance of Clanranald's people to lose sight of it, I got it conveyed to Loch Arkaig, and it has been buried there against future requirements. – I know what you are going to say, "If only we had had that money earlier, when we needed it so!"'

Those were indeed the words which leapt to the young man's lips. Yet since over the ruined fortunes of today there still danced, like will-of-the-wisps, the hopes of tomorrow, he fell to discussing the possible uses of this money with the man to whose endeavours (as he soon discovered) it was due that the French had not carried it off again when they heard the news of the disaster at Culloden. Archibald Cameron had indeed played post and banker to some purpose! Ewen looked at him with admiration not free from concern.

'Archie, are you duly careful of your own safety in these constant journeyings of yours, seeing that you are proscribed by name?'

His cousin smiled. 'You may be sure that I am careful. Am I not pre-eminently a man of peace?'

Nevertheless not even Balmerino, the dauntless old soldier, was to make a more memorable end on the scaffold than Archibald Cameron. But his time was not yet – not by seven years; though, all unknowing, he had just been talking of what was to bring him there – the belated French treasure, fatal as the fabled gold of the river maidens to nearly every man who touched it.

'Now for your getting off to France,' he resumed. 'There has lately been a French privateer off Loch Broom, and she may very well be hanging off the coast farther south, therefore you should start for Moidart without a day's delay. Since the twenty-fifth of July the coast is not so closely watched for the Prince as it was; the cordon of sentries has been removed. Make for Arisaig or Morar; at either you will be able to find a fisherman to take you off at night to the French vessel if she is still there. You speak French, so the rest should be easy.'

'And will Lochiel and the Prince try to leave by her?'

'I doubt it, for I fear she will be gone by the time Donald

could reach the coast, or His Royal Highness either. But do not delay your departure on that account, Ewen, for the larger the party getting off from shore the more hazardous is the attempt – at least, if there are any soldiers left in those parts now. (There cannot, at any rate, be many.) Now I must be getting on my way.'

'You will not pass the night with us?' suggested Ewen. 'Aunt Margaret seems to have a high opinion of the garrets as a refuge.'

Dr Cameron shook his head. 'I must push on; 'tis only five o'clock. God bless you, my dear Ewen, and bring us to meet again – even though it be not in Scotland!'

'I wish I were coming with you to Ben Alder,' said Ewen rather wistfully, halting after his visitor down the stairs

'Trust me to do your business with Donald as well as you could do it yourself – nay, better, for I suspect that you would leave out certain episodes. – You'll be rid of this fellow at last, Miss Margaret,' he said to the figure waiting at the foot of the stairs. 'I've sorted him!'

' 'Tis you have the skill, Archibald Cameron,' replied the lady, beaming on him. 'None of my prayers would move him. You'll drink a health with us before you go?'

And under the picture of King James the Third and Eighth the three of them drained their glasses to the Cause which had already taken its last, its mortal wound.

Next day Ewen kept his word, and set about his departure. A garron was found for him to ride, and two of his men who had followed him through the campaign were to accompany him to the coast. Yielding to pressure, he had agreed to take young Angus MacMartin with him to France as his personal servant. He could not refuse it to Neil's memory and to old Angus's prayers that a MacMartin should be about him still.

He was to leave at dusk, since travelling by night would be less hazardous, and a little before sundown he went up to Slochd nan Eun to take leave of his foster-father, with whom he had had little converse since his return, for Angus had been ill and clouded in mind. But he had borne the loss of his two sons with an almost fierce resignation; it seemed as if he had asked no better fate for them, especially for Neil. He had recovered from his illness now, but he was rather frail and still at times a little confused. A daughter looked after him in the old cottage which had once rung with the laughter of many children, and with Ewen's own; but the old man was alone, crouched over the fire, with a plaid across his knees when Ewen, helping himself on the ascent with a staff, arrived at the door.

Half blind though he was, Angus's hearing was as keen as ever, and, even with the unfamiliar halt in it, he knew his foster-son's step.

'Mac 'ic Ailein, is it you? Blessings on your head! You have come to say farewell to me, who shall never see you again.'

Tremblingly and slowly he arose, and embraced the young man. 'Neil and Lachlan shall go with you, son of my heart, that you take no harm before you embark on the great water.'

'Neil is dead, Foster-father, do you not remember?' asked Ewen gently. 'He gave his life for me. And Lachlan – I fear Lachlan is dead also.'

'It is true that I do not see them any more,' replied the old man, with a singular detachment, 'for I grow blinder every day; yet I hear Neil's pipes very well still, and when the fire burns up I know that Lachlan has put on a fresh peat for me. Good sons both, but I have between my hands a son who is dearer, though I did not beget him – O my tall and beautiful one, glad was the day when you came back after the slaughter, but gladder this day, or you carry your head out of reach of your foes!' He passed his hand lingeringly over the bright locks. 'And yet . . . all is not well. I do not know why, but all is not well. There is grief on the white sand . . . grief and mourning, and a sound of tears in the wind that blows there.'

'Indeed there is grief,' said Ewen sighing, 'grief enough in my heart at going, at leaving Alba and my father's house. I was almost for staying, Angus, did I take to the heather; but the brother of Mac Dhomhnuill Duibh has been here, and he bids me go. The Chief himself is going. But we shall return—'

'Some will return,' broke in Angus, sinking his head upon his breast. 'Aye, some will return.' Sitting there, he stared with his almost sightless eyes into the fire.

Ewen stood looking down at him. 'Shall I return?' he asked after a moment.

'I shall not see you, treasure of my heart . . . But these eyes will see my own son come back to me, and he too grieving.'

'But I fear that Lachlan is dead, Foster-father,' repeated Ewen, kneeling on one knee beside him. 'Is it not his wraith that puts the peats on the fire for you?'

'It may be,' answered the old man. 'It may well be, for when I speak to him he never answers. Yet one night he stood here in the flesh, and swore the holy oath on his dirk to be avenged on the man who betrayed you to the *saighdearan dearg*. My own two eyes beheld him, my two ears heard him, and I prayed the Blessed One to give strength to his arm – for it was then that you were gone from us, darling of my heart, and fast in prison.'

'But you surely do not mean, Angus,' said his foster-son, puzzled, 'that Lachlan came back here after I was captured? You mean that you saw his *taibhs*. For in the flesh he has never returned to Slochd nan Eun.'

'Yes, for one night he returned,' persisted the old man, 'for one night in the darkness. None saw him but I, who opened to him; and he would not go near the house of Ardroy, nor let any see him but his father, because he was sick with grief and shame that he had left you on Beinn Laoigh to the will of your enemy. Ah, Mach 'ic Ailein, did I not feel that many things would come upon you because of the man to whom the heron led you! But that I never saw – that he would betray you to the *saighdearan dearg*! May Lachlan soon keep his oath, and the raven pick out the traitor's eyes! May his bones never rest! May his ghost—'

Ewen had sprung up, horrified. 'Angus, stop! What are you saying! That man, the English officer, did not betray me: he saved me, at great risk to himself. But for him the redcoats would have shot me like a dog – but for him I should not have escaped from their hands on the way to Inverlochy. Take back that curse . . . and for Heaven's sake tell me that you are mistaken, that Lachlan did not swear vengeance on *him*, but on the man who took me prisoner, a Lowland Scot named Guthrie. That is what you mean, Angus, is it not?'

But Angus shook his grey head. 'My son swore vengeance on the man who was your guest, the English officer who found you in the bothy on Beinn Laoigh, and delivered you up, and told the soldiers who you were. Lachlan found this out from the talk as he skulked round the Lowlander's camp in the dark.

Vengeance he meant to have if he could, but he swore it for certain against the other, the English officer, because he had broken your bread. So he took oath on the iron to rest neither day nor night till that evil deed was repaid to him – he swore it here on the *biodag* on which you both saw blood that day by the lochan, and which you bad him not throw away. I think he meant to hasten back and lie in wait for the English officer as he returned over the pass of Corryarrick, and to shoot him with the musket which he had stolen from one of the redcoats. But whether he ever did it I do not know.'

Bewildered, and with a creeping sense of chill, Ewen had listened mutely in order that he might, perhaps, contrive to disentangle the true from the false in this fruit of the old man's clouded brain. But with these last words came a gleam of comfort. No, Lachlan had not succeeded in any such attempt, thank God. And since then – for it was in May that Windham had returned over the Corryarrick – his complete disappearance pointed to one conclusion, that he was gone where he could never keep his dreadful and deluded vow. Ewen drew a long breath of relief; yet it was rather terrible to hope that his foster-brother was dead.

Still, he would take what precaution he could.

'If, when I am gone, Angus,' he said, 'Lachlan should return here, charge him most straightly from me that he abandon this idea of vengeance; tell him that but for the English officer I should be lying today where poor Neil is lying. – I wonder if anyone gave Neil burial,' he added under his breath.

But Angus heard. He raised himself. 'Lachlan buried him when he came there after yourself, *Eoghain*, and found you gone, and was near driving the dirk into his own heart, as he told me. Yes, he stayed to bury his brother, and so when he came to the camp of the redcoats they had taken you to Kilcumein. But all night long he prowled round the tents, and heard the redcoats talk – he having the English very well, as you know – and tried to get into the tent of the commander to kill him while he slept, and could not. So he hastened to Achnacarry, and found Mac Dhomhnuill Duibh, and besought him to go with the clan and besiege the fort of Kilcumein and take you out of it; but the Chief had not enough men. So Lachlan came here secretly, to tell me that he had not been able to stay the redcoats from taking you, and that Neil had been happier than he, for he had died outside the door before they entered to you; and all that was left for him was to slay the Englishman – and so he vowed. But now, it seems, the Englishman is not to be slain?'

'A thousand times, no!' cried Ewen, who had listened very attentively to the recital, which certainly sounded as if it had come originally from Lachlan's own lips, and some of which, as he knew from Archie, was true. 'Remember that, if Lachlan should come here. – But I cannot understand,' he went on, frowning, 'how, if Lachlan overheard so much of the soldier's talk, he did not overhear the truth. and learn how Major Wind-him ran in and saved me from being shot. Surely that is the matter which must have engaged their tongues, and in that there was no question of delivering me up.'

'I do not know what more my son heard,' said Angus slowly, 'But, when a man hates another, does not his ear seek to hear the evil he may have done rather than the good?'

'Yes, I suppose he did hate Major Windham,' said Ewen thoughtfully. 'That was the reason then – he wanted a pre-text. . . . Indeed I must thank God that he never got a chance of carrying out his vow. And, from his long absence, I fear – nay, I am sure – that he has joined poor Neil. Alas, both my brothers slain through me, and Neil's children fatherless!'

'But Angus *Og* goes with you, is it not, son of my heart, that he too may put his breast between you and your foes?'

'That he shall never do,' thought Ewen. 'Yes, he goes with me. Give me your blessing, Foster-father; and when I come again, even if your eyes do not see me, shall your hands not touch me, as they do now?' And he guided the old hands to his shoulders as he knelt there.

'No, I shall not touch you, treasure of my heart,' said Angus, while his fingers roved over him. 'And I cannot see whether you will ever come back again, nor even whether you will sail over the great water away from your foes. All is dark . . . and the wind that comes off the sea is full of sorrow.' He put his hands on Ewen's head. 'But I bless you, my son, with all the blessing of Bridget and Michael; the charm Mary put round her Son, and Bridget put in her banners, and Michael put in his shield . . . edge will not cleave thee, sea will not drown thee. . . .' He had slid into reciting scraps of a *sian* or pro-tective charm, but he did not go through to the end; his hands fell on to his knees again, and he leant back and closed his eyes.

Ewen bent forward and threw some peats on to the fire. 'Tell me one thing, Foster-father,' he said, looking at him again. 'Even if I never leave the shores of Moidart, but am slain there, or am drowned in the sea, which is perhaps the meaning of the wind that you hear moaning, tell me, in the days to come shall a stranger or a son of mine rule here at Ardroy?'

Angus opened his eyes; but he was so long silent that Ewen's hands began to clench themselves harder and harder. Yet at last the old man spoke.

'I have seen a child running by the brink of Loch na h-Iolaire, and his name is your name.'

Ewen drew a long breath and rose, and, his foster-father rising too with his assistance, he kissed him on both cheeks.

'Whatever you have need of, Angus, ask of Miss Cameron as you would of me.'

'You are taking away from me the only thing of which I have need,' said the old man sadly. 'Nevertheless, it must be. Blessings, blessings go with you, and carry you safely away from the white sands to her who waits for you . . . and may my blessings draw you back again, even though I do not greet you at your returning.'

When Ewen came slowly down the path again he found himself thinking of how he had descended it last August behind Keith Windham, nearly a year ago. The story of Lachlan's vow had perturbed him, but now he saw it in a far less menacing light. Either his foster-brother's unquiet spirit was by this time at rest, or the whole thing was a dream of that troubled imagination of the old seer's, where the distinction between the living and the dead was so tenuous.

Soon he forgot Keith Windham, Angus and everyone. Loch na h-Iolaire lay before him under the sunset, a sunset so tranquil and so smiling that in its sleepy brightness, which mirrored all the mountains round, the loch seemed to hold the very heart of content. Ewen had the sensation that his heart, too, was drowned there. And by his own will he was saying farewell to loch and mountain, island and red crag. He remembered how Alison had said that he would be hard put to it to choose between her and them. Was she right?

There was a place where for a little there was no bank, but marshy ground, and where the water came brimming into the reeds and grasses, setting them faintly swaying. He went to it, and, stooping with difficulty, dipped a cupped hand into the water and raised it to his lips. Perhaps that sacramental draught would give him to see this scene as bright and sharp in dreams, over there in the land of exile whither, like his father, like all who had not counted the cost, he was going.

As he drank there was a loud croak over his head, and, looking up, he saw a heron winging its slow, strong way over the loch towards the sunset. It might almost have been the same heron which he and Alison had watched that evening last summer, when it had seemed to arrive from the western coast like a herald from him who had landed there. Now it was going towards the coast once more, as he, the outlaw, was going, and as his Chief and his fugitive Prince would soon be going. In a little year, between two flights of a heron seen over Loch na h-Iolaire, the whole adventure of ruin had been begun and consummated.

Well, if one's life remained to one it was in order to come back some day and renew the struggle. Ewen took off his bonnet. 'God save King James!' he said firmly, and turned away from the mirrored mountains to take the same path as the heron.

Chapter Five

T H I S sea-fog, Keith Windham decided, was worse than the inland mist; thicker, more woolly, more capricious. Yesterday, for instance, one had wakened to it, and all day it had cloaked sea and shore and the wild tumbled mountains of the 'Rough Bounds'. Yet towards evening it had suddenly lifted, and the night had been clear and moonlit. But this morning the white veil was down again, and only now, some hours after sunset, was it clearing away.

And this was all the more vexatious because in the silver clearness of last night he had distinctly made out a strange vessel – a Frenchman, he was sure – anchored somewhere off the Isle of Rum. But in the day, thanks to that muffling fog, who knew whether she was still off the coast or no! Yet in a few minutes more, when the moon came up from behind the mountains, he hoped to be able to see as far as her anchorage; meanwhile, followed by his orderly, he rode slowly along the flat shore in the direction of Morar.*

No one could accuse Major Keith Windham of neglecting Lord Albemarle's instructions; if anything, he went beyond them in his ceaseless vigilance. Quartered himself at Arisaig, he thence patrolled the coast in both directions, from Loch nan Uamh, the Adventurer's original landing-place, to Morar of the white sands on the other, and had his grumbling men out in all weathers, at all hours of the day and night, and for any kind of false alarm. But he spared himself still less than them, taking little sleep and covering miles every day, often on foot. If fatigue, like virtue, were its own reward, then he had that recompense. And so far it was his only one.

But at least Keith felt tolerably certain that no fugitives had yet made their escape from his strip of coast, no fugitives of any kind. For, apart from using every endeavour to secure the person of the Pretender's son, he had been instructed to prevent all communication with French vessels, of whom one or two might always be hovering off the coast. These nights, therefore, that this ghostly ship was visible, it naturally behoved him to be extraordinarily vigilant, since it was unlikely that she was there by chance; she was probably hanging about in hopes of taking off the prize that he was after, and he was duly grateful to the moon last night for showing her to him. And surely it was time for the moon to appear now! Keith put his hand impatiently into the breast of his uniform for a little almanac which he carried there, and, encountering a packet which he also carried, was swept at the touch of it away for a moment from shore and ship and moonrise.

Having left Fort Augustus for the coast so soon after Ewen Cameron had confided to his care the letter to his wife, Keith had had no opportunity of despatching it; moreover, why send that farewell letter now that its writer had escaped? So not knowing where else to dispose it, he still carried the packet with the lock of hair upon him, a material token of the tie between him and the foe who had captured him a year ago, and had held him in a species of bondage ever since. The

* Pronounced Mórar.

thought had never formulated itself so definitely until tonight, but, by gad, it was true!

He had been hard put to it to conceal his exultation when, just before setting out from Fort Augustus for Moidart, he had heard of Ewen's escape and disappearance; and this news had, ever since, been a source of the most unfeigned pleasure to him. His sacrifices had not been in vain; they had been well worth the making. He thought of Ewen back at Ardroy – *his* doing, that! Ewen would recognize it, too. He had not failed in everything!

And now he pictured Ewen lying hid in the mountains round Loch na h-Iolaire until the worst of the storm had blown over. He could not imagine him leaving Ardroy unless he was obliged. and surely, not being on the list of proscribed, he could contrive to elude capture in those wilds. His wife would doubtless get news of him somehow, return to Scotland and visit him secretly; and in the end, when the price had been paid by those who had not had his good fortune, and there was for the others an amnesty or some act of indemnity, he might be able to occupy his home again in peace. It had so happened, Keith believed, after the Fifteen.

Was then his hope that they should meet again some day so impossible of fulfilment now? It was true that if he himself succeeded in capturing the 'Prince', Ewen would not readily take his hand. However, no need to face that dilemma yet. But, in a sense, every day that 'the young gentleman' was still in Scotland brought nearer the hour when he must try to leave it, and if Lord Albemarle were right in supposing that he would make for this stretch of coast, already familiar to him, he must soon approach the snare laid for him there.

And the presence of that unknown ship last night seemed to indicate that the actual moment of that approach was very near. Ah! now at last he would be able to look for her, for the moon had pushed up over the craggy eastern summits at his back into a cloudless sky.

Keith gave his horse to his orderly, and going along a low spur of rock gazed out to sea. The fantastic peaks of Rum were even more unreal in the moonlight than in the day, and the Isle of Eigg of an even odder shape. At first he thought that the stranger was gone, and then all at once he saw her, a ghostly bark on the rippling silver. She seemed to be off Morar, and,

since some of her square-sails appeared to be set, he doubted
if she was at anchor; but she was certainly not sailing away.

Keith had to make a rapid decision. At Morar he had an
officer and thirty men stationed. That, surely, was enough. He
could, if he wished, send back to Arisaig and bring up some
more from there; yet should Arisaig and not Morar prove after
all the destined spot, and he had denuded Arisaig of watchers,
he would be undone. Loch nan Uamh, the original landing-
place, was also provided with a quota, but the distance did not
admit of bringing any soldiers thence tonight.

He returned to his orderly and mounted his horse. 'I shall
ride on to Morar. Go back to Arisaig and tell the Captain so;
desire him to keep a close watch on the shore, for the Frenchman is lying off the coast again and nearer in than last night.'

The man saluted and rode off along the rough sandy road,
and Keith was left alone with the ship, the moonlight and his
own excited thoughts. Not that he stayed to contemplate any
of these; he pushed on at a smart trot for Morar, turning over
the question of a boat, without which no fugitive could,
naturally, reach the ship. He had temporarily confiscated every
boat on this stretch of coast except such as were genuinely
needed for fishing, to which he had granted a permit. Even
of the owners of these he was not sure, for they were all Mac-
Donald of Clanranald's dependents. It would no doubt have
been better to have burnt every one of their craft. Yet even
then a vessel could easily despatch one of her own, at the risk
of being fired on.

Keith took a last look at the burnished and gently moving
expanse of which he must now lose sight, for here the track
turned sharply to the right to run round the deep little inlet
of Morar. But there was no visible speck upon the sea which
might be a boat.

And before long he was approaching the shoreward end of
the inlet on the rough sandy track of a road, bordered by dense
undergrowth, which ran round, a little higher than the level
shore, under trees of no great stature. The tide was coming in
fast over the dazzling white sands of Morar, snow under the
moon, and drowning the little river which tumbled from the
wild, deep freshwater loch behind, where Lord Lovat had
sought his last refuge. It was so intensely quiet, and the tide
was slipping in so noiselessly, that the roar of the double falls

was carried very clearly over the water. Reining up, Major Windham listened for some sign of the patrol which should be going its rounds from the quarters on the other side of the bay, across the river; and, to his displeasure, could detect none. This on a night when a French ship was off the coast! The men must be got out at once.

He touched his horse with the spur and then pulled up again. What was that dark shape down there on the sand? A small boat, and so near the incoming tide that in another quarter of an hour or so it would be afloat. No fisherman could have been so careless as to leave it there, unless it were secured in some way. Brimful of suspicion as Keith was tonight, he had jumped off his horse in an instant, and thrown the bridle over a convenient branch. He knew better than to take the animal plunging into the soft, dry sand of the slope; he was almost up to his ankles himself before he was down.

Yes, he was right; the boat was there for no purpose authorized by him. It had only recently been brought there, for it was not made fast to anything. There were oars in it, but no nets or fishing-lines. It needed no more evidence to convince him that the little craft had been placed there in readiness to take off some person or persons tonight to the strange vessel.

The most lively anger seized Major Windham. What was that damned patrol about not to have discovered this? He must certainly gallop round to their quarters without a moment's delay and turn out the lazy brutes. His pulses leaping, he plunged up the yielding sand to the tree-shadowed road, turned to throw himself in the saddle – and stood staring like a man bewitched. His horse was gone . . . gone as if swallowed up!

'It is not possible!' said Keith to himself. 'I have not been down there two minutes!'

But, evidently, it was possible. Black though the shadows were under the trees, he could tell that they held nothing so solid as a horse. He looked up and down the empty white track, streaked and dappled with those hard shadows; he examined the branch. It was not broken, and the beast could certainly not have twitched his bridle off it. Someone had been watching him, then, and human hands had conveyed the animal away – whither?

Furious, he began to run back along the road; its sandy surface was already too much churned up to show any hoofmarks. He did not remember passing any crofts as he came. Though a man could hide in the thick bushes on the seaward side, a horse could not be concealed in them. He turned abruptly and went back again, remembering that there was a dwelling or two farther along, between him and the river. If some of these MacDonalds had stolen his horse and hidden it there, by Heaven it should be the worse for them!

What, however, was of paramount importance now was not the finding of his horse, but the beating up of the patrol with the least possible delay. Yet by the time that he, on foot, could get round to their quarters, or at least by the time that the soldiers arrived on the spot, the boat would probably have put out with her freight. That was why his horse had been spirited away by the ambushed spy in league with tonight's fugitives.

Keith set his jaw and cursed himself most fervently for having come alone. The extraordinarily skilful way in which his horse had been made to vanish, joined to the inexplicable lateness of the patrol, only confirmed his conviction that it was the Pretender's son for whom that boat was waiting. Then, at all costs, he must delay its putting out. . . . Could he disable it in some way? Not easily, without tools, but he would do his best.

Once more he plunged down the sandy slope. But the boat, though old, was solid. A knife, a sword, could make no impression on those timbers. Keith had a moment of angry despair; then he remembered having seen in one of these craft the other day a plugged hole, designed to allow water to drain out if necessary. Suppose this boat had one!

Getting in he peered and felt over the bottom, and at last, to his joy, his fingers encountered, towards the after end, a round peg of wood sticking up like a cork. After some tugging he succeeded in wrenching it out, and slipped it into his pocket. He could get his thumb through the hole he had thus unplugged. He leapt out and ran towards the slope again in triumph. One of two things would happen now: either the Pretender's son and his companions would discover what had been done, and a new plug would have to be fashioned to fit the hole, which would delay them not a little, or – what seemed to Keith more probable – they would launch the boat and pull off without examining it, on which it would almost immediately fill and sink, and its occupants be forced to struggle back at a disadvantage to a shore by that time, it was hoped, straitly guarded.

Keith was half-way up the slope again when he stopped abruptly, for in the stillness he had distinctly heard voices – low voices at no very great distance. The patrol at last perhaps? He did not think so. The speakers seemed to be coming along the tree-shadowed road between him and the end of the inlet, the very road along which he was preparing to hasten. A party of Jacobite fugitives would most certainly not allow a soldier in uniform to run past them if they could help it. Was the prize going to slip through his fingers after all?

No, hardly, in that unseaworthy boat! But he must perforce let the owners of these cautious voices pass him and get on to the beach before he started for the quarters of the patrol. Had the tide not already been so high he could have cut across the sands and swum or waded the river, but that was out of the question now; he could only go by the road. He looked round for shelter, and slipped cautiously into a high bush of hazel which itself stood in a patch of shadow so deep that he felt sure of being invisible.

Not only voices, but muffled footsteps were audible by this time, and presently a man – a fisherman, he thought – ran down the slope towards the boat. He had scarcely passed before it came to Keith with a gust of despair that he had set himself an almost impossible task. Now that the fugitives were already here, before he had even started, he could never get round and fetch the patrol in time, for if the Jacobites were left to embark undisturbed they would discover and repair the loss of the plug – that man down there was probably discovering it now. But there was another way of rousing his dilatory men, for, unbelievably negligent as they were this evening, they could not fail to hear a pistol-shot. That would bring them to the place in double quick time; and although to fire would naturally alarm the fugitives, and make them embark with all the greater despatch, there was gain in that, since – if it were not already done – they would pretty certainly not discover the loss of the plug. Keith drew the loaded pistol from his belt, but he put it at half-cock, because he must wait until the party was well past him before firing, seeing that he was only one against he knew not how many.

Centuries seemed to pass while he waited, and considered, only to dismiss, the idea of deliberately shooting at the Pretender's son with a view to disabling him; for he could not in this light be sure of stopping short at that. His heart beat faster than ever it had done at Fontenoy or Culloden Moor, for this business was fraught for him with issues more momentous than any battle. What happened in the next quarter of an hour would decide his whole future – and no fighting had done that for him.

A sudden fall of sand behind him startled him for a moment, but he dared not turn his head to look what had caused it, for three . . . four dim shapes were coming at last out of the shadows above and beyond him, and beginning to descend the slope. The tallest was limping badly; and he was also the principal figure, for the others, he could see now, were only gillies, and one was a boy. Had the Pretender's son gone lame in his wanderings? It was quite possible.

Or . . . or . . . God of Heaven! The sand seemed to swim under Keith's feet. It was not Charles Edward Stuart, it was Ewen Cameron who had walked into his trap, Ewen Cameron who had just limped down past him on the arm of one of the gillies . . . Ewen, his friend, whom he had thought safely hidden in Lochaber!

The bitter disappointment and the disastrous surprise of it overwhelmed Keith, and he stood there stupefied. Once more he had come on a fool's errand – not the first since he had watched the coast. This was Edinburgh over again . . . but a much more sinister repetition of it. For the net which he had spread for the arch-rebel was not empty; it held a lesser but indubitable prize – a chieftain, Lochiel's kinsman. With a wild sense of being in a net himself he realized the cogency of the arguments which he had used against Guthrie; Ewen Cameron was too important to shoot out of hand, he was also too important to let go. . . . And he saw Ewen sent back to the scaffold after all, and by him: tied on a horse, by his hands. . . . Or since the boat was holed, and Ewen was lame, he would drown, perhaps, when it sank . . . the men were already pushing it nearer to the water. . . .

Stabbed to alarm by that thought he stepped almost unconsciously out of his sheltering hazel bush, and stood at the edge of the shadow with some vague notion of shouting to warn Ardroy. No, what he had to do was to fire, and bring the patrol here quickly and arrest him. He was to stop all communication, to allow no one to leave . . . much less a chieftain and a kinsman of Lochiel's . . .

'God help me!' he said aloud, and put a hand over his eyes.

There was a sudden crackling of broken stems, a fierce exclamation behind him, something glittered out of the shadow, and Keith swung quickly round just as the man who had been tracking him for over a week sprang down upon him. And so he did not receive Lachlan MacMartin's dirk between the shoulders, as Lachlan had intended, but in his breast.

Leaning on young Angus's shoulder by the boat, Ewen watched the Morar fisherman hastily fitting in the spare plug which he had brought with him (because, as he had explained, the redcoats had played the trick of removing one from Ranald Mor's boat the other night). The fates had indeed been kind – no patrol this evening – if they were quick they would get out of the bay without a single shot being fired at them.

The boat was being pushed down to the water when all at once the lad Angus gave a little cry, clutched at his master's arm and pointed up the beach. Ewen, turning his head, saw two men locked together on the sandy slope, saw one drop and roll over, had a dim impression that he wore uniform, and a much clearer one of a wild figure running over the sand towards him with a naked dirk in his hand. Young Angus tried to throw himself in front of his chieftain, but the grip on his shoulder, suddenly tightening, stayed him. Moreover in another moment the spectre with the dirk was on his knees at Ewen's feet, holding up the weapon, and, half sobbing with excitement, was pouring out a flood of words as hot as lava:

'Mac 'ic Ailein, I have kept my vow, I have avenged you – and saved you, too, though I knew not till the *biodag* was bare in my hand that it was you who had passed. The Englishman would have betrayed you a second time . . . but he lies there and will not rise again. Oh, make haste, make haste to embark, for there are redcoats at Morar!'

Despite his disfigured face, Ewen had recognized him at

once, and the meaning of his words, for all their tumbling haste, was clearer still – horribly clear. Frozen, he tried to beat that meaning from him.

'God's curse on you, what have you done!' he exclaimed, seizing his foster-brother by the shoulder. 'If you have really harmed Major Windham—' But the moon showed him the bloody dirk. With a shudder he thrust the murderer violently from him, and, deaf to young Angus's shrill remonstrance, started to run haltingly back towards the slope. Surely, surely Lachlan had mistaken his victim, for what could Windham be doing here at Morar?

But it was Keith Windham. He was lying on his side, full in the moonlight, almost at the bottom of the slope, as if he had been thrown there . . . stunned, perhaps, thought Ewen wildly, with a recollection of how he himself had lain on Culloden Moor – though how a dirk could stun him God alone knew. Half-way down the slope lay a pistol. Calling his name he knelt and took him into his arms. Oh, no hope; it was a matter of minutes! Lachlan had used that long blade too well.

As he was lifted, Keith came back from a moment's dream of a shore with long green rollers roaring loudly under a blood-red sunset, to pain and difficult breath and Ewen's arms. He knew him.

'I . . . I did not have to . . . fire,' he gasped: but Ewen could not realize what lay behind the words. 'Go . . . go before . . . they come from Morar . . .'

'My God, my God!' exclaimed Ewen, trying to staunch the blood which that spotless sand was already drinking. 'Oh, Windham, if I could only have warned you – if I had known that *he* was here . . .'

'There is a hole . . . in the boat,' said Keith with increasing difficulty. 'I . . . took out . . . the plug.'

'They have put in another – one they had in readiness. Windham, for God's sake try to—'

Try to do what? 'Your letter . . . is still . . . I had no . . .'

'Duncan – Angus!' called Ewen desperately, 'have none of you any brandy?'

But his men, who had run up, were intent on another matter. 'Come, the boat is ready – and I think the redcoats are stirring over the river,' said Duncan Cameron, laying a hand on his shoulder. 'Come, Mac 'ic Ailein, come!'

Ewen answered him in Gaelic. 'I shall not stir while he breathes.'

But the dying man seemed to understand. 'Go . . . Ardroy! . . . I implore you!' He began to fumble at one hand with the other, and managed to pull off the signet ring which he always wore, and to hold it out a little way. Ewen took it, not knowing what he did.

'I was watching for . . . the Pretender's son,' went on Keith, lower and lower; 'then I saw . . . it was you . . . and I had to try . . . to decide . . . duty . . . no, it is just as well . . . I could not . . . have borne . . .' He sighed and shut his eyes.

Ewen held him closer, still trying to stay the flood, and trying, as he knew, in vain. Yet Keith only seemed to be going to sleep. He was murmuring something now which Ewen had to stoop his head close to hear. And then all that he could catch were the words: '. . . desire . . . friends . . . always . . .'

'Yes, yes, always,' he answered in anguish. 'Always!' But there would be no 'always'. 'Oh, if only you had not been in that madman's path!'

But that, at least, was not fortuitous. Yet to Keith the assassin had only been some man of Morar in league with the embarkation.

He opened his eyes. 'Your hand . . .' Ewen gave it to him, and saw a little smile in the moonlight. 'Have you been . . burying any more cannon? . . . I always liked you,' said his enemy clearly; and a moment after, with his hand in Ewen's, was gone to that place 'where an enemy never entered and from whence a friend never went away'.

Ewen laid him back on the patched sand, and, getting to his feet, stood looking down at the man to whom the heron had brought him – foe, enigma, saviour, victim of a terrible mistake. And friend – yes; but it was too late for friendship now. It had already been too late at their last meeting – which had not been the last after all – when he himself, as he thought, was standing on the threshold of death. But it was Keith Windham who had gone through that door, not he. . . . Had he known that he was dying? . . . Every word of the few he had spoken had been about *him* . . .

Then through the haze of shock and grief penetrated the sound of a distant shot, and he remembered that there were other lives than his at stake.

'Go – go and hide yourselves!' he commanded. But the two Camerons shook their heads. 'Not until you are in the boat, Mac 'ic Ailein!'

'I will come, then,' said Ewen. He would rather have stayed, now; but he knelt again and kissed Keith's forehead. And that it should not be found on him, an equivocal possession, perhaps, he drew out his own letter to Alison and slipped it, all sodden, into his pocket. Then he suffered the gillies to hurry him down to the boat, for already it was clear that the soldiers were crossing the river, and some twenty yards away a couple of ill-aimed bullets raised spurts of sand.

By the boat was waiting Lachlan, Lachlan who, directly he was recovered from the result of his first attempt by Loch Tarff, had once more set about the fulfilment of his vow, who had hung about Inverness through July and found no opportunity, lost track of his quarry when he went to Fort Augustus, picked it up again in Moidart, and had hardly let him out of his sight since. It was he who had removed the horse.

'Ewen, my brother, forgive me – forgive me!'

Ewen turned on him a terrible face. 'Never! You have killed my friend;'

'Never? Then as well have my life, too!' cried Lachlan. The reddened dirk which a year ago he had been moved to fling into the loch spun glinting through the moonlight and splashed into the sea, and its owner, turning, ran headlong towards the road and the oncoming patrol.

Soon the noise of shots and shouting could be heard no longer, only the creak of the oars in the rough rowlocks as young Angus and the fisherman pulled hard over the moonlit sea towards the French privateer. But Ewen sat in the stern-sheets of the little boat with his face buried in his hands, and cared not that he went to safety.

The day would come when, pondering over his memories of those broken sentences, recalling the pistol lying on the sand, he would arrive at a glimpse of the truth, and guess that Lachlan's blade had saved Keith Windham from a decision too cruel, and that perhaps he had been glad to be so saved. But he would never realize – how should he? – that the tide which for a year had been carrying the Englishman, half ignorant, sometimes resisting, among unlooked-for reefs and breakers, away from the safe, the stagnant Dead Sea of his choice, had borne him to no unfitting anchorage in this swift death, devoid of thoughts of self. For Ewen saw Keith only as a loser through meeting him – a loser every way – whereas in truth he had been a gainer.

A hail came over the water; they were approaching the privateer. He tried to rouse himself from his stupor of grief and regret, and from the self-reproach which stabbed scarcely less deep because it was causeless. And as he did so the kind moonlight showed him his friend's ring upon his finger.

EPILOGUE

Harbour of Grace

T H E fresh wind scouring the mouth of the Seine kept the fish-
ing-boats from Honfleur lying well over, and at the foot of
the cliffs of Ste. Adresse the waves were shivering themselves
in a joyful welter of foam. Long pennants of cloud streamed
and vanished in the blue; all the shipping rocked at anchor,
and Alison Cameron, crossing the market-place of Havre-de-
Grâce with a basket on her arm, had to clutch at her black
cloak lest it should be whirled off her shoulders.

She had reached the French port in time to see her father
alive; in time, indeed, to give him nearly six weeks of the most
devoted care. But in May he died peacefully, ignorant of the
catastrophe which had torn for ever the webs that he had
helped to weave. Since he was ill it had not been very difficult
to keep from him the news of the downfall of Jacobite hopes
and the fugitive state of the Prince, and to invent reasons for
the absence of any news of Ewen Cameron. Of Hector's
capture he had known before leaving Scotland. It was the
thought of Ewen, to whose care he knew Alison now definitely
committed, which had made his last hours easy. 'Your man
will never let you want for aught, my lass,' he had said, near
the end; and Alison had the strength to keep from him the
anxiety which racked her.

And so one morning she found herself left alone in the
lodging where her father had lain ill, a little house belonging
to a youthful married couple, kind and sympathetic enough,
and glad that the Scottish lady should stay on there, waiting
for the husband who, Madame Grévérend was privately sure,
would never come now, having without doubt been slain in
the deserts of l'Ecosse. And when, later on, a gossip would
ask her why the young Scottish lady did not voyage back to
those deserts to find her husband, or to procure news of him,
or at least to have the solace of weeping on his tomb, Madame
Grévérend would explain that the poor creature was so per-

suaded that her husband would in the end come to Havre-de-Grâce seeking her that she feared to miss him if she went away.

'But she will wait for ever, one fears,' Madame Grévérend would finish; 'and she left without even a good-for-nothing like this to plague her!' And here she would snatch up her fat, curly-headed Philippe and kiss him. 'Yes, she has lost everything, poor lady, and she only five months married.'

But one has never lost everything. Alison still had that possession which Madame Grévérend could not understand, the certitude which had come to her in the cabin of the brig at Inverness. Sooner or later Ewen would come for her.

Yet it was hard, sometimes, to cling to that belief when the weeks went by and there was not the slightest crumb of authentic news of him. All she had was negative; for there was in Havre-de-Grâce another Scots refugee, a Mr Buchanan, who had served in the Duke of Perth's regiment, and he had convinced her, on evidence that seemed conclusive to a mind which only longed to believe it, that Adroy had not been among the slain or massacred in the battle. Where, then, was he?

Her marketing finished, Alison took her way homewards through the bright windy weather, and came, down the little Rue des Vergers, to the small, sanded courtyard with the pear tree where she dwelt above M. and Mme Grévérend. In that sunlit space there was at the moment only the grey cat curled in a corner, a pair of pigeons promenading, and Philippe, seated easily upon his mother's doorstep, deliberately pouring sand on to his curls, as if in penitence for some misdeed, by means of an old tea-cup.

'My bairnie, don't do that!' called Alison, half laughing, half horrified. 'Fi donc, quelle saleté!'

Philippe gave her a most roguish glance, scooped up and emptied upon his locks a sort of final bumper cupful, and then rose uncertainly to his fat legs and came to her, lifting a beaming, smeared face for a kiss. Alison wiped his countenance and gave him one.

'Are you all alone, Philippe?'

The child intimated that he was, and then entered unasked upon a long explanation of the complicated reasons which had led him to make a garden of his head.

'I think you had better come up to my room with me and

let me brush out that horrid sand, my pretty,' said Alison, wondering what would happen if she held him upside down and shook him. '*Veux-tu bien?*'

He nodded, and Alison held out a hand. But neither of his were available, since one still clutched his tea-cup, and the other was tightly closed over some small object.

'What have you there?' asked the girl. It might so well be a beetle or a worm.

Philippe was coy about revealing his treasure, though he evidently desired to display it. But at last he opened a fat fist. '*De l'argent!*' he said exultingly, for, though immature, he was true Norman. And indeed there lay in his pink palm a small coin.

There was something about that piece of money which caused Alison's heart to leap suddenly into her throat; and, to the infant's dismay, she snatched his treasure from his hand and looked at it closely. It was no coin of France; no coin of any realm at all, in fact, but a Scottish trade token of the town of Inverness.

'Who gave you this, Philippe?' she asked, looking almost frightened. For Mr Buchanan, who might otherwise have been the donor, had gone away three days ago.

But her plundered companion was plainly making preparations for one of the most resonant howls of his short life. 'There, there, darling,' said Alison hastily, going down on her knees and restoring him his token. 'I am not going to take it away. But who in God's name gave it to you?'

It required time for the little boy to master his emotion, but when this was done he embarked upon another tortuous narrative, from which a close attention could gather that a strange gentleman had come and asked for Madame Cameron and had presented him with this earnest of his regard.

'And where is the gentleman now?' asked Alison breathlessly.

Philippe turned his rotund person and pointed up the stairs with the tea-cup.

Next moment he was alone in the middle of the courtyard, alone with the pigeons and the cat and Madame Cameron's abandoned basket, and Alison was flying up those stairs to her room. But half-way she stopped, with her hand to her heart, for her own light footfalls had not prevented her from hearing those others going impatiently to and fro above her – unknown steps, belonging to a man with a halt in his walk.

No, of course she had been too sanguine. It was not Ewen. The tumult of her heart died down again to the old sad patience. Yet it must be someone from Scotland, someone from the Highlands, too, for the token proved that; and if he asked for her it was because he came with news of Ewen, or of Hector.

And perhaps because at the bottom of her heart she trembled to think what that news might be, Alison turned and went down the stairs again and picked up her basket from the courtyard (and none too soon, for it had already riveted Philippe's attention as well as the cat's) and went a great deal more soberly up the stairs once more, and opened the door.

It was she who recovered speech the first, but scarcely coherent speech.

'Oh, Ewen, darling of my heart . . . you look so thin, so ill! And why are you lame? I thought it could not be you. . . . I knew you would come. . . . Sit down, for pity's sake!' She dragged him to a chair. 'Are you hungry – when did you eat? I must get you—'

But she was powerless in the arm he put about her, though the arm was trembling a little, and she fell on her knees beside the chair and cried into his coat; and then Ewen dried her eyes by a method which he had just discovered.

'I am neither thin, nor ill, nor lame, nor hungry, and I have all I want. Open your eyes and look at me like that again!'

His dear voice, at least, was not altered. 'I shall tell Madame Grévérend, when she returns, to make ready—'

'How concerned are women with food! I have no wish to eat at present; I only want to be sure that I am here,' said her husband, half laughing. 'If you go away to give orders, m'eudail, I may perhaps fancy I am back on the sea again, or . . . back on the sea,' he repeated rather hastily, turning his head a moment aside.

'You are here,' said Alison earnestly, as if he really needed the assurance; 'you are here, Ewen, heart's dearest, and I always knew that you would come!'

·   ·   ·   ·   ·

Long, long afterwards, that is to say, when Philippe and the pigeons had gone to roost, and the windy day had flamed itself out in a royal sunset, Alison, in her husband's arms, where she had been clasped for fully five minutes without stirring or speaking, fingered the back of his hand and said half dreamily: 'How came you by this strange ring, dear heart?'

Ewen moved abruptly; something like a shudder ran through him. 'I will tell you some time,' he said hesitatingly, 'but not yet. Oh, Alison, I cannot speak of it yet. . . .'

Some dreadful remembrance of the defeat, she thought piti-fully, then, seeing how pale he had become, slipped off his knee, and, bending over him, drew his head with a lovely gesture to her breast. And Ewen hid his eyes there like a child.

But leagues on leagues away the tide from the Outer Isles was beginning to fill the silver cup of Morar, and he stood there once again, helpless and heartbroken, looking down at Lachlan's handiwork. Not even Alison, whose arms held him close, whose cheek was pressed on his hair, not even Alison could stand with him in that place, where Keith Windham had come to the last of their meetings, and the bitter grief of Angus's prediction had reached its real fulfilment.

Yet he must not sadden Alison on this, of all days. It was Keith who had given it to him.

He lifted his head from its resting-place. '*My dearest on earth,*' he said, but not as he had said it a year ago, for the gift he asked meant even more now, – '*my dearest on earth, give me your kiss!*'

TITLES IN THE NEW WINDMILL SERIES

Georgette Heyer: *Regency Buck*
Alfred Hitchcock: *Sinister Spies*
C. Walter Hodges: *The Overland Launch*
Geoffrey Household: *Rogue Male; A Rough Shoot; Prisoner of the Indies*
Fred Hoyle: *The Black Cloud*
Irene Hunt: *Across Five Aprils*
Henry James: *Washington Square*
Josephine Kamm: *Young Mother; Out of Step; Where Do We Go From Here?*
Erich Kästner: *Emil and the Detectives*
John Knowles: *A Separate Peace*
D. H. Lawrence: *Sea and Sardinia; The Fox* and *The Virgin and the Gipsy; Selected Tales*
Marghanita Laski: *Little Boy Lost*
Harper Lee: *To Kill a Mockingbird*
Laurie Lee: *As I Walked Out One Mid-Summer Morning*
Ursula Le Guin: *A Wizard of Earthsea; The Tombs of Atuan; The Farthest Shore*
Doris Lessing: *The Grass is Singing*
C. Day Lewis: *The Otterbury Incident*
Lorna Lewis: *Leonardo the Inventor*
Martin Lindsay: *The Epic of Captain Scott*
David Line: *Run for Your Life*
Kathleen Lines: *The House of the Nightmare*
Joan Lingard: *Across the Barricades*
Penelope Lively: *The Ghost of Thomas Kempe*
Jack London: *The Call of the Wild; White Fang*
Carson McCullers: *The Member of the Wedding*
Lee McGiffen: *On the Trail to Sacramento*
Wolf Mankowitz: *A Kid for Two Farthings*
Olivia Manning: *The Play Room*
James Vance Marshall: *A River Ran Out of Eden*
J. P. Martin: *Uncle*
John Masefield: *Sard Harker; The Bird of Dawning; The Midnight Folk; The Box of Delights*
W. Somerset Maugham: *The Kite and Other Stories*
Guy de Maupassant: *Prisoners of War and Other Stories*
Laurence Meynell: *Builder and Dreamer*
Yvonne Mitchell: *Cathy Away*
Honoré Morrow: *The Splendid Journey*
Bill Naughton: *The Goalkeeper's Revenge*
E. Nesbit: *The Railway Children; The Story of the Treasure Seekers*
E. Neville: *It's Like this, Cat*
Wilfrid Noyce: *South Col*
Robert C. O'Brien: *Mrs Frisby and the Rats of NIMH*
Scott O'Dell: *Island of the Blue Dolphins*
George Orwell: *Animal Farm*
Merja Otava: *Priska*
John Prebble: *The Buffalo Soldiers*
J. B. Priestley: *Saturn Over the Water*
Lobsang Rampa: *The Third Eye*